The Haunting of Matty Buhrmann

The Haunting of Matty Buhrmann

Yvonne Whitney

iUniverse, Inc.

New York Lincoln Shanghai

The Haunting of Matty Buhrmann

Copyright © 2005 by Yvonne Whitney

iUniverse books may be ordered through booksellers or by contacting:

iUniverse
2021 Pine Lake Road, Suite 100
Lincoln, NE 68512
www.iuniverse.com
1-800-Authors (1-800-288-4677)

ISBN-13: 978-0-595-37544-8 (pbk)
ISBN-13: 978-0-595-67525-8 (cloth)
ISBN-13: 978-0-595-81938-6 (ebk)
ISBN-10: 0-595-37544-8 (pbk)
ISBN-10: 0-595-67525-5 (cloth)
ISBN-10: 0-595-81938-9 (ebk)

Printed in the United States of America

1

The last wisps of cloud from last night's storm had drifted eastward, leaving the golden spires of the Mormon Temple to shine gloriously against the unbroken blue of an early September sky. Somewhere someone noticed this but not Matty Buhrmann. Her world for the last half hour had been restricted to the shining concrete, the big green signs and the hot steel vehicles that ran, too fast and too close together, around the nation's capital on Interstate 495. Right now, Matty had ceased to be a part of the moving necklace. Her car and the green Toyota that had been in front of her had been driven off the road by a semi that had almost missed its turn and, with confidence born of size and power, had dived from the middle lane onto the exit ramp. Close calls were common, but this was as near as she had come to a real accident since the big one just over a year ago.

Calm. Stay calm. I'm all right. So's the other guy. I think. And this isn't my fault. It isn't my fault. Isn't. The other one wasn't either. Will I ever have to stop telling myself that?

That last thought brought the familiar stinging behind her eyes that threatened tears. After a few moments in which it was impossible to move, even difficult to breathe, she took the cell phone from her purse, unbuckled her seat belt and got out. The small Toyota was tipped at an uncomfortable angle halfway up the far side of the wide drainage ditch.

Still breathing hard and aware that the hand clutching her cell phone was trembling, Matty ventured onto the grassy slope, tiptoeing to keep her high heels from sinking into the earth, still damp from last night's shower.

"Are you all right?"

The man didn't turn to look at her. The sound of the traffic was deafening. Had he heard her?

To avoid slipping, it was necessary to use her heels now, digging them into the few spots of mown weeds and grass on the slope not covered by the usual roadside debris: gravel, crushed soda cans, bits of paper and ubiquitous cigarette butts. She stopped where the ground turned marshy.

"Do you want me to call someone? I have a cell phone."

He looked at her without interest, a beefy man, too large to be driving the little Toyota, wrapped in a wrinkled, gray suit. A predictable red tie hung loosely around his neck. He looked hot and tired and as if he hadn't been happy for a long time. The back seat of his car was piled with cartons.

Salesman. New Jersey license plate. Probably late for an appointment.

Life's a bitch.

She wished she could say that to him in sympathy, but a woman had to be careful when approaching a strange man, even a sad sack in trouble.

Life's a bitch...How did the sticker go? And then you die? No, that wasn't quite right. Was it? My memory is lousy. Ever since the accident. Everything is "ever since the accident." Life's a bitch. Why?

She was rushing from a computer class that kept her from the office too long, late for an appointment with a psychiatrist and shaking with emotional baggage left over from the last accident. The emancipated, modern woman. Funny, in a way.

She didn't laugh much any more.

It was absurd to say that hardship made you strong. It made you aware of your vulnerability. For an endless time, they had said the accident was her fault, that the woman had died because of her mistake. Every piece of registered mail sent out a bolt of nausea. Endless hours of sitting in orange or brown plastic cup chairs in small, airless rooms waiting to see people who would decide whether or not to destroy her life—These things carved into her for the first time a feeling of helplessness. For almost a year she swam through that nausea. Then they asked the questions she had been told they would ask and she gave the answers she had been told to give and it was over and they said she was exonerated. Free. But not free of guilt. Or free of fear.

The offer of a cell phone apparently unwanted, Matty pulled a business card from her suit coat pocket and waved it at the unattractive piece of humanity across from her. He waved back once, dismissing it.

"Don't you want to go after the truck driver?" she yelled over the traffic's howl. "I remember the name on the truck."

A shrug told her he lacked the energy or will to pursue justice.

Shit. He isn't even mad. At least, I'd be mad.

◆　　◆　　◆

"Sorry I'm late, Neil."

"You're usually a little late," the small man said with a forgiving smile. It was an observation, not a criticism. Psychiatrists didn't criticize.

Neil Osborne, M.D., P.A. sat in a comfortable, overstuffed chair, not behind a desk. He was a friend. This was a social visit. The pretense almost worked, helped along by the fact that Neil was the wrong temperament for a psychiatrist. He projected neither strength nor comfort. He was nervous. His eyes, wide and set too far apart, like a doll's eyes, tended to move constantly, from the patient to the window, to his desk, to his shiny black shoes but, carefully, never to his watch. What he did have was the ability to see inside his patients, an often irritating talent.

"Traffic," she said, an excuse scattered like litter across life in Washington, D.C. Matty sat down in the chair opposite him, slipped off her pumps, tucked her feet under her skirt and leaned her head into the corner formed by the wing and the back. She didn't want to be here, but at least she did like this chair, wide enough for sitting in her favorite position.

"Anyway, it's more efficient," she said. "I can't waste time waiting outside your door. And actually—" She started to mention the near-accident, then stopped. She didn't want to get into that. It would bring more tears. It had been a year of tears. *Enough.*

The silence became long, but Matty was not going to finish her sentence. *He's the professional. Let him handle it.*

"You're exceptionally tense today. Or..." Neil tilted his head to the left "...perhaps jittery is more accurate?"

Matty realized she was playing with one dangling earring. She stopped, then felt defensive. Although clearly a reaction from the accident, nothing Neil had said, the anger could not be suppressed. There were no social barriers here. She could criticize, too.

"This is like sitting in mud," she said, waving a hand around the room.

"Mud?"

"Brown. Brown paneling, brown leather furniture, brown wood. Everything's brown but the drapes. They're sand. Don't like brown. Mud."

That felt good. A smile touched her lips briefly.

"I thought it was…That it created a sense of ease," he said mildly.

"Green. Green does that. That's why schools are painted green. You should know that."

But the kick had gone out of challenging Neil. The huge bulk of the truck was back, prickling the nerves of her arms. Neil had said something. She didn't know what.

He leaned toward her.

"…a strong woman. You got back up on your horse and rode again—"

"Into my car," she corrected.

"All right. Into your car. Fine. But the life you're leading is not going to heal you. It's too frantic."

"The business is going well. Very well." Her stare dared him to deny it.

"It seems to me that everything is going well except you. You're getting thinner, for instance."

"So I wanted to lose a few pounds."

"Are you enjoying food?"

That caught her by surprise. "Sure," she lied.

He sat back in his chair again.

"Are you still having trouble remembering words?"

She didn't want to admit that. Only this morning she had called to order more toner for the copier and couldn't come up with its name. "The black stuff," she had said with a forced laugh and the man had laughed with her. It hadn't been funny.

"You need to get away from the pressure."

"Standard advice for all your patients?" *Sarcasm. Nasty. Why am I angry with Neil? He wasn't driving that damn truck. He's like Tom. I can be a bitch and he's so kind, so understanding. Asshole.*

He nodded agreeably. "For a good many of them. Some of them really can't. I think you could. You're not by nature an aggressive woman, Matty. Do you hear how confrontational you're being with me?"

No, Neil. Haven't a clue. But guilt was taking the edge off her anger. This was a nice man. It wasn't his fault that she resented having to take time see him, that she still needed him.

"I can't. It's my business. Okay. So you pushed the right button. That word thing. It is bothering me. But it will go away." *Like crying too much, too easily.*

"It's been—What?—almost a year since the trial was over? The anxiety isn't going away, is it? And it's no good telling you to slow down. Your property management business, with calls all hours of the day and night, the constant interruptions, endless complaints and problems to solve—Wouldn't it be healing to get away from that?"

Matty sat up straight in her chair and stared directly at him.

"You mean take a vacation? I'm paying you two hundred dollars an hour for you to tell me to take a vacation?"

"No. You're paying me that much to get a prescription for Diazepam. The vacation advice is free."

That jolted a quick laugh out of her. It helped, just a little. "You know I can't. Not for a whole week."

"I was thinking, perhaps…a month?"

"A month?"

"Six weeks would be better. If you go for a week, you'll be planning what to do when you come back even before you go."

"Impossible!"

"Sit back, please, and consider. You said last week you were about ready to put all your records on computer. Did you finish that course?"

"Next Friday."

Immediately she saw the possibilities.

"No dressing up each morning, Matty. No rush hour traffic. Forget your hair and manicures and the phone calls. You can work without interruption—"

"Yes. I remember. Constant interruption can literally drive you insane."

She closed her eyes and in the silence addressed each problem and solved it. After a few minutes, she looked at him and said, slowly, "But where? Not a resort!" In her mind, laughing couples played in the surf.

Neil leaned forward and, lifting her hand from the arm of her chair, held it between both of his, something he had never done before. She felt a rush of sympathy. He was such a funny-looking little man and she knew he was attracted to her.

"I have a little place in mind," he said. "A cabin. It belongs to a cousin of mine. He told me to lend it to any reliable person. It's better for it to be occupied. I warn you it'll need some cleaning—"

"But not a month!"

"Look," he said, holding up her hand. "This hand is perfectly manicured. It is also cold and rigid. The manicure tells me you're coping. The rigidity tells me that you're not making the progress we're trying for."

"What happened to warm heart?" Were his words a cover-up for the inappropriateness of holding her hand?

"I suspect that's as buried as a lot of your other nicer aspects"

"Ouch!"

"Why so rigid?"

"I'm not used to your holding my hand."

It was, in fact, becoming uncomfortable. Matty was repelled by the fact that his was softer than her own, which, if not callused, was at least firm from housework and constant minor repairs to the properties she managed. She pulled her long, copper-tipped fingers away, not so quickly as to be insulting.

Neil steepled his hands and tapped the fingertips together, a sign, Matty now knew, that he was a little nervous himself.

"My taking your hand is a new situation and you've lost the flexibility to deal with new situations. Your life is contracting. That often becomes necessary as we get older, not at the age of thirty-four. You need this time, believe me. You can take walks, admire the view, the wild flowers…"

Mentally, Matty fast forwarded through the next few weeks, envisioning the work that she could get done if left alone.

Neil was still talking. "—the late seventeen hundreds. West of Frederick in the mountains. Beautiful country. Not far away…"

Matty was thinking her own thoughts. *I can stay in touch by phone. Rosemary to handle the paperwork, Consuela the people. It would save time, loads of time, at the office once I have everything on computer. And Tom. Awful to think of a loving husband as a burden, but the laundry and meals and adapting to his schedule…Neil has some good points. Especially about the traffic.*

He was saying something, but she didn't hear it.

"I'll do it," she said.

Neil raised his eyebrows, looking even more like a doll.

"Excellent," he said, not surprised at the suddenness of her decision. Her decisions were always sudden. The cabin is…" He frowned. "I'm not sure this is the right word, but it seems to be…There's something—" He smoothed the frown from his face and finished, "—magic. Sort of magic."

In the outer office, key in hand, Matty waited while Neil's secretary, Erica, drew a neat little map and wrote an unnecessary quantity of directions, frequently looking up at Matty with lips pressed together as though repressing something she wanted to say.

"Have you been to this place, Erica?" Matty said, giving her an opening.

"No. Not really." The dark eyes were on the paper under her hand now, revealing nothing.

The invitation had not been accepted.

Matty went to the door and opened it, feeling for her car keys in her purse as she stepped into the hall. They didn't seem to be there. Had they been left on the desk as she got directions? Turning, she found Erica's chair empty. At the same moment, her fingers found the keys.

"Should she go there?" Erica's voice, coming from the direction of Neil's office, sounded troubled.

There was no doubt in Matty's mind who "she" was. She leaned inside the door and saw Erica's back framed by Neil's door.

The psychiatrist's soft voice was barely audible.

"I cannot discuss my patients with you, Erica. You know that."

"But Louisa—!"

"My sister is easily frightened."

"I know. It's just that Matty—"

"I cannot discuss my patients with you." The tone was firmer this time.

Erica's head lowered slightly and her hand moved to the doorknob. Reluctant to be caught eavesdropping, Matty stepped back into the hall and carefully pulled the door shut.

Scared? At this cabin?

Her mind sought possibilities. *An intruder? An animal? What kind of animal would frighten—No. Neil wouldn't send her where there was any real danger. Isolated, maybe? That wouldn't worry Erica, surely.*

Strange.

Matty resisted the impulse to go back in and ask what they were talking about, but it wasn't a conversation she was supposed to have heard and, given Neil's reaction, one that his secretary was not likely to explain. Finally, she decided that, if there was anything she should have known, Neil would have told her. Erica probably didn't know the whole story about Neil's sister.

Slowly, Matty walked down the hall, still not quite certain she was ready to leave. Or go to that cabin.

Magic. That was an odd word for a psychiatrist to use. Could that have something to do with Erica's concern?

The idea led nowhere. Men in black capes waving batons, rabbits and puffs of smoke seemed to have little to do with a cabin in the woods. She pushed the button for the elevator, trying to wave away the little gust of fear the conversation had sent through her. It was probably as groundless as all her other incessant anxieties.

2

Rockville, Maryland was full of colonial style, commercial townhouses and proud old homes converted to impressive offices as the Washington, D.C. sprawl pushed into the town's residential areas. Matty's office was in none of these. Her car bumped across railroad tracks and pulled onto the asphalt that blackened what was once a front yard. She climbed the six front steps of the flaking stucco bungalow, pulled open the ill-fitting front door and then climbed two more sets of stairs. Montgomery Management had no national image to maintain. Its humble attic office made possible the lower fees that attracted clients, who liked the convenience of meeting in their own homes. As for tenants, in Montgomery County they would go anywhere for a good rental.

"Hello, Rosemary."

A grossly overweight, bleached blonde looked up slowly, her eyes acknowledging Matty's presence without welcoming it. They were beautiful eyes. All Rosemary's features were beautiful, delicate, punched into a Pillsbury doughboy face. Rosemary Hahn was a mystery to Matty, a totally alien nature, envious of everything Matty had and was doing, as far as Matty could see, all the wrong things to achieve happiness. She covered herself in glitz and paint, bleached her hair and painted her nails strange colors overlaid with ornate pictures rather than cutting out the doughnuts and putting in some time at a gym. Envy was a fire that burned up what little good will she might have shown toward her employer. But she worked. She wasn't good with people, but she was efficient.

"Where's Consuela?" Matty asked brightly. Rosemary always seemed to force her to make an extra effort.

Consuela Segundo was the third member of the office staff and Rosemary's foil. She was haphazard about paper, unpredictable with grammar, but made warm connections with all kinds of people.

"Went home early. Eddie was sent home from school. Sick. Told her I'd take over if anything came up." There was no resentment. Consuela was unattractively skinny, homely of face, wire-haired and poorer than Rosemary.

"Ah. Too bad." Matty sat down at her desk and turned her swivel chair toward Rosemary. "I've decided to go away so I can concentrate on getting forms and records on disk for the computer. Otherwise, they'll never get done." It was her idea now, not Neil's, she noted. "Anyone who needs to talk to me about anything will have to catch me before next Friday. Between now and then, I'll get ready what I need to take. You'll be in charge while I'm gone."

This evoked a real smile.

"How long will you be gone?"

"A month, probably." That brought a little jump of anxiety that had to be soothed. "If you have a question, you can reach me by phone."

"I'm sure we'll be just fine."

"I'm sure you will."

Matty smiled again, but Rosemary had turned back to her work. Encounters with her assistant always left Matty with a feeling of failure. She glanced at the unoccupied desk by the window, missing Consuela. Dippy. That was the word often used to describe the other half of her staff. Not a fair description of a woman who, left to support a child when her husband deserted her, forced to share a rented apartment with another woman in the same situation, nevertheless managed to find every day full of happy distractions. Her plants needed more water than a tropical forest, every phone call was a social occasion, each new item of clothing Matty wore an excuse for prolonged admiration. So much joy; so little cause. Maybe that was why she valued Consuela, to observe that quality of joyousness she had lost herself.

Suddenly aware she was wasting time, Matty turned to her desk and reached for the mail.

◆   ◆   ◆

"I think that's a fine idea."

Irritation rose in Matty, recognizably the same irrationality that had risen with Neil. Why was everything she did always all right with her husband? And why in the world should that be irritating? Lately, everything Tom did annoyed her, especially his constant, predictable agreeableness. He was aware of her feelings and said nothing. Maybe that was what bothered her, that he didn't complain, that he was so damned understanding. It implied that she needed to be understood, needed careful handling. It's human nature to want admiration, not pity.

"Bloody ground," Tom said, his finger moving across the map to her destination.

That didn't sound good.

"What does that mean?"

"Turner's Gap. Not a major battle . But something happened there."

It was one of the things Matty most respected about her husband. His knowledge sometimes seemed encyclopedic. Tom Burhmann was a writer for one of the science departments at the National Institutes of Health. He loved his peaceful, undemanding work and that helped make him a gentle man. He was just over six feet tall, still lean and reasonably fit from a four-year stint in the Air Force, but that was years ago and now his broad shoulders were beginning to curl forward from constant reading and long hours at his computer. In another five years there would be a noticeable pot belly.

"Bloody ground, huh? Must have dried up by now. Do you think it's a good idea, my going?" she asked out of kindness, to let him know he mattered.

"Yes, I do," he said, knowing the decision was entirely hers.

"Friday," she said.

"No Saturday afternoon delight for us?" he asked.

"We'll have Saturday afternoon on Thursday night."

They smiled at each other, enjoying the easy communication.

"Want me to go along the first day? Just to check out the place? Make sure it's okay?"

"Okay? What wouldn't be okay?"

"It doesn't bother you to go alone? A lot of women would be at least a little leery."

"Of what?"

"I don't know. Bugs. Mice. Strange men. Isolation. The unknown. The unknown is supposed to be a little frightening, isn't it? Or exciting, depending on what kind of person you are."

"Forget frightening. And exciting. For me it's a place to work, to catch up. And to unwind."

"You're not put off by this Louisa's experience, whatever it was."

"No. I can trust Neil."

"And you don't believe in this magic."

"Not really," she said. "But a little magic might be nice, don't you think?"

◆   ◆   ◆

Matty spoke to Consuela next morning and that left only one goodbye, which she put off. She tore through the next week and a half, held together by the thought of a whole month away. She was both fearful of and irritated with traffic, angry with anyone who took longer than three rings to answer the phone and absolutely furious with the copier, which went streaky again. Water took forever to boil, too many clothes needed ironing and papers hid in the depths of files with demonic purposefulness. Thursday was the last day before leaving. She had called her father to explain why she hadn't seen him the week before: she had to get ready. Conscience required a visit before leaving.

◆   ◆   ◆

The nursing home was a different world. Above all, it was a world that kept her from the one where she belonged. People moved in slow motion.

Here, in the last days of life, when time was short, time had no value. Pills were taken slowly, one at a time, by shaking hands, visitors sat for endless hours in silence with nothing to say, just "being there." The only things that moved with any speed were the minds of people like Matty, churning with unbidden lists of chores that needed doing somewhere else.

"Addison Francis Bancroft" was the name on the brass plate outside the private room. They had to have it especially made. The home's usual ones were too short for the full name her father insisted on having displayed. An atheist, he was nevertheless an admirer of St. Francis of Assisi.

"Hi, Dad."

"Mathilda."

Would the day come when he would look up and not know her? There were days, many days, when his memory was unreliable, when he repeated the same news items three or four times during a single hour's visit. That was the time she made herself stay, no less than an hour. Sometimes she had to reassure herself that she still loved him. She certainly cried about him often enough. But he was less and less often the father she used to know.

"You look good today, Dad."

He did look good. Days like this, Matty was sure he would live many years yet. He had stopped taking good care of himself when her mother died, claiming that old people claimed too much of the nation's wealth keeping themselves alive long beyond the time when life was good. Now, from the knees down, his legs had been lost to diabetes.

Matty leaned over and kissed the shining pink forehead.

"Would you like to get in your chair and I'll take you outside?"

"No, thanks."

Matty almost mouthed the response with him. It was always the same, probably because he didn't want to be too much trouble. She would much rather have something to do.

She held her father's hand as she talked. Touch was supposed to be important, but he seemed scarcely aware of it. There was a lot to say about the proposed trip and all she intended to accomplish, but his eyes became impatient and she knew she had gone on too long, that he had something to say.

"Jimmy's son called last night. Jimmy Nelson."

Matty searched her memory. She had no idea who Jimmy Nelson was.

"I'm glad he called, Dad." She was. There were few events in his life. A single phone call could give meaning to a week.

After he had reviewed two or three times all the things Jimmy's son had said, his attention drifted, as it always did, to the television set that was rarely off. With the remote control he turned the sound up a little. From a room down the hall, an eerie crooning began, like something from a low budget ghost movie. It was Mrs. Grogan. The sound always distressed her father. He said it sounded like his future calling to him.

Matty began mentally to run through all the things she had to do before she left. Her fingers itched to take out a pad and pencil and make some notes. Instead, she sought some topic that would divert her father's attention from the television.

"Tom has a new project at work. A big one. A study on memory and they want a lengthy report, almost a small book. It should be interesting." She leaned forward, ready to recite the discoveries relevant to aging and the medications he was taking that might affect memory. Surely that would be of interest.

"Oh," her father answered, but his eyes stayed on television. "*Jeopardy*," he said.

Her eyes turned to the screen. She watched with him until *Jeopardy* was over. Then she leaned over and kissed the hard, fleshless forehead again.

"Bye, Dad."

"Must you rush off, Mathilda?"

He always said that no matter how long she stayed.

"Matty, Dad. Mathilda doesn't suit me."

"It should." He looked at her, puzzled. "We meant that it should."

She smiled and left, her shoulders dropping in relief. She could get on with things now. Getting into her car, she thought again of what her father had said. Mathilda was supposed to suit her? An old-fashioned name like that? Maybe it would suit her better in that old cabin. No doubt it would be a little like going back to the past.

3

It was really dark now. Matty was tempted to look at her watch, but was afraid to take her eyes from the ruts. This couldn't be called a road. Though the potholes made her wince in sympathy for her poor car, it was comforting that the grooves were like guiding hands that wouldn't let the tires slide down the mountainside. On her left, a nearly full moon whitened the edges of the leaves and branches of the slender, thickly crowded trees that clung to the steep slope, holding it together with their roots.

It almost seemed that the disintegrating driveway intentionally tried to evade the straight beams of her headlights as it curved up, down and around. Tree branches fingered the roof and crickets' shrill sound accompanied the hum of her car's motor. At some point on Route 270, music had become just noise and she had turned off the radio. Another time, this alien world made silver and blue by the moonlight would have been captivating, mysterious. Tonight she was too tired. She just wanted to get there.

It had been a hell of a day. The plan had been a quick getaway from the office, then a stop at some pleasant inn in the country for dinner, pampering herself a little. Neil would have approved. But Consuela had brought Eddie to the office, as she often did when he wasn't well, which was often. He was a serious seven-year-old who liked to "play business" and neatly arrange the paper clips and other paraphernalia that Consuela threw haphazardly into her desk drawers. Today, Consuela had spent most of her time comforting him, trying to get him to take fluids and eat something until she gave up and took him home. Unwilling to leave a new tenant due to come in at the end of the day to Rosemary's drill instructor treatment, Matty stayed to explain how the requirements of the lease related to their particular property. Expecting to leave, she hadn't brought lunch and couldn't deal with Rosemary's usual *Pizza Hut* delivery. That had been a mistake. Going without food always made her tired.

Traffic had been the usual slow torture. A quick stop at a *7-11* in Frederick netted a few groceries, including a granola bar, which she had eaten as she shopped, eliciting a disapproving look from another shopper. At checkout, paying for the bar, Matty had waved the wrapper like a flag of honor, announcing the fact that she was paying for it. Behind her, her critic looked away, refusing to be reproved by her honesty.

After a sharp left turn, the driveway ended, finally and suddenly, in a small level clearing and the house thrust itself into view on her left, not the cozy cabin she had imagined, but an uncompromising, rectangular log home, two stories sketched in alternating strokes of light and dark against the blue-black sky, unsoftened by foundation plantings. The moon was on the far side, turning the edges of the tin roof a bright silver. A stab of fear went through Matty until she realized the eerie blue lights in the upper windows was the moon, too, shining through. It wasn't welcoming.

So this is home for a while.

She sat in the car, reluctant to unlock the doors and get out.

Okay, Neil. You were right. I don't welcome new experiences. Maybe especially not this one.

She tried to rearrange her mind, envision a new adventure or at least a rest, but all she could do was wonder why the hell she was about to leave her luxurious car, far away from her clean and comfortable home, and enter this intimidating pile of logs.

Matty backed up a little so the lights from her car illuminated the door. The silhouette of a porch on the far side of the house had been visible as she pulled in. There would be a nice view down the mountain from there, so this perhaps was considered the back door. It was made of four vertical planks held together by two narrower horizontal ones. There were wide, shallow gouges, the evidence of crude planing. This must be the original door. Seventeen hundreds, Neil had said. How many hands—and what kind of hands—had pushed open those planks? For the first time, Matty felt a stirring of curiosity that overcame her reluctance. She opened the car door, got out and walked over to the house. The entrance was barely higher than her five foot six inches.

Anxious to get in now, she dug in her purse for the key. The lock was inappropriately new. The key turned easily, but it took a hard shove to open the door and she lurched into a swirl of dust particles, sparkling in the moonlight, that the movement brought to life. At first she saw only the pale rectangle of a single window across the room and then, as her eyes adjusted, low white forms moved out of the shadows. A metal pole threw back the light from her car headlights and she headed for it quickly, hoping it was a floor lamp. It was. Feeling for a switch, her hand became wrapped in a spider web and she recoiled in disgust, wiping her hand on her slacks. The need for light took on a new importance and she stubbornly reached again and found a chain and pulled. Light swept the surrounding area, revealing several inert insects in the web but, at least, nothing alive. She took a Kleenex from her pocket and wiped her hand more carefully.

She had been holding her breath and now let it go in relief. The lamp was at the end of a couch. It and two lumpy chairs, covered with white sheets, circled a low coffee table. These were ghosts she could deal with. In front of them, in the position designated for a TV set in most homes, squatted a pot bellied stove. The stove was a disappointment, the death of the dream of reading in front of an open fire on cool evenings. The living room ran from front to back, the full width of the house, perhaps fifteen feet. Directly across from her was a twin to the door she had entered. To her right, thigh-high homemade bookshelves, boards across stacked bricks, ran the length of the wall. On them were books, magazines and assorted odds and ends. Its lone decorative item was a small white bust that, for the moment, she identified only as not Beethoven. The books should have been covered, too, she thought. She always felt protective of books. An old cupboard in the far corner held nothing visible behind its clouded glass doors. No curtains or drapes. That was okay, quite the thing in elegant old houses, although these windows had flat planks for woodwork, nothing decorative enough to avoid covering. Stairs behind the bookshelves, narrow and steep, marched up the middle of the house and, to her right, just past the bottom of them, an open doorway.

The kitchen, surely. Yes. Check the kitchen first. Then, definitely, the bathroom.

There was no optimism in either thought.

Matty went through the doorway, less intimidated now by the spider web that caught her cheeks and nose. The lamp had failed to reveal the web, but would have shown any residents. On the far wall sat the sturdy bulk of a small refrigerator. Anxiously, she opened its door and was reassured by the wave of light. Its small bulb revealed more promising sources of illumination, a lamp on a small table below the front window and a bare bulb over the sink under the opposite window lit by her headlights. The tap squeaked as she turned it, but water gushed out at a responsible rate. Her shoulders dropped in relief.

Okay. We're in business.

Walking back to the car, her mind gathered together all the tasks that needed to be done and formed them into a manageable timetable. Food, a clean bed and bathroom headed the mental columns. The kitchen would have to wait for tomorrow.

Not sure the refrigerator would be cold, she had bought little that needed to be kept cool and those items were quickly put away. A cup of yogurt provided dinner while the remaining items were dumped on the small amount of counter space by the sink. It hurt to leave them there in disorder, but they were not a priority tonight. She took stock as she ate standing up, as much to avoid the dusty furniture as for efficiency. Turning on the lights had revealed a room exactly the size and shape of the living room. Looking like something from the "Before" picture in an aged issue of *Better Homes and Gardens*, it held a chipped sink with a skirt, the rounded-top yellowing refrigerator, a square column of brick chimney beside it, and a mint green stove on legs that produced the hiss of gas when the handles were turned. Faded gold and green linoleum covered most of the floor, but was worn down to wood in front of the appliances and the sink. Oilcloth meant to match the linoleum, strings dangling from the cuts made with pinking shears, covered the small table-for-two under the window. Experience told her the hot water heater in the corner would hold forty gallons. That was adequate. It and the stove probably ran on propane gas. The chimney would be in the kitchen in a house this old, of course, but why, she wondered, was there no fireplace? This would have been where they cooked. No open fire here, either. So much for the…Matty couldn't come up with the word. Somehow worn linoleum, dust and spiders had not been part of her dream getaway cabin.

Ambiance. That was it. The ambiance here stinks.

Floor to ceiling open shelves with dusty cans and dishes covered the taller part of the triangular inner wall. To its left, a door with an upper edge slanted to conform to the stairs ended almost at floor level. Stooping, she opened it, peered under the stairs and found an old brown canister style vacuum, a mop and broom and, below them, various odds and ends, including some welcome cleaning supplies as Neil had promised when she picked up the key.

Matty quickly scraped up the last of the raspberry jam at the bottom of the yogurt cup and pulled out what she would need from under the stairs. The rest of the kitchen didn't bear thinking about tonight, not the bad smell and especially not the insects, live and dead. It was time to go upstairs and face the bathroom. What kind of a horror would the toilet be? No doubt better than some her job had introduced her to. With hands firmly holding the paper towels, toilet cleaner and a Lysol spray bottle, her bladder drove her upstairs.

◆　　　◆　　　◆

Two hours later, Matty had a headache from the whine of the old vacuum and her muscles were weary from unaccustomed exercise. The bedroom over the kitchen was as clean as it was going to get tonight. The wide floorboards were hazardous in the places she most needed to walk; the planks had worn down and the heads of square, handmade nails protruded. Tomorrow she would get the hammer from the toolbox every property manager kept in a car trunk and pound them down. The iron double bed was made up with her own white sheets and her toilet articles lay in orderly patterns on the dresser that had one drawer missing. The mirror needed resilvering and the image that stared back at her seemed afflicted with some dread disease.

Cleaning the front window, she had been bothered by a flagpole in the front yard with a tattered rag of cloth. Girl Scout training had taught her never to leave an American flag up at night without a light. But was this even an American flag? It fluttered enough in the breeze to reveal ragged edges and a few holes, but not enough for Matty to determine the pattern and the colors were pale, certainly not a vibrant red, white and blue. It should be taken down, but what was the point after all this time? Maybe it wasn't an American flag. Either way, she was too tired.

She left the window for the fourth time and went into the bathroom that occupied half the space over the living room. Next to the kitchen, this was the most depressing room in the house. She knew it well from an inch-by-inch scrubbing, but it would never feel clean. Perhaps it was the memory of all the dead bugs that had been sucked into the vacuum or all the hidden live spiders that had probably killed the other bugs. Matty would have preferred to have the spiders dead and the other miscellaneous and innocuous insects alive. Spiders were her least favorite crawling thing and she had some reservations about sleeping with all the ones still moving around downstairs. Just as in the kitchen, many feet had worn the ugly yellow, orange and brown linoleum in front of the toilet, tub and sink down to bare boards impossible to sanitize. Maybe some cheap throw rugs could be found at the general store Neil had described. For now, a few of the towels she had brought would have to do. At least the tub had some appeal. It was deep, claw-footed, with a comfortable-looking slanted back and, unlike the toilet, rust stains were limited to a few tracks below the spout. The taps no longer shrieked at her touch as she started her bath.

No quick showers here. No shower at all. A luxurious soak was probably better, anyway. Matty poured an overdose of almond oil into the water and inhaled deeply as, eyes closed, she sank chin deep into the hot water.

Moments passed.

She wasn't relaxing.

It was too quiet. No hum of vehicles or voices of passing neighbors. No music from a nearby townhouse. When had the crickets stopped shrieking? Was anyone anywhere near her at all? She had a sudden vision of herself, naked in the tub, suspended one story above two unfamiliar rooms in the only brightly lit spot in a dark world. Why did nakedness make one feel so vulnerable?

Matty let out a long breath. *This is not me. Is this the magic Neil had mentioned? That you turned into someone else? Into a sissy? Enough!* She buried her thoughts in an article about rental insurance.

By the time she crawled into bed, her head was comfortably full of business, bugs and silence and moonlight shadows forgotten. Her own clean sheets were cool, the rough tan blanket necessary, though it would still be hot in the city this early in September. Carefully turning the sheet over the top of what was probably not a clean blanket, Matty tucked it under her chin, reached over and pulled the chain on the wrought iron lamp, the twin to the one in the kitchen. The last light in the house went out.

The moon took over. There were no curtains upstairs, either, and the light lay across her chest like a living thing, pulsing with every breath. She looked at the offending window. The moon was high in a cloudless sky, illuminating that worrisome limp rag hanging on the flagpole. *Not right. Check that out in the morning.* She had worked hard, had earned that nice, groggy feeling that foretold sleep. Not that she really expected it. At home, the minute her head hit the pillow, her mind went into overdrive and she reached for the Diazepam. *No tranquilizers,* she ordered. *Doesn't matter if you sleep or not. Neil said so.* She smiled in the dark. That sounded like something she said often years ago: *Dad said so.* The smile didn't last long. What Dad said these days had, sadly, little authority.

She flipped over, turning away from the distracting window. But there, distorted on the log wall, was that rectangle of light with the shadow of the flag, waving in wordless communication. She closed her eyes. Only for a moment. She had to open them again. Yes, the flag was still there, moving a little more now.

"Damn!" She said and sat up. "Flag. Rag. Whatever. How can something stupid like that keep me awake!" Surprisingly, her voice sounded good to her in spite of the sentiments she had expressed. There had been too much silence. Taking her boom box and CD's into the house had seemed unnecessary work this first night. She lay back down again and issued a firm invitation to sleep.

"Please," she whispered. "I'm so tired I'm going nuts." She turned to the window and the flag flipped her a greeting.

"Okay, okay," she said, beginning to wonder if talking to herself was going to become a regular part of her stay. "This I can deal with."

A pull on the lamp's chain sent weak light flooding over the primitive room. Slippers and robe seemed necessary, both for warmth and the rough floors and whatever hid in the grass outside. Holding her robe away from the dusty steps, she went carefully down the steep stairs that would never pass an FHA/VA inspection and went outside, using the familiar back door for no good reason except that it was familiar. It pushed open with its usual creaky complaint.

Matty walked around to what she now thought of as the front, noting for the first time the two high-backed wooden rocking chairs on the porch that ran the length of the house, and headed for the flagpole. It wasn't tall, not even roof high, made of roughly finished wood. The pulley near her shoulder was rusted and the rope dark with age or grime, probably both. Which side of the rope? She always guessed wrong adjusting the vertical blinds at home. A hard pull met with equal resistance. No give at all. She tried the other side. Not much movement here, either, but it didn't fight back. She yanked hard. The pulley screeched in protest, but the rope moved a little.

"Damn you!" she said. "You're coming down!"

By the time the limp fabric was draped across her arms, she was trembling with exhaustion. It was an American flag, so faded there was little contrast, though she could see that it had far fewer stars than today's nation required. The cloth was linen. Linen was tough, but it hadn't been able to last as long as time had demanded.

Bundling the flag in her arms like laundry, careful to keep it from touching the ground, she carried it back to the house and dumped it on the chair across from her bed. It sent up a lazy billow of dust. Matty brushed off the front of her robe and defiantly took the bottle of Diaz-epam from the dresser, went into the bathroom and threw one of the yel-low pills down her throat, followed by a sip of water. She marched back to the bed, got in and folded her arms across her chest. The rectangle of light from the window had moved to her thighs. It seemed less threatening there. Her eyes went back to the flag and, as the tranquilizer gradually took effect, looking at the gray heap of linen eased her anger at the overall mis-ery of the day. Or was that the tranquilizer? Whatever the cause, a sense of history, of time passed and passing, came over her. The books downstairs roused a sleepy curiosity. Surely one or more of them had something about the history of the area. Gettysburg was near. Probably some fighting here. Perhaps in the Revolutionary War, too. *History was important, wasn't it? Or was going to be.* She didn't know why that thought passed through her mind.

4

At six thirty, Matty woke for the second time. The first time, she had taken another tranquilizer and now found herself enmeshed in the usual combination of nervousness and reluctance to get up. Every day started like this. But this was certainly not her usual day. Outside the front window was the flagpole, harmless now, and the flag merely a dirty pile of dull colors on the chair by the bedroom door. How could she have become so worked up last night? The work ahead was intimidating. Not the paperwork. That was welcome, an opportunity for progress, accomplishment. But before that lay the cleaning of the rest of the house. Tom's comment about mice—*Were snakes a possibility? They ate mice. Was that thought good or bad?*—came back to her. She lay in bed another half an hour, again, the usual thing, a reluctance to start the day that had begun just after the accident. It would always be that, THE accident. Since then, she lay in bed in the morning until tension became unbearable and forced her to get up. Neil had explained that, an unwillingness to face possible problems, but it still sounded nuts to her.

After a quick trip to the bathroom, she pulled on jeans and a tee, heavy duty sneakers and extra lotion to protect her hands and did not hurry downstairs.

It looked a little better in the sunlight. Pausing at the bottom of the stairs, she could see the white shrouded furniture in the living room to her right, the dingy, outdated kitchen to her left. It was the view that helped, the sunlit expanse of green foliage and blue sky beyond the windows.

"No curtains. Good choice," she said aloud, noting that there was another reason for bare windows besides elegant woodwork. "Especially since I would have to wash the bloody things." Then a less happy thought struck her. There was, apparently, no washer or dryer. "Shit," she commented. Not driving had been one of the major lures of this vacation and now there would have to be a search for a laundry. "Vacation? Hah! Some damn—"

"No," she corrected herself as she was about to enter the kitchen. "Adjust attitude."

She turned instead to the back door and opened it, finding the solid presence of her car a reassuring sight. *How could one love a car and hate driving it? One would have to be nuts.* That was not a good thought. Neil's advice had been to take walks and look at wild flowers. Later, of course, but she scanned the thick undergrowth for a flash of color. The wild flowers didn't look like much. Mostly that stuff they used to dye with food coloring when she was a child. The name wouldn't come to mind. She never stumbled on words used every day, but the ones rarely needed too often hovered on the fringes of her consciousness, stubbornly refusing to surface. One of Neil's touchstones.

I've got to try. I've got to try. I need this.

She wasn't surprised to find tears running down her cheeks. Any emotion at all brought them. It hadn't helped that the night's sleep had been inadequate, as usual. She inhaled deeply and told herself to relax, to linger a few moments and enjoy the view. It seemed an appropriate, healing thing to do.

Not feeling healed, she walked back in to the kitchen.

◆　　　◆　　　◆

An hour later, the cleaning had to be abandoned. She had washed the cereal bowl and spoon with the bar of soap from the bathroom and downed tasteless but healthy bran cereal, had more or less successfully pounded down many of the offending nails in the floorboards and started to clean, but too many supplies were missing. Here less than a day and it was necessary to climb back into the car. Neil's directions to the local general store were in her purse. Obsessed now with the need to get some "real" work done on the computer and stop playing housekeeper, she banged the old door on her way out, defiantly refused to lock it and left at a not quite safe speed back down the mountain.

◆ ◆ ◆

A run-down dump. That was Matty's initial reaction to JOSEPH'S COMMODITIES. *Commodities? Somebody's nuttier than I am!* Selection would be limited, but at least there would be no long lines.

The inside was predictable, narrow aisles, shelves crammed to the ceiling, dusty wooden floors. Not so predictable were the angry voices.

The woman, heavy-voiced, slow: "Well you should'na told her she had butt-sprung shorts!"

Then the man, sharp and quick: "Coulda said worse. Damn women don't know how to dress any more. Belly button stickin' right out at me. Clothes either too big or like somethin' they stole from their kids! Nothin' fits!"

Matty peered around the corner of an aisle and saw them. The woman was red-faced, sturdy, wearing a pink-flowered dress, the kind her Grandmother used to call a housedress. Matty didn't think they made them any more. The man was smaller, pale, all bones. They didn't see her and she backed behind the shelves again and began collecting.

"You're just mad 'cause we didn't have what she wanted!" the woman taunted.

"Never do these days. Always wantin' somethin' different. Stuff from every country in the world but this one! What's this organic cereal she wanted with no salt, no sugar, no preservatives, no fertilizer, no nothin'? Sounds like an empty box to me. What the hell's wrong with oatmeal? Or corn flakes? Or Rice Krispies?" His voice rose higher with each cereal. "Turnin' up her city nose at wine 'cause it's got a cap on it. What the hell difference does it make what kind of lid it's got?"

Matty moved quickly through the aisles, sympathizing with the unknown woman. Murphy's Oil Soap sounded just right for those old floors. Just for fun, she picked up a box of oatmeal and held it prominently in her hand as she approached the couple at the cash register.

"What about you? Findin' what you need?" the reedy voice challenged.

In the field of property management, dealing with angry people was routine.

"Absolutely. You have all the necessities."

He didn't like that. She knew he wouldn't. He was looking for a target and she wasn't going to give it to him. Matty countered the narrow, angry eyes with an innocent smile. Up close, he seemed even older. His bones looked ready to jut through finely cracked, lifeless skin. In the city, she would have wondered about AIDS. It didn't seem appropriate here. The woman who must be his wife had all the flesh, ample but firm. Her sturdy fingers were picking up the items one at a time very slowly and punching the old black register's keys.

"Judgin' by this stuff, not just passin' through, are ya?" she asked.

"No. I'm staying up the mountain in an old log house." Matty gestured in the general direction.

The woman's eyes grew. "That so," she said, drawing the words out. "Now there's a inter'stin' place for ya. Ain't it, Joseph?"

"Mr. Briggsley to you." The man was staring straight ahead and spoke in a disinterested way.

"Don't mind him."

There was no trace of anger in her voice now. A woman who forgot and forgave easily, Matty concluded.

"He's not like anybody. Some day when he's got less poison in him, you got to talk to him. He knows all about history. That house—It's got a lot of history to it." She kept on punching the keys but with a frustrating slowness. "Headquarters for some soldiers. Civil War, y'know. Me, I wouldn't stay there for the world, would I, Joseph? 'Scuse me," she corrected. "Mr. Briggsley."

"He's not your husband, then?" Matty spoke as though the man weren't there which, in a way, he wasn't.

"Oh, yes. He is. Forty-seven years now. But, like I say, he's not like any-body. Leastways, nobody around here. Forgettin' my manners. I'm Mary Briggsley and this here's Joseph Briggsley."

Matty couldn't resist. "Of Joseph's Commodities."

Mary smiled. It was a good smile and Matty warmed to her for the first time.

"Just so. Joseph's idea. Got some tone to it, he said."

But what about Mary, who is doing all the work? Matty took the woman's outstretched hand. She looked toward Joseph, but no hand was offered there.

"Matty Buhrmann," she said.

Mary was now bagging the groceries with much rearranging and pok-ing. A quick look at her watch made Matty's skin itch. The cleaning had to be done before tackling the computer and there was always the nagging worry that some program wouldn't cooperate. She willed the worn hands to move faster.

"Anyway–" Every word stopped the hands. "—you wouldn't get me stayin' there. Not with all them dead soldiers."

"What?" This comment was so unexpected, Matty had no emotional reaction at all.

"You know. Civil War. Whole graveyard for just them what died around here. Poor lost—youngsters, some of them. Joseph can—" She turned, but Joseph had gone without a word. From a back room came the sound of a manual typewriter.

"Good." Mary Briggsley leaned toward Matty and sighed the word. "He'll get it all out on the typewriter. Nasty stuff he writes. Regular Stephen King."

"He writes novels?"

"Well now, maybe no. Short stories once't in a while. Mostly poetry. Disgusted is what he is. Hates the whole world most days. People ain't always so—Oh, I don't know…respectful, I guess you'd say. And he's so smart." Mary was obviously impressed with her spouse. "All A's in school. Reads, writes, all that stuff. But he couldn't go to college, ya see. Had to take care of his mother. Kind of turned him. Sour, I mean. Knows he's better than most of the people who come in here, but they got so much, y'know? Where do so many people get so much? Big cars. On their way from one house they own to another they own somewheres else. Wearin' diamonds with sweat shirts, y'know?"

Matty had often wondered, too, how so many got so much, but, unlike Mary, she had enough for comfort and had no interest in continuing the conversation. The money lay on the counter, but Mary made no move to pick it up.

"You go to church of a Sunday? Nice Lutheran Church up on over by the Larken's horse farm if that suits you. But we got—"

"No. Thank you, but I don't go to church as a rule."

"Pity," Mary sighed as though Matty had said she had cancer. "You might mention it to the others."

"The others?"

"Them what's with you."

"Oh. No. I'm alone." Matty immediately realized that that wasn't a wise thing to say, but it was too late. She pushed the money a little closer. The woman picked it up, but didn't seem to know what she was holding.

"Alone? Oh, my." Mary leaned closer. "Then you really might want to go. To church, y'know. Kind of protection." It was almost a whisper now.

But Joseph heard. "Let the woman go, Mary."

Mary turned toward her husband's voice.

"Now we're havin' a nice conversation out here. You just get on with your writin'!"

"Woman wants to go. And quit tryin' to scare her with silly talk about dead soldiers and such idiocy."

"Nothin' silly about the dead, Joseph. And where there's violent death, souls walk. Any fool knows that."

Matty's need to get back to work was like another being inside her straining to get out.

"Mrs. Briggsley, I do need to go."

The woman was immediately apologetic.

"Why it's so, then! That Joseph! Ornery don't keep ya from bein' sensitive-like. He could maybe earn some money if he'd just write somethin' that didn't make you curl up inside. I'll be real quick."

She counted out the change at a speed that was probably rapid for her, offered it to Matty and then leaned over and whispered "He likes ya. Wouldn't care about ya bein' in a hurry if he didn't like ya."

She leaned back and beamed at Matty. "Now you remember church." Her expression became serious and her voice dropped to a whisper again as she added, "It might do some good, y'know. What with all those unrested spirits. At least, say a prayer now and then."

"Pray to the devil. Do just as much good," was the verdict from the back.

Matty took her change and fled.

5

On her knees, scrubbing the wide planks of the kitchen floor with Murphy's Oil Soap and a stiff brush from the closet under the stairs, Matty compared herself to Robinson Crusoe, a perfectly absurd comparison, she knew. She hadn't built this old cabin or foraged in anything more wild than an old-fashioned store for food, but compared to the life she lived in Rockville, this was primitive, even disgusting. There *had* been a mouse, as Tom had threatened, small, gray and slowly liquefying, under the kitchen sink, hidden by a curtain whose flowers were no longer recognizable. It accounted for the unpleasant smell and she was grateful now for the more acceptable aroma of Lysol and Murphy's Oil Soap. Centipedes had become as repulsive as spiders. There was something threatening about too many legs.

At first it was as if the house fought her. At home, housework was done in bits and pieces that gave her time to think through office problems and make plans. It was satisfying to accomplish two things at once. Household chores were readily abandoned when her thoughts were urgent enough to grab a piece of paper or the telephone and switch to business. Here there was no escape. There were always more small invaders, moths, beetles, spiders, live and dead, unidentifiable dried remnants, windows that kept producing new streaks and dust that moved only to resettle somewhere else. She had never before realized that a vacuum sweeper, while picking up dust, blew a certain portion of it back through the fabric bag. The air was constantly filled with dust made golden in the sun, like minuscule fireflies.

Then, sometime around mid-afternoon, the task ceased to be something to get out of the way and became a source of satisfaction. There was a great deal of room for improvement, something that didn't exist at home with Ellen coming every other week, and it was gratifying to see a dusty museum become a livable, if shabby, home. She slowed down and began to hum occasionally. Running the sweeper hose over the tops of the books, she noted that more than one dealt with the Civil War and these were set on top of the bookcase for evening reading. American Heritage's *Picture History of the Civil War* was intimidating in size in spite of the reassuring quantity of pictures, but the small pamphlet titled only "Gettysburg" looked to be a good start, maybe to be read out on the front porch.

Grateful for a chance to sit down, Matty plopped onto the floor with a hand towel and began pulling out the books, dusting them and putting them back in organized fashion. Most were novels, so they went on the top of the two shelves, alphabetized by author's name, paperbacks at the right side. Then, on the shelf below, four autobiographies, then one of the loose bricks that had been used as bookends, then a dictionary, another brick, a stack of old magazines, not hers to throw away, another brick and, finally, a small set of do-it-yourself home repair books which she vowed not to use.

The final book, *Historic Homes of Carroll County*, appealed to her because it might have a house with similarities to this one. It went on top of the bookcase with the Civil War reading.

The third room upstairs was saved for last. Her office was to be in the small room in the front, exactly the same size as the bathroom. Setting up her office felt good. A screwdriver from her car kit provided the means to remove the mirror from a large kneehole dresser that became her desk. It was then shoved across the room to the window to take advantage of the view over the tops of the trees and down the mountain. It took several wads of paper to make it stop rocking. The single bed along the wall would be a handy place to organize papers. An extra lamp was pilfered from the living room and tests had to be made to determine the right chair and pillow for the long hours she planned to put in on them. Then the scrubbing and dusting. It was frustrating not to be able to clean the outside of the upstairs windows. The project seemed promising at first as there were no screens except several narrow sliding inserts set against the walls, but the windows all stuck half way up or down and it was impossible to reach more than a few inches of outside surface.

The bottles of Murphy's Oil Soap and Windex were more than half empty by the time Matty stood and surveyed her new workroom and mentally patted herself on the back. It wasn't often she took time to stand still and appreciate something. She made herself stay a few moments longer than instinct dictated.

A short rest was in order. A few minutes on the old iron bed with a copy of *Realtor* magazine sounded good. The flag lay on the ladder-back chair. It was tempting to wash it, but it might fall apart. Safer to leave it just carefully folded. Taking it down had been a good decision. Someone had taken endless time to sew those now grayed stars and stripes. How long had it been since she had tackled any task as slow and painstaking as that needlework? Was their sense of time different then? The mystery of time had fascinated her even as a child. On vacation trips with her parents, she would watch the roadside from her back seat window, the blades of grass, weeds, asphalt and occasional bits of trash flashing by and would think, "When we come back, it will look just the same, but the vacation time will all be gone. Where will it go and what makes now now?" "The thoughts of youth are long, long thoughts," Longfellow wrote. They were, she decided. She had no such thoughts now. Oh, well. She didn't much like Longfellow anyway. It was a good sign that the specious dismissal seemed a little humorous. She almost laughed.

Queen Anne's Lace. That's what it was, that ragged roadside weed that they had dyed.

Matty sat down on the bed with the flag on her lap, not minding the dust it held in its old fibers. There was plenty of dust in her old jeans. Her days of dying Queen Anne's Lace and the fancy needlework were long gone. When did she become so practical? Not in the early years of marriage. She and Tom used to dream together, tackle creative projects around the house. There was a sudden surge of guilt, of sympathy for Tom. Has he lost the wife he thought he had married? The hour with Father went so slowly, but one hour in a week and an occasional Sunday dinner out wasn't much to give the man who had been a loving and supportive parent. Was her job more important than these two men? Was business more interesting? Maybe it was. That hurt. The thought was quickly dismissed. Yet this was surely what Neil had in mind, taking time to sort things out.

She was surprised to find her thoughts interrupted by the sound of passing traffic. But no. Traffic was the more familiar sound, the Rockville sound. This was thunder. The window framed well-defined, fast moving clouds of black and blue and gray.

A familiar pounding returned to her chest. All her office gear was still in the car! She jumped up, dumped the flag back on the chair and ran downstairs, pressing a hand against the wall as she slipped a little on the third step, and out the door.

"Damn!"

It *had* started to rain.

A quick reach into the back seat netted the umbrella and then, from the front seat, a push of a button popped the trunk. It took six awkward trips from the car to the door with the umbrella held unsteadily between her arm and ribs before everything was safely placed just inside. After one last trip to slam the trunk lid, she switched the umbrella to her hand, turned at the door to shake the water from it, kicked the door shut and set the umbrella on the kitchen floor to drip dry. It now had one broken spoke from bumping the door frame. She sat down at the small table by the kitchen window to take a breath, pulled off her wet sneakers and watched as the clouds were blown to the east and the rain went with them.

Heart still pumping hard from the exertion, the absurdity of her actions overwhelmed her. How often this last year she had rushed to accomplish something only to find it would have been better to wait? Only a few minutes ago it had seemed the kind of progress Neil wanted was going to happen. Sitting on the bed, just letting her thoughts drift, she had become the Matty of years ago. Why the need to run into the rain? She took a deep breath that a novelist would call a sigh and again looked out the window. Some distant western clouds made patterns with others of various shades of gray, but the light no longer had an ominous yellow cast. Consciously, and with some effort, she forced herself to sit and enjoy the view.

Last night had been much too short and today a much more physically demanding day than she was accustomed to.

"Why don't you take a little nap?" she asked herself, making an effort to ignore the drive to take those boxes upstairs and organize her workspace.

"Because I am a driven, totally nutty female and I can't," she answered. "I just can't lie down and do nothing. And why am I talking to myself again?"

God, I am driven!

And hungry!

Screw the office!

Good advice.

Begrudging the time it took to prepare a proper dinner, Matty settled once more for something simple, this time a can of sardines, a kiwi she had been surprised to find at the general store and a small glass of the Pinot Grigio she had brought from home. They needed something bland and starchy to compliment them, but the loaf of bread was rejected. It had been impossible to explain to Neil or to herself why she was still limiting carbohydrates when she needed to gain weight. Maybe here she could begin to eat a little more sensibly. It just didn't seem possible yet. At least, she took time to sit down at the little kitchen table, leafing through a *Realtor* magazine for the few minutes it took to eat.

This evening was supposed to be a time to relax with one of the history books, but there were those boxes at the bottom of the stairs and her office upstairs crying to be fed. In spite of weary muscles, this was a job Matty looked forward to and she worked into the dark hours, arranging with care, gratified to see her workplace take shape. It occurred to her that, had she waited until the next day, she might actually have enjoyed the work. As it was, she was merely tired and relieved when it was done. Bedtime had to come much earlier tonight.

◆　　　◆　　　◆

Deciding to be realistic, Matty took a tranquilizer after her bath, but only one. Sleep should be no problem after a day of unaccustomed physical work. Silence broken only by the cricket chorus was a little strange but welcome. There was once more a heavy cloud cover and no moonlight shadows invaded her room.

She plumped her pillow and let her head drop back on it, adjusted the covers and laid her arms along her sides. This was how the quest for sleep usually started. She shut her eyes and mentally wandered through her inventory for a fantasy. There was always a small store of them waiting, little, familiar stories that would move her away from worries and the stimulation of planning tomorrow's tasks and into a less demanding world. They were the sort of thing you never told anyone and she wondered if everyone did this. Sometimes imagination rewrote parts of her life with the wisdom gained later, avoiding the excruciating embarrassments of the teenage years or sailing through college because she had learned not to procrastinate, correcting her mistakes, weaving a better life than she had lived. Sometimes her thoughts picked up a piece of a plot from a book or television and made it her own. Tonight, she imagined what it would have been like to have been the mistress of this house when it was new.

It was working. She began to relax, no longer a modern businesswoman, but a hard-working, relatively prosperous farmer's wife who had just cleaned one of the best houses in the area and had settled down in front of the hearth (Where was the hearth?) to do some mending.

She rolled over into the position she always slept in, on her right side. In her half-dream, the story lines mixed and changed and pale shadow figures with pants stuffed into high boots or long, full skirts moved and talked. Only one remained still and constant, a girl in a blue dress and white apron, sitting in the chair by the door of her bedroom holding the old flag.

6

Waking brought the usual tension. It was almost fear. But this morning Matty's mood lightened a little. The sun shone in the bedroom window and visible through the door across the hall was her office table, arranged and ready. She smiled to herself. Working without interruption was even more wonderful than Neil had predicted. Yesterday she had progressed purposefully and steadily toward an end that, with minor unpleasantness, had been achieved. One more pill had been necessary during the night, but only two for seven hours sleep was cause for rejoicing.

Without waiting for her usual extra half hour in bed, she welcomed the day, sat up and reached for her robe. This was going to be great!

◆　　　◆　　　◆

Two hours later, Matty was marching back and forth across the few empty feet of floor space in her small office, her face puckered by intense thoughts punctuated with verbal "shits" and "damns." The pleasure of a good awakening and initial long, happy look at the lovely view out the window had all disappeared. *Mail Merge* wouldn't work. The columns wouldn't stay where they belonged; addresses wandered over the page with wills of their own. And, stupidly, she had not thought to bring any of the phone numbers that might have brought help, the computer support number, the store where she had bought the machine, Ted Offenbach, her teacher. *Shit!* She could get the numbers by calling information or the office, of course, but there was a stubbornness in her that refused to admit she had more or less failed the class.

Never able to sit still for any length of time, Matty could no longer stay hunched over the Dread Machine. There were no errands, no running to the files or to the deli for coffee. Being alone had seemed an entrancing dream, but this was really *alone!* Not a single soul to bitch to! She ran down the steep stairs, slipping on the third step from the top again. It slanted slightly forward. For the first time, she took a moment to see if it was something she could fix. Maybe a couple of shims? But there was no crack to insert them in and, in any case, there were no shims, no odd pieces of wood of any kind. She could be careful.

Her boom box was on the coffee table. She carried it upstairs with her box of CD's and put on Brahms' violin concerto. Exquisitely beautiful. Distractingly so. It came out, replaced by Schubert's *Trout*.

Now. Mail Merge. Black Death.

No, not that serious. Maybe the Asian Flu.

Nah. Black Death.

She was pleased she could insert a little playfulness into a serious attack of frustration. *Thank you, Neil.* Reluctantly, she got out the instruction manual, the one for dummies. Manuals were always her court of last resort. Realization came late that she didn't have to do this particular chore in the uncomfortable straight-back chair. Irritated by her inefficiency, she went back downstairs, stretched out on the couch and, with an exaggerated grimace, opened the hateful tome. The music sounded faintly from above.

◆　　　◆　　　◆

Two hours later, the first page of addresses lay evenly spaced on the computer screen, more beautiful than the window view above them. Matty scrolled through with satisfaction and some relief. Her muscles were crying out for movement. She stood up, stretched her arms high overhead, scraping her knuckles on the low, rough ceiling, scowled and then laughed at herself. Then she laughed again with pure pleasure at the ease with which her laughter had come.

"Neil, you are a genius," she told the window. "You said take walks and by George, I will!" Not for the first time, she wondered who this George was that her grandmother always swore by.

Downstairs, Matty pulled back the bolt on the front door and went out onto the porch for the first time. It was a glorious day with that special fall light that sharpens outlines, clarifies and intensifies color. The trees wouldn't begin to turn for weeks yet, but a few leaves were airborne and, by the time she left, the reds and yellows would have appeared. It might be hard to leave.

It seemed necessary to walk carefully down the unpainted old steps, but someone had put a few new, shiny nails in them, probably the same person who mowed the weeds that were the front yard. At the far edge of the lawn, the ground angled sharply down and the sky disappeared as she reached the tree line. The house looked different from here. The severity of line was softened by the narrow porch across its front. The windows and tin roof glittered in the sunlight. A tough old house. No flowers, no shrubs, just thick logs that had lasted two hundred years or so. She lived in a townhouse. Is that why this house looked lonely? It needed that flag on the flagpole and someone in one of those rocking chairs.

The girl from last night would have looked just right. Odd how she had appeared unbidden. Matty always selected the cast for her fantasies, but she had not created this girl. Blonde, wasn't she? Yes. Her hair pulled back. Mary Briggsley had said they were mostly Lutherans here. Germans, then. Her dream had been historically accurate. An odd idea.

It was rough walking, the ground steep and rocky, but Matty persisted for almost an hour. She noted the time on her watch as, simultaneously, she realized it was silly to be wearing a watch. A control thing, Neil would have said. She approached the house from the kitchen side, the only side she hadn't seen before. Because of the slope of the land, the stone foundation became gradually higher towards the porch and Matty wondered if the house had a basement. She would have to investigate later, although she didn't much like basements and this one, with no windows and probably a dirt floor, was bound to be more unpleasant than most. Not long ago, she would have looked forward to a search. Neil's test again, her dislike of new experiences, the lost desire for adventure. She determined to find a basement if there was one.

Lunch was quickly thrown together, a ham sandwich and a glass of skim milk. Work was going well and the next chore was a particularly interesting one. It would be a Godsend, especially at the end of the year, to push a button and let the computer print the checks and a financial summary.

She started with considerable trepidation. The multiple-column accounting system had been a bugger in class.

◆　　　◆　　　◆

The setting sun was an unnecessary reminder that it was time to quit. Matty had worked with intense concentration, the manual beside her, determined to beat this puzzle and she had. Nerves were jumping beneath her skin, but it was done! Already fourteen of her clients' records could be pulled on screen, beautiful to see.

She sat back in her chair and took a deep breath. This was the most difficult task she had set herself. Tomorrow would be just more of the same, a nice, easy day. She realized she was uncomfortably thirsty and reached for her glass of milk. It was empty.

Frowning, Matty tried to remember drinking it but couldn't. The plate was empty, too, but for a few crumbs. There was no memory of eating the sandwich, either. No. Not quite true. She could remember eating it, just not tasting it. That was bad. One of Neil's questions, one of his tests of mental health, was whether or not she enjoyed eating.

Purposefully, she concentrated on the taste of the ham, the multi-grain bread, the cool milk, but drew a complete blank. She shook her head as if to clear it and ran a hand through her hair. It wasn't the first time she had been so absorbed mentally that she performed a physical function unconsciously. At home, she would go to the kitchen to wash dishes and find them done or cart the laundry basket to an empty hamper. But usually, once prompted, the memory came back. This time it seemed incomplete. It was a little disturbing. Was this an indicator of how far she had to go yet? Surely the ability to concentrate was not an emotional problem. And she wasn't going to take a month to heal! The pleasing thought of how much she had been able to accomplish in one afternoon returned and she gave one quick nod of her head in approval, picked up the dishes and walked carefully past that third step down to the kitchen.

It was time for a proper meal. Maybe lamb chops, spinach and a baked potato? That seemed too much work. Some time in the last year she had lost interest in cooking. Maybe change the potato to a roll. The return of the carbs was underway!

It sounded good. And lonely. A book was good company, but out of the question. Too much time at the computer had created a headache and burning eyes. Another problem she hadn't anticipated. And there was no television. She felt like calling Tom.

Oh, Good Lord! Why haven't I called Tom? Because stress causes memory lapses. I know, Neil, I know!

He had promised not to call her, to leave her alone to mend. How could she have forgotten to let him know she had arrived safely?

The cell phone was in her purse on the coffee table. She pressed the buttons and paced the living room, waiting for the connection.

He was there and grateful for her call. No recriminations, of course. As they talked, she put the frozen spinach on to steam and ate it. It was nice to have company for dinner. He knew much more about the Civil War than she did and wanted to know exactly where this house was. She didn't know, but gave him the nearby roads so he could look it up. Her complaint about the lack of a fireplace prompted him to explain that settlers often dug a basement first and lived there until the rest of the house could be built.

"Then that's where the fireplace is?" she asked.

"Possible. They usually put one in the first floor, though, and the second floor, too. For heat."

"The chimney runs through both floors and up through the roof, but no fireplaces. Maybe they took them out to make space. My bed is against the chimney upstairs and the stove is right next to it in the kitchen."

"Check out the basement."

"I don't see how to get in."

"Looked outside?"

"Kind of. I'll check again. I don't like basements. Except finished, livable ones. This one's bound to be creepy."

"No doubt. Low ceiling, old steps, too. Be careful."

"I will. I'm going dead."

"What?"

"My battery. Haven't thought to plug in my phone since I got here."

He laughed. "Do that. You may need it all alone up there."

No doubt she would.

It was almost dark, but curiosity demanded another look for signs of a basement. The spinach hadn't been enough and she didn't want to think about broiling lamb chops this late, so Matty grabbed a banana and, in the fading light, walked slowly around the front of the house where the foundation was higher because of the slope of the land. It was too dark to see anything under the porch and she had no desire to get a flashlight and crawl around. Finishing the last bite of banana, she waved her hand in dismissal. This was a problem she didn't have to solve. It wasn't fun to solve problems any more. There used to be enough energy to leap over whatever hurdles property management put in her way. Now those challenges created a dull ache in her middle and an unuttered groan of complaint.

"Screw you," she told the basement that might or might not have been there and went up the front stairs and into the house.

Passing the chairs, she had an idea that it would be nice to sit and watch the moon come up. With a bucket of suds and a rag she gave the old chairs a badly needed cleaning and carefully dried one of them. She sat for almost three minutes. Watching the moon come up sounded delightfully romantic, but in the doing was like watching grass grow.

It was cool. Not really chilly enough for a fire in the wood stove, but she built one anyway, for something to do, wondering at the same time why it was always necessary to accomplish something, especially when she was so tired. A fireplace would have been much nicer. A fire in the fireplace, a glass of wine, a comfortable sofa and a good book. A little bit of heaven on earth.

However, it was an ugly stove, not a fireplace, she skipped the wine as that would mean she couldn't have Diazepam later, the couch wasn't that comfortable and the first houses of Carroll County didn't seem to have much in common with her house. She was only good for ten minutes of reading at a time, then restlessness and itchy eyes drove her to her feet. There was always some excuse, a noise to identify, a drink of water, a trip to the bathroom. Once she went outside to see if it looked like rain. When she could read for an hour without a break, she would know she was healing.

Matty flipped through the pages and came to a house that was covered in attractive scalloped shingles but was similar in size and shape to hers. The house was in Mayberry, Maryland. *Mayberry? Wonderful!* It was a helpful chapter. The layout was the same as this house. Homes of that time were built so that the owners slept in one of the small upstairs rooms, the equivalent of her office or the bathroom, and the other small bedroom was for important visitors or sometimes the parents or one of the married children and spouse. All others slept together in the room she had presumed was always the master bedroom. The builders of this particular house had lived in the basement while the upper stories were being finished and the kitchen remained in the basement for many years. Chalk one up for Tom!

Matty smiled and gave a quick nod of her head. It was clear this house followed the same pattern. It only remained to see how to get into the basement. The house in the book had those awkward, almost-horizontal exterior cellar doors, Bilko doors, some people called them. She had broken a few fingernails on those! One illustration showed the original beams made from tree trunks of an appropriate size, the marks of the adz that squared them off clearly visible as they were in the ceiling above her and throughout her house. The walls were of chestnut logs. Matty suspected both houses had this in common, judging by the rich, dark brown of the logs of her walls. In between was a large amount of off-white chinking. Horsehair was used to bind the chinking, according to the book. She remembered a friend who had visited Stratford-on-Avon telling her that the guide had corrected her. "This is not wattle and daub," the guide had said in her correct English accent. "It's wattle and manure," pronouncing the final word, "manyou-ah." Her friend—June. It was June—always had to repeat that a few times, enjoying the accent. Matty got up and inspected the chinking next to the door. It seemed to be ordinary, smooth plaster. Definitely, thankfully, not manure.

She was suddenly very tired. It wasn't late, but nervousness ate up her energy these days and she wasn't surprised to find this day of office work had drained her almost as much as the house cleaning. Deciding to skip a bath, she picked up the little brochure, "Gettysburg," and locked up the house.

By ten o'clock, Matty sat reading by the inadequate light of the small lamp by her bed. Initially, the little guidebook was disappointing. Almost all the pages were devoted to ads for lodging and meals and it was almost ten years old. Not that that mattered. The battle hadn't changed. In a way, though, the pamphlet was appropriate. She knew almost nothing about this important moment in American history and the booklet's limited amount of information provided an overview and a small quantity of facts that could be quickly absorbed. The fighting covered twenty-five square miles, but the small maps didn't give her any idea where she was in relation to where the battle had taken place. Something must have happened here if, as Mary said, soldiers were buried nearby. Or had they been brought back home to be buried?

The battle occurred on the first, second and third of July, 1863. It was the bloodiest battle in American history, with 51,000 casualties, and a turning point in the Civil War. The only detail that rang a bell was Pickett's Charge, but she hadn't known that of his 12,000 Confederate soldiers, 10,000 were casualties. A statistic heavy with pain and grief. There was no clear picture of a flag to compare to the old flag here. Matty set the little book down and picked up the American Heritage volume. Her eyes were too tired to read any more, but she flipped through the pictures. In some, mountains were in the background. Was one of them her mountain? Probably not. This was too far from Gettysburg. The flags were all too small to count the stars. She set the book aside on the bed and closed her eyes.

Her own country at war. What would it be like to see people killed all around you, your home a hospital or headquarters or destroyed? Why didn't people take time to be grateful for the most important things in life like peace and safety? Why did one unhappy thing contaminate all of life as her car accident had contaminated hers? She remembered a period of several months when her mother was focused on what a great gift water was, discovering its many uses one by one. "Look!" she had called one day to her four children. "I am cooking with water, drinking a glass of it and washing my hands in it while outside the rain is making everything grow! Isn't that amazing?" They had merely been impatient to get back to their Monopoly game. But it *was* amazing. Mom had led the way, but Matty hadn't followed. It was time to try. In memory, she went back to those days. Something else to be grateful for. How many people never knew a home like hers with only the normal amount of sibling rivalry and happily married parents? Until Mom died. Matty had been sixteen. It still hurt. She reached over and took a pill from the night stand. She knew herself. From the dead at Gettysburg to her Mother. She was going to need help sleeping tonight. Still, thoughts of her family were mostly happy ones and, as she slowly succumbed to the tranquilizer, her mind stayed on those years, the boxes of comic books they kept under Dan's bed, trudging to the grocery store with a sled after a big snowstorm, hot summer nights together on the floor of the living room soothed to sleep by the cool and the hum of their only window air conditioner. It didn't bother her that there were five children now, two blondes instead of one.

7

Her car spun around once, twice. She was helpless, unable to think what to do. The steering wheel spun in her hands. Her ears were tortured by the shriek of metal smashing, scraping across metal. The bus was big. Monstrously big. She was thrown against the window, the steering wheel, the safety belt scraping her neck, and then pain shot from her head down to her waist. The sickening thud of the car against a human body and the screams, the high-pitched, stabbing, unbearable screams...

Matty woke shaking and sobbing, her heart battering the front of her chest. The bed was soaked with sweat and where her hand clutched the blanket, the nails of her left hand had broken through the worn fabric.

Gradually the crying subsided and her grip loosened, but tears kept coming.

"Oh, God," she whimpered. Then a long, mournful sound came from deep in her throat. "This has to stop. Why won't it stop? She's dead, oh dear God, she's dead. It's not my fault. It's not. It's not."

Matty's breaths were deep, long, audible. How easily it could have been her fault. One small miscalculation, a momentary distraction and someone else could die. How was it possible to drive day after day through that menacing horde of lethal weapons? *I'm sorry. I'm so sorry. It's not my fault. It's not.*

After a while, the memory shifted into past tense and she was thinking, *it wasn't my fault. Maybe somehow I could have prevented it, but it wasn't my fault. They said so.* Finally the tears stopped, leaving her weak, the nerves all over her body prickling...

◆　　◆　　◆

Another pill and two hours later, as the first pale light lit the windows, Matty got out of bed determined to "take steps," as her grandmother used to say. Neil had been right. She was still shaky and mildly ill from her nightmare and the waking memories of the accident. Waiting for the tranquilizer to calm her, she had done once more what she had done so often: put her fears to rest, one by one. The trial was over. Tom and she had umbrella insurance now. Never again would they have to fear losing everything they had worked for. Dad wasn't going to die. Not right away, anyway. She had come to terms with that. Physically, she had healed. Her back hadn't been seriously damaged. It had been a bad time, but it was over. What she had now was about as good as life got, wasn't it? Unless…They had once talked about having a baby. She had protested that the business needed her full attention while it was building. And then the accident dropped on their lives like a bomb.

Over a dish of bran cereal, Matty made a daily schedule for mental health. No more leaning over the computer for eight or ten hours a day. That obviously wasn't helping her, engrossing though it might be while she was at it. "DON'T RUSH!" she wrote at the top of the page. "DO ONE THING AT A TIME" went right under it. Then, "Take a walk after breakfast (Look, don't think!)" *Like that's possible.* She refused to change it. Next: "Computer: two hours maximum." Then, afraid she couldn't live with that, she scratched off "two" and wrote in "three." It occurred to her that she should have taken yesterday off. It had been Sunday. She added, "Get up, walk around, stretch at least every half hour." Then lunch. Lunch outside seemed a good idea. There was something nourishing about the outdoors. After lunch, professional reading or more computer but with at least one big break, maybe the exercise tape or a household chore. She remembered how much better she had felt the first day. Tired but limp. A long walk maybe. Then another three hours on the computer. "No work after dinner." She could listen to music, sing along to a CD, read a book, give herself a manicure, wash her hair. Saving time by limiting grooming had been one of the temptations of this getaway, but maybe personal maintenance was good for morale.

The thought that yesterday was Sunday prompted another idea and she wrote, "See somebody once in a while." For a few more days, she could avoid that last one. People filled her life at home, closed her in, but being alone for too long wasn't healthy. Maybe she would take Mary up on her invitation to church, sing a few hymns, sit back and listen to a sermon, hopefully not too boring, chat a few minutes with some new people. Maybe corner Joseph for some information. Or didn't he go to church?

She sat back and looked at her list. Therapy. That was the main thing, not getting business done. Her attitude had done a hundred and eighty degree turn since she had accepted Neil's offer. Maybe that was the magic he spoke of. Things—She didn't want to define "things"—were a little out of control. There was no denying that the hand that wrote this list was not steady.

The cell phone played its bit of Mozart beside her, shattering her carefully fashioned calm into tiny needles that jabbed first into her heart and then ran down her arms.

"Right. Nerves of steel," she said bitterly before answering.

It was Rosemary.

"Freedmans are having a fit." The voice was flat, unmoved by any sympathy for the Freedmans. "Refrigerator went out Saturday afternoon. They want to know why you weren't at home when they called and they want a new refrigerator, like, yesterday."

Out of habit, Matty swung into her business mode.

"Check the file to find out what size the refrigerator is and what features it has. Call Sears and order the equivalent. One on sale if possible. White. There's not enough money in the owner's account so put it on the office charge account. Figure out how much we need to cover the refrigerator and also leave a two hundred dollar balance in the emergency account and then call, uh…" *What the hell was his name? Blair. Ed Blair.* "—Ed Blair at his office—Don't talk to his wife—and ask—"

"Bitch," Rosemary interrupted.

"Yeah, she is. Ask if he wants to send us a check or have us take it out of the next month's rent."

"He'll want it out of next month's rent."

"Of course. But he'll feel better if he's made the decision himself. If he wants you to buy a cheaper refrigerator or a second hand one, tell him a superior quality house—He'll like that—requires good appliances, especially with the rent that high."

"Then call the Freedmans back and make sure someone's there when the 'fridge comes, right?"

"Right. They'll squawk 'cause it won't be tomorrow. You know what to tell them."

"Take the frozen stuff to the neighbors or a relative, buy ice for their cooler and enjoy eating out for a few days."

"Exactly. Come to think of it, have Consuela make that last call."

Consuela would give the Freedmans at least ten full minutes of dramatic sympathy after giving them the bad news.

"Anything else?"

"I'm handling things."

There were quick good-byes. There had been no "How's the cabin? Having a good time?" Even so, Matty felt slightly cheered by the call. Granted, when she was in the office, too much came at her at once, but these few minutes had reminded her that she was a competent woman who knew how to deal with her growing business. Confident in her role, she marched upstairs to the computer.

◆   ◆   ◆

Preparing dinner that night, Matty decided it hadn't been a bad day, considering the start. She had followed her own orders and taken a long, slow walk in the morning, climbing up behind the house in hopes of finding a view across the valley. It had been a tough climb, over rocks and through scrub, ducking under low branches that caught in her hair. Her knees and hands still burned from numerous scrapes. She had fought the land and it had fought back, but it was worth the effort.

The view had swept over her like a caress. It was a narrow valley, the low blue mountains on the other side allowing only compressed, elongated farms below. The sky was a fall blue, deeper than in summer. Ponds glittered, tin roofs shone among the farms' squares and splotches of varied shades of green and tan. The road she had traveled to get here curved in and out of stands of trees down the center of the valley. She had felt grateful to be up high, watching, rather than encased in one of the glittering spots of metal moving in neat lines along its surface. The house had probably had this view at one time before the trees grew tall. They weren't first growth. Those old trees had probably gone into the making of this house. Fatigue should have made it easy to stand still and calm, but restlessness had driven her back to the house once the landscape had been surveyed and classified. She had been conscious of her idle hands hanging at her sides.

The time at the computer had gone reasonably well, although her level of irritation when it didn't was off the charts. She made herself take breaks and lunch had been eaten on a blanket on the front yard. Lying back on the blanket afterwards, she had rolled over and found herself staring through the deteriorating lattice under the porch at two tiny, grimy windows. That prompted the first smile of the day. There was the basement. Its entrance would reveal itself eventually. In the meantime, she felt much better about having spent the day profitably.

◆   ◆   ◆

Sleep held no appeal. It was always like that after a bad nightmare. It might come again. She read a little, lying on the scratchy couch with one of her bed pillows for comfort. A long bath was an acceptable delaying tactic.

Pulling off her jeans while brushing her teeth, Matty knocked a plastic glass off the side of the sink. It made her remember that the schedule advised doing one thing at a time. She forced herself to stand still and just brush, a discipline that took a surprising amount of effort and was, she decided, one of the truly boring details of daily life.

She stepped into the hot bath, slid down into the water, closed her eyes and began to think about what should be done tomorrow after the monthly financial forms were finished.

A sudden awareness thrust her upright. She was numb! There was no comforting warmth on her skin, no feeling at all!

Matty looked down at her bare flesh, its image rippled by the moving water. What was going on? Of course, she could feel the water! She moved her hand in and out, sensing the change in temperature. Her heart began to slow to normal and she lay back again, trying to come to grips with what had just happened. Or not happened.

Had she fallen asleep?

She tested the idea. Her eyes had been closed, so there was no visual memory. But her mind had been working. Hadn't it? She felt the burn of growing tears. Was something wrong with her? Really wrong with her physically? Not an acceptable idea, even in the form of a question. She dismissed it. She was tired. The trip, adjustment to a new place, was all more than a little wearing. Call Tom? And say what? It wasn't fair to worry him. Call Neil, maybe. *Damn his magic!* There had never been this problem at home. Had there? Maybe she was just becoming aware of her problems with this slower pace and the lack of distractions. Maybe this is what Neil wanted.

Neil wanted her in a state of panic all alone?

Thank you, Neil!

She was beginning to feel normal again. What had happened, after all?

She didn't know.

Not knowing was definitely scary.

Matty got out and dried herself with intentional slowness even though she was shivering in the coolness of the September night. She was grateful for feeling, even feeling uncomfortably cold. It was reassuring after that odd moment in the tub.

Once in bed, she hefted the big Civil War history onto a pillow on her stomach. Buford and Reynolds and Howard…The men of the Battle of Gettysburg didn't really register, failed to distract her from herself. She put the book aside and reached for the precious bottle of escape. Two pills? Twenty milligrams was a lot to start out with but seemed necessary.

The world outside her window was alive with moonlight again tonight. The flagpole thrust starkly upward toward slate-gray wisps of clouds that floated eastward against a sky so black it seemed opaque. Jackson and Ewell and Early...How many would die before the end of the chapter? Death couldn't be so bad. Too much Diazepam would bring only a lovely sleep without nightmares.

8

A copy of *Realtor* magazine in her hand, Matty lay on the couch doing nothing. A few tears were drying on her cheeks. Tears had become so common she wasn't even aware of them. Neil had reassured her that they were her way of releasing not only unhappiness but also tension and that it was healthy.

It had been a bad morning. The fear that had jerked her upright in the bathtub last night had left a residue impossible to shake. Four times she had walked to her cell phone, twice picked it up and dialed a few, but not all, of the numbers that would ring Neil's phone. Matty was a person who rehearsed what she would say on an important call and the rehearsals hadn't gone well.

Neil, I couldn't feel the bath water for a split second last night? I think. Impossible. I think something may be wrong with my...my what? Nerves? Well, who didn't know that?

A simple statement that she thought something was wrong that she hadn't been aware of before was fine, but what came after that? The experience had been so brief, it was almost possible to believe it hadn't happened. But no matter how hard she tried to dismiss it, the memory crept between the lines of the article she had been trying to read, made her keep stopping to reassure herself that she could feel everything, the tightness of the band of her bra, the worn-to-softness jeans, the coolness of the air on her face and hands. She was unable to resolve whether she really had not been able to feel or whether her brain was...What? Somewhere else? Not picking up the signals?

Around ten o'clock, she had put an exercise tape in the boom box and faithfully followed the irritatingly exuberant instructions, but the routine had left her mind too free to wander in uncomfortable directions and failed to leave the usual relaxed aftermath.

Now, trying to relieve the restlessness, she got up and went to the window. The sky was overcast, threatening rain again. Perhaps the weather was affecting her mood. Any excuse would help.

She felt listless, lacking the energy to go upstairs and complete her three afternoon hours at the computer. It required concentration. Lying around accomplishing nothing was not the answer either. She should call Neil and talk this thing over or make a firm decision to wait and see if anything else happened and get on with life in the meantime. There was a reluctance to phone and speak aloud of the mini-event. It would make it more real.

She decided to find the basement.

Armed with a flashlight and hammer, Matty marched onto the front porch and down the steps. With a section of the grayed lattice pulled away, the flashlight beam revealed clearly the two small, very grimy windows, but no other opening along the rough stone foundation.

"Cellar doors," she said aloud. "The house should have those damn Bilko doors."

She sat down cross-legged on the ground, propped one elbow on a knee and leaned her head on her hand. If the windows were cleaned, the flashlight would reveal where the entrance to the basement was, but that would require crawling over the dirt and through the cobwebs. There were enough of those in her hair already from just looking in. The windows were too small to provide access in any case.

Think. You need something to think about besides the bathtub. Now if I were building a house...living in the basement...no fireplace upstairs...In that other house, the one in the book, they were still cooking in...

She jumped up. Still cooking in the basement? If so, wouldn't there be an interior entrance? Somewhere there was a trapdoor. Under a rug or...A better idea surfaced. In almost all houses, stairs were stacked. The basement stairs should be under the stairs to the second floor. In which case...

It took twenty minutes, including the first aid required for a badly cut finger, before everything was out of the closet and onto the kitchen floor, but there was a reward. The floor was a crudely cut piece of fairly new plywood with, in some places, over an inch gap between it and the wall. Somebody had wanted a closet more than a basement.

Three splinters and a broken fingernail later, the board was out. Cold, damp air circled Matty's ankles, moved up her legs, brushed her hands. It smelled of earth deep in the ground far from sunlight. She stared down the hole for a moment, more put off by the dank odor than by the darkness.

The flashlight beam revealed a set of stairs as steep and narrow as those to the second floor but rougher. Below, only earth gray with age and dust.

She set a foot carefully on the top step. It was always more difficult going down these narrow steps than going up.

Her cell phone sang its song, jarring her.

Matty realized she had been holding her breath. Maybe it was just as well the phone had brought her back from wherever her mind was going. She took a deep breath before backing up and out onto the kitchen floor.

"Mrs. Burnam?"

"Buhrmann."

"Oh. Yeah. O.K. Uh, this is Christy's Florists." The voice was young. It had cracked slightly on the "Christy's." "I mean, I'm delivering for them. Christy's Florists. Just makin' sure you're t'home. This road don't look so good."

"You're—Where are you? At the end of the—" Matty stopped, not sure what to call the road that led to the house.

"Yes, ma'am. End of your road. They gave me a cell phone. Ain't they great? Gimme a coupla minutes."

Her eyes were wet almost immediately. She knew what the florist meant. How often had Tom sent her roses after the accident? It was a welcome emotion affecting her now, not fear. She quickly brushed her eyes with the back of her hand, went to her purse and pulled out two dollars. As she opened the door, a white van appeared where the road turned before leveling out a short distance from the house.

An awkward jumble of long, skinny arms and legs emerged from the white van. Matty felt an instant sympathy. He was everything a teenage boy didn't want to be, scrawny and narrow-shouldered, with limp red hair and a case of acne that was painful to see. He seemed unaware of his aesthetic handicaps, jumping out of his skin with delight and eagerness to please as he approached.

"Oh! Gosh!" was all he could get out for a few seconds as he fumbled with the long white box. "Uh..." His eyes ran over the outside of the house for a few seconds, then came back to rest on Matty. "It sure is a beautiful house."

"Beautiful?" Not an adjective Matty would have used.

"Uh. Well, no. Inter'stin' is what I meant. Real inter'stin'. Old. Uh, no." His eyes dropped to the ground. "That beautiful thing, that—that came out because—" his eyes came back to her face. "Cause you—Well, you know, you're beautiful," he finished with his eyes focused on the ground again.

Matty smiled. Surely her eyes were red, her clothes hardly flattering, her hair full of cobwebs.

Thank you," she said, reaching for the box

He had forgotten it. "Oh, yeah, sure."

"Have you been here before? Do you know anything about the history of this place?"

He was so eager to please, he jumped in without thinking. "Oh, just kids who come here breakin' in..." He slowed down, realizing where he had taken himself. "Uh...with their dates. You know."

"Yes, I know." Another day, it would have been funny. She handed him the money.

"Oh, thanks. Really, thanks. Best ask Aunt Jane about this house. Jane Goodman. But she's, like, a little, uh, odd, so maybe..." He frowned. "Maybe it's not such a good idea, you know...I mean, she's, like, not really nuts about anything else. It's just..."

It was clear he wasn't going to be able to finish the sentence.

"I'd better get these in water."

"Oh. Yeah. Sure." The boy backed away, bobbing a little. It seemed a form of politeness, the historic remnant of a bow.

Matty smiled. She took a certain amount of male admiration for granted, but this boy's unguarded reaction was refreshing.

She set the box down on the kitchen table and opened it, already certain of its contents. The expected yellow roses showed through the green tissue paper. The note in the little pink envelope read: "I know you're trying to stay away from the phone so I sent these instead. May I come see you this weekend? Feel free to say no. All my love always, Tom."

She went straight to the phone.

"They're beautiful. I love you!"

"Love you, too. You okay?"

She hesitated. It would be a relief to share that odd moment in the bathtub, but there seemed to be no acceptable way to describe the incident. Tom would insist on coming here—or that she come home—for what was probably nothing.

"It's different. You can get a lot done when you're left alone. I have lots of free time. Found the basement."

"Anything special?"

"Haven't been down yet. I was just on my way when the flowers arrived."

"Neil had a good idea then. I've decided it's odd, though, sending you to that place. Do psychiatrists do things like that?"

Matty took a moment to think before responding.

"It is a little unusual, maybe. But he knew I would only go away if I could work. Where else would I go to be alone? And also, I suppose, he's become something of a friend as well as a doctor."

"Is that supposed to happen?"

Again she hesitated, thinking of the moment Neil had taken her hand. "Actually, I suppose it's inevitable. With some people. Anyway, he was right about this. I'm getting things done and also finding things out about myself." It took effort to sound cheerful.

"Good." He sounded relieved. "You were getting, uh…" Tom wasn't often at a loss for words. "Or maybe I should say you weren't getting over the accident. It changed you. And you weren't changing back. Neil got you to ask the right questions, to try the right things, but they didn't seem to be working, did they? So maybe that's why he's doing something a little off the beaten therapeutic track. If this is good for you, would you rather I didn't come this weekend?"

Matty was surprised how much she did want Tom to come.

"Yes, come. Really."

"Great!" He sounded more than pleased, perhaps relieved. "Are Neil's directions good?"

"Until the last turn. It's just hard to see in the dark. Try to get here while there's some light. If you come to an intersection with a drug store and a funny little general store called "Joseph's Commodities," you've gone too far. Better yet, don't come Friday after work. Traffic was hellish. Wait until Saturday morning and enjoy the scenery."

"Right. Shall I bring anything?"

"A washer and dryer." She was smiling now. It was comforting, talking to Tom about something as ordinary as laundry.

"Ouch! Don't have one, huh? How about I bring you some clean things and take home your dirty—Excuse me. Ladies don't get dirty.—used stuff."

"Dirty was accurate. Good idea. Jeans, sweat shirts and tees, socks and underwear will do it. Thanks."

"See you Saturday, then. Take care."

"I will. Bye."

"Bye."

Matty stood for a few moments with the phone in her hand. She felt a loss and wanted Tom's voice back, but the conversation had to be cut off before she said something that would compel him to come flying up here. They had never intruded on each other's work and she didn't intend to now for something as…She searched for the right word. "Intangible" came to mind and she gave a quick snort of a laugh that had no humor in it. The word was doubly appropriate. Didn't the word literally refer to feeling, touching? She went back to the kitchen table and inhaled the perfume of the roses. It was the scent she loved above all others and each rose was a different perfection, bright as the sun. They were some consolation for Tom's absence.

Among the debris from the closet now spread out on the kitchen floor were three old-fashioned, round milk bottles. A single one wasn't large enough for the dozen and a half roses, so she washed two bottles and made bouquets for the kitchen table and the office.

The smell of earth from the basement was at war with the flowers. Matty leaned over and inhaled once more the sweet scent and then gave in to the basement's less appealing aroma.

There was no railing as there was for the upper stairs. It was necessary to hold the edges of the steps to the second floor overhead as long as possible and then move slowly down the last few steps, setting her feet sideways on the narrow treads.

It's not a basement. It's a cellar.

She was stooping, in case the ceiling was low. Turning the flashlight upwards, she found that, although there was enough room for her to stand upright, the spiders had claimed much of the space for their webs. After waving the flashlight over her head to clear them, hoping for no live residents, she straightened up and let the flashlight do the exploring.

The fireplace was on the outside wall across from her, jutting out into the room, large, roughly rounded stones held together with a gray material. The hearth was over a foot high and across the top of the opening, a huge wooden beam at least a foot wide served as a lintel recessed into a chimney that went to the ceiling. Had there ever been a fireplace in the kitchen? The chimney there showed no evidence of one.

She could see the gray rectangles that were the windows under the front porch. They were too dirty to let in an appreciable amount of light. Matty couldn't imagine living here. It was a tomb, a silent, dark, stone room.

Going back to the kitchen to get the matches needed for the stove, Matty lit the oil lamp that had been part of the closet's contents. With this and a broom, going down the stairs was hazardous, but the cellar had some light now, enough to see the whole room at once rather than one flashlight beam width at a time. Waving the broom at the ceiling ahead of her, she walked to the fireplace.

It was disappointing. There were no interesting details, no hole for fire-wood, no bread oven, no shelves or old iron cooking pots. On the floor, there were a few odds and ends, a bucket, some curtain rods, four rusting collapsible lawn chairs, a pile of lumber. This was no Williamsburg resto-ration. The top of the huge lintel, partially covered by old whitewash dark-ened by smoke, was higher than her shoulders.

Matty wondered if the original family had been stuck here for a winter like the one in the book. Setting the oil lamp on the floor, she turned to the right side of the room where a section of the floor about six feet long was raised. There seemed no reason for the elevation except perhaps, since this would have been the higher side of the mountain, they had decided it would be easier to leave it for a bed or sitting area rather than dig it out. The lamp threw her flickering shadow across the room.

Why is it flickering? Cold air doesn't rise.

The light at her back, Matty stared into the looming shape of her own distorted shadow and tried to make sense of the shapes in the darkness. There seemed to be too many shadows moving in the unstable light.

Suddenly, unreasonably, she was afraid. The dank smell had become sickening. The silence was gone, replaced by a pounding in her ears. It no longer seemed an empty room.

Cursing her overactive imagination and the ease with which fear took her over, she walked deliberately back to the lamp, picked it up and climbed carefully back up the stairs. She didn't look back.

9

As Matty grabbed the big slab of plywood to wrestle it back into the closet, a corner fell into the dark opening and it was a struggle to get it back up and into place. The small job could have been done in a single minute, but anxiety didn't breed efficiency. She leaned against the wall, feeling foolish. There was nothing down there but shadows thrown by the flame of an oil lamp.

Diazepam was not permitted during the day. Her own rule. A glass of white wine was definitely in order. She poured a few inches into a tumbler, sat down at the kitchen table and took a moment to look out the window, trying to dig up some pleasurable response to the crisp green of early autumn. Then she dove once more into the uncomfortable regions of self-analysis. Evidently for some time things had been going on that she hadn't been aware of, obscured by the many distractions at home and in the office. The business had made it possible to avoid taking an objective look at herself in spite of Neil's proddings. Here, imagination coupled with raw nerves were revealing her true condition. More than anything else, she was disgusted with herself, appalled at the weakness, the fearfulness. Her heart was still beating too hard. It was tempting to drink the wine quickly, but that was not a solution. That would have been merely another symptom.

Time was supposed to heal if she did the right things. She smiled at the roses. Tom knew what the right things were. She leaned over and inhaled deeply.

For a moment, she was merely puzzled. There was no odor. Granted, the basement smell dominated the room, but...

She tried again, burying her nose into the mass of soft petals, demanding the familiar, comforting scent.

It came. It came suddenly, potently, after too long a delay.

Matty pressed her fingers against her forehead. There was no denying what had just happened. She could smell the roses now, even a foot away with her hands covering her face. Yet she couldn't smell them when her nose was buried in them. Something was very wrong. The moment in the bathtub and now this. And—maybe—the sandwich? Taste, touch, smell. It made no sense. Not to her, anyway. She didn't even want to think about the possible causes.

She went quickly to the coffee table for her phone. Neil was with a patient, of course.

"Have him call me. As soon as possible." The attempt to sound calm didn't work.

Erica assured her that he would be able to call very shortly, her comforting response born of many calls like this.

Matty paced the living room, tempted, yet afraid, to go back to the roses.

"They can wait," she whispered to herself. "Wait for Neil. Wait for Neil." The phrase was repeated over and over, mentally pushing away more fearful words and thoughts.

When the phone played in her hand, she didn't even wait to make sure who it was.

"My senses are screwed up! Neil, listen! I couldn't smell roses. And I think I didn't feel the bath water. What could do that, Neil? And maybe I didn't taste a sandwich. Neil?"

"Matty." His voice was a verbal caress.

Matty knew it meant nothing. It was his professional, calming sound. It always struck her as odd that it worked in spite of her awareness of its manipulative intent.

"Are you all right at this moment?"

Matty stopped pacing. *Am I?*

"What do you mean, all right?"

"I mean, do you seem to be your normal self at this moment?"

"I think so." She was walking to the kitchen. "I think…" She leaned over and smelled the roses, daring to do this now. They were there for her. "Yes. I'm—Everything is working now."

"Why don't you sit down? You're standing up, aren't you?"

"Yes, damn it! This is a standing up conversation!"

"All right. But take time to tell me what has happened."

"Shit, Neil, I don't know what's happened. That's what *you're* for, aren't you? I couldn't smell Tom's roses. Now what does that mean?"

"You're describing it in the past tense. That means you can smell them now?"

"Yes. I did before, too. And then I couldn't. And then I could. What's that?"

"Please just sit down, Matty. Then we'll talk."

She returned to the living room and dropped onto the couch, irritated with the delay.

"Okay, I'm sitting. What the hell difference does that make?"

"Now take a deep breath, organize your thoughts and then tell me exactly what has happened, in chronological order.

She did take a deep breath. That was as much of his instructions as her impatience allowed.

"There was a moment—I was in the bathtub and I suddenly felt that I couldn't feel the water. No. I felt that I hadn't felt the water. You know what I mean. I could feel it when I thought about it, but I had the sense that I hadn't been feeling it. You understand?"

"Yes. I get your meaning. And the sandwich?"

"That one's a maybe. I couldn't remember the taste of a sandwich. Or milk. Or, you know, chewing it, the feel of them. I could have been distracted. That happens all the time. But the roses Tom sent. Yellow roses. My favorite. I couldn't smell them. That's a definite. I tested. I could smell them and then I couldn't and then I could again.

It was Neil's turn to take a deep breath. She waited. It was like being in the courtroom waiting for the jury's decision. Her heart was pounding and she clutched the phone like a life preserver.

Finally, he spoke, thoughtfully. "Sensory losses—You are absolutely sure of this?"

"Of the roses, yes. Really only the roses."

"I'm assuming you took into consideration the possibility of a draft—"

"No. I didn't. But that wasn't possible. I was too close."

"And you could breathe freely? You weren't congested?"

"No. It was sudden. I couldn't smell them. Then I could. Is that a brain thing? A ministroke or something?"

"So you're not sure about the bathtub incident or the sandwich."

Matty hesitated. "I don't know. Why would I even think of something that hadn't happened? And then, it seemed as though I could see—" She stopped. Her fear in the cellar was just nerves. She didn't like basements. "No. That's just silly. I got scared—a little scared—in the cellar. Just shadows. Nothing."

"Are we dismissing this absolutely? It sounds as though you have reservations."

"No. It was just my imagination. Forget the cellar thing. So what are the possible explanations? I need to know. This is scary, Neil. Is it a brain tumor or some damage from the accident? Isn't it too late for that?"

Again, Neil's silence made her impatient.

"Neil?"

"Matty." He drew her name out with irritating slowness. "Don't worry about a brain tumor. You've been under medical supervision much of this last year and a tumor is not likely."

"Well, what is then? What?"

"I can't diagnose over the phone. I need to see you."

"Tests?" Matty had a sudden vision of herself in a hospital explaining to some technician that she couldn't smell flowers. "I don't want any tests. Just tell me the possibilities. As long as it's something I can live with..."

"I'm sorry, Matty. I imagine these things are frightening when you're all alone up there—"

"Alone is fine. I'd be just as scared anywhere."

"Don't you think we'd better arrange for you to come home?"

"Arrange? What arrange?"

"If—No, let me change that. Since we don't know for certain what the problem is, it wouldn't be wise for you to drive yourself home."

There was silence for a moment. All this because she couldn't smell roses for an instant?

"No. No big production, Neil. No rescuing Matty. Actually, I feel really good today. Better than usual. Just—It's strange when your body—I don't know—doesn't behave the way it has all your life. It's a kind of betrayal. But, no…No. Is this likely to be a life threatening thing? Is something going to go horribly wrong with me?"

"No, Matty." His reassurance sounded genuine. "I'm almost certain it's something we can deal with, just the two of us, although it might be wise to schedule some tests. It's probably more a matter of time. Or perhaps 'place' is the better word." The tone shifted into regret. "I'm sorry I sent you there. Obviously, it was the wrong thing to do. Your need for control should have told me you needed familiar places, routine more than you needed to get away from pressure."

Matty could see the frown that went with the note of guilt in his voice.

"What do you mean? You know what this is?"

"I know the most likely explanation, given your history and what I know about you. In your case…"

"Hurry up, Neil! In my case, what?"

"Let me ask you a few questions. All right, Matty?"

"Don't baby me. Ask!"

"How are the nightmares?"

"Not great."

"Is it the usual one, your car hitting the woman?"

Matty couldn't hear those words without a rush of nausea.

"Yes, yes. It wasn't my fault."

"You know that in your mind. Your feelings haven't accepted it."

"I know, I know. We've been over this before. Move on."

"You haven't sustained any physical injury?"

"Broke a fingernail! Cut a finger, too. Big deal!"

"Nothing more than that?"

"No! Move on!"

"Are you enjoying the cabin?"

"No. Trying to. It's a lot of work."

"Would you say you were depressed?"

Am I? "I thought I was doing better. But, no, maybe not. You said, 'In my case.' You had something in mind. For God's sake, what?"

"I think it isn't, as I said, anything we can't deal with. Sometimes after a traumatic experience, there is a delayed reaction. There are medications that will help and we need to talk about—"

"This is all in my head?"

He didn't answer immediately.

"This *is* all in my head. Psychological, I mean. Not physical. That's what you're saying, isn't it?"

"This is very uncomfortable, having this conversation when I know you are in a strange place alone. I can't diagnose this problem for certain from a distance, but your situation could have triggered what is happening to you."

Matty began to relax a little. This didn't sound too awful. Odd, certainly. But not *too* awful. She looked around the living room that had taken so much work to clean and thought of the other rooms, of her productive work in the office upstairs, of the view from the mountaintop.

"My situation. Alone, you mean. Strange place. Seems unlikely, but you're the doctor. I don't think I want to come home."

"We do need to talk, Matty. And Tom should bring you back."

"Talk about what?"

Again that irritating silence. Then, "Have you been taking more Diazepam than usual?"

"Yes, a little more. Hard to sleep in a strange place. But I'm not going to make Tom come and get me. I've put him through enough and I'm perfectly capable of driving home myself. But I don't think I'm going to. I think I'll just get used to this place. That's bound to happen, isn't it? It will become familiar? In any case, he's coming this weekend and he can bring me home if this stuff doesn't stop."

"This is Tuesday. I guess that will be all right with certain provisions."

Neil spoke slowly, as though trying to come to terms with her decision. Matty could picture him, head back, eyes shut, his hand stroking his throat. He exhaled audibly.

"First, it seems unlikely, but Diazepam has been known to cause hallucinations when taken intravenously and we have found you are exceptionally sensitive to a number of medications. Please keep to dosage instructions. Better yet, stop taking it. Arrange to come home if you find yourself increasingly depressed. And you will call me if there is another incident? This is an absolute must."

"I will. Yes, I will." This was a very small concession, considering the relief she was feeling. It was all right for her to stay! It couldn't be too serious!

"And note all the circumstances. How you're feeling. Note if you have any forgetfulness, whether or not you're working well, efficiently, what you'd been doing, whether or not you'd been drinking or failed to follow my advice and were taking any Diazepam. This is not to be construed as meaning it's all right to ignore my advice, you understand. You probably ought to flush the medication down the toilet right away and come home. You don't have any other drugs there?"

"Just Tylenol."

"Your work on the computer—That's going all right? No problems?"

"Like?"

"Concentration. Memory."

"I don't—No. I don't think so. There's always some of that since the accident. I seem to get frightened easily. You know that. I was uneasy coming into the house and the basement. I got really stupidly scared down there for no reason at all. But I've had some light moments, too. I'm working physically. That's good, isn't it?"

"Yes. But you need to have control over your life. I'm afraid that's what I've taken away from you by sending you there. I want you to start working some structure into your day. Make a schedule and stick—"

"I've done that! Just today!"

"Good. Good. You realized that need. And it's very important that you call me, especially if you become more depressed or if there are any more incidents. You must promise me this."

"Yeah, sure. So I'm kind of reacting to a—a sort of loss of control, the loss of the familiar, a delayed reaction to the accident? A strange reaction, isn't it? Unusual?"

"Not that unusual, actually. There are some very effective medications—"

"Then prescribe me some! There's a pharmacy here."

"I can't do that over the phone. I must see you."

"I know. I know. You can't."

"Is someone calling you on a regular basis? At least daily?"

"I can arrange that."

"Yes. Do that, please."

He still sounded reluctant to let her go. She started to say goodbye, but, instead, took time to thank him. It had been comforting to talk.

Matty set the phone on the coffee table, suddenly immeasurably grateful there were such things as cell phones. Muscles began to relax, helped by a few deep breaths. There was the rest of the wine waiting in the kitchen. A mistake. A tranquilizer would have been better, but Neil's orders were not to take any and, of course, never to mix them. They weren't going to be thrown away. That had never been a possibility.

Then something in her rebelled.

"No, damn it!" She got up. "Work your lazy ass off, you messed up nut case! You've got a healthy body. You do! Now work it!"

It was a grueling afternoon. The exercise tape came first and then Matty grabbed several Granola bars and a bottle of water and stalked the mountain as though her life depended on seeing every blade of grass, every bush, tree and rock it had to offer. With her went her new mantra, "I will not cry, I will not cry. I will *not!*"

◆　　　◆　　　◆

Later, standing at the kitchen sink, her legs trembling slightly from exertion, Matty washed up the day's few dishes and tried to figure out what would keep her awake until bedtime. She was exhausted. Defiantly, she had sniffed the roses several times since returning to the house and Tom's gift hadn't failed her. The computer chores were laid out for the next day, several pieces of furniture with no dust on them had been dusted anyway and her cell phone was already on the kitchen table, plugged in for recharging overnight. At some point, the realization surfaced that Neil hadn't made a definite diagnosis. Something psychological. That was okay, something to work on. No tumor. No strokes. Why eliminate strokes? Adrenaline surged uncomfortably. *Trust Neil. He had something in mind. Trust Neil.* Still, the experiences, added up, were frightening. It had taken physical and emotional determination to carry on today and there was now a reassuring feeling of pride and confidence. She turned, leaned her back against the sink and dried her hands. The sun was setting beyond the window over the table and the roses shone. She smiled and went over once more to inhale the scent.

It wasn't there.

Matty felt as though her insides were collapsing. The tears she had denied all day came pouring out. She fell sideways into the chair, knocking the roses onto the floor. Her mouth opened, a great wail of grief ready to slice the silence—

It was stopped by a small hand with stubby fingers reaching out to her across the table. Behind it, a white apron surrounded by blue.

Matty raised her eyes and saw hair as golden as the roses and blue eyes that looked at her with infinite pity.

10

She didn't move. It seemed safer not to move. She breathed slowly and carefully. Sound didn't seem safe, either. That initial startled yelp couldn't be helped, but now there was only the sound of the crickets and her own heart. There was an impulse to pull her legs up under her, as though they weren't quite safe stretched out under the table. Her arms wrapped around her knees. She stared straight ahead at the stained kitchen wall. Thoughts tried to form, but couldn't because the main thought, the huge, overwhelming thought, was unthinkable. What she had just seen did not, could not, exist. A name for it kept intruding on her mental defenses and the name was "ghost."

Matty didn't believe in ghosts.

Eventually, it was possible to begin to examine more or less calmly what had just happened. The kitchen looked, felt normal. There was dark beyond the windows. The moon wasn't visible yet, but the rectangle next to her was lighter than the one over the sink, so it was out there. The one bulb in the lamp weakly illuminated the green and yellow square of oilcloth on the table, the roses lying in a pool of water and broken glass on the floor, the dark logs and white chinking of the wall on her right, the door to the storage closet and the unlit opening to the living room on the left. She wasn't yet ready to get up and look further.

A ghost? Jesus! It was not an expletive she used. *What else could it have been? It certainly wasn't real. It couldn't have been real.*

There was a word Matty's mind searched for but couldn't find. It was better than "ghost." Ghost was something from comic movies. "Vision" wasn't acceptable. It implied that the thing had been, at least to some extent, created by her own mind.

Matty examined her fear and accepted it. It was natural to be afraid of anything this abnormal. Fear belonged, was right and proper. It may have been enhanced by, but was not the creation of the nervous leftovers from the accident. There was only the question of how to deal with this. And that depended on what that…that…the word she had been searching for popped up suddenly. *Apparition.* What was that apparition? And what was It going to do?

It hadn't just disappeared or evaporated or faded away as such things were supposed to do. She—Why call it an it? It was a girl—ran away. Like a frightened child. It was almost as if they had frightened each other.

"Whenever people die violently, souls…" What was it Mary Briggsley had said? Mary believed in ghosts.

But Matty didn't.

The only alternative was that it was her imagination. That would be an hallucination. Could she have imagined this sympathetic little girl? It struck her suddenly that, if so, perhaps she had imagined her twice, once as she went to sleep Saturday night and again tonight. They were the same, weren't they? Matty searched her memory and came up with the conclusion that they were, at least, much alike. But how dependable was her mind?

No! Matty's rejection was violent and certain. There was an enormous difference between not smelling roses and seeing visions. *Apparitions,* she corrected. A minutely detailed apparition, if not quite entirely solid. The blonde hair was pulled back, but several wisps had escaped and curled around the young face. She couldn't have been much more than sixteen. Her eyebrows were light, but rather thick, her lips pressed together, matching her eyes, half-closed in sadness and sympathy. Pity. The girl had looked as though she pitied Matty before Matty had uttered that little bark of fear and the eyes had widened in fright. Even as she ran, Matty was aware of a dark stain on the skirt, a smudge on the blouse and the way her waistband had become wrinkled the way they do when their wearer has been sitting or bending. This picture could not have grown from her imagination. This was no image produced by jangled nerves. But they were related. Her expression said clearly that sympathy had prompted that outstretched hand.

Fear began to melt. Her subconscious, Matty realized, had been considering jumping into the car and driving home. Rejecting flight left an option that became gradually acceptable. She could get up and look for this strange visitor. The growing realization that she was really going to be able to do this was surprising. If this little girl wanted to help her, why shouldn't she look for her? A nervous laugh started to grow, but died before it gave birth to sound. If she didn't find the girl, she would go and talk to Mary Briggsley again. Get her away from that irritable husband of hers and find out something about this…phenomenon. Phenomenon was good. It sounded scientific.

She couldn't call Neil. Or Tom. Perhaps Tom would find out for himself this weekend. It would certainly help to have someone else see this thing. In the meantime, she would…What? Make friends with the ghost? The jolt of adrenaline was wearing off and Matty realized she was becoming a little punchy. The attempt at physical exhaustion today had succeeded. The search had better get started.

She stood up, finding her muscles stiff. How long had she sat paralyzed in the uncomfortable chair? With a look at her watch came another question. Did ghosts appear only at certain times? What silly movie had given her that thought? On the other hand, wasn't the girl like a character in a silly movie? Apparently there was a lot to learn about these things she had never believed in.

Had the girl run to the doorway? Perhaps, after all, she had run and then evaporated as such things were supposed to do. Matty shook her head. Switching one's mind to a different reality had elements of the absurd. Such speculation was almost easier when she was afraid. *More afraid,* she corrected. Fear had become a little soft around the edges, but it was still palpable.

It was painful to step over the roses. Even in this astonishing situation, Tom's gift couldn't be left lying there. Neither could it be given much time. She ran a little water in the sink, picked them up a few at a time and laid them there and then turned impatiently to the living room.

A quick pull of the chain and the floor lamp revealed a dull room that looked just as she had left it, shabby furniture with faded colors, dark rectangles that were windows, the intrusive little pot-bellied stove. Matty walked through the room, touching the back of the couch, the top of the stove as if to reassure herself that it was all real.

"Hello?" she called softly. "Are you there?" And then, "It's all right. It was—" She was going to say that it was nice of her to be concerned, but the words wouldn't come. She walked back into the kitchen and stared speculatively at the storage closet door. She wasn't going down there. Not tonight.

There was the upstairs to check, of course, maybe near the flag, but it seemed almost certain that the girl was gone. It just felt that way. Something else impossible to explain. It was disappointing. Was it confirmation she sought or the sympathy the girl had offered? She didn't want this child to be as elusive as the fragrance of yellow roses.

Matty climbed slowly to the second floor and stood for a few minutes at the top of the stairs, glancing into her office and bedroom. Tension drained away, leaving her stunned and emptied. Too much emotion had come and gone this day. She walked slowly, turning out lights. She needed a bath but was too tired. It would be something to do tomorrow, cleaning up the mess on the kitchen floor, making the bed, fixing breakfast just as if nothing extraordinary had happened. That's what you did when secure beliefs turned upside down, she supposed, ordinary, everyday things. The only difference was that, for a change, you were grateful to them instead of resentful. They grounded you. She took off her jeans, tee shirt and underwear and threw them in a heap on the bathroom floor. Using the toilet made her a little self-conscious. Could the girl see her? Dropping her nightgown over her head, she climbed into bed and turned to the night stand to down two small yellow pills, grateful she had ignored Neil's advice to flush them down the toilet. Surely no one could sleep with a ghost in the house without help, exhausted or not.

There was only one more chore to be done tonight while the pills took effect. Matty picked up the legal pad and pencil she had taken from the computer room and wrote:

Tues, after lunch. Couldn't smell roses. Jumpy from first look at basement. Not depressed. I think. Not happy, either. Tues., 9 PM. Couldn't smell roses for second time. Sitting at the kitchen table doing nothing. Physically active all aft & eve. V. tired. Seemed fine mentally. Efficient? Don't know. Prob. not. 2 pills at bedtime. Sorry, Neil

She held her pencil in her hand for a few more minutes, but it balked at writing anything about the apparition. Neil wouldn't believe it, anyway. She set the pencil and paper back on the nightstand, turned off the light, arranged herself for sleep, arms at her sides, and waited for the pills to take effect. Outside the front window, the moon was behind some clouds, edging them with its light. Her gaze kept going to the chair by the door, the chair where the flag lay.

There was no one there.

11

Immediately upon waking early in the morning, Matty lifted her head and looked at the chair even before forming an opinion as to whether or not she wanted the girl to be there. Disappointment gave her the answer. No one—no Thing—had been anywhere in this room any of the many times Matty had searched the room by moonlight, nor was a young girl waiting for her in the yet pale light of day. Eager to search the house, she got out of bed, pleased at having come to terms with last night's encounter while sleeping. Odd how the mind did that. You went to bed wrought up about something and in the morning, the edge was gone. Did dreaming do that? What dreams had come last night? This morning, oddly, the memory of the ghost—apparition?—spirit?—wraith? Wasn't it indicative of its importance in human experience that there were so many words for the same thing?—wasn't the least bit alarming. There was another that seemed good yesterday, but she couldn't remember it now.

Spirit. That was rather nice. Matty hadn't thought of that one last night. Apparition was perhaps more accurate but unwieldy. In a way, the experience was quite wonderful. Off and on, Matty had read with an open, but critical, mind about afterlife and reincarnation, the Seth books, Kubler-Ross, the light at the end of the tunnel. Wasn't everyone trying to believe these days, trying to find a substitute for stale religion? All these theories lacked proof. There had to be proof because the desire to believe in something beyond everyday life was strong enough to create belief without grounds. That business about man's having to invent God if he didn't exist. Who said that? And something about a God-sized hole in people. The need had arisen when her mother died. Her father had never spoken to her about Mom being happy in heaven the way Aunt Lois and a few friends and neighbors had. The existence of this girl proved something. Proved, maybe, everything. It could mean death wasn't the end.

Something else had come into her mind during sleep. Neil's sister. Eloise? No. Naomi? Damn! Would her memory ever be dependable again? At least, she had remembered that the woman had been afraid here. Perhaps the explanation had appeared in the kitchen last night.

The morning sun coming in the window turned the motes of dust in the air golden as it usually did, but today it made her think of angel dust. Had an angel been sent to her? It was a nice thought, but not quite a believable one. Funny how angels seemed to have reappeared in modern culture.

Mary had said souls walked after a violent death. Had this young thing died violently? Poor child! Matty wanted to know more about her. She must have been one of the earliest inhabitants, judging by her dress. Colonial times? Civil War? No little cap like they sold in Williamsburg. When did they wear those and did they wear them all the time? Could Mary Briggsley tell her more? Surely, this little ghost must be famous in the neighborhood! She had to get Mary away from Joseph. Mary and Joseph! That coincidence had escaped her before. Was everything pushing her toward a faith she had never had? Matty smiled and wondered if they had a son.

She jumped out of bed, feeling light as air in spite of a broken night's sleep, buoyed by the thought of what the girl's existence promised, a radical change from her mood when she went to bed. Would the girl be downstairs? Wait till Tom heard about this!

No! Matty stopped abruptly, one leg halfway into her jeans. She was so caught up in this now that she had forgotten to consider the skepticism she was bound to encounter. Never mind. He would see for himself.

Matty stopped at the bottom of the stairs. Entering the kitchen was an Event. But the kitchen was empty.

"Hello?" she called, her voice carefully schooled to an unthreatening gentleness. "Please come back. I'm sorry I scared you."

The birds chirped and a dog barked somewhere in the distance, nothing more.

"My name's...Mathilda," she said, deciding it was more appropriate than Matty.

Did the girl appear only at night? Had it been some cabalistic, ritual hour when she had appeared those two times?

Gradually, the excitement of anticipation drained away and Matty went about the humdrum business of making coffee, pulling out a piece of paper to make a list of what was needed from the grocery for Tom while she waited for it to perk. He wouldn't settle for bran cereal and skim milk. There was that box of oatmeal she had bought because of Joseph. At some point, she would have to eat her joke.

Three hours later, the required three hour stint at the computer was over. Not much had been accomplished. It was impossible not to keep looking around for a sign of the girl. Matty hated to leave for the grocery store without seeing her again.

The jeans were rejected in favor of an outfit chosen with Joseph in mind, a full, navy blue cotton skirt and matching scoop-necked blouse adorned only with a delicate line of embroidery around the hem and neck-line. It occurred to her that she did a lot of this, adapting clothes, language, even attitudes to suit the tastes of her clients. It was more a game than a burden. At least, it used to be.

With one last, reluctant look around the house, she headed her car into the guiding ruts that led to the main valley road.

◆　　　◆　　　◆

The general store was weather-beaten wood, so long unpainted that paint seemed inappropriate. The roof had been patched with unmatched shingles. A dented old milk can, brick red with an eagle decal, stood by the front door, full of American flags. Matty sat for a few moments, her car on the gravel in front of the door, surprised that she had been here before and hadn't really seen these details. There was a red neon "Pharmacy" sign on a small addition to the farmhouse diagonally across the intersection, too.

She had noticed that before at least. Diazepam was never far from her mind.

A bell jingled as she walked through the door, startling her a little. It hadn't been there before. It brought a panting Mary Briggsley from the back.

"Oh, good! It's you! I got to rush so these days, what with these kids grabbin' somethin' and runnin' when no one's up front. Used to be we could go out back in the garden and not worry at all. Folks'd just leave the money on the counter." She shook her head. "Now. What can I—Why, don't you look nice! Joseph'll have to see you 'fore you leave. Cost much, did it? I could fancy that myself!"

The outfit had cost just over two hundred dollars, an amount that suddenly seemed outrageous.

"It's old, Mrs. Briggsley. I doubt you could find it now."

"Oh."

Mary Briggsley's disappointment showed in every feature. Not a difficult woman to know, she decided. Mary was patting her hair now and Matty searched her memory. Mary's hair was mostly gray, only bits of a medium brown showing here and there, but hadn't it been straight and falling in her face before? Now it was coiled in limp corkscrews like a depressed Afro.

"You've had your hair done," she offered cautiously, not sure whether congratulations or condolences were in order.

Mary beamed. Matty smiled back, sure of her approach now.

"Done it yesterday. Not m'self, o'course. Norrie and me, we always give each other our do's, y'know. Kind of wild. But that's the style now."

Matty smiled brightly. That had been the style. How many years ago? Finally, from the back of her throat, she dragged, "Goodness! You did it yourself!"

Mary didn't notice. She patted her sagging steel wool again with satisfaction. "Little hard to comb out, but it'll relax."

"Your husband is here? I wanted to ask him if he had any books on the history of this area, the early settlers. He was typing before and I thought he might be a man who had some reference books."

"My, yes. Loads. You can ask him."

"He's here then?" Matty supposed he was always here, but had held onto a small hope of getting Mary alone to talk about those restless spirits.

"He's got a delivery and then he's goin' over to the Moose to play chess with Walter. Has lunch there, too." She turned to the back and called his name. Where there had been silence, now the typewriter clacked.

"I'll go tell him."

It was obvious Joseph had heard and dismissed them. Mary seemed to take this kind of behavior for granted.

The woman's whispered words were indecipherable, but Joseph's' voice came loud and clear and angry.

"What the hell do I care what the woman's got on!...I don't lend books! God dammit, Mary, you know I don't lend my books!...Tell her myself!"

And there he was, as dried up and red-eyed as Matty remembered.

"I don't lend books!"

"I think I heard that somewhere," Matty said.

The old man cocked his head suspiciously. "Meant to be humor, is it?"

"Partial to it, myself," Matty replied, getting in the swing of the thing now.

"Smart-ass woman. Who likes a smart-ass woman?"

"So don't like me. Just loan me some history books. I'll leave a deposit."

"Hah!"

This seemed to be a laugh. He put his elbows on the counter and leaned toward her. His breath smelled of stale coffee. "Tell you who likes a smart-ass woman. I do. Always damn did!"

He turned and headed for the back again. At a loss, Matty looked at Mary, who nodded vehemently and gestured for her to follow.

The room seemed to be a dining room that had become an office. The walls were lined with bookshelves of all kinds, stacked bricks and boards, as in Matty's cabin, metal storage shelves, one oak glass-doored bookcase. The books were neatly arranged, all the same distance from the front edge of the shelves. On the oak table were a few scattered volumes, stacks of paper, mugs full of pens and pencils, one half full of coffee and an old manual Remington typewriter.

"History, huh?"

"Of this area, if you have anything."

He went to the oak bookcase, opened the door and pulled out two faded books. "How fast you read?"

"Fast."

He pulled out two more.

"Keep a week. No more. Hundred dollars."

"A hundred dollars. Right." Matty put all the sarcasm she could into the few words.

"Hah!" That laugh again. "Fifty, then."

It was outrageous, but these books were important to her and they did look old, not something she could get from the public library. Matty took two twenties and a ten from her wallet and handed them to him.

"Till next Wednesday."

He didn't answer. The money was stuffed into the pocket of his plaid flannel shirt. He was through with her.

Matty became aware of a delicious smell in the air. She was hungry. Her small breakfast hadn't made up for the lack of food yesterday. *Get the groceries,* she told herself, *including a snack to munch on here in case I have to kill time till Joseph leaves.*

"You say you deliver?" she asked Mary once they were back in the room that served as the store. There was a possibility of killing two odd birds with one stone here.

"Joseph does. Dollar a mile. Some of the older ones, they stock up about once a month. You can freeze milk and butter, you know. Lots of people don't know that. And eggs keep forever when they're fresh like our'n. Lots of people don't know that, either. How else you got so many for Easter? Chickens don't lay more that week, y'know."

Matty was content to let Mary run on. She needed to fill time until Joseph left. But Mary, perhaps remembering that she had kept Matty too long the first time, gestured toward their three undersized, rickety carts and smiled her on her way.

She began collecting what she needed for Tom, dawdling, wishing Joseph out the door. A locally baked apple coffee cake. Duncan Hines devil's food cake mix. She would make that for Tom with her own mocha icing. She got some cocoa and confectioner's sugar but passed the cooler with the screw-top wine. Tom would bring better wine. Mrs. Briggsley saw her looking at the skimpy selection in the meat counter.

"We got any beef or chicken you want in the freezer in the back. From Carl Schuler's place. You just name it."

Matty named it. Tenderloin steaks and chicken breasts, two of each.

The woman looked pleased to be taken up on her offer. Or did she just smile at anything? While she was gone, Joseph came in and, without a glance at her, began collecting the items on a list he held in one hand. He moved quickly, not bothering with a cart or basket, but grabbing an armful one aisle at a time and dropping each load on the counter. He rang up the order without looking at the keys, setting each item in an empty carton with his left hand while the right hand flew over the keys.

Opposites attract, Matty thought, without believing the words. She couldn't imagine anyone being attracted to either of these two. *Not fair*, her conscience protested. Mary said Joseph was smart. That was attractive to a woman and Mary was a pleasant sort who might have been pretty as a girl. Tom would never have settled for her, common sense argued. She probably drives Joseph crazy, the two sides agreed.

The bell jingled as a young couple entered, red faced and windblown.

"Can you get us to Gettysburg?" the young man demanded of Joseph.

The old man took in the Docksiders, the white duck pants and designer polo shirt very slowly.

"Got no car," he drawled.

"No, no! We've got a car! We need directions!"

"Got no map?" Joseph asked innocently.

"We thought we knew the way."

"Can sell you a map," Joseph offered pleasantly.

The young woman decided to take a hand.

"Look, actually, we're not very good at maps. Couldn't you just tell us how to get there please?"

Joseph looked her up and down, taking in the full, pink shorts, the white sweatshirt with "Take Me, I'm Yours!" scrawled in pink, pink socks and white Reeboks with pink trim. He smiled.

"Surely, Ma'am."

Matty went on collecting her groceries until she heard him telling them to take 70 West toward Myersville. That couldn't be right. She hurried to the front of the store, uncertain whether to chase the couple or ask Joseph. She didn't know this part of Maryland well. She settled for Joseph.

"Are you sure about those directions?"

He was smiling. "Sure they'll get 'em back here."

"Back here?"

"Too cheap to buy a map." His smile widened, revealing irregular, gray teeth. "By the time they get back here, they'll need something to eat, too. They'll spend some money on food. And a map." He threw back his head and uttered another "Hah!" Then he picked up the heavy box with ease and went into the back room. A few seconds later, a door slammed.

Matty was appalled but amused, too. Whatever the man was, he was an original. Mary had arrived and the laugh was stifled. It might be uncomfortable to explain.

"This'll be all?"

"Yes, thank you, Mrs. Briggsley."

"Mary. Don't no one call me Mrs. Briggsley less'n they're under ten. Even then, I'm Miss Mary."

"Mary, then. Call me Matty."

"Oh, yes. Matty. I remember now." She was proud of remembering rather than embarrassed at having forgotten. The thick fingers hovered over the keys and landed on one, then a second, then, after a little wriggle, a third.

Matty picked up a bunch of grapes.

"Would you weigh these first?" she asked. "I'm starving. I'll eat some while you ring up the other things."

"Why, sure." Mary put them on the white enamel scale. "Tell you what, though. Why don't you have some lunch with me?" She was clearly delighted at the idea.

So was Matty. This would give her plenty of time to pick Mary's brains without admitting she'd seen anything unusual until she was sure of a sympathetic reception. Maybe not even then.

"I'd love to. That's real neighborly of you."

Matty winced. She deplored her habit of dropping into the speech patterns and accents of anyone she was speaking to. It was useful. There were courses for Realtors that taught the effectiveness of adopting the vocabulary and body language of customers in order to make them more comfortable and trusting. She did it unconsciously.

"Good! Good!" Mary grinned with pleasure. "I'll just put your cold things into my refrigerator. I thought to fix a nice fruit salad for lunch. Joseph don't care much for fruit salad so I have it when he's gone."

"That sounds wonderful!" Matty's enthusiasm was genuine. "But don't go to too much trouble for me. You're sure you were going to do that, anyway? I'll be glad to help."

"No, no. You be the guest."

Each time she spoke, Mary stopped punching the cash register. Matty decided to be quiet until the order was checked out.

The kitchen looked a lot like the one at the log home except the cabinets were metal, an old Youngstown kitchen, the once-white baked-on finish now yellow. Mary gestured her guest into one of the caned chairs at the scarred oak table and set to her task.

"You said an interesting thing last time I was here, Mary. You said that you wouldn't stay where I am, that the souls of people who died violently walked. Did you really mean that? Are there any stories about my house?"

Mary, slicing a banana into a big yellow bowl, stopped to say, "Oh, yes. Bound to be, house that old." Then, in the act of rinsing a handful of fresh raspberries, she stopped again, her head tilted back as she stared at the ceiling, thinking. "Lots of stories," she said slowly, as though imparting a world of information.

This was going to take time. At this point, Matty wondered which appetite took priority, hunger or curiosity.

"Have you had any personal experience?" Matty asked. "With ghosts, I mean. At the house. Or anywhere," she added quickly. Was she being paranoid about revealing what had happened to her? She had had enough of feeling like a nut case.

"Oh, sure." The ball of steel wool bobbed violently. "When mother died, you could see her spirit go. Just like steam from a kettle, it was. Course not everyone saw it. There's some as is sensitive and some as isn't." She turned to Matty. "Don't do to mention such things to Joseph. He's not a believer."

"In ghosts? Or God?"

"In anythin'. Wrote me a poem about it just this mornin'."

"I see."

She didn't.

"Then there was that time over to Yolanda's. Nothin' to see, mind you, but we all heard it. Moanin'. Sad-like. Happens all the time. It's a woman died hundred years or more ago. Her children all died in a fire and they rebuilt the house and she mourns 'em."

"Did she die, too?" Matty wondered how to steer the conversation to her own house.

"Not in the fire. She got saved by somebody. Died a crazy old lady near ninety years old. But she stuck around. After dyin'. It's guilt makes her stay. Wants to live it over, save the kids."

"But no one *sees* her." Matty wondered why she had difficulty believing this story after her own experience. "So spirits stay if they have some reason? Something they want to do?" Anyone who went to the movies knew the answer to this question, but she had to keep Mary talking.

"Oh, yes! For certain!"

Mary had taken three cans from a lower cupboard and opened them. She was now draining off the juice into a glass. The cans went upside down over the bowl and neat slices of oranges, pears and peaches fell out.

"I save some of the juice, don't you?" Mary asked. "To thin the mayonnaise just a bit."

Matty, who never put mayonnaise in a fruit salad, nodded and said, "Oh, sure. Much better."

After the mayonnaise, Mary took a plastic bag from overhead and shook out a few cups of miniature marshmallows, sprinkled sugar over the pile and began stirring with a wooden spoon.

"Almost ready," she promised.

"I'm a light eater. Just a little."

Matty briefly wondered if there was a diplomatic way she could get a little of whatever was cooking on the back burner of the stove instead of the salad, but couldn't come up with an acceptable approach. Tom said her obsession with healthy eating wasn't healthy. He was right.

"I can tell." Mary shook her head from side to side. "Wish I had your will power. But then, you're young and supposed to be thin."

Matty took a bite of the sweet salad. No point avoiding the marshmallows. They would have to go eventually. Ghosts. She was here for ghosts. Marshmallows were a small penalty to pay.

"You're saying spirits don't depart…" That didn't sound right. "Why do they hang around? What do they want?"

Mary had downed half her salad and looked as though she would just as soon not be interrupted, but she stopped eating long enough to say, "Got to be a strong reason."

That wasn't very helpful. Matty just said, "I see," and stared at the steam rising from the big pot on the stove, wondering if that was what Mary's mother looked like when she died.

"What you're cooking there smells wonderful," she ventured.

"Green beans. Nice piece of pork. I like 'em to simmer all day on a low heat, don't you?"

Simmer them all day? Would they have any nutritional value at all? Matty murmured an "um" that was the best she could do in the way of a positive response. It was becoming difficult to feel positive about this woman in more ways than one. There seemed to be no useful information from this source and Matty wondered how she had gotten herself into the position of asking questions that, more and more, seemed irrational. She decided to try one that was slightly more scientific.

"I've heard of cold spots, for instance."

Mary blinked rapidly and her eyes wandered. Matty knew the signs. It was a search for the right answer. She had seen it often enough in prospective tenants. It was hard not to get up and leave immediately. The girl might be there, waiting.

"I know a good deal," Mary said as if to reassure herself as well as Matty. "But if you want an expert, I guess you'd have to go to Evelyn Morris. She's a real expert."

"Oh? Where do I find Evelyn Morris?"

"She works in Frederick doin' somethin' or other. Over to church a lot, too. Lots to do without a pastor. Four years now we been makin' do with these travelin' ones and Father Courland what's retired. I can get you her phone number. Only she's not home a lot." Mary got out of her chair.

"No. Never mind. I'll catch her at church. Don't interrupt your lunch."

Actually, Mary wasn't interrupting her lunch. Astonishingly, her bowl was empty and she was getting up for more. Matty tried to hurry.

"Have you—" Matty, about to ask if Mary had ever been to the cabin, caught her mistake. Courtesy would require an invitation if she hadn't. "—ever heard anything about the house I'm staying in? About it's history?"

"Oh, sure. It's old."

Right. Thank you very much.

"Hasn't no one lived there for some time now," Mary continued. "Since't I was a girl. Just a vacation place. Just as well. No cable."

No cable? "Oh! Television."

"Never could figure someone wantin' to vacation where there's no T.V. I mean, you finally got the free time and can watch all you want to and there's no T.V. Now does that make sense to you?"

It apparently hadn't occurred to Mary that she had just described Matty's situation.

"I read a lot myself."

"Oh! I suppose you're like Joseph. I sort of think of him as one of a kind."

"I think that's a safe thought."

Mary smiled, comfortable now with the turn of the conversation and ready to be sociable.

"He is a funny man, isn't he? Like nobody else. Around here, anyways. I don't mind doin' most of the work so's he can do his writin'. Have it in mind some day, maybe after both of us is gone, he'll turn up famous, y'know? You should read what he writes! Give me a poem just this mornin', that one about religion. Can't make head nor tail of it, but I think it sure shows he don't believe in God nor ghosts nor nothin'. Scary sort of thing. Maybe you can make somethin' out of it. He never will explain. You wait here!"

Mary moved as fast as she ever moved to a pile of papers and magazines on the counter. After a little shuffling, she returned with a single sheet of typing paper, which she dropped in front of Matty.

"There, now! What do ya make of that?"

Matty read:

That stony law I stamp to dust and scatter religion abroad
To the four winds as a torn book, and none shall gather the leaves.
But they shall rot on desert sands, and consume in bottomless deeps
To make the deserts blossom and the deeps shrink to their fountains,
And to renew the fiery joy and burst the stony roof.
That pale religious letchery, seeking Virginity,
May find it in a harlot, and in coarse-clad honesty
The undefiled tho' ravished in her cradle night and morn.

"Now ain't that awful stuff?" Mary asked when Matty raised her head. "Ravished, now. You know what that means, doncha? An' harlot?"

Matty nodded, subduing a smile.

"I mean, it sounds like sorta poetry, but it don't rhyme nohow, but imagine talkin' like that about religion. I suppose you don't have to believe if you just can't, but there's no call to be talkin' about it like that, harlots and such."

It wasn't awful stuff. It was powerful stuff. And hardly anti-religious. Clearly, Mary didn't understand it. Matty wouldn't have recognized it if it hadn't led up to the next line, the line that Joseph apparently hadn't wanted to include about all life being holy. She had used it in a paper about the romantic poets in college.

Matty pled ignorance as to the poem's meaning, said her thank-you's and goodbye's as quickly as possible without rudeness, collected her groceries and left. Her shoulders dropped in relief. Adapting to Mary was a bit of a strain. And Mary, obviously, wasn't going to be any help with her ghost.

Maybe Joseph would.

A man who pretended to have written the poetry of William Blake ought to have something interesting to say.

12

Driving back to the cabin, Matty remembered she had meant to call the office from time to time. Even at her most nervous and overworked, she never forgot things like that. It was hard to believe that now it didn't even seem to matter much. What was more important than finding clear evidence of life after death? *Mom.* That was the first thought that followed. The woman in the accident. And after that, *Dad.* Death, as yet, had little to do with Matty herself.

The evidence was clear, wasn't it? Why was belief so difficult? Dad had once said that Westerners needed data to support faith, unlike people of some cultures to whom spirituality came more naturally. She was undeniably a Westerner. Here was proof and still acceptance was difficult. Matty sat in the car outside the back door, wanting an explanation for her reluctance before another encounter. Finally, she decided that it was because this manifestation—There, that was another word for it!—contradicted her previous experience and fit with none of her beliefs. She found she doubted enough to keep wondering if her own mind hadn't somehow created this ghost. She and Tom had wanted a child. Could this be a projection of some emotional need? But surely she would have imagined a baby or a toddler or perhaps an engaging child she had just seen somewhere. The problem with her nerves—How she hated thinking about herself as someone with nerves!—contributed to lack of faith in herself. Or would anyone have this conflict when meeting the impossible face to face?

Matty picked up Joseph's books, handling them carefully. Two were very old, the covers splitting down the spines, strings of the fabric bindings hanging from the edges. The door to the house was unlocked, more evidence that she was too focused on her new mission and not in touch with the world. She loved that phrase, having first heard it from the mother of a boy who had bumped into her cart at a grocery store. "Stay in touch with the world, son," his mother had said and Matty had treasured the phrase ever since. It took on a new meaning now. Had her view been too limited? Had she not been at all in touch with an elusive but vital part of her world? The impossible was, apparently, very possible indeed.

"Get in touch, Matty," she told herself. "Get in touch."

Dad had to be wrong.

As soon as she shut the heavy door, silence shut out all sounds but the most raucous of bird calls. It made her realize this was no moaning ghost like the one Mary had described. This was a silent one. Matty had heard personal accounts of other ghosts that were both silent and invisible. A restaurant in Westminster, she was assured by one of the waiters, was undoubtedly haunted. Its ghost had never been seen or heard, but for over a hundred years it had taken pictures off the walls at night. One particular picture? She couldn't remember. Then there was her cousin...

Matty set the books carefully on the coffee table and returned to the car for the groceries as memories of other similar stories flooded her mind. Setting the purchases in appropriate places, amazement grew that this evidence been around her all her life. How could she listen to stories told by reliable people and then dismiss them, put them into a special category of good social tales, entirely divorced from her beliefs about life and death?

"Holy sh—" She broke off. Somehow it didn't seem right to say "shit" if the girl might hear. Had she heard?

Matty uttered a quiet "Hello?" and waited. The kitchen faucet dripped once. She shook her head again and began picking over the raspberries, throwing away the few with white fuzzy growth. They would be nice after dinner, on a little ice cream maybe. Matty rarely allowed herself desert, but this seemed a special occasion, though a confusing, difficult to define occasion.

◆   ◆   ◆

Evelyn Morris was in the phone book, but, disappointingly, not at home. Mary had said she worked. In a way, it was a relief. With Mary, she had worked her way into a conversation about ghosts and she knew Mary at least slightly. It was going to be much more difficult to initiate this phone conversation.

The sun was warm and welcoming and she had opened the windows that offered the least resistance, but she wasn't sure the ghost would come outside, so she quickly changed into jeans and a tee and settled onto the bumpy couch, stretched out fairly comfortably and opened the first book, a glass of wine by her side.

Early Residents of Maryland looked the most promising. "Chapter One: Indians." Of course. Flipping rapidly, she came to: "Chapter Three: English and Scots." The English and Scots had settled heavily in Maryland, many more English than Scots. The following chapters told her that the next groups came from Northern Europe, the Netherlands, France and Sweden. The Germans had drifted down from Pennsylvania. All mildly interesting, but it didn't tell her who built or lived in this house. She set it aside.

The next book didn't seem much more helpful initially, *The Civil War in Eastern Maryland: Washington and Frederick Counties*, published by a local historical society. She was almost ready to fall asleep after skimming through nine chapters.

Then she was very much awake. Had Joseph known what was in this book? Her house! She sat upright, leaned over the book and read the passage again. At the end of the chapter, detailed directions to each of the houses discussed were given for those who wanted to drive by and one set of directions was almost certainly to this house. Matty turned back to the earlier pages. Some general named D. H. Hill made his headquarters nearby in an old inn known as Mountain House, which provided an overview of Turner's Gap. From there he saw the Union troops coming. A battle started on the morning of September 14, 1862. He held off the advance until General Longstreet arrived with help. Matty had to stop and think. *When was the battle of Gettysburg?* She remembered the movie and that it was summer, but the details from her reading this week had not stuck. *July. Definitely July. But was it the same year?* She ran upstairs and got her little pamphlet. 1863. Not the same year. Why was that disappointing? Because she felt the need for connections to familiar things? *Silly.*

Was the girl here then? Matty pictured her in her mind. *What did women wear during Civil War times?* Matty grabbed the American Heritage book. A quick flip through the many pages showed women working, but there was no definitive item of clothing, only the long skirts and big aprons.

Matty realized she was cold in her tee top. She looked out the bedroom window, aware for the first time that the sky was darkening. Rain was coming again. Choosing the quickest remedy, she slipped into her warm blue velour robe and went downstairs and back to her book. She read every line in the chapter three times. There was no mention of the owners of the house. Not really much mention of the house at all, except that it had been here then and was used to house some of the wounded. Disappointed at a dead-end so soon after her great discovery, she turned to the next book.

It was no help at all, an account of the rise of industry in Maryland. Lots of information on the Chesapeake Bay and its varieties of seafood. Matty skimmed it, bored, but afraid to miss anything. At the office, she played with a paper clip or pen while she read. Here, she rubbed her fingers against the soft velour of her robe, but her fingers were cold or her hand asleep. She rubbed harder and feeling came back.

Her gaze wandered to the window. The sky had darkened even more. Tree branches were now bent in a strong breeze, the first raindrops making black spots on the weathered porch railing. She looked around the room for the girl as she had dozens of times during the day and listened without expecting to hear anything.

Sitting too long had created an uncomfortable restlessness. The title of the remaining book wasn't promising, *First Families of Maryland.* It sounded snobby and no doubt was a kind of social register. It also looked fairly new. She had saved it for last and now decided it could wait. It was time to check the basement again. She needed to move and it was the only part of the house left unexplored since the girl's appearance. It wasn't a pleasant prospect.

First, there was all that stuff. Matty made a little of her own thunder as she threw boots, buckets, the broom and all the other carelessly heaped odds and ends onto the kitchen floor for the second time and lifted the plywood board. The now familiar odor of cold stones and earth rose to meet her. Pressing the wall with one hand as she gathered up her robe in the other to avoid dusting the stairs with it, she walked sideways, carefully, one step at a time. She had forgotten the flashlight, but there was some daylight in addition to the light falling down the stairs from the kitchen. She closed her eyes and waited for them to adjust. When she opened them, the two dusky windows seemed almost to move toward her.

"Are you here?"

Out loud, it sounded idiotic. Why would she be here? Because she wasn't anywhere else in the house? Or because she had first appeared after the basement had been uncovered? At least, there was some logic in that. Matty listened and waited for the shadows that had frightened her before. They were gone. The same shapes still inhabited the cellar, the fireplace, the harmless odds and ends. Some energy seemed to have gone. Climbing back up the stairs, Matty wondered why, then, she was so anxious to leave.

By the time the closet was back in order, she was ready to return to her reading. The wine glass was empty, offering a temptation that should be resisted.

Her last book. It was certainly going to be no problem to get them back to Joseph in a week. Surely no "First Family" had inhabited this humble abode. Still, they were undoubtedly among the first in the historical sense. The index showed a list of family names which were the chapter headings. Maybe there was hope here. But which family was *her* family? With a grunt of displeasure, she began with "Chapter One: The Steelmans." She soon discovered that the key as to whether or not the chapter was of interest lay in the location of the house. Fortunately, this was usually one of the first facts given. Most homes were around the Chesapeake Bay and those chapters could be quickly eliminated. Those whose descriptions didn't relate to her knowledge of the state were marked with little pieces of a

Kleenex she took from her robe pocket. If nothing jumped out at her, she would have to go through those more carefully.

Going back through the marked chapters, a major problem remained: the method of property description. She was accustomed to the standard lot, block, subdivision and county identification usually followed by "also known as" and the street address. Most of the chapters used place names she didn't know and the county was rarely mentioned. Matty went to the car for a map and settled down, expecting a tedious and unproductive search. Town names easily eliminated some of the entries. Finally she found a reference to South Mountain. A little leap of hopeful anticipation sent her back to the beginning of the chapter. A few pages into it, she sat back and stared at the lines that had made her catch and hold her breath. In spite of the fact that the family who built this house must have been early settlers, it was almost impossible to believe that they were really here, in this book. This was her chapter, her family! How many houses of this age could there be on this part of South Mountain? She had a name!

"Birdie," she said out loud. "Is your name Birdie?" She rather hoped not. She wanted something more…dignified?…romantic? *Silly,* she chided herself.

There was no reply.

"It is, isn't it?" *Please,* she added silently.

Or perhaps not. Matty went back to the book and read quickly. "…one of the larger log homes in the area for some time…no definite date of arrival, but known to have been there in 1773." The source of the family name was a soldier's diary, which said "mayd camp ner house ownd bye a farmer naymed Birdie, reddy enuf to be rid of English rul." No mention of the first name or of his family. "Nothing further is known about this early settler. The house was next occupied by Horst Rochenbaugh (See Chapter 14.)"

Quickly, Matty leafed forward in the book, looking for Chapter 14. *Why didn't the book give a page number?* A familiar impatience swept through her, but all was forgiven when she found the chapter that began: "Horst and Julianna Rochenbaugh purchased a home on South Mountain from the original settler, Clotworthy Birdie, on July 19, 1784. The Rochenbaughs were from east of Philadelphia…" Matty scanned. "…their only child, a son, Nathaniel, became a well-known miller after moving near…" Much about Nathaniel followed, but Matty wanted the inhabitants of this house, which appeared to be only Horst and Julianna after Nathaniel left, then only Horst until he died in 1811. Apparently the next owners weren't considered a first family. Matty was irritated. 1811 seemed early enough for that designation.

Where in the span of time did my girl fall? Birdie? Rochenbaugh? Was she of Revolutionary times, Civil War or neither? Why a war at all? Because Mary had said those soldiers walked and so did her ghost? This was not good detective work. She was jumping to conclusions again just as she had when assuming that first families were so-called because of their importance.

Matty stared at the book in frustration for a few seconds until realization hit her.

"Hey!" she said out loud. "You know real estate! You can do this!" Then she had to add, ruefully, "Not without considerable trouble." Title transfers could laboriously be searched backwards, but such records provided limited information. Perhaps the local people were her best source after all. Whatever the era, the clothing told Matty that she had to go back a long way in time. Could that gap be crossed?

It was long past dinner time. Now that she had gleaned what could be gotten from the books, she set them carefully in a small pile on the coffee table, surveying them with satisfaction. There had been more there than she had hoped for. There was fighting here during the Civil War, the house dated from Revolutionary War times and the first two owners were named Birdie and Rochenbaugh. Matty turned her wrist to check the time. The fact that there was no watch there brought a smile. It was a sign of progress.

Matty hummed "As Time Goes By," as she started dinner, singing snatches of the lyrics as she remembered them. She paused, ripped a sheet of aluminum foil from its box and tried to think of something more appropriate. What songs did they sing then? Maybe "Amazing Grace." She knew a few words. Very few. She shrugged. At least "As Time Goes By" was somewhat old-fashioned, she thought, and the title was apt.

"It's still the same old story, a tale of love and glory, a case of do or die…" Her mother used to sing this sometimes as she did her housework. Good lyrics, Matty thought as she quartered a potato and dropped it into the pot of cold water and set it on a burner, pleased with herself that once more carbs were included in dinner. Wouldn't Neil be happy if she came back a little plumped up? She sautéed a garlic clove with "woman needs man and man must have his mate" and then had to stop to think of the next line. It came. "This no one can deny," she sang dramatically as she waved her spatula like a baton.

Suddenly, she felt silly. Was this supposed to be entertaining the ghost? Trying to attract her? *Good God*—a phrase she now had second thoughts about using—*I am!* At least, she was trying to create a friendly atmosphere. A chopped, fresh tomato went in with the garlic in self-conscious silence and, when it was hot, a pile of fresh spinach, stuffed into the pot with the lid. Time to put those two lamb chops on the broiling foil. They had come from home and were getting a little old.

Matty surveyed the various spittings and boilings with satisfaction. Good dinner. She had gone back to humming the tune.

Damn! She still hadn't called the office!

A familiar little stab of panic hit her in the chest. This was automatic, erased only when the problem was deemed inconsequential, as this one was. It didn't really matter that Consuela and Rosemary would have gone home by now. Tomorrow would do. A bigger stab of fear attacked her as she thought of the loss of the smell of roses. Any small fear invariably invited others. Mentally, she thanked the sweet little ghost who had appeared to sympathize with her. It occurred to her that in her life in Rockville, there was no one to offer such sympathy because no one was told of this ongoing anxiety about even trivial things. This was the need Neil filled. Psychiatrists were paid to put up with irrational fears one couldn't admit to the important people in life. They would worry too much. At least, Tom would. The search for the girl's identity had served an important purpose, had almost made Matty forget her problem. That should continue. And the schedule must be honored. A little work, walks, exercise. Those things were necessary for getting well. They just weren't nearly as interesting as this ghost. What did her little spirit think of the exercise routine, she wondered? The girl's family must have worked hard just to stay alive. All that exertion, accomplishing nothing visible, must seem absurd.

Matty almost gobbled her dinner. She couldn't remember the last time she had enjoyed a meal so much. The raspberries were on the counter, waiting for the ice cream.

"Be good," she cautioned herself as she dipped into the vanilla ice cream. "Not too much now. Oh, what the hell! Loosen up!"

She went to the cupboard for the Hershey's syrup she had bought for Tom. *Just drizzle a little...*but she kept on drizzling until she laughed. Neil would love this! She was sorry she hadn't started a pot of coffee. Too late now.

The first bite was heavenly.

The second bite wasn't there.

It wasn't there at all. No tart raspberry. No sweet ice cream. No luscious chocolate. No cold, either, or the feel of little raspberry seeds.

Matty stared straight ahead, trying not to panic. She had to order herself to try another bite. It was like sucking an empty spoon. Somehow, this was worse, much worse, than not smelling roses. She squeezed her eyes shut, but the tears came out anyway.

"Damn, damn, damn," she began and the "damns" wouldn't stop. She put her elbows on the table and pressed her palms against her eyes. She would have to call Neil. This was serious. This was scary as hell!

Matty sat immobile, unsure of too many things. She started for the phone, then stopped. Neil would tell her to come back. How could she explain the importance of staying here? She needed to know this, this...apparition, this child, was real. She had made a start. From the library, the courthouse, from Mary's friend, from Joseph might come the verification that mattered so much in more than one way. There was life after death.

These problems are all in my mind. Neil had said so, hadn't he? Matty tried to remember exactly what it was that Neil had said. *He said he thought he could deal with it. That would make it a psychological problem, wouldn't it? This is something my brain has created? That would be a sort of hallucination, wouldn't it? Could not tasting or feeling be a form of hallucination? It didn't seem right. Hallucinations would be feeling or tasting what wasn't there*

Or seeing.

No. The girl was real. I won't have Neil telling me this little bringer of hope isn't real!

Neil hadn't mentioned hallucinations. But then, Neil hadn't offered any diagnosis at all. How could she have missed that, not pressed for one?

Matty sat down to finish her sundae, not for pleasure, for there certainly was no pleasure. She ate in defiance. She was going to keep on going, at least for a few days. What difference could just a few days make? Neil seemed to think it was all right to wait.

As long as I report if there are any more incidents. Will I?

She kept lifting the spoon although every bite was tainted with the metallic taste of fear.

At least, every bite had some taste.

13

Matty woke with familiar little shafts of anxiety running through her chest and down her arms, softened but not eliminated by the tranquilizers taken to get through the night. She felt now as though she were walking two tightropes. One foot was on the hope the girl had brought, the other on the fear that something was irreparably wrong with the circuits in her brain. The ropes kept getting farther and farther apart. It was impossible to stay on both of them for long.

She stared at the rough beams over her head, the dirty white parallel lines between. The pattern was potentially hypnotic as her eyes ran back and forth following the bumpy, stained white, the chipped and nail-studded brown, every foot a little different from the one before. Why the hook there, the splash of red over the window? Relics of lives that had been lived here. Tempting just to lie there and wonder…

Distractions didn't work for long.

Choose.

Call Neil. Go home, anxiety ordered.

Stay, the sympathetic eyes of her little spirit seemed to plead, *I offer hope.*

Fear was a powerful motivation. Nothing bad had happened for a year after the accident, but it had left a residue of unreasoning anxiety that drained the joy out of life. Now sensory losses provided a very real reason for fear. Bed was her refuge. Was it even possible to get up? She lay rigid, gripping the blanket with her fists.

Slowly, her fingers uncurled. She was able to breathe deeply. Muscles began to loosen.

Eventually it was possible to sit up on the edge of the bed. She pulled a Kleenex from the box beside her and wiped her eyes, blew her nose. After a tortured night of arguing with herself, the debate finally drowned in Diazepam, it was reassuring to feel quite normal. Bad nights were not unusual. She could see clearly, hear the birds announcing day, feel the soft sheets and the rough blanket, smell the scent of the musty old house beginning to crawl through Murphy's soap and Lysol.

Why don't I sleep with the windows open?

Because it feels safer.

She laughed humorlessly at the ability of mundane thoughts to push their way into the morass of fear and dilemma. It was time to go downstairs and see if taste worked this morning. *Just some lousy residue from the accident, a psychological glitch.* It was that reassurance that had made staying in the house, in this bed, possible.

Get on with it.

The planks were cold on her bare feet, colder than they had been before. The days were moving into winter. It was Thursday. Tom would be here in two days. She could make it through two days. Maybe he would see her girl and they could go home and Neil or somebody could fix her and life would be all right again. She squelched the thought that life hadn't been altogether all right for some time.

Follow the routine, she told herself and found that she could.

Bran cereal and skim milk. A walk. It wasn't a calming walk. Trying to keep fear at bay, Matty tried to decide where to begin the search for historic proof of the girl. Every possibility would take her away from the house and she didn't want to leave. What better source of information than the girl herself? If only she would appear again!

To the top of the mountain and back down without a rest on the big rock at the top. She was doing better at the end. Calling the office, something she had hoped to avoid, had a sudden appeal. It would be comforting to touch a more familiar world. As the office phone rang, it occurred to her how ironic it was that the office was now the escape rather than this so-called vacation.

Rosemary's voice projected a combination of boredom and irritation, a note of "Why are you bothering me?" It would have been annoying if she weren't so accustomed to Rosemary.

"The Gurrhas say their hot water heater is broken again."

"Meaning the pilot went out," Matty interpreted.

"Right."

"Damn it, I've shown them how to light it twice!"

The Gurrhas, from somewhere in the middle east, were encountering modern home appliances for the first time. They loved them when they worked, ran them without need as children would play with a toy, but considered it a failure of American culture when something went wrong.

"Oh, well. Call Fred." Fred was the office jack-of-all trades. "Tell him to tell them again not to leave the basement door open. It's the breeze blowing through that blows out the pilot."

"If my house stunk like that, I'd leave the doors open, too. Anyhow, Fred won't go. Says he can't stand the bugs."

"Tell him there aren't any—aren't so many—in the basement."

Matty would never forget her revulsion the first time she had entered the Gurrha's kitchen on a routine "insurance" inspection, the usual excuse for checking up on how tenants were maintaining a property. Sacs of roach eggs lay all over the stove and were festooned from the hood. Matty told Mrs. Gurrha the family would have to clean and she would send in an exterminator. It had been a temporary fix. Fixes were always temporary in her business.

Property management was an education in culture clash. There had been a group of assorted Asian students who loved birds and let them nest in the drapery rods, an African family who had always cooked over an open fire on an earthen floor and assumed it was all right to do the same on the tile floor of their American kitchen and a delicately beautiful Vietnamese couple who, with neither the owner's permission nor a permit, built a bathroom in a small corner of the basement with a door so narrow they were the only adults who could get through. One of the reasons she had come to love this business, though, was the fact that while headlines screamed of ethnic wars, there was, with only a few notable exceptions, a reassuring niceness about almost all of them. She liked the Gurrhas.

"Nothing I can't handle. Thought you might want to give permission before I spent money."

Rosemary sounded ready to defend herself.

"How's Eddie?" Matty slid past the challenge.

"He's a kid. Got over it fast. Consuela's got it now."

"How sick?"

"Not very. Came in anyway. I'm taking care of her."

Matty knew she was being shut out. She gave up and said goodbye.

The roses were pushed to one side of the sink. Petals littered the oak floor, their edges beginning to brown and curl. One quick sniff had been reassuring, but one was enough. It occurred to her that problems didn't happen in the morning; it was always later in the day. Was that significant? Did tiredness trigger these things? No matter. Neil had told her to note the time of day and she had. Except for last night.

Matty went upstairs for the other roses, came back down and threw them all in the trash. Raspberries and roses. Neither lasted long. Two of her favorite things in the world. Would they ever bring the same pleasure again?

At the computer, she worked in a way totally unlike herself, without concentration, making careless mistakes. This all took a back seat to a new and more pressing interest.

No. Two new interests. My head and my ghost. There's good news and there's bad news...

Her duty done, she took a sandwich outside as her schedule dictated. Not bothering with a blanket, she wandered the yard, the sandwich in one hand and a glass of wine in the other and allowed her mind to focus completely on how best to approach her research. The wine brought the first real pleasure of the day.

Mary had been no help and, according to Mary, Joseph didn't believe in ghosts. The best proof would come from people who had experienced this same girl. Stories written down would be best, but might not exist. Second best would be first-hand accounts. Local legends might be informative, but were useless as evidence. It was possible to get the names of all the former owners of the house. The current owner would be listed at the county courthouse, the most recent grantee. From there she could work back from grantee to grantor repeatedly until she had a list of those who might still be living. At least, that was the way it worked in Montgomery County. Hopefully, some former owners would still be in the area and would be in the local phone book. She could pretend an interest in history as an excuse for calling and from there direct the conversation without being too obvious. There seemed no other avenue at the moment.

A sudden thought stopped her walking. *All those magazines!* Stacking them out of the way, she had noticed they were men's magazines, cars, sports figures on the covers. They belonged to the owner! Matty ran into the house and pulled them off the bookshelf.

The same name appeared over and over. John Durham. A Maine address. If he wasn't the owner, she was going to disturb the wrong guy. Information provided the area code for the address on the magazines. His name was listed. First hurdle jumped. Adrenaline shot through her as the phone rang.

What should I say? He won't be home. Why would he be home? But, just in case, what should I say? Okay. How about—

"Yo!"

She couldn't believe it. *He's there! How could that be on a Thursday afternoon? He has two homes. So...rich maybe? Doesn't work?*

"Yes," she said hesitantly. "My name is Matty Burhmann. I'm—Actually, I'm in your house. Your house on South Mountain. I—"

"Matty, huh?" he interrupted. "I like that. You sound delicious. What do you look like?"

What was this? "What do I look like?"

"Yeah. You sound good to look at. Sexual confidence. It's always in the voice. Right?"

Shit!

"You're at my house, huh? Always get horny in that house."

Oh, double shit! She tried to get the conversation back on track. "I thought you might know something about the history of the house. It—It's so old," she finished lamely.

"You're avoiding my question. You are a fox, aren't you? If you weren't, you wouldn't mind my saying so. Oh, hey, I know women! I might just come visit that old house of mine." His voice was heavily suggestive.

"I have lovely features and I weigh only a little over 300 pounds. It's very well distributed," Matty replied earnestly. *Pardon me for using you, Rosemary.*

Silence on the other end.

"You're kidding, right?"

"No. Why would I kid you? Seriously, can you tell me anything about the house?"

The voice was a little wary this time. "Neil said—But he didn't describe you. Wouldn't. Come on now, you—"

She hung up. She couldn't help it. Maybe it was too soon. Maybe he knew something, but it wasn't in her to put up with him any longer. Thank God for cell phones. He couldn't call her back. Unless he had caller I.D.

Shit!

Best to go to Frederick, but she hated to leave the girl and really didn't want to search for a courthouse, especially in a crowded old town with confusing, one-way streets.

Matty walked into the kitchen and refilled her glass. Two glasses were all right. No more. On the way back to the couch, she passed the bookshelves and eyed them speculatively. The slimy character on the phone didn't match up with the titles she had read while arranging them. How did Neil manage to have a cousin like that, anyway? She was a visitor here. Could some local people who knew about her girl have loaned books to visitors? A long shot. The furniture didn't match the voice, either. Perhaps some people sold the contents along with vacation houses. Maybe not quite as long a shot.

With a pad and pencil, she flopped down in front of the books now neatly lined up. What a waste of time that had been! Time to pull them all out.

"Mildred Hodges." Spidery writing, long, thin letters penned with a fine point identified the owner of one of the romance novels. The writing looked old-fashioned, like that of someone long dead. She wrote down the name anyway.

"Beverly Gruston" was next, printed carefully inside the cover of a Sandra Brown mystery. Matty prayed fervently that she had been an owner, not just a friend or a guest.

Fifteen minutes later, she had four more Beverly Grustons, a Westminster Public Library, a Ken indecipherable and a red sailing ship with "Marjorie Buford, Her Book, 1909" written on the hull. Forget Marjorie. Beverly looked a good bet.

The phone book was old, but for her purposes probably just as good as a new one.

There was no Beverly Gruston or any other Gruston. Plenty of Hodges, but no Mildred or M. Should she call all the Hodges? *Do you know Mildred? Sorry to have bothered you.* Well, some people did that, but she didn't want to. Was there time to drive to the courthouse? Was this even Frederick County? It took only a quick look in the front of the phone book to confirm that it was. She had hoped that it might be another county with a smaller county seat, someplace with little traffic.

Two thirty? Gratitude flooded Matty. No problem with her senses today! She put her arms up in the air and then jabbed down with her elbows in the sign of triumph.

"Yes!"

It occurred to her that it wasn't yet significantly "later in the day," but that thought was shoved aside. Everything had worked so far. That was good.

It was too late for Frederick today, but she could leave early in the morning and still have the afternoon to phone any former owners. Church was important for catching Joseph or perhaps someone else who would offer information when told where she was staying.

No. Wait. Tom would be here Sunday. If he saw the girl Saturday, they could both go to church. If he didn't, it would be best to stay here hoping the girl would appear. Two thirty had seemed like good news. Now it brought a worry that the girl would never appear again. It was the first time this thought had surfaced and it brought with it a feeling of dismay. Bad enough if she didn't appear to Tom. What if she never came back at all? She had to come! Tom had to see her! That would provide indisputable proof of her existence to a psychiatrist, to Dad, to anyone. Then she would head to Rockville immediately to see Neil. It would be hard to abandon this shy little spirit without finding out something about her. Maybe Neil would let her come back another time. Why was arranging these thoughts so hard? Decision-making used to be one of her strengths.

The cell phone called, startling her. Strange how quickly she had become accustomed to silence.

"Fred, he so dronk!"

It was Consuela. Matty wasn't surprised. No doubt Rosemary had asked Consuela to call. Rosemary didn't like Fred, didn't want to deal with him. The only man Rosemary had ever expressed admiration for was an office equipment salesman, short, slim, a disreputable version of Valentino with blackheads who perched his shiny polyester trousers on the edge of Rosemary's desk and gave her a sales pitch once a month. He seemed to know that he would never connect with Matty.

"No hope, Consuela?"

"No way." The short response was delivered with Consuela's usual drama.

That meant Fred was on one of his major binges again. It didn't happen often. They were the reason Matty could afford him, so she put up with it.

"How about Ralph?" Ralph was a general contractor who rarely was able to get contracts.

"Too busy, he say."

Of course he was busy. Low mortgage rates had everyone in the construction business busy.

"Any ideas?"

"Pilot light, yes? No big deal."

"No big deal at all if you've got someone to light it."

"Okay. Eddie and me, we fix. No problem."

"Well, I'm sure you can, Consuela."

Matty wasn't at all sure. Consuela had always lived in apartments and one didn't learn much about hot water heaters in apartments.

"You worried, huh? I know you. No problem! Honest! Eddie and the super, they big frien's. He know that stuff."

"Eddie? Consuela, gas and flame can be a dangerous combination. I wouldn't let Eddie mess with it."

"Okay, then. I get Gomer maybe."

"Gomer?"

"We call him Gomer. Soun' like the guy on Andy Griffith. The super. No problem. Nice guy. You know anybody wan' marry a guy like that? Fix everything. Forty year old. Wants kids. Real nice guy. I tol' him I look for somebody, but, you know, is hard."

Matty laughed.

"What about yourself, Consuela?"

"Who, me? No, than' you. Too tall, too white, got a head like a cucumber and not Catholic. Real nice guy for a frien' but no husban'. Hey, how you doin' down there? Or over there? Where the hell are you, anyhow? All alone on some damn mountain! Soun' like a terr'ble place. Who you talkin' to beside me an' Rosemary? You go squirrely!"

"I'm already squirrely. That's why I'm here."

"Nothin' wrong wi' you, hey! I should be so smart! Course you kinda nervous here an' there, but you got it all together, seem to me. Crazy worl', you know? You know—"

What Matty knew was that Consuela would go on forever if she let her.

"You can solve my problems when I get back, Consuela, if I haven't solved them myself by then. Thanks for the offer to light the pilot, but I don't want you to take chances. If you can't get cucumber-head, call the tenants tomorrow and tell them to read the instructions and do it themselves. That's the logical thing to do, anyway, though they might blow up the house. And take care of yourself. If you're sick, you should be at home."

"No problem. Rosemary drivin' me home so I don' ride the damn bus. Me, I'm fine. You be good, too. If you can enjoy bein' alone on a damn mountain, you go ahead and do it. You get lonely, come back, okay? Bye now!"

Consuela could happily go on forever, but she was accustomed to Matty always being in a hurry.

"Bye, Consuela," Matty said affectionately.

She switched the phone off. God bless that dear woman! Consuela put a smile on everyone's face. What a gift! For a few minutes, fears and decisions had been pushed aside and normality had entered this old log home. Not for long. The house began to take over again. Then Matty wondered where that thought came from. The house was not to blame for her problems or her indecision. Matty rubbed her fist against her forehead, as though that would somehow force some order into her mind.

It was time to try Evelyn Morris again, but there was still no answer.

Damn! Why didn't I think to try her this morning before she went to work? That's an easy one. Because I am seriously messed up. At least, I stuck to my schedule. That's a necessity right now. Something to hold onto.

She looked at the toy-like silver phone still in her hand. It had become another something to hold onto and she set it back on the coffee table with reluctance.

◆   ◆   ◆

There was no sign of the girl until dinner time. Matty had taken a short walk, returned about four and skimmed through all the copies of *Management Review*. There had been a mild satisfaction in throwing them in the trash, minus a few articles torn out and set aside for reference later.

Hunger had turned into a gnawing stomach ache before Matty made herself face dinner. Breakfast and lunch had been fine, without loss of taste, she reassured herself as she set out foods normally on the taboo list because Tom disliked them, eggplant and liver. Even as a child, she had liked food that was a little different.

It was while first opening the refrigerator that Matty sensed someone. She took out the liver and put it in on the counter, surveying the room as much as possible without turning her head. Her heart began to beat faster. Had her singing attracted the girl yesterday? An old hymn, something the girl might recognize, might make her feel welcome. This inspiration pleased her, but what hymn was old enough to be familiar to her spirit? "Amazing Grace" was still the only one that she could think of that was sure to be old. Tom said it had been written by a ship's captain, a slave trader who had repented and found religion. Turning to the counter for the shiny purple eggplant, Matty caught a flash of blue and her heart took a jump. She began humming with more enthusiasm.

Between excitement at knowing the girl was present and fear of losing taste, it was almost impossible to enjoy the meal, which was a shame. The eggplant was perfect. Every bite brought a surge of gratitude for the ability to taste the rich flavor. Her mind jumped back and forth between the girl and her problem. Would a different song have been more appealing? The word "tumor" had popped up several times in the last few days and was pushed to the back of her mind. Somehow strokes had retreated as a possibility. They seemed to belong to old people. Was the girl shy? Hiding from her? Why? This wasn't Matty's first experience with a major worry about her body, but the injury from the accident, they had told her promptly, could be fixed. All those people with cancer and heart disease and AIDS. One did get on with life. But didn't it spoil everything a little? Did you ever get over that? Did the girl die of some such disease? She looked healthy. Sort of not quite there but undamaged and healthy. Was that a flash of blue? No, just a shadow from a tree moving in the wind. Would she ever be able to enjoy anything again if this turned out to be something medical and permanent rather than psychological? Why was it so hard to hold on to Neil's reassuring words? Tonight wasn't bad because it had been a good day. Why did the girl never make a sound? It was nearly seven now and still there had been no loss of sensation. If only she could believe it was over! God, she would be grateful! Which would be better: if she had no further problems or if the girl made real contact or, better yet, if she could prove to herself and anyone else the girl really existed? Odd

that it seemed impossible to choose. It seemed that any sensible person
would choose to ditch a medical problem, but the girl was a miracle. How
not choose a miracle? She lifted her fork to stab another bite and found
that she had eaten it all.

*Stupid. I have no choice here. Out of my hands. Neil. God. Whoever. I'm
certainly not in charge.*

When the dishes were finished, she took one last look around the
kitchen and then the living room. She shook her head a little in disappointment. Were there to be further "sightings" today?

Something had to be done about her appearance before tomorrow's
visit to the courthouse. That meant washing her hair and a manicure for
her ruined nails. What would the girl make of shiny red polish and a curling iron?

◆   ◆   ◆

Once comfortably in bed with a Faye Kellerman mystery, Matty was
able to make the entries she had been too upset to write the night before:

*Wed dinner: Lost taste of two bites of raspberry
& choc sundae. Absolutely no sensation at
all! No problem before or after. Particularly
happy & relaxed!*

Let Neil deal with that one. She couldn't resist adding:

Thurs: no incidents!

No incidents. Not quite accurate. It should have read "No bad incidents." The girl was not to be mentioned in this diary for Neil. In any
case, there had been only the one brief glimpse of the girl. The nail polish,
hair dryer and curling iron apparently had been insufficiently interesting
or the girl had remained invisible or out of sight. Matty thought about
starting a list of the spirit's appearances, just for herself, but dismissed the
idea as being compulsively organized. Some things were unforgettable.

Others, she realized too late, were all too forgettable. It was too late to call Evelyn.

At eleven, she turned out the light. In spite of the fact that there was nothing calm about her situation, in which hope, fear, excitement and anger chased each other through her body like kids let loose on a playground, she was determined to fall asleep without help.

My brain worked today! Not very clearly, maybe, but it worked!

The thought was a caress of hope, softening fear.

The clouds were lit by a moon not yet in sight. Amazing how quickly the position of the moon changed. She thought it might be pleasant just to lie patiently and wait for it, a nice change from the usual urgency of feeling that, once in bed, she had to hurry up and get a good night's sleep to be ready for the next day.

Whenever there was no other distraction, the girl was in her mind. *My mind is haunted by a ghost.* She smiled a limited little smile.

Matty remembered what Mary had said. Did this girl have some awful regret, something to fix, something uncompleted? Would she then cease to exist anywhere in any form if it were accomplished? Not a good thought. In college, she had written an essay on the subject of death in early Christian literature. It had struck her then that the characters spoke glowingly of the wonderful gift of heaven, yet death scenes were laden with anguish. Matty wanted to hang on to the belief that this girl's presence promised some kind of continued existence. But even if she did, it failed to ease the fear that sensory losses were causing. Matty was no more ready to die than those Christians.

14

The clock in the circle of outdated avocado green on the kitchen wall had a tarnished brass hour hand that, today, stubbornly refused to move past seven. An hour ago, the anonymous taped voice that responded to her call had crisply announced that the Frederick County Courthouse would open at 9:00. Matty had jumped into a pair of khaki slacks and her best polo shirt, regretting that it hadn't seemed necessary to bring more business-like clothes, and was now pacing the kitchen floor. One attempt to work at the computer had failed, but there seemed nothing else to do but go back upstairs and try again.

By eight o'clock, an awkwardly phrased form letter glared back at her from the computer screen. Its primary message was there was no point in punching any more keys this morning.

Back downstairs, the hand that wasn't holding a coffee cup kept reaching towards the phone. Country people rose early, didn't they? By eight thirty, Matty could wait no longer. She dialed the numbers wrong and started over. Somewhere a phone rang. And rang and rang.

Shit! Is this woman ever at home? Screw this Evelyn Morris!

Not sure where she was going, Matty got into her car and headed for Frederick. The familiar prickling of nerves and ache in her gut were there even before she hit rush hour traffic. Neil had hit that one on the head. At nine, she pulled off the road and used her cell phone to call for directions. The courthouse was in the middle of town, at the corner of Patrick and Court.

Middle of town. Of course. Shit!

◆　　　◆　　　◆

Although Matty knew how things were done in her own county, she spoke tentatively to the courthouse receptionist, in appearance a slightly younger version of Mary Briggsley.

"I want to research an old house. A very old house."

The woman's smile was pleasant, making her look even more like Mary, but there was more intelligence in her countenance.

"You might want to try the Historical Society."

Matty was disconcerted. She didn't have time to be in the wrong place.

The woman responded to her frown.

"Tell you what," she said. "I always keep a few of these on hand." She handed Matty a small manila trifold titled "How to Research Your Old House."

Matty laughed. "This isn't a government publication, is it? The title is much too sensible!"

The woman laughed, too.

"Thank you. I insisted on that title. Some of the others wanted something fancier. We're all volunteers at the Historical Society. I'll be working there tomorrow."

Funny, Matty thought, how quickly you recognized someone who could be your friend. She also realized that she was missing the company of women like this.

There were an astonishing number of sources in the little pamphlet. The land records she had already targeted were there, of course, but the list went on: birth, baptism and marriage records, tombstone inscriptions, obituary files, census reports, will and probate records, equity court records, orphans' court proceedings, rent rolls, debt books, Archives of Maryland in Annapolis, tax assessments, maps and atlases, newspapers, railway directories, the Historical Society's collection of photographs, an old manufacturing and agriculture census and some local histories, including the books of early families and homes that Joseph had given her. Matty became more sure that she could eventually collect quite a lot of information about her house and its inhabitants. Just not in one day. And it seemed unlikely that ghosts would be included in any census. She decided to stick with the original plan: get the names of recent owners to call and also work back to the names of early families in the hope of getting the name of this girl. Whether the latter would be of any use to her was doubtful. Matty just wanted it. This plan had the additional advantage of limiting her search to one set of records, probably all in one room. She got the directions to the Land Records.

◆   ◆   ◆

John R. Durham. For no reason Matty could identify, it was always a mild surprise to find in public records exactly what was supposed to be there. She had looked up her own title transfer record once and sat staring at her name for some time, knowing it should be there and yet finding it odd to see it in print. Here was the name on the magazines. Remembering his voice, his offensively suggestive tone, it was almost unpleasant to start the search with his name. Matty sat back in her chair for a moment. The room was large and still. Only one other person, a little man in a gray suit who looked very much at home, was moving about with a pleased air of authority.

This was the start of a long process. She was sorry no drinks were allowed. They would not have hurt the heavy oak table, but there could be no risk to the precious original documents. A huge piece of history sat in this quiet room. What havoc a fire would inflict! She leaned over the computer.

John R. Durham had purchased the property from Mildred S. and Josephine L. Snyder. Sisters? No such information was ever given. She jotted down their names and the reference for the previous transfer and moved on.

After an hour, the search had moved from the easy computer entries to the oversized books that lined the walls. Taking them on and off the shelves, carrying them back and forth to her table, was work. Matty set the next book on the table and stopped to stretch. The little gray man came over to her.

"You seem to be doing fine, but is there anything I can do to help?"

He was shorter than Matty by half a head. She had seen him before many times, in many places. The world seemed to produce these men by the harmless thousands. She smiled.

"No thank you. It's just a matter of time."

He brightened. "Everything is, isn't it?" He made it sound as though she had just uttered a profound philosophical truth. Unfortunately, he didn't know what to do with it and looked at her expectantly.

"Yes," Matty said agreeably. "I'm working back to the original owners of—" She decided to simplify "—my house. You wouldn't know anything about the older homes just west of here, would you?"

"My mother's house is almost a hundred years old. It's west of here." He looked embarrassed. "But I'm sure that's not what you want, is it? You want…" He nodded towards her.

"Yes. Information about *my* house. On South Mountain."

His pale lips opened and closed a few times, trying to catch some words. His eyes widened and he smiled now with confidence. With one emphatic nod of his head, he advised, "You should try the information desk."

"I'll do that," Matty said respectfully.

The lips curved into a delighted and somewhat silly smile.

"That's what I'm here for."

As he walked away, Matty wondered if he was an employee, as he had implied, or just a lonely man looking for a place to be somebody.

◆   ◆   ◆

A little over two hours of handling the heavy blue books resulted in a surprisingly long list. Most owners had kept the house for no more than a few years. Unusual. She had often advised people to buy a home with the future in mind. A hefty commission went to Realtors every time you bought and sold. It seemed that no one was giving these people that advice.

The stays in the house became longer as she moved past a tax sale and into the first half of the nineteenth century. Then, the house had been part of a huge property from the sound of the metes and bounds description: "From a clump of alders by the northern end of the stream called Bear Run westward for four hundred feet thence to a rock set in the ground bearing the initials FBA thence to a common roadway leading to Marker's farm proceeding along the north side of said road for a distance of..." It went on for a full page. The County had sold it for three hundred and sixty dollars. Matty slowed down, feeling a reverence for these older books, the careful, elegant penmanship. Soon it would all be computerized. How boring for future researchers! Penmanship was pretty much the only interesting thing about these entries.

She was near the end of her search now. The familiar name overflowed its allotted space with elegant, slanted, parallel lines, artistic curves and flourishes. It had to be here, of course. The records went back to 1743. Yet finding it was a discovery to be cherished. She couldn't resist carefully touching the letters. *Rochenbaugh, Horst R. and Julianna M.,* written when these two were living in her house.

Her tired arms replaced the book on its upper shelf and took down the final one with a mix of gratitude and excitement. At last, the transfer of title from dear old Clotworthy Birdie to the Rochenbaughs. Matty savored every heavy, crafted letter. What a shame that calligraphy had deteriorated into modern scribbles.

Grantors, grantees. That was all she was going to get from these books. The stories behind the names remained a mystery. Matty closed the last book reluctantly. These heavy tomes could tell her no more. The long list of former owners on the paper beside her was satisfying and yet she was disappointed. Had she expected the name of the girl to leap out at her, that she would somehow recognize it?

On the way out, she stopped at the information desk to ask for directions to the Historical Society. The woman smiled as Matty approached.

It would be pleasant to have lunch together, to talk about unimportant little things, and maybe eventually about more important things, over a glass of wine and a salad. A luxury there was no time for now. A smile, a quick question, a quick answer and Matty turned away. The Society was only a few blocks away, but she had only this afternoon and perhaps a little time in the morning before Tom came.

Walking down the courthouse steps, the pull of the Historical Society slowed her. They would know her house, but without a time period or name, there would be no clue to the girl unless they kept records of ghostly appearances, which seemed unlikely. Matty shook her head in silent rejection. It was already one o'clock. She picked up her pace, the decision made. It made more sense to grab a bite of lunch at that little café she had noticed on the way in and then head home to make phone calls.

Matty slid onto the red vinyl seat of a booth by the window. It wasn't an impressive place. Without the liquor license, it would have been a diner rather than a café. She needed a glass of wine. Surprisingly, they had a phone book that covered her area. If none of the names at the top of her list were there, she might reconsider the Historical Society.

◆   ◆   ◆

The drive back to the house was a journey away from reason and purpose and a descent into doubt and confusion. Writing down data, clear facts, from a public record was one thing. Using those facts to chase down a ghost was another.

I don't believe in ghosts!

This, too, seemed to be a fact, a fact that now stood in direct opposition to her own experience. Her time in Frederick had returned her to a more familiar world. With that had come the return of more familiar convictions.

Matty was surprised to find herself at the house. Absorbed in thought, the return trip had gone quickly. Around her was the familiar, small swatch of mowed weeds surrounded by locust and oak trees tall above a tangled mat of mountain laurel and sumac woven together by insidious vines.

Full circle. Back home as confused as ever.

She leaned her head on the steering wheel. Beside her, the list with fifteen phone numbers seemed a waste of time. Some would not be the same families that had owned the house. There were four Taylors, a common name. Some would have moved, some died.

"Shit," she mumbled without energy. Even with the daylight, coming up the rutted driveway, there had been a return of the unease of that first night. Now, looking at the grayed planks, they seemed more than the door to an old house. This was the door to a different world and she didn't belong here. She had felt comfortable, competent, in Frederick, going about familiar tasks. Eating her lunch in that café, it hadn't even occurred to her she might lose taste. That made a day and a half now without a problem, a thought that lifted her spirits a little, but the strong conviction stayed that she belonged in places like the Frederick courthouse where sensible people went about doing rational things. Was the girl waiting inside? Why was that possibility no longer appealing, even a little frightening? Tom would be here tomorrow and she would go home and…and what? Not tell Neil about her ghost, that was for sure! Maybe just take things a little easier.

"Just till tomorrow," she told herself. "You were wrong to send me here, Neil. Bloody, stinking wrong."

◆   ◆   ◆

"Do you mind telling me why you sold? I mean, why your father sold?"

"I tol' you. He went down to Florida," the old man said irritably.

That wasn't what Matty meant. How could she put this?

"There wasn't anything about the house he didn't like?"

"Plumbin' was real bad."

"I mean, anything that couldn't be fixed."

"Like what?"

"Like…the atmosphere, or where it was, up here on the mountain, or anything like that."

"Yeah, come to think on it."

Matty's heart gave a jump.

"Yes?"

"Soil wa'n't good. Too rocky. You want to farm, you got to come down in the valley. Anyhow, no sense doin' any farmin there now. Land cost too much."

Matty was getting desperate. Some of the others she had called weren't related to the former owners of the same name. Two had been small children here and either couldn't be drawn into a meaningful admission or had nothing to admit. This was the last name and it belonged to a bone-headed idiot.

"It wasn't spooky or anything, being up here alone?"

"Wa'nt alone. We's together."

The voice of T. Roger Rudenick said clearly that he was a nice guy, but there was a limit to his patience.

Matty gave up.

"Thanks, Mr.Rudenick."

She wondered what her little ghost thought of her phone calls. Did she understand what was going on? Matty felt that she was always near, hearing, seeing everything. It was a little uncomfortable. Perhaps that was why she felt the need to get outside once in a while.

Evelyn Morris still wasn't home. It seemed inappropriate to call the church and useless as well. She would undoubtedly still be at work.

Getting up from the couch, Matty was surprised to find how stiff she was. Driving, working over the land records and hunched over the phone with pad and pencil ready for information that never came, had left her with sore neck and shoulder muscles and too much pent up nervous energy. She also realized that somewhere in dialing those fifteen numbers and talking to the five who had been home, her little spirit had once more become real to her. She frowned as she stretched. Why such a radical change in attitude since those last moments in the car? Now *this* seemed where she belonged. Was it the house? Or was the girl exerting some strange pull?

What brought the girl out? Matty's unhappiness? Certainly she seemed a sympathetic child. Or was it the opposite, happiness? Appearances had occurred when Matty had been singing or humming, puttering about fairly cheerfully after her office work was done. Or would it be more accurate to say, with stubborn determination, putting up a good front? At first, Matty had used words like "phenomenon" to make the appearances seem more reasonable. Then she had moved to "spirit" because it was short and, in some odd way, kinder. Now it was "the girl" or "the child." The apparition had become human.

"I'm going to take a walk now," she announced. "Then I'll be back for dinner. About seven. See you then," she finished airily, looking around the empty room.

The room that looked empty, she corrected herself.

◆   ◆   ◆

Matty walked hard and was starving when she got back. She made a quick sandwich of last night's leftover liver with a little Dijon mustard. That went down just fine, but it wasn't quite enough. She lifted the raspberries out of the refrigerator and eyed them speculatively. Should she have another sundae? The decision was easily made. The joy had been sucked out of raspberries. They looked colorful on top of the discarded roses.

When she turned, the girl was standing in the middle of the kitchen, watching, silent as always.

This time it was Matty who held out a hand, slowly, not wanting to frighten her. It was hard to breathe. She searched her memory for the names on her list.

"Is your name Rochenbaugh?" she asked softly.

The girl tipped her head very slightly to one side. It was the first time she had reacted to Matty in any way except running away and Matty felt her chest tighten in excitement.

"Snyder?"

She had been right about the age, Matty thought. About sixteen. Maybe an immature seventeen or eighteen. A plain face, but with nice, regular features, the cheeks full as a child's, though her figure was certainly well developed. The eyes were dark blue, the brows the palest, though fairly wide, brush line, blonde like the almost kinky hair that was pulled back loosely.

Did the girl speak English? Or was she an early German? Matty searched her mind for the few words she knew. *Ich bin ein Berliner. Ein, zwei, drie, fier, fumf, danke—shit!* Names would have to do.

Matty pointed to herself. "Mathilda," she said.

Then she pointed to the girl. "Birdie? Taylor?"

The girl was gone. She didn't run. She didn't fade. She just, suddenly, wasn't there.

Matty uttered a soft, meaningless sound of disappointment and stared for a long time at the spot where the girl had stood. Was she still there, but invisible?

Wiping sweaty palms on her slacks, Matty wondered how long she could stay on this seesaw. Yes, there was a ghost. No, there wasn't; it was all in her head. But there she was. Or had been.

Her hands shook slightly as she poured a glass of wine. It was almost dark outside the window as she sat down at the kitchen table. Leaning her head on one hand, Matty watched the darkening sky. She felt exhausted. It was too much. Too much uncertainty, hope, fear. A distorted vision of herself stared back at her from the old, wavy window glass and she could see as well as feel the familiar tears drifting slowly down her cheeks.

"I need you, Tom," she said to her image. "Please come early." Her voice dropped to a whisper. "I don't want to be alone any more."

15

By ten o'clock the raised four foot square slab of concrete over the cistern had been warmed by the sun. Matty sat cross-legged in the middle, holding her third cup of coffee and watching for Tom's car. Last night he had said he would come early. Why wasn't he here yet? She was becoming impatient and that wasn't the way she wanted this day to start.

By the time she heard the sound of an engine, she was no longer willing to jump up and run to greet him. Didn't he know how much she wanted him here? Common sense answered her instantly. Of course not. As far as Tom knew, she was just having a nice, relaxed holiday. Common sense wasn't quite reaching her emotional center.

It took the sight of the old Cutlass that Tom wouldn't give up creeping over the last big bump in the road and pulling to a stop behind her Acura to erase the last trace of irritation.

"Hey!" she called, filled with a sudden happiness at the sight of his lanky frame unfolding from the car. It caught her by surprise and she felt her eyes moisten. This was new. She wasn't normally sentimental, but here, at this old house, she was jerked daily through a gamut of emotions, leaving them like loose muscles, responsive, ready to react. Tom would have loved knowing she had nearly cried at the sight of him, but she was unable to give him that gift. It was probably pride, but she told herself he might worry. Matty opened her eyes wide so the moisture didn't spill, set her cup on the cement and walked to meet him.

His long arms went around her and held her more tightly than usual. His lips were against her ear.

"You feel wonderful," he said.

Tom said things like this so often it sometimes didn't touch her. This time, it did.

"You, too," she murmured and meant it. It had been like this just after the accident, but hugs were awkward, limited by her injury. Then she began to keep feelings at a distance. Matty tightened her own arms. Something was exchanged between them, hard to define. She gave over tension and worry to him and got comfort and ease in return.

He pulled back to look down at her face, searching.

"I guess it's okay I came," he said with a trace of surprise.

He didn't add that she hadn't made him feel this wanted in a long time and that he had missed it. She was grateful for the omission.

"Cup of coffee?" she offered.

"Afterwards?"

Matty grinned. "Okay."

"Can we skip the bath and just get down and dirty?"

"We can even skip the bed. I have a blanket on the porch."

Tom looked at her suspiciously. "That doesn't sound like you. Right out here in front of God and everybody?"

Unknowingly, Tom had pinpointed why she had made the suggestion. The eyes of God didn't worry her, but the eyes of the girl did. Maybe the girl wasn't limited to the house. Then again, maybe she was.

"You won't be cold?'

Matty shook her head and ran to get the blanket.

Whatever the reason, it was a good idea. Their lovemaking over the last year had taken on a pattern, like an oft-repeated dance. They knew the steps and in what order they were most effective. It bothered Matty a little, knowing this lack of novelty was another offshoot of the fear left by the accident. Even in this, she needed control, familiarity and predictability. But the routine worked. It was satisfying, comfortable and, today, there was an unusual strength to the emotions it generated. The feel of Tom meant more than it had in a long time. The physical exchange of caresses both excited and calmed her. It was one of those times when she was aware of the oneness of the two of them. For her, it was always in the beginning, in the holding, the soft, slow touching, more than at the end, when she was caught up in the excess of her own sexual release. Tom's body was white in the sun, fuzzy seen through the lashes of her half-closed eyes and falling hair. The novelty this time was in being outdoors. Even the sounds were different, their moans and cries punctuated by the bright, sharp calls of birds until the final roar of feeling that drowned out all sound.

They lay back, eyes closed against the sun, hands locked, arms, hips, thighs touching for several minutes before either of them wanted to speak.

"Silence is the finest compliment after a great concert," Tom said finally.

He was often in a humorous mood after sex.

"And I suppose you're the conductor, since you've got the baton."

He laughed. "*Had* the baton. You haven't looked in the last few minutes, have you?"

"I have, actually." She rolled onto her side. "You look funny in the sun. You're so white!"

"So are you."

"So am I." She nestled her head contentedly against his shoulder and pulled the blanket over them.

"You're not worried about being here naked, are you?" Tom asked. "I take it we're really isolated."

"Really isolated."

"Strange woman."

He meant that he thought most women wouldn't be comfortable being isolated. She wondered if that were true.

"Intimidating, isn't it?" he asked.

"What? Being naked here?"

"No. The house."

Matty remembered the first time she had looked up at the house from the front yard. It had seemed taller than it was, stark, strong, not quite friendly, but not intimidating and, now, it was familiar.

"It's a good house." She felt a little defensive about it.

"Would you want to live like this? Out here, I mean, in a decidedly unmodern house with no shopping malls or Kennedy Center?"

Matty didn't have to think about that. She already had. "I think it just might be quite wonderful."

"You'd get bored!"

"Probably. But not for a long time. It might—"

Matty stopped, but the tone of her voice had created too much curiosity for Tom to let it go.

"It might what?"

"It might be nice to have a little land and a house. Just a small one. Not too much to take care of."

Tom rolled over and studied her. His pale blue eyes were even paler in the bright light.

"Now that's a change. You want to buy another house, Matty? God knows we can afford more than our townhouse."

"I don't know. It's just…It's been good for me, getting outside every day, sitting on the grass, climbing this little mountain instead of pumping away at that boring bike in front of television. More peaceful than I would have believed. You can't sit in the back yard of a townhouse without a dozen people watching, kids running through the petunias."

"You once said you would like to own ten acres and take care of two square feet, just enough to grow a few…What were they?"

"Dahlias. Why are you staring at me?"

He lay back down and Matty knew it was to break eye contact. This time, it was she who propped herself on an elbow and stared at him.

"Come on! What were you thinking?"

"I wondered if this was tied to wanting a family. It's not, I assume. It just sort of sounded like something from the past."

"Oh."

This time it was Matty who lay back quickly. There had been a time when they had talked about a house and some land and a family. That was why she had gotten her real estate license. It seemed a good way to learn the market and make some commission money on the purchase while keeping her job as a lab assistant at NIH where she and Tom had met. Then she had found the new job more interesting and, just as she was beginning to understand what they meant by "real estate burnout," her broker had asked her if she was interested in running the small property management division, offering to sell it to her when he retired in a few years. Her decision had been to postpone children and the house. Tom wasn't happy about it, but Tom wasn't a man to interfere with her life. The day came when, driving down the road to an appointment to take a new management listing, it hit her that she was waiting too long. She had pulled off the road, too disturbed to go on. After phoning to postpone the appointment, she had sat for an hour at a drug store watching a cup of coffee get cold, trying to force a decision. She had failed. Matty had never mentioned the moment to Tom. They had just gone on. Then there had been the accident and now she was thirty-four and Tom was forty-two. Not too old. Not yet.

"I really hadn't thought of that," she said and then added something that struck her as odd the moment she said it. "We could adopt an older child, one who needs a family and a home."

Silence from the other side of the blanket. Then, "Would you really like to do that? Kind of iffy, isn't it? Wouldn't they have problems of some sort?"

"I don't know. We could just think about it." The tone was dismissive.

"Okay."

Tom's was the last word, but it was really she who had ended the conversation. Was it unfair to drop the idea so abruptly? Maybe he wanted his own child. It would be like him not to say so, to feel that it had to be her decision. How long had this idea been in her head? Had the girl put it there? Yes, she had. How very odd. But it was absurd to think of adopting a child when these funny things were happening to her senses. Or were they? There had been no problems in the last two days.

Matty had been almost ready to fall asleep in the sun, wrapped in Tom and the blanket. Now these new thoughts made her feel jumpy. She sat up and turned to him, feeling the coolness of the air for the first time.

"I want to show you my house!"

They put on their clothes, not rushing, hopping about on one leg at a time, laughing as they pulled on their jeans. Tom was busy buttoning his shirt and didn't notice when Matty froze, her eyes locked on the open front door of the house. The girl was there, watching.

Matty didn't like it. It wasn't fair to resent the girl, but she didn't like it. She tried to be forgiving. After all, they had made love outdoors. Anyone was free to watch, really. She stifled the resentment and sat down to tie her tennis shoes. *Turn it around. Be happy that, apparently, this ghost is going to show herself to Tom.* That was what this weekend was all about. Then, thinking back to the tenderness of their lovemaking, she corrected herself. That wasn't *all* the weekend was about.

◆   ◆   ◆

"So this is it, huh?"

The tour of the house had ended in the computer room.

"You don't have to stoop, Tom. It isn't that low," Matty said as he ducked back out the doorway.

Tom grinned. "You think not?" He stood upright, framed by the flat woodwork surrounding the door. His hair touched the top board. "I need a little more clearance to be comfortable. No wasted space in this house, is there? Just these four rooms plus the bathroom. You've told me you don't count bathrooms in real estate, but I think you have to count this one. Big."

"I love the footed tub, don't you?"

"Yeah." He looked at her quizzically. "But not as much as you do. This place seems to fill a need I didn't know you had." He pulled her to him. "Maybe I'd better get to know my wife. You seem different."

"You know your wife. Not to worry."

"Okay." He pulled back, but left his hands on her hips. "If I know my wife, I ought to know what she wants, then. I think..." He paused, head cocked to one side in pretended thought. "I think she wants lunch."

Matty nodded, accepting the role reversal. "Of course *she* does. *She* got up early at...?"

"Eight o'clock."

"Eight o'clock? That's early?"

"Early for a Saturday."

"A Saturday when you're going to come make love to the wife you haven't seen in over a week?"

Tom grimaced. "Actually, I set the alarm for six, but I set it for six PM by mistake."

"So then I jumped into my clothes and ran to the car—" Matty interrupted.

"Shower. I had to have a shower."

"Good thing, too. Okay, never mind. I'll just give in and agree that it's time for lunch."

But Tom was not finished exchanging roles. "Screwing always did make you hungry."

Matty started to kick him lightly, but saw that he was on that slanted step and instead, said "I just saved your life."

"Thanks, but I'm not that hungry."

"No, I meant—"

They were at the bottom of the stairs now and he turned to face her. Standing on the last step, she was as tall as he. She looked directly into his familiar face, too pale and too long, but with a good, strong nose and chiseled mouth and broke off to finish with "I love you, Tom."

Tom ran his finger across her lower lip. "Something's going on here, Matty. What is it?"

She smiled to reassure him. "I just wanted to say I love you."

"But you said it as if you had just discovered it."

"I forget once in a while."

"I never do." he said without resentment.

"I know. And I—It means a lot to me."

"I still think something's going on. Or maybe I just didn't expect you to loosen up so quickly. Was Neil right? Is this cabin magic?"

"No doubt about it, though I'm not sure I'm that loosened up." Matty debated whether or not to tell Tom she would be leaving with him, decided against it and instead led the way into the kitchen. "You'll have to look around outside, too. There are some—I don't know—heaped up piles of stone that might have been used in a war. To hide behind."

"Breastworks. Revolution? Civil War?"

"Don't know. Would you? Know, I mean?"

"Probably not. This house goes back to the Revolution? I suppose you wouldn't know."

Matty hesitated. She couldn't yet talk about the primary reason for her research, but it seemed safe to admit to this much. "I do know, as a matter of fact. It does date to before the Revolution so the breastworks—Isn't that kind of a dumb name?"

"I kind of like it."

Matty laughed as she took a wicker basket out of the closet. "Okay, but isn't there something simpler? Shorter maybe?"

"Sure." Tom's eyes drifted to the ceiling. "Fortification—No. That's hardly shorter. Bulwarks? Not ramparts, I take it."

"Why do you take that?"

"Ramparts are major constructions. How high are these?"

Matty thought a moment, then brought her hand to her chest. "Like so. The ones that are intact. Some are lower."

"Ah, yes." Tom ostentatiously subdued a grin. "Just about breast high. If reference to anatomy is totally repellant, you could, in a pinch, call them barricades, I suppose, though that implies—"

"I know. Keeping something out, which they did, in a way. But these were mostly for the protection of the soldiers while they were shooting, right?"

"Exactly."

"Thank you, Dr. Buhrmann."

"Always a pleasure to lay my erudition at my wife's feet for her—"

"If you say edification, I'll kill you! Worse!" She waved paper napkins in his face. "I won't fix your lunch!"

"Service. I was going to say service. Are we picnicking?" he asked as Matty dropped the napkins in the basket.

"We are. There's this wonderful rocky outcrop on the top of the mountain—"

Tom's face portrayed dismay. Matty ignored it.

"It's not far, oh literate but unathletic one. You drove all morning. Very sedentary."

"Ah. True. But not after I got here."

"I was on top."

"Not all the time."

"Quibbling."

"No." Tom overacted, smiling dreamily. "Reliving."

"Accepted." Matty dropped silverware into the basket and went to open the refrigerator. "Nevertheless, there's a gorgeous view and we can explore the, uh...Oh, what the hell, breastworks."

"Of my choice?"

"Tom! Don't tell me you're still interested?"

He came up behind her and put his arms around her. Matty leaned her head back on his shoulder. How long had it been since they had bantered like this? Tom was right about her being different. A silent thank you to the girl passed through her mind. Or did she owe that to Neil? And was this house, the country to be thanked as well?

"What can I do?" Tom asked.

"I'm making roast beef sandwiches. You can open some wine. You brought some, didn't you?"

"Always do."

"There's some fruit and cheese in the fridge. Pickings are slim, though. Our local grocery owners believe Swiss, Cheddar and American constitute a complete tour of the world of cheeses. Tom?"

Tom had run out of the kitchen. The door banged behind him. He was back in a matter of seconds with a box under one arm, a suitcase in the other hand and a proud smile.

"Clean clothes!" Matty said as Tom set the suitcase inside the door.

"Better yet—goodies!" he said, dropping the box onto the kitchen table.

"Wonderful! What? What? What?" Matty demanded, machine-gun style.

Tom named the items as he took them out. "A fine Pommard, too good for sandwiches. We'll have the Beaujolais for lunch. Stilton *and* camembert. A loaf of real French bread. Anchovies for you to eat after I'm gone, please. A bottle of Chivas Regal. Also—"

"I'm not drinking scotch."

Tom looked at her inquiringly and then put the bottle back without comment. "Wine okay?"

"Wine is fine. I drink it for the flavor and to enhance food. I don't think of it as emotional support."

The words were stilted, the tone defensive. Neither of them was happy about that. She knew he was thinking about her tranquilizers, but she didn't say anything and that answered his question. There were times when the understanding in a good marriage was annoying.

Discretely, Tom returned to his recital. "Fresh basil for pesto sauce. Also fresh parmesan and olive oil. Pasta, in case you didn't have any."

"How did you know what to bring for pesto sauce? That's wonderful!"

"Looked it up. Do you know how many cookbooks you have?"

"Thirty-seven. Do you know how many of them I use?'

"About three, is my impression. Fortunately, I also knew which ones. I think I got the right ingredients, but I didn't bring the book."

"I can wing it."

"I rather trusted you could. Chicken liver pâté from Sutton Gourmet. The French bread is to go with that."

"I love you!"

Matty gave him a hug. He held her tightly.

"You know," he said into her ear, "We've touched more in one morning than we normally do in a week."

"I know. It's vacation. No." She looked straight into his eyes. "It's me. I'm sorry for the way I've been, Tom. I'm getting better." *Don't I wish.* She had to fight tears and the impulse to tell him what was happening to her. *Please don't let bad stuff happen until we leave, until I can get back to Neil.* She reminded herself that there were no indications of trouble in the last two days and the tears receded.

For once, Tom seemed to lack the right words. He held her again, his face hidden in her hair. Matty wondered if, this time, there were tears in

Tom's eyes. She gave him a little time. When he pulled away, he was smiling.

"That's it. The whole inventory. Doesn't seem like much, does it? Seemed an awful lot when I was running around last night."

"It's more than enough with what I have. We'll have a wonderful dinner. I got the ingredients to make your favorite chocolate cake—"

Tom groaned. "Chocolate! Food for the gods. But—" He shook his head. "Not tonight. You're here to rest. I didn't come to make work for you. I called South Mountain Inn. We used to go there, back in the days when we wandered around the countryside, remember? Made a reservation for tonight."

Matty had a fleeting regret. That meant they would be out of the house much of the day, limiting the chances of Tom meeting the girl. But, if not today, tomorrow.

◆   ◆   ◆

They came back from their explorations about four o'clock, hot, tired and with a light covering of mountain dirt, vegetation and stone dust. Tom proclaimed the deep tub as luxurious as Matty had promised, sighed in gratitude as he sank into the lumpy mattress and fell asleep almost immediately. Not wanting to be tired at dinner time, she took a Diazepam as soon as his breathing became regular and wasn't long in following him to sleep.

◆   ◆   ◆

"Look! The fountain! And remember the stone church?" Matty looked across the road.

"How long has it been since we were here?" Tom asked.

"Since I got busy with the business. Too long," she added.

They crossed the little bridge and entered the restaurant. Signed photographs of familiar faces greeted them at the hostess' station.

"Would you prefer inside or outside?"

"Outside," they said together, knowing that the patio room was glassed in and no bugs would disturb their dinners.

Everything about the restaurant struck Matty just right. After a week of solitary meals on ugly oilcloth, she was ready for too much rich food cooked out of sight and served by someone else on a clean, white table-cloth shining in candlelight. The tall glass vase holding miniature gladiola was admired, then set aside so they could see each other better. Tom ordered quail stuffed with sage dressing and Matty decided to skip the decision-making process and just said, "Me, too."

The history of the Inn was printed on a long sheet of paper and she began idly to read it aloud to Tom, a lazy way of creating conversation. The history was mildly interesting, dating from 1732, but it was the paragraph beginning "During the Civil War..." that made her sit upright.

"Tom! This place was a general's headquarters in the Civil War! Hill! Confederate General D.H. Hill was here!"

"And...?" Tom said, his lifted eyebrows indicating that an explanation as to why this was of such importance was in order.

"No, it's just...I've read some history. There was fighting here. Civil War." The impossibility of explaining to Tom why this might be important was frustrating. "My house was a hospital after the battle and the northern general, Hill, was right here. Right here!" She read on, careful to keep her voice calmer. "The Battle of South Mountain was just before Antietam, it says."

"Really, Matty! You didn't tell me you were into local history. What happened to the office stuff? The computer?"

Matty folded the single piece of paper carefully and put it in her purse.

"Can't do that all day," she said, trying to tailor her smile to the situation. She wanted to grin broadly. What a marvelous coincidence! Yet how almost predictable. *Soldiers walked. And so does my girl. This could be the time, the Civil War.* Hill had appropriated the best building in the area and, of course, it had become a landmark. The countryside of Maryland and Pennsylvania was sprinkled with historic bed and breakfasts and restaurants.

This small piece of evidence seemed immeasurably important to her. It seemed, just for a fleeting moment, that this might be the time to tell Tom. Common sense struck down the impulse. This was no proof, really, just a clue to follow. She could almost see the happiness in Tom's eyes fade, replaced by concern, the creases between his eyes growing deeper.

He would have to see for himself. There was no proof her little spirit was connected to this place, this general, this battle. She was clutching at straws. Reluctantly, she let go of her excitement.

It was late when they got home. They were groggy from food and wine, but not sleepy because of the afternoon nap. They made love again, delighted to want each other so soon. It had been a long time since this had happened twice in one day. Afterwards, they went downstairs to collect a bottle of wine, glasses and books. Tom said something about this being what vacations were all about and fell asleep almost as soon as these comforts were arranged around the bed. Matty held a book for a while without reading, enjoying the way she felt, the peace of the evening and Tom's presence beside her. She wondered why the girl hadn't appeared again, at least to her if not to Tom. She had seemed a curious child. Had she really watched them make love? Or was she a considerate girl who didn't want to intrude on their privacy? An interesting thought. Could she observe while invisible? Had she been here in this bedroom but out of sight?

I'll worry about that tomorrow, she decided, borrowing the philosophy from Scarlett O'Hara.

It was a bright night, the clouds scudding across her moon just the way she liked. Matty paused to give thanks for what would surely be remembered as one of the most perfect days of her life. She turned out the light and dropped her book on the floor. Then she lay down, rubbed her cheek against Tom's arm, wrapped her hands around its reassuring girth and went soundly to sleep.

16

The light, full rather than the stingy gray of early morning, told Matty it was late when she woke. A rare, lazy feeling filled her. Gone was the morning anxiety of the past year, replaced, in this house, by a gamut of emotions that ran from something near stark terror to, for this first time, a slow, relaxed waking, the days a series of ups and downs rather than the tight, even tension that had brought her here. One pill, only one little yellow helper, had been necessary at three o'clock, but that was less than usual and an encouraging sign of progress.

Tom wasn't beside her. The aroma of coffee beckoning from the doorway was proof that he had been up for a while, probably now on the front porch in easy contemplation of the terrain that Matty marched doggedly through. She stretched full length and put her hands beneath her head. The contentment that had come with Tom was amazing. It was clear now that, at home, she had been overworked and overstimulated by too many people and too much to do. Tom had been a barrier between herself and the solitude, the freedom from responsibilities, that she needed. Now her needs were different. She smiled. Tom had never made coffee before. Perhaps it was time to consider asking him to do more around the house. Matty had always denied the need for help, stubbornly proud, but also not wanting to emphasize the fact that she was now busier and made more money than he did. She made light of the chores, at the same time feeling resentment that he didn't help more. This was a nice little insight she would take to Neil.

The fact that there had been no sensory losses for three days now caused little explosions of joy every time that thought passed through her mind and that was often. Life was going to get better. It would be perfect if the little spirit would just introduce herself to Tom and she could go home to Neil. Or…was it really necessary to go home to Neil?

She got up without haste, pulled on jeans and a sweat shirt against the cool of the morning and went barefoot down the splintery stairs.

"Are you there?" she whispered to the kitchen. "Please come out. Don't be afraid. He's a very nice man, really."

Matty could see Tom through the window, leaning against one of the porch posts, warming his hands around a coffee cup.

"I need him to know I'm not crazy. Can you understand that?" Maybe not. Was she one of those ghosts that didn't even know she was dead? What book or movie had that idea come from? Matty looked at the pantry door that hid the entrance to the basement. Was that her hiding place? Should she try to get Tom down there today?

"Please," she said again and waited, searching the kitchen and then the living room for a glimpse of the blue skirt, the yellow hair and then stood for several seconds still and silent at the bottom of the stairs, trying to sense the girl's presence. What brought her or kept her away? Matty needed to talk to Mary's friend and it seemed now as though it would be safe, medically, to stay long enough to see her. Please, she prayed silently, let her be an intelligent woman who really knows something, not just a superstitious fool.

There was nothing that indicated the girl was here. What was that something that made Matty turn and look, anyway? She shook her head in defeat, went back to get coffee and joined Tom on the porch.

"Nice, isn't it?" she asked.

"Yeah. Watched the mists come up from the valley."

"You've been up a while then."

He looked at his watch. "Almost two hours. Since seven."

"Seems as though I get up later every day I'm here." *With some notable exceptions.*

"Silence woke me."

She laughed. "I know what you mean. But weren't the birds making a racket? The country is surprisingly noisy in its own way."

"Not like Rockville racket."

"Ah."

Trash trucks, garage and car doors, children playing until the squeal of school bus brakes ended the laughter, horns calling riders, riders yelling "I'm coming, I'm coming" were part of their usual mornings. Birds, crickets and an occasional distant dog barking didn't amount to much by comparison.

"Maybe you're right, Matty."

"Right?"

"About getting a house. It wouldn't be isolated like this, though. We couldn't afford this much land anywhere near Rockville."

"I know. It's just that mowing grass and tending gardens needn't be such awful chores now. We can afford to hire some help if we want to." She didn't add that it was her business that made this possible. Tom loved his job, was very good at it, but he didn't earn much by Washington, D.C. area standards.

"Freedom is the best thing money can buy," Tom said.

"You stole that from my father!"

"I've learned a lot from your father. I had dinner with him at the nursing home Thursday night, by the way. Dinner was good, but he wasn't at his best. Have you talked to him?"

"No. Tom, he wouldn't remember if I had. His short-term memory is getting worse fast. Have you noticed?"

Tom nodded. "Not unusual. According to one of the studies I—"

"Not today, Tom. I want today to be wonderful, like yesterday. Is it awfully selfish of me to want to get away from Dad, from worrying about him, for a while?"

"Probably a big part of what you need and why you're here." He leaned over and kissed her on the tip of her nose. "Sorry I brought it up. Back to where we were. I was thinking it would be great to live a creative life in a place like this. I could write articles, maybe a text book. You could get back to pottery, writing poetry and—"

"And earning no money. You sound like Neil. I haven't written poetry in over ten years. It never was much good. I haven't the talent to justify hiding away in the country."

"Neither have I."

"You write beautifully."

"Not beautifully. Clearly. Accurately. Flexibly. They tell me the audience, give me the facts. I move the words around. Tell how to examine breasts so the stupidest of women can understand, condense the results of the latest cancer studies for doctors with no time to read. Press releases, pamphlets, articles."

She could hear Tom's mood going down. "I fell in love with a funny old tree," she said.

"What?"

"Remember?"

It was a game they used to play with points for originality and speed. One would give a line of verse, the other had to add the next.

Tom smiled. "I do remember. Any particular old tree?"

Matty pointed. "That gnarly, tired-looking old pine. But I have the next line, too. Can I give the next line?" Without waiting for an answer, she continued. "And I think the ridiculous thing likes me."

He laughed. "Okay. So...how about, "So early one day as I went on my way..."

"Frail, Tom. Been done."

"You're using up time."

"Okay." There was a breeze blowing her hair in her eyes and she used it. "Wind. Yes. Something about the wind. A wind came by...sigh...I'll go with that. A wind came by and I heard it sigh."

"A sappy tear fell from its knothole eye." He laughed.

"Tom! How did you do that so fast? Are you watching the time?" She turned over his wrist to see his watch.

"We're on vacation. Forget speed. Anyhow, you fed me the right rhyme. Why are you grinning like that?"

"We are proving we could retire and earn fame writing poetry—"

"Verse."

She grimaced. "Verse. You're right, of course. But it's fun to think about, isn't it?"

"Dreams are free entertainment."

"And nourishing."

"That, too. But breakfast would be even more so."

They made a big breakfast, the kind Tom liked, pancakes and sausage and fried eggs and orange juice. Matty dropped an egg on the floor and muttered a quick "Darn!" The girl seemed to respond to music, so she began to sing snatches of "Nearer, My God, to Thee" as she wiped up the mess. It wasn't quite the appropriate tune for the occasion, a bit lugubrious for her light, Sunday morning feeling, but she remembered some of the lines from the church-going years with her mother and an early movie version of the sinking of the Titanic. She got up to find Tom eyeing her with exaggerated suspicion.

"Is this place changing your personality?" he asked. "What was that you said when you dropped the egg?"

"Mm…darn?"

"What happened to 'shit'?"

"I thought…bad habit. Apt to pop out with clients. I decided to work on that while I was here."

"Okay. Good idea. Now explain the 'Nearer, My God' thing."

"Not a thing. A hymn. A nice hymn. The sausages need turning. Whistle me a background."

Tom had a beautiful, mellow whistle. Maybe it would reassure the ghost. *Or intrigue her. Or something. Anything.*

They sounded good together and moved on to "Rock of Ages" and then "Amazing Grace" with Matty filling in the gaps in the lyrics with da da's and Tom adding grace notes. The phrase "blind but now I see" came back to her and it seemed prophetic. Was she now seeing a truth she had denied before?

During breakfast, she laughed a lot, trying to pull the girl in. It made Tom happy, but it became uncomfortably phony and she decided just to let the day happen.

◆　　◆　　◆

Tom liked the basement. He couldn't stand up, but was curious enough to poke around, waving the oil lamp, for some time, noticing a lot of details that she had missed. The original horsehair chinking had been replaced, at least as much as they could see, with modern concrete. Several beams had shims to prevent squeaking and a few had angle irons added for support. She had heard this sort of thing during house inspections many times, but still didn't know why it was of more than passing interest to anyone.

"Look at the size of the beam over the fireplace!" Tom admired, running his hand over smoke-blackened wood. "Imagine cooking here! You'd love that, wouldn't you?"

"I can't imagine having a wood lintel over the fireplace. It would burn too easily."

"You'd be surprised, Matty, at how much heat and time it would take to burn through a foot-thick piece of oak like this. Steel I-beams would bend long before this would burn through. Why a fireplace only down here, I wonder?"

"You were right about people living in the basement according to a book I found here. I guess they kept on using this as the kitchen."

"Poor woman. Not a nice place to spend a big part of a day." Tom sat down on one of the lower steps to give his back a break from bending over. "Makes you wonder what it was like to live then, doesn't it? Imagine living down here. Not much daylight. Bare earth floor. Grateful for any shelter in the early days, I suppose. Isolated, probably. I wonder if the women went crazy here, too. In the West, every Spring, they used to bring to the nearest town women who had gone insane over the winter."

"Tom! Are you serious?"

"Absolutely. Loneliness was probably awful. Children might have helped, but could cause problems, too. No peace. No quiet. Everyone crammed into one room. Kids would get irritable. Constant fear of illnesses they didn't know how to treat. A lot of children died."

Matty squeezed in next to him on the step. They sat in silence for a while, the oil lamp feebly lighting the lone dark room some family once called home. She was grateful she had a husband like this, one who could sit and dream with her. Mentally, she placed a table, opened the windows to fresh air, put soup to simmer in the fireplace, made a bed in the corner over that raised earth. Not an impossible life. Unless children died.

"We're so pampered. Wimps, aren't we?" It wasn't really a question. "Why didn't the men go crazy?"

Tom didn't answer right away.

"Because they worked outside, even in winter? Cows had to be milked, livestock fed. They probably took on all that uncomfortable responsibility, but it also got them out of the house. Good to be alone once in a while. Or maybe men just deal with solitude better. But I'm guessing."

"Sounds reasonable."

Matty longed to tell Tom of her first experience here, the odd shadows, the unexplained flickering of lamplight, but knew it wasn't possible. Just as the second time she came down, nothing like that was here now. Disappointed, she followed Tom up the stairs.

"You know what strikes me?" he asked.

Not what strikes me, I'm sure, she thought as she dutifully responded, "What?"

"Everything is at human level."

"Human level?"

"Yeah." Tom brushed off the seat of his pants. "I can see myself building this place, repairing anything that went wrong, except maybe for the appliances. It's a simple place. You could be independent here. Can you see me trying to fix anything at our townhouse? That useless two-story foyer looks fancy, but we can't reach it to paint. You can't even get up to dust the picture there or clean the window over the door without the step stool. Plumbing and wiring are behind drywall and I wouldn't know how to fix drywall if I had to rip some out to get to something." He touched the cables running up the wall of the kitchen.

"Not very pretty, though," she protested. "I don't want a hot water heater in my kitchen."

"But you wallpaper. Wouldn't it be easy to do these seven-foot walls? You wouldn't need to keep moving a stool. I like the simplicity of this place. Not big. Not complicated. I bet those settlers felt a strong bond to the houses they built themselves."

Matty laughed.

"Why funny?"

She was caught. How to explain that one early settler had never left?

"Not funny, really. I'm just in a good mood. Wondering if they had time to make up silly poems the way we just did."

◆   ◆   ◆

She showed him the flag.

"When were the first flags made, Tom? Do you know?"

I remember when it was adopted because it was the day after my birthday, June 14th. Slightly different year, also easy to remember. 1777. Why?"

Because it might help me find out when she lived. The way she held this flag..."I was wondering how old it was. When did the flag have this many stars?"

"How many?"

"Thirty-four."

"I don't really know."

Matty ran a finger around one of them.

"Look at the stitches. It must have taken forever to make this." *Did she make this?* "Now, machines do it all."

"Don't regret that, Matty. It just means a lot more people can have flags. And anyone who wants to sew one like this can still do it."

He was right, of course.

◆   ◆   ◆

The special sense of reuniting left them, replaced by a comfortable companionship. After lunch, Tom sat on the porch reading one of Joseph's books. Matty would have preferred to read stretched out on the couch, but thought there was a better chance of the girl appearing to Tom if she was with him. By dinner time, she was worried. Passing up going to church on the assumption that it was better to give the girl a chance to appear might turn out to have been the wrong decision. Surely the atmosphere was right, calm and loving. She had whispered invitations at every opportunity. She wasn't saying "shit" out loud, but it was beginning to punctuate her thoughts.

Tom wanted to take her out to dinner again, but was more than content to stay. Matty threw the pesto sauce together with an impatience she was feeling for the girl. "Please" was getting to be an irritating word.

She poured the water off the pasta and called Tom to come in to open the wine as she set dinner on the table.

"You look sad," Tom noticed.

She smiled. "You're leaving soon."

"But you really want to stay."

The sensory losses had disappeared. There was no reason not to stay. She would—she *could*—find the proof she needed somehow.

"There's no reason to leave."

Tom shook his head. "No. Of course, there isn't. This is obviously just what you needed."

◆   ◆   ◆

With a sense of loss, not just of Tom, but of what had seemed an important opportunity, Matty watched the old Cutlass move slowly into the shadow of the trees that overhung the rutted road and stood several minutes looking after the car that passed from sight too quickly. Then she went into the house and leaned against the door, studying the kitchen and living room.

"Why?" she asked of the shadowed, silent rooms. "Why couldn't you show yourself? You knew I needed you to. I know you did. Why couldn't you do that for me?"

She moved slowly into the kitchen and knew instantly that the girl was there. Out of sight, but there. Matty stopped, afraid to continue accusing her, not wanting to frighten her away, but angry that she should be here now, when it was too late.

"Why?' she asked again, sadly.

There was no answer.

17

"This is my religion. Don't care to provide entertainment for anyone."
The voice was firm but not angry.

Matty was taken by surprise. It had never occurred to her that she
would be put on the defensive.

"I'm quite serious about this," she assured Mary's friend. "Really."

"You'd like to join our group?"

"No. No, not that."

Matty wished she had put more thought into planning this phone conversation. It was clear that Evelyn Morris was a great deal more serious
about ghostly phenomena than Mary. An elderly woman, from the sound
of her slightly ragged voice. Matty pictured someone small, probably
white-haired and with, definitely, a strong chin.

"It's just that I've had an experience I can't explain. I won't take much
of your time. And I would very much appreciate your not mentioning this
to anyone."

It was the right thing to say. The voice became more relaxed, interested.

"In that case, I'd be glad to see you."

"Oh, good!" Matty jumped in. "Tonight? Tomorrow?"

"I'm down with something. Prob'ly flu. When I do feel better, I got to
get back to work and catch up on stuff at the church, too."

"The church?"

Matty had repeated it only to keep the conversation going, but the
woman was defensive again.

"I know. You're wondering how I can attend a Lutheran Church and be
a Spiritualist. Well, let me tell you, there's a lot of people don't understand

about us. Grant you, some people don't have any belief except Spiritual-ism, but there's nothing in it says you can't believe in God, too. Anyhow, around here, you got no social life at all outside church. I can prob'ly see you Saturday."

"Saturday?" It was only Monday, but an ill woman could hardly be pressured for a favor. "Yes, of course, if that's the earliest possible time." The response was phrased to elicit an offer of an earlier date, but no such offer came.

"I may be tired still. Meet me at my house then? I'll give you directions to where I'm at. Then we might want to meet again wherever this experi-ence of yours happened."

Not a plan that suited Matty.

"I don't know my way around very well and the—It happened here. You know the old log home on South Mountain? Would it be too much to ask you to come here?"

"Really? That house? Now that does get my interest! Look here, you must know how much any contact with the spirit world matters to some-one like me. If you think you've had a contact at that house, we should talk about it now, on the phone. Might be some equipment I should bring."

"Then you would rather meet here?"

"Not saying what happened, are you? Never mind. In fact, your reluc-tance is the preferred attitude. I'll see you at your house Saturday. Ten o'clock?"

"Yes. Thank you. Thank you very much."

The woman's grammar left something to be desired, but otherwise she sounded just right.

◆　　　◆　　　◆

Her next call was to Tom, to make some excuse to keep him from com-ing again this Saturday. Evelyn Morris could become a group of ladies from an historical society who wanted to see the house. Had to be Satur-day, of course, because some of them worked, worked too far away to come on a weekday. That sounded plausible. It would be so much better if she could just bring Tom in on this!

It was not a comfortable phone call. They both wanted a repeat of last weekend and her excuses sounded weak to her own ears.

"How about Saturday afternoon or dinner in the evening?" Tom asked.

"Well, I don't know how long they'll stay and, if they know some history about the house…I don't want to hold them to a deadline."

"Okay. Sunday?"

Sunday. Sunday. Damn, I hadn't thought about Sunday! Will I be ready to leave Sunday or will Saturday's visit lead to something else? Or will I want to go to church to talk to some other people? Sorry, Tom.

"Sounds wonderful, but someone said something about dinner after church. Sort of a thank you for the house tour. Kind of vague, but I should leave the time open." *Liar, liar!*

"Okay, Matty. Sorry if I'm pushy. I'm not supposed to horn in on your therapy. I'll wait to hear from you. You can call—Hell, you know that!—at the last minute. I can pop up Sunday if it turns out you're free later in the day. Just…This last weekend was something to remember, wasn't it?

About that, she could be honest.

"If was, Tom. It definitely was."

◆   ◆   ◆

Elation lasted as she worked at the computer, ate lunch outside and took her usual afternoon walk, anticipating Saturday, pleased that her head was working again and holding close the weekend's promise of a return to a more loving life with Tom. Life was good.

Matty returned from her walk with energy left over and a joyous feeling that needed expression. The soothing CD's were left in their box as she turned on the radio. Loud, unexpected rock music shoved her away with its energy, but left her laughing. She began to move, tentatively at first and then more energetically, making the movements larger, less controlled than aesthetically desirable, but no one was looking and it was the movement that mattered.

Until there was no music and no movement.

It lasted only an instant, but it was the most frightening instant of Matty's life. Her arms moved in space, but her mind sent contradictory messages. Her eyes told her they were there; her muscles and nerves said they weren't. Her feet no longer felt the floor and there was complete silence. There was no way she could keep her balance.

The fall was awkward, an elbow and then her forehead banging the coffee table. Then she was on the floor and the music was back, accompanying a new sensation, pain, along with the more welcome ones. For a few moments, she was unable to sort out what had happened or what to do. She sat up and hugged her knees. A few drops of blood fell onto her knees and arms.

Her heart was hammering so hard she could feel it in the back of her head. *I was a mind floating in space. A mind without a body. But I could see parts of myself! See, yes, but not feel. Or hear. What the hell? What the...I am here. I am all here now. Fingers, toes...* She wriggled them, touched her arms and legs. *God, my head hurts! I should go fix it. No. Stupid head, what does that matter? Banging my head—That was when I could feel everything again. What does that mean? Head wasn't working? Like kicking a piece of machinery? Made it work again?* She looked down at the body she could now feel. *Blood. Heads bleed a lot. Bled at the accident, too. Ruined my best sweater. Should wash jeans before the blood sets. Couldn't wash the sweater. Was at the hospital. Stupid. Sweater didn't matter. Jeans don't, either. Oh, God, Neil, what's wrong with me?*

Matty dropped her head on her knees and rubbed her hands up and down her shins in mindless, catatonic repetition, tears mixing with blood. Her breathing slowed to normal but not her heart. She leaned back against the hard edge of the table, her hand still moving reassuringly over her legs.

Why now? It's been so good. Why this? Even people with amputated limbs sometimes still feel them. Because they have a brain, stupid! They have brains that work and yours doesn't! Neil can't be right. This can't be psychological. Tumor. No! Can't be a tumor. It would always be there, not coming and going like this. Wouldn't it? What do I know! Late in the day. It was late in the day before. This is morning. And this was worse. Dancing. Movement aggravated it? Jogged something? Dad had gray clouds over his eyes when he had his ministrokes. TIA's. That's what they called them. Am I having something like that? Oh, God, could there possibly be a little logic in this?

As the minutes passed, it became harder and harder to recapture the unreal moment. Matty stood up and moved all the muscles of her body, slowly, easily, in unconscious imitation of a cool-down routine after a workout. She pulled a Kleenex from the box on the coffee table and mopped up the blood on her face and arms. The bleeding had almost stopped. The pain hadn't. It didn't seem to matter. Her body was working again. That was the big thing. Everything felt normal.

But it wasn't.

I have to go home.

Now.

Damn! I could have gone with Tom!

Neil.

Wiping her damp hands on her jeans, she picked up the phone from the coffee table and punched the numbers for Neil's office with a shaking finger. It was busy. They had two lines, so Neil was on one, Erica on the other.

She paced, trying to wait for a little time to pass before phoning again. She was angry. Everything had been going well. She really wanted to talk to this spiritualist. And there had been no loss since the raspberries and ice cream days ago.

The line was still busy. Neil and Erica must both be dealing with emergencies not nearly as important as hers.

Be real. You're not dying. Not right away. Head feels much better. What could they do over the phone anyway?

But the feelings of urgency and irritation only deepened as the minutes passed. She fed Neil's phone number into her instant dial list and hit the assigned number over and over, the adrenaline building until she forced herself to stop. Tom might have to take her home, but a call to him was no more productive. He was not at his desk and more information from Neil was needed before scaring the hell out of Tom anyway. Without leaving a message, she walked outside.

Cross legged on the sun-warmed concrete over the cistern, Matty stared at the uncaring sky and tried to think more calmly. Could this wait until next week? Maybe Neil could tell her. But even if he could wait, could she? This was too frightening. *Please, Neil, have something reassuring to say. Tell me you can fix it.* She tried Neil's number again and this time got him and blurted out her story quickly, loudly and in a severely disorganized way. But then, it didn't make sense to her no matter how it was told.

"Matty this sounds a little more serious than last time—"

A little more! Always trying to baby me! Tell it like it is!

"It sounds awful, Neil. Say it! And you haven't a clue, have you?"

"All right. It sounds like a terrible experience for you, but, yes, I have a clue although the dancing…You felt like dancing? You were happy?"

"Yes. Very."

"I wouldn't have expected that. Would you say you have been experiencing mood shifts rather than an overall depression?"

"No. Not exactly. It was a very good weekend with Tom."

"And this happened after he left?"

"Right."

"Yes. After he left. You were fine until he left. My advice is the same as before. You should come back and someone needs to drive you. And yes, I could be wrong, of course, but…This is the first incident since you called last time?"

"Yes."

"And Tom has been with you?"

"For the weekend. Yes."

"It's not ongoing, then."

"Is that good?"

"Yes, I would say so. How are you doing overall? Has your work been going well?

"Not really." *Can't tell him why. This little ghost is distracting? Oh, sure! Still, I can't lie, either. I need to know what's going on with me.* "It's been a little difficult to concentrate. Different…place."

"Yes. I'm sure that's a key factor. I shouldn't have sent you there. This can't be done satisfactorily over the phone. Can Tom bring you home?"

She had to ask. "What you think is wrong with me—Would that cause hallucinations? You know. Seeing things?"

"Possibly. And you would know they were hallucinations. You are completely aware that these experiences are unnatural. Has anything like that happened?"

"No," she said quickly. "I just thought I'd ask. I would be aware of them. I see." *Do I? Damn! Is this girl an hallucination? If she is, why don't I know she is like I know something is wrong with me when I can't smell or feel? Why is she different? Should I tell Neil about her?*

"Then these things…I thought hallucinations were seeing things that weren't there or smelling something that isn't there, things like that. What's happening to me is just the opposite."

"They can be related, but, Matty, all I want you to understand right now is that this is something we can deal with."

"Psychological. Trauma. Like you said before." Matty's heart was almost back to normal. She had a doctor to deal with psychological stuff. Neil would never believe this girl was real. This was not the time to talk about her.

"Yes. We'll work together."

"I don't want to come home yet unless it's really necessary."

"Why, Matty?"

"I just don't. Do I have to leave now?"

Silence on the other end.

"I don't quite understand. It's difficult to reconcile your wanting to stay with what is happening to you. I think we need to explore this although…"

"Although, yes, okay, although what?"

"I'm leaving tomorrow for a seminar in Chicago." He was obviously reluctant to say this. "Can you possibly have Tom or someone bring you to the office today? I'll be glad to come in late if necessary."

"No." It wasn't true. Of course Tom would come if she needed him. Her response came from an irrational anger that Neil was going away. It didn't help that she knew it was irrational.

"I can have someone else see you tomorrow. Dr. Lyman is on call for me. David Lyman."

"This isn't a sore throat, Neil! This guy doesn't know me. What's the point in starting all over with him?"

"The point, I think, is your being here where help is available and there are medications—"

"You said that before. You also said I'll know if it gets worse."

"Yes. If I'm right. That's what concerns me. We need to be sure my assumption is right. You need to come back."

"And Tom needs to drive me. Yes, I can understand that now after what just happened. But I trust you. You think you know what's happening. Some kind of trauma."

"A delayed reaction to trauma. Yes, that's my best guess. You've lost the usual controls over your life. I didn't realize how...Just coming back might help."

"Is this true or are you just trying to calm me down because I'm all alone up here?"

"I'm fairly certain I'm right. But you must understand I can't be positive."

Matty made her decision. "When will you be back?"

"Thursday."

"Then I'm staying. Screw your...your..." The word wouldn't come. "This other guy." *Substitute. That was what she had been trying to say.* "Can you see me next Monday? Then Tom won't have to take off to get me." *And I can talk to Evelyn and maybe some other people before I tell you what else is happening.*

"Yes, of course I will see you Monday if you refuse to return until then. But—Is there any point in arguing with you? I really—"

"No. You know how stubborn I can be."

"I—ah, actually recognized that particular tone. Well...Can you come in before my usual appointments? At eight thirty?"

"I'll be there." Her voice softened. He did care about her. "Thank you, Neil."

"But I insist you be prepared to have Tom bring you home if this problem progresses. I'll fill in David Lyman. Do I have your word on that?"

"Progresses. There was quite a gap between...Is this likely to progress, as in happen more frequently?"

"It could."

"Or not."

"Or not."

"Or go away?"

"That, too, is a possibility. I don't like to give you guesses. How do you feel now?"

"Perfectly normal. A little more nervous than usual, but that's normal under the circumstances."

"You're limiting the Diazepam?"

"Yes." This was true. "Only took one Saturday and last night. Little more wine with Tom but not much. And you said that was no problem as long as I didn't mix them."

"Good. That's wise. I don't understand your reluctance to deal with this now. It's not like you. Wouldn't you be more comfortable back here? You can have the cabin again another time."

What could she say? *Yes, I would, but there's this other thing? My little ghost might go away?*

"I know I sound a little more nuts than usual, but I really want to stay here. I've...met some people. We've made some plans that just won't work any other time and I'd like to take time to close up shop and come home when I'm ready and Tom won't have to take off work. He's really busy. Anyway, you're not going to be there and you're the one who really knows me."

The longer they talked, the less anxious she became. There was apparently no need to rush her in an ambulance for emergency help. A delayed reaction to trauma could wait.

Neither spoke for several seconds.

"You haven't made that promise to call Dr. Lyman if there are any further sensory losses," Neil reminded her.

"Then I'll be an emergency?"

"Then we can appraise the situation in light of new information."

"That came straight from a text book."

"The chapter titled, 'Communication in Times of Crisis.'"

Matty was able to laugh. Just talking to someone who could take control of the situation made her feel better. Still, she had never felt so alone as when the phone was dropped back onto the coffee table.

18

Several times during the week, Matty wanted to call Neil again, but Neil wasn't there and she had neatly avoided promising to call this Dr. Lyman, who didn't know her. Sticking to her prescribed routine, the mornings went well as usual. The tranquilizers were tempting, but she wouldn't take them during the day, not wanting to disguise any abnormalities that might occur. She cursed herself for letting Tom take home the Chivas Regal. The losses of taste or feel were rarely more often than once a day, were relatively brief and she learned to hold in the panic. At least, the most frightening experience, the loss of awareness of her whole body, was never repeated, nor the loss of hearing. The radio stayed off.

It was strangely comforting that she was not alone. The girl appeared regularly, never showing her full self, never staying long, was often nothing more than a flash of moving color. It did seem that she was a presence that could be sensed when out of sight more than any living individual Matty had ever known. She seemed to prefer to position herself where she could see but not be seen. Matty spoke to her regularly, but it wasn't clear whether or not the girl heard. There was never any response.

It would have been one of the most wonderful and exciting weeks of Matty's life if she hadn't been afraid of what might be wrong with her. There was a pattern, she found as she religiously kept the diary Neil had advised. Sensory losses occurred later in the day, loss of taste at dinner, rarely at lunch, loss of touch in the evening. Once she couldn't feel her silk nightgown as she lay on the bed. Tom sent yellow roses again. She took them to the trash, still in the box, and cried long after the trash can lid closed over them. The effort required to maintain control and the constant fear of another loss produced near exhaustion by the end of each day. It was hard to get off the couch and go to bed, though, once there, sleep was elusive and would have been impossible without medication. She was breaking some of the little yellow pills in half now, adding only five milligrams at a time, her only concession to Neil's admonitions. She held onto the thought of his return on Thursday and by that morning it was clear the progression of which they had spoken was happening. She had to go back and yet seemed unable to call either Tom to come get her or Erica to make an appointment. It would be the final admission that this wasn't going to go away.

For too long, Joseph's books had been sitting on the coffee table, a quiet reprimand. They had to be returned.

Outside, in her car, she gripped the steering wheel and prayed she could get down and back up the mountain safely. Thank God it wasn't far. Then she would call Tom and start to pack. The accident had told Matty that nothing frightened her husband as much as something wrong with her and she dreaded doing that to him again.

It seemed a long time ago that she had last stood outside the graying old store. Matty braced herself for the onslaught of Mary's sociability.

"Did you ever get Evie? She's got the flu somethin' awful." Mary's expression said she was hoping for a really good story to pass on.

Setting the books on the scarred counter gave Matty a moment to think. It seemed doubtful that Evelyn would have told Mary what they had talked about.

"I did reach her, but we didn't talk long. She was too sick. I didn't want to keep her." Matty made a mental note to cancel the Saturday appointment.

Mary's face fell. "Too bad. She's a awful interstin' woman. Little touchy, though, did you find?"

"A little, but she was sick after all. Did Joseph tell you about the deposit?"

"Ain't he awful? Fifty dollars! Though I was surprised he loaned you these books at all. Couple are worth somethin,' he says. Find what you was lookin' for?"

"Just interested in information about the area. Yes. They were helpful. Thank him for me, please."

After a few meaningless bits of social chatter, Matty extracted the money from Mary, forced a cheerful smile and left.

◆   ◆   ◆

Back at the house, she sat for a few minutes in the car, grateful to be safely home, but reluctant to make the call that would end her time at this amazing place. *Afraid to stay; afraid to go. Afraid, afraid, afraid! If I died now, that ought to go on my tombstone. I've been afraid for a year of another car accident. How foolish fear is. What happens is never what we fear.*

The phone was caroling as she opened the door, reminding her that she had forgotten to take it with her. Probably Tom.

"Miss Burhmann?"

It wasn't Tom and she didn't want to talk to anyone else.

"Mrs."

"Sorry. Mrs. My name is Jane Goodman. I'm a friend of Evelyn Morris."

"She gave you my phone number?"

"No, no. She would never do that. I wouldn't ask. My nephew, the boy who delivered flowers—He was quite taken with you. He said you asked about the house and I got your number from him, from the florist's records."

"Isn't that illegal or something?"

"Well, they're not medical records," Jane Goodman snapped back and then the voice returned to a more equable, if not conciliatory, tone. "Anyhow, I thought you'd want to hear from me. I'll hang up now if you don't. I'm not sure I should be calling anyway. Evie—That's Evelyn—told me you—Well, this is going to sound odd, but she told me you called her and when I put that together with the fact that you're staying at the old log house on the mountain, I...I suppose it would be nervy of me to ask why you called her, wouldn't it?"

Matty was in no mood to play games.

"Maybe I should ask why putting those two facts together were so interesting to you?"

Silence.

"It would help if we knew each other, wouldn't it?" Jane Goodman asked.

"Maybe."

There was a long sigh and another period of silence before the woman continued.

"I'm interested in the house because my grandmother used to live there."

Matty was jolted. This was one of the people she had been looking for. Was it too late? "And?" was all she could think of to say.

"Your turn."

Oh, shit! What do I do now? Would a few hours make a difference? I don't even know if Neil could see me right away. Did he say what time he was getting back today?

"Mrs. Buhrmann?"

"Yes. Sorry. Maybe we should get together to talk. Are you free now?"

"Why don't we wait until you've talked to Evie."

Matty had lost her earlier mental note to cancel that appointment.

"Why? So she can tell you what we talked about?"

"No. If it's what I think it's about, Evie doesn't talk, at least not to me even if we are friends. Sort of."

"Then how do you—"

"She couldn't resist a little gossip, admitting she'd talked to you. No one else has heard from you except Mary Briggsley. We're all curious. She said you were asking about church services, but I knew she hadn't been manning the church phones this week. I've been taking her food and I know she's been so sick she hasn't even been answering her own phone most of the time."

"What's the point of waiting?"

"What she tells you might be useful to us. I think she goes too far, but she's no fool. I'd kind of like to see what she finds up there." Having given that much away, Jane Goodman let down the barriers a little further.

"Look, Mrs. Buhrmann, I have to live here for the rest of my life. What I want to talk about is kind of personal and nobody—*nobody*—knows anything about what I've been doing and I don't think I want them to. Will you promise me, please, not to mention my call to anyone, not even Evelyn?"

The temptation to stay had never completely disappeared. This woman was feeding it.

"Of course. There's no one I would want to confide in and, frankly, I'd like to exact the same promise from you."

Matty knew she wasn't going home today. Not unless something awful happened.

"Done." Jane Goodman sounded relieved. "Good. Good. Why don't we meet 'by accident' at church Sunday? Did Mary tell you where the Lutheran Church is?" Without waiting for an answer, she gave directions. "Go past Mary's store about a mile and a half. Turn left onto Severing Trail. Then another left onto Red Oak Lane."

"Wait."

Matty knew she wouldn't remember the directions. Not now. She got a pencil and one of the pages she had torn out of *Realtor* magazine and wrote them in the margin. As she wrote, it occurred to her that Jane Goodman had called *Joseph's Commodities* Mary's store. Odd. Odd marriage.

"Red Oak Lane?"

"Right. I'm very tall, almost six feet, skinny as a rail, a real plain Jane and I'll wear my pink suit."

"Fine," Matty said. "I'm—"

"You'll be the one I don't know."

"Till Sunday then."

"Till Sunday."

Matty pressed the button to end the call. Why had she neglected the delivery boy's comment about the aunt who was "nuts" about this house? Evidently this Jane Goodman's interest was not as much a secret as she thought.

19

Saturday came at last.

Matty wasn't proud of the way she had held up during the last two days. Neil had been right about being at home. Even if there were no quick fix, it would have been comforting just to be working with him, knowing he was near. She was erratic, unable to concentrate and tears flowed at the slightest provocation, often from mere tiredness. Thursday, she had cautiously driven to the drug store at the same intersection as Joseph's store. The pharmacist had been a rotund, pink-faced man with the kind of mustache that collected food. He hadn't approved of Matty's prescription or the fact that she downed a pill and waited for it to take effect before leaving, but she could not face getting back in the car without one. The thought of losing the sense of touch or awareness of her body while driving was terrifying.

She had stalked grimly through these last two days, constantly steeled against further sensory problems, her mind frequently debating what would be bad enough to force her to leave before she could see Evelyn Morris and Jane Goodman. Especially Jane Goodman. It was a relief to record, at the end of both days, that nothing had happened. Nothing at all. It now seemed possible that the problems arose from some disturbance in her nerves calmed by the Diazepam she was now taking during the day. So much for Neil's advice!

◆　　　◆　　　◆

Matty was in the kitchen laying out the mismatched, chipped cups for tea when the car stopped outside. She walked to the door and waited for the knock, knowing that she didn't open it and go out to welcome her visitor because everything spontaneous and natural in her was gone.

"I'm Evelyn Morris."

Matty's first reaction was to wonder why this woman was calling herself Evelyn Morris. Where was the old woman on the phone? This Evelyn was about Matty's height, full-figured, red-haired and had beautiful, clear white skin. With makeup, she would have been exotic, even in her blue denim shirt dress.

"I thought—I expected—I thought you were older."

"Sounded as old as I felt the day we talked. 'Bout a hundred." The comment was humorous but the tone was not. It said she was a person to be taken seriously.

Matty wondered how she and Mary could be friends. Perhaps there weren't many choices in the country.

"Please." Matty stood back and gestured for the woman to come in, thinking that this was going to be awkward. They would sit down and exchange a little personal information, the way women did, and then someone would have to find the courage to say something meaningful.

It didn't go that way. Evelyn Morris didn't sit down. She wandered as though in her own house, into the kitchen and back to the living room, touching things as she went, absorbed in what she was doing. She went upstairs without an invitation. Matty followed, feeling a little foolish, like a pet dog, and also just a little resentful at the way her visitor touched personal things as if they were her own. Finally, they were both seated in the living room, Evelyn on the couch, she in the old recliner.

"Don't feel a thing," Evelyn said.

"Do you usually? If something is there, I mean."

"Mm. Sometimes. I'm not all that sensitive. Got to touch something that belonged to the entity that is trying to make contact."

Entity. That was a word Matty hadn't come up with. Safely non-specific.

Evelyn Morris looked at her directly for the first time since she had begun her travels through the house.

"You may be more sensitive than me."

"I'm sensitive? Nothing like this has ever happened to me before."

"Like what?" Her direct gaze said it was time.

Matty wasn't quite ready.

"I forgot. I was making tea. Would you like a cup?"

"Sure."

"I have Lapsang Soochong or Earl Gray."

"Anything past Lipton's is beyond me. Let's do that first one."

"Kind of smoky."

"Fine."

Matty got up.

The woman's voice followed her into the kitchen.

"You can talk from there if you want to. Sometimes people can't look me in the eye when they talk about these things for the first time. You embarrassed?"

The kettle was steaming over a low fire. Matty poured water over the teabags. The heavy scent moved to her face along with the steam and she recoiled. It had become almost a reflex to avoid nice aromas for fear of losing them.

"I don't think so. But maybe. Do you take milk? I don't have cream."

"No. Little honey if you got some. Why don't you ask the questions?"

"If you don't mind," Matty said as she set a tray with the teapot, cups, a jar of honey and a spoon on the coffee table.

"Most people call me Evie."

Matty smiled. "I guess it's about time for that, isn't it? I'm Matty. It's just—" Matty leaned forward in her chair, elbows on her knees, hands clasped. "I have to be honest here. I was in a serious car accident. I killed someone. That is, my car killed someone. It wasn't really my fault, but I had a kind of breakdown. That's why I'm reluctant to tell anyone I know about this. They might just think—I'm not sure I'm a very believable person right now."

"You saying I shouldn't believe you maybe?"

"Oh, no. I'm sure of what's happening myself, but...but—" *What the hell is that word?* "You know..." It came. "Confirmation would be nice."

"Then shoot with the questions. Or tell me your story." Evie sat back against the couch, waiting.

"Okay. I feel really stupid asking this, but what is a ghost? I mean, are there any, really?"

"Depends on what you mean by 'ghost'."

It took a while to come up with the right words. Evie was patient.

"I mean a dead person who doesn't go...wherever he or she should go. Who stays here for some reason and becomes—or is something a living person can see or maybe hear?"

"Good. Wanted to see how you defined 'ghost.' Yes, darn right there are ghosts! Think we'll work on that definition, though. There are different kinds of what you call ghosts."

"There are? You really believe there are!"

"Of course."

"How can you be sure? Is there some way you can prove this to me?"

Evie laughed shortly. "Think maybe you've proved it to yourself. But I'll go along with you. Experience. Lots of stories from reliable witnesses. Photos. Recorded sounds. Recorded temperature changes without what you would call logical explanation. Same with smells. That's why I asked about bringing equipment. We don't have any of the expensive, sophisticated stuff, but we can record sound, measure temperature, take photos with different kinds of film. You even know what Spiritualism is?"

"Maybe not."

"We believe we can contact the dead. And we do. Through a sensitive, a medium, mostly. We do different things to get to 'em. But sometimes they try to contact us. That's what you call a ghost. A manifestation of some kind. Sometimes there's no trace of the entity itself, just a sense of its presence or its effect on something in the living world."

"Why do you need a medium? Because they're more sensitive to the ghosts or, excuse me, entities?"

"That's it. Other side needs 'em, too. Sometimes the dead can't see or hear us too good and they don't talk much. You've prob'ly seen kind of wispy spirits on TV or in a movie. They actually look that way to us sometimes. And we look that way to them sometimes, too, because they're not seeing clearly. A medium usually sees better and hears better, too. Kind of like an interpreter."

"My spirit is clearly here. A little...cloudy maybe but quite detailed. But why are they here? And why are they limited to one thing, sight or sound or cold or something? If they're here, aren't they totally here?"

"Not sure they're here at all."

Matty was stunned. *Well, that wraps that up, doesn't it?* "I'm sorry. What have we been talking about?"

"Maybe it's time for the tea?"

"And then we start all over?"

"Not entirely."

Matty had to force herself to be careful pouring the tea. The tranquilizers weren't working; adrenaline overpowered them. She could almost feel the nerves under her skin and it was necessary to concentrate on deep, even breaths. Where was this conversation going?

"Now," Evie said, accepting the blue cup and pink saucer from Matty's shaking hand. "Let's begin again with what I believe."

"Let's do that," Matty said a little too emphatically for courtesy.

Evie took one sip, looked up and said, "Nice." Then her eyes went to the ceiling. "I believe—No. Let me start with—There's them what believe some people remain on earth for a reason, need for retribution, need to correct a mistake, inability to separate from someone or something. I believe—" Her eyes came back to Matty. "I believe they all go on, but we can reach 'em—"

"But that would mean—"

"Let me finish. They sometimes leave traces. I believe that strong emotions, strong needs have their own lives. *They* can remain. Some of us believe they're like electrical impulses. They've been measured. Myself,

I'm not sure of the form. I think what remains is kind of like energy. In New Oxford, Pennsylvania, not far from here, our group saw a one-room log home that had been expanded to six rooms. The original room wouldn't let itself be redecorated. Wallpaper was tore down during the night. Dishes thrown. Chipped the new paint. Lots of witnesses. Big family in the area. They all saw what happened. Some of 'em had helped with the work. Lot of energy there. But no one felt threatened or was hurt. The child, four years old, especially liked playing there. They gave up making it the living room. Used it as her playroom. Seemed like a kind of poltergeist, something you've prob'ly heard of. But poltergeists are usually malevolent. You know what that means?"

Matty nodded and Evelyn nodded back, approving.

"This one seemed to only want her house as she knew it. Desire must have created the energy. No scent, no sound, no cold, no sense of presence, no misty anything. Just will. Energy. That's what I believe. It was just left behind."

"But that seems such a pitiful reason for—for, I guess you'd say, all that energy. I thought there had to be a violent death or some such thing. *Decorating?*"

"Don't seem like much, does it? There are other, scientific kinds of explanations. One's about living on different planes of possibility or time, parallel planes of existence."

Her tone was dismissive, but Matty found this explanation interesting.

"So a ghost may be from another plane of existence?"

"So some say."

Matty stared at her teacup. The thought of drinking its contents was far from her mind.

"Could we go from one plane to another and relive the same life? I mean, go back to the same time? I'm trying to understand why ghosts appear in the same place all the time."

"Actually, all of 'em don't. You're talking about recurring ghosts."

"They're not all like that?"

"No. That's called a haunting. Same manifestation appears repeatedly in the same location. Or is associated with some physical thing."

Matty was struck by the mixture of simple, uneducated language with the more sophisticated phrases obviously picked up from her particular field of interest.

"Like houses."

"That's the obvious one. You got your haunted pieces of furniture. Lots of planes, ships and trains."

Some of what Evie said rang little bells in Matty's memory. Yes, she had heard of these things before. "That haunted flight. Flight 401," she said.

"You got it."

Matty didn't add that she hadn't believed the story. In any case, what she believed was doing some flip flops right now.

"But if a place were haunted, that business of parallel planes—"

"Remember it's been theorized that parallel planes can also be of two sorts: possibility planes, where we lead a vast number of lives, the results of different decisions or some kind of turning in our lives and also different *time* planes. Maybe some people can't move on in time. Just get stuck where they are. Some scientists don't believe time is linear. Only seems so to us ordinary people."

Matty was struggling to apply these new ideas to her own experience. "Except that the world turns, so how—"

"Revolves around the sun, too. Don't do to try to figure it out. Leave that to the scientists. And we're earth-bound, aren't we? I mean, our experience is limited to our own bodies and what we can touch and deduce from our limited experience."

Matty sat back in her chair and Evie gave her time to think.

Finally, the woman said, "This hasn't helped none, has it?"

Matty looked up. "No. But you explain things neatly. Like my husband."

"I've done this before."

"It shows. But, no, I can't apply this to my situation. Except maybe that thing about a form of energy. Energy can come in bursts, can't it? Appear and then dissipate? That might apply. But why is the energy here?"

"We're back to strong emotion."

"A need, like the New Oxford thing."

"Maybe. Lots of needs. People aren't always real logical about what they feel strongly about, you know."

This didn't suit Matty. The girl didn't seem a remnant of one strong emotion. There was sympathy, interest in everyday doings and, for the first time, there was the realization that the girl's expression was one of sadness.

"If someone were, say, killed violently, would the ghost be the remnant of that violence or something more like the person before she died?"

"A *she*, then." For the first time, Evie allowed a slight smile. "Don't know. Most apparitions I've heard of don't seem to exhibit much emotion at all. Very subdued, they are. Never heard of a happy one."

"And they don't talk."

"Oh, yes. Some do. There's a well documented one at a college in Westminster that's talked to students. Touched 'em, too. That's unusual, though. Like I say, most times you need a medium."

"I'm beginning to feel silly not telling you what this is all about. I've already given away that it's female."

Evie just waited. Her usual expression was not welcoming and Matty wondered why anyone told her their strange stories. Maybe they were desperate, too.

"There's this girl," she began hesitantly. "This girl dressed in a long blue skirt. With a white apron. Pretty girl. Lots of blonde hair. She doesn't make a sound. Not quite as clear as a real person, but clear enough. Hanging around. Interested. The oddest thing..." Matty looked at Evie earnestly. "I told you about my problem. Sort of. When I'm having a particularly difficult time, crying or whatever, she looks so sympathetic. She has even reached out to me, but then she retreats as if she's afraid to touch me. And she won't, or at least, didn't, appear when my husband is here."

Evie drained her teacup. "That was good. That tea. Good of you to open up, too. Thank you." She leaned over to set the cup on the coffee table. Her long red hair fell into her face and she brushed it back with an obviously well practiced flip of her hand. "There may be something about you that she likes—"

"How can a form of energy have likes?"

"We are both forms of energy, just not exclusively. We are also matter. But burn a lump of matter called coal and you have—"

"Energy. I think I need my husband in on this."

"And about your husband, maybe she feels intimidated by two people at once. Maybe she's afraid of men. A girl, you say. An abused girl? Maybe she just doesn't find him sympathetic. Or maybe she does appear and he isn't aware of her."

"No. I was always with him and I would be aware if she were there."

"Then you sense her presence whether you can see her or not."

Matty nodded.

"And she responds to you."

"Mm." Matty nodded again emphatically, trying to make the woman realize how incredible this was, but Evie only smiled slightly, leaned towards her and said, quite calmly, "How wonderful for you. That has never happened to me. Can't you ask her some simple questions?"

"I have. She doesn't answer. Not even a change in expression. Does she hear me?"

"You'd know that better'n me. The connection between us and them isn't like between you and I. She may hear you and maybe not."

"But she sees me. Why not hear me?"

"Don't touch you, though, does she?"

"Well, no, but—"

"What kinds of questions you been asking?"

"Her name. I have a list of former owners."

"I see." Evie leaned back and frowned. "Maybe she didn't have one of those names. Have you asked her if she's happy? If she died violently? If there's something you can do for her? Also could be she can hear you, but not real good, you know? Maybe your voice is kinda faint. Maybe speak up a little. You say you see her pretty clear?"

Matty shut her eyes and tried to picture the girl.

"Actually...She's clear, but not like you are. Just a little...sort of transparent. Just a little."

"Is she here now?"

"I always assume so, but, no, I don't sense her here now."

170

"Ah. So maybe I chased her away like your husband did. Wonder if she'd run from our equipment. Could we set something up for next week?"

"Can I call you? I have to leave tomorrow and I'm not sure when I'll be back. I need proof, Evie. Maybe I just need to prove to myself I'm okay mentally."

"Doesn't seem to want another witness, does she? Even if I'd seen her, I'm no good. Good witnesses are skeptics, people everybody knows are hard to convince. Even then, they probably wouldn't convince anyone—"

"But it would help me."

"You do doubt yourself then."

"I do and I don't. She's so real. But I know I have some problems that haven't been identified. I would love someone else to see her."

"All right. I can get others in our group, trip-wires, infra-red film, a volt-meter. I may be able to borrow a thermograph and a machine that registers vibrations from some people from Frederick. You got a tape recorder?"

"There's nothing to record."

"Sometimes we tape stuff we didn't hear."

"Oh? Yes. I could bring one back with me. Is it all right that I'm not sure when I'll be back? You'll be here for the next few weeks?"

"Sure. Try to give me some warning and I'll set up something with our medium in Gettysburg. She may be all you need. Maybe if you tried together and then she tried alone, one of them combinations might bring your girl. That would give you your peace of mind, but you understand I want to get more. Our group likes to have real proof, good enough for outsiders."

"I'd like to know more, too, though it's probably just curiosity. I feel I know her and I'd like to know when she lived, why she is still—Well, you say she isn't really here, but it looks as though she is. Do you know anyone who knows a lot about the old families here? Their history?"

"Frederick Historical Society."

"I have their address. Maybe on the way back from Rockville…"

"There's that old bastard, Joseph Briggsley. He reads a lot of local history."

"Old bastard?"

Evie nodded vehemently.

"Leech. Never worked more than twenty minutes in any one day. Mary's father left her the store and he's lived off of it ever since. Mary does all the work."

"I've noticed that."

"Don't take long."

"Mary and Joseph. Not the Biblical kind."

Evie smiled for the first time. "Mary might be right for her. Certainly is a long-suffering woman. They had a son, too. Michael. He was only twenty-two when he died in a car accident. Long time ago now."

"Long time ago? Mary doesn't seem that old."

"She was sixteen when he was born. That's why they got married. Joseph was the hero that saved her from shame. And himself from poverty. He's not—wasn't—Michael's father. That marriage is still running on gratitude."

Evie got up. "But I'm getting into local gossip now. Not what I came for." She moved toward the door, then turned. "Try to figure out what she responds to. Check the weather, time of day, what you're doing."

"For a while I thought she came when I was unhappy."

"Possible. There was an apparition they called The Nanny Ghost in a house in the valley. Took care of a baby from the time it was born. Bedclothes were tucked in, pacifier put in his mouth. Somebody saw her rocking the child. Holding him at the window, too. The mother told her to go one day and the Nanny disappeared. They can be caring." Evelyn shrugged her shoulders in dismissal. "Not the usual thing."

"But she might have come to help me, to comfort me."

"Mm. Might be what you might call a side line. Don't think she'd come back just to help you. You never knew her. Not like family or something. Let me know when you're coming back?"

"I will," said Matty. They were both at the door now. "I'm sorry to be so vague." She decided to be honest. "I'm seeing a doctor and I don't know what will come—What may need to be done."

"I'll say a prayer for you."

"Oh." That was not something Matty's friends said. "Thank you."

Evie was halfway out the door before Matty remembered what Evie had said earlier.

"Oh, wait! You said if you could touch—Would you wait a minute?"

Matty ran upstairs and got the flag out of the dresser's bottom drawer where she had put it for protection. Hurrying back downstairs, she slipped a little on the third step again. It was not a good place to move quickly.

"Here. Would you touch this and see…?"

"A flag? American. Not exactly red, white and blue, is it?"

It took a moment to realize what Evie meant.

"Oh, yes. More like pink, tan and gray, isn't it? It has thirty-four stars. Do you know when that would have been?"

"Yeah, more or less. We're in contact with a soldier who died in the battle of Gettysburg. Thirty-four stars when he was fighting. I believe the last was the star for Kansas. And then at least one more was added during the War, maybe two."

Matty held out the cloth with a genuine smile. She had a time. Not colonial days, then. Later. A lot of years had just been eliminated. There was an instantaneous surge of need to check her list of names.

Evie held the flag with one hand underneath, the other lightly caressing the top as her eyes closed slowly. Her face took on a strange tension that added years to her appearance. She held it a full minute before the lines eased and she became young again. When she spoke, her voice was softer and her eyes had a special excitement in them. It was the first time Matty had sensed real warmth from this oddly aloof woman.

"Don't know if it was your ghost, but someone has left extraordinary energy in this cloth."

Both women stood in silence for a time, lost in the potential of those words.

"Thank you," Matty said, finally.

"Thank *you*," Evie echoed fervently.

20

Back in the house, Matty spread the flag across the couch and looked at it gratefully. Evelyn Morris had sensed energy here! *Thank God! Validation!* The tears that blurred the faded stars and stripes were testimony to how much she needed this reassurance. Strange that what came through to each of them was different. Matty had handled the flag repeatedly, yet felt nothing, and Evelyn couldn't sense the girl. She reached down and touched the worn linen again. What had it felt like to Evelyn?

A crossover from another time plane? This idea had appeal. It sounded reassuringly scientific. But she liked Evelyn's belief better: everyone moved on, but sometimes, as in this house, something was left behind. Not a completely satisfying explanation, though. This little ghost of hers seemed too real to be a lingering remnant of energy.

Matty dropped onto the recliner, leaned her head back and closed her eyes. It was too much effort to pull up on the wooden handle that would raise her feet. She was tired all the time now. There was too much tension for sleep. She wanted a scotch. Or some wine. She was taking too much Diazepam.

The first time the girl had appeared, she was holding this flag, looking at it sadly. The thought rose that, buried beneath Matty's own need to prove she wasn't hallucinating, was a desire to help this child. The intimation grew, became certain knowledge and it felt good. There was a need to know what kept her little spirit here, even a need to somehow care for her. That was why Matty had wanted to touch her. The girl seemed to want to touch, too. What was it that denied them both a mutual desire?

A child. Matty smiled ruefully. This wasn't the first time it seemed another instinct was surfacing here. She had never felt this way about any living child. What outrageous twist of fate had offered her a dead girl—painful words—to mother? Was it crazy to pursue this ghost thing when she had her own psychological—perhaps physical—problems to deal with? But you had to go on, didn't you? Every day people with terminal illnesses got up and made breakfast. A disease shouldn't become your whole life. Mack had multiple sclerosis. Anne had cancer, barely under control. Diabetes had caused Carol's mother to lose a leg. Yet they went out to dinner, did housework, earned a living. They laughed. All these people behaved in a perfectly ordinary way with appalling shadows darkening their lives. Where did they find this elusive source of strength?

I can't do that, act normal. Nothing could make me laugh. But I can keep going. I'll cry all the damn time, but I can keep going. Wine. Joseph can bring me some wine. I can't drive. Too scary. Some of that awful screw-cap wine. And groceries, too. I need groceries. Don't want them. Need them. Not eating enough.

It almost seemed that fate was handing her a perfect excuse to get Joseph alone to pick his brain.

She went into the kitchen. The clock told her that it was still early, only eleven. Evie had been businesslike, brief. In spite of fatigue, adrenaline pumped her up as she leafed through the thin telephone book for the number.

"Oh, he don't deliver on Saturdays. What?"

The last word wasn't said into the phone. Mary was talking to someone in the store.

"Well it's that new woman on the mountain. Yeah. Matty. She wanted you to deliver and I—Well, you never—Well, all right, all right." The voice was aimed at the phone again. "He says he'll deliver, though I don't know. Always said as how he deserves the weekend off, though the good Lord knows the store's open all—Yes, yes, I'll get the—" The last to Joseph, apparently. "Just a minute. There's a pencil here somewheres."

Matty waited. There was more mumbled conversation in the background before Mary was on the line again. She explained, when Mary finally thought to ask, that she couldn't get the groceries herself because of car trouble. The lie fit beautifully with the fact that Tom would be coming to get her on Sunday. She was beginning to see that lying was a kind of art, or at least a craft. *Crafty.* Was that word entirely coincidental? She didn't much like thinking of herself that way.

"He says he won't be there till late. He's writin' somethin'."

Meaning, Matty thought, that he's putting me in my place. He'll come, but not promptly.

"You mean after lunch?"

"After lunch, Joseph?" Mary yelled, forgetting to move the telephone away.

Matty winced and pulled the phone from her ear.

"After dinner. About five thirty, prob'ly."

After dinner? Why so late?

"That will be fine," Matty said, feeling she was getting the better of the deal anyway. Joseph didn't know what he was coming for, did he? And maybe, if she took a pill, she could get a nap and be more alert. Manipulating Joseph was not going to be easy.

A picnic lunch up on the rock sounded right. She could take her blanket and maybe fall asleep in the sun. *Yeah. Right.*

The girl was there as she fixed a sandwich, always behind her, only a piece of blue skirt or an arm, such a young arm, visible. Matty talked to her, being sociable, not expecting or trying for a response now.

"I haven't much left to eat, have I? Good thing I like odd stuff. This isn't bad. Cucumber sandwich with a few of Tom's wonderful anchovies. No mayonnaise, but I have butter." Always before, she had assumed the girl could hear. Now she wondered. Evelyn believed—How had she put it?—help was sometimes needed for the other side. Maybe the girl couldn't hear her, or perhaps couldn't hear clearly, although she certainly could see. She was always watching.

Matty felt guilty leaving the girl. She always did at lunch. It was like abandoning a guest in your home while you went out to eat. But a walk was part of her therapy and there was something nourishing about sitting in the sun on that rock. Nature's tranquilizer, she thought, and immediately it sounded like sarcasm. Nature's tranquilizers didn't work very well.

◆　　　◆　　　◆

Joseph arrived at six. Matty imagined him typing away at his pseudo-occupation, enjoying making her wait. What author was he copying today, she wondered?

"Groceries," he said, offering her a bag from the back of his station wagon.

Evidently, she was to carry them inside herself. But no, he picked up the second bag and followed her into the kitchen.

"Thirty-seven forty-three plus eight dollars delivery."

It was an outrageous delivery charge and Matty was sure Mary would never see any of it.

"Forty-five forty-three," was all she said.

He nodded approval of her addition and stuck out his hand. Matty went to her purse, wondering how she was going to keep him here. Evidently, he intended a fast departure.

"Will you have—" What did she have? Not much to drink. She had a fleeting thought that the Chivas Regal would have held him. "—some fruit juice or the wine you brought?"

"Coffee," he corrected.

"Coffee. It should be in one of these—"

But Joseph already had it in his hand. She hadn't specified what brand when ordering from Mary. He held an expensive coffee that she had been surprised to find at the store on her first visit.

This would take a few minutes. So much the better. Joseph pulled a pipe from his pocket and wandered into the living room to light it. Matty started the coffee and put the perishables away quickly as it brewed. She wished he would go outside to smoke.

Joseph wasn't concerned about being polite. He was being curious. He wandered around the living room, glanced up the stairs and came back into the kitchen.

"Wouldn't stay here alone, my wife wouldn't," he announced.

"So she said. A lot of women wouldn't," Matty said, defending Mary as she set the last cup of yogurt into the refrigerator.

"Mary wouldn't stay an afternoon alone, much less overnight."

"And you don't approve of that caution."

"Chicken."

The malevolence in that one word stabbed at Matty. Her back to Joseph, she made a face out the window and then turned to him.

"Mary seems a nice enough woman. But if I may say so, you two don't seem particularly compatible."

"Don't take long to figure that out, does it? We say what's on our minds. Not like city people."

It was impossible to avoid confrontation with this man. Matty took a deep breath, reminded herself of her mission, and responded as calmly as she could.

"Some city people say what's on their minds. They're no different from country people. People are people. If you're talking about husbands and wives arguing in front of strangers, most people—"

"You can't talk about most people. Don't know 'em all, do ya? City folks, now, you can tell me about city folks."

Matty realized her fingernails were digging into her palms. On a good day, she would have made a game of this. There hadn't been many good days recently.

"Okay, then, the married people I know who happen to live in the city don't argue in front of strangers. As a rule." Even as she said it, she knew it wasn't true, especially in her business. It just seemed necessary to counter this confident ill will.

"Phony. All on the surface, city people."

"We call it polite."

"Sure you do."

She had to fix this. The aroma of coffee was doing its best to create a sociable atmosphere, but Matty was too easily provoked by this dried up piece of irritability. When he walked out of the kitchen, she was afraid he was leaving. It seemed like him, to leave without saying anything. But he turned right, instead, to go onto the porch. She took another deep breath, shut her eyes and ordered tight muscles to relax, starting with her shoulders. Time to start over. Be more pleasant.

Or maybe not.

This was a new thought. Maybe Joseph enjoyed a good argument. She doubted if Mary argued very intelligently. Those had been invigorating times on the high school debate team. Maybe a good intellectual fight would keep Joseph here. With a little help from the coffee.

She walked out onto the porch and sat down in the rocker next to Joseph. Neither said a word.

It took only a matter of seconds before Matty felt the discomfort of silence. Joseph seemed completely at ease, taking an occasional pull on his pipe and looking at the trees as if he could see through them all the way down the mountain.

A memory crept in from the summers in Ohio when neighbors had gathered in her grandparents' back yard and sat and smoked and sipped lemonade or beer from bottles. They talked off and on, but sometimes just sat in comfortable silence watching the fireflies and the kids running around, occasionally calling out a caution. When they left, the adults said "goodnight," a few words, perhaps, about seeing each other again as they walked slowly toward home, gathering children and dogs on the way, their bare legs marked by the plastic strips on the aluminum chairs. When did this kind of peace become wasting time? Apparently, for Joseph, it hadn't yet been replaced by television.

Matty's sense of timing told her when the coffee was ready. She got up, went into the kitchen and filled the two least chipped mugs.

"Black?" she called out, pretty sure that would be right.

"Black," the echo came back.

The coffee seemed to be a signal for him to talk.

"Can't stand anything unfamiliar," Joseph said. It seemed to be a continuation of his former theme. "Got no imagination. You'd think imagination would be what'd make you afraid to stay here alone, but it don't seem to work that way. Now me, I could sit here and entertain myself for days, thinkin' on what went on for hundreds of years here—"

This was promising. Matty couldn't stop herself from jumping in.
"Yes, what—?"

"But Mary, now. No imagination. No vision. If she ain't seen it and her mama didn't tell her about it, it never entered her head. Now me, I been everywhere and thought just about every thought there is from right here. Bein' a reader does that."

"You wish Mary was like that?" Matty wanted to get back to "for hundreds of years here," but knew now that Joseph was going to go his own way.

He chewed on his pipe a while before saying, "You don't want a married couple to be too alike."

"And you certainly wouldn't want a modern city woman like me."

He looked at her appraisingly.

"Can't beat a modern woman when she gets it just right. Not so likely to be fat, as a rule. Seems though, they mostly go off the track. Get too wild in their dress or their thinkin' or the way they act and forget to be a proper woman. Nothin' wrong with 'em workin', either, mind. Poor sits hard on a woman and she might's well earn some of what she needs to spend. Mary does that, at least. Lots of Marys around. Plump up first time they get pregnant and keep on addin' from there. Won't look at the bills or the checkbook. Has to look at the register keys and punch 'em one at a time after forty years of it. Not much to hope for in a stupid woman. Didn't know that early enough. Never said an interestin' thing in her whole damn life." He drew deeply on his pipe and blew the smoke out forcefully. "People hereabout reckon her a good wife."

His voice said he didn't, but Matty was impressed that he even would offer that small token. He seemed to be finished for the moment, so she made a second attempt to steer the conversation.

"I haven't thanked you for the books. They didn't tell me much about the families around here. Do you know anything about them?"

"Sure. Knew most of 'em before they started using us as a bedroom for D.C. Still know the locals. Dull. Talk about crops and the weather and animals. Farm animals," he said in a flat voice that indicated his lack of interest.

"I meant the early ones. There was fighting here during the Civil War. I suppose the owners of this house were affected. There was something about this house being used as a hospital but not much else. Not even the owner's name."

"Rest is rumor."

Rumor! Then there were stories! Matty tried to keep any excitement from her voice. "Rumor has some basis in fact."

"You can lose a lot of facts in a century and a half."

"But there are stories," she insisted.

"Sure."

"For instance? Can I get you another cup of coffee?"

Matty fervently wished she had baked the chocolate cake planned for Tom. Joseph would have been good for at least two pieces. It was darn good cake.

Joseph handed her his mug and she went in to fill it. By the time she returned, he had decided to talk.

"Rumor has it—" he stuck out his thin lower lip and leaned his head over the coffee, making four little steps of his chin. "—when the people here heard the Confederates and the Yankees were about to..."

"Yes," Matty prompted as he paused to take a sip. "I read, for instance, that the Confederates—"

Joseph silenced her with a blank look.

"Rumor had it," Joseph repeated in exactly the same tone of voice to underline the fact that he had to start over, "—that when the people in this house heard the Confederates were comin' they hid in the basement—"

Matty couldn't help herself. "Even the men?"

This time, at least, he didn't start over.

"Don't know about that. But they all got themselves killed. All of 'em. Whole family."

"Oh." Matty wanted to ask if he knew the ages of the family members, but it seemed safer to let him continue.

"Women like the other version better. Weren't all killed. Men went off to fight. Left behind a girl engaged to a boy from over there—" His pipe stem pointed into the trees.

The silence went on too long.

"And?" Matty ventured.

"Dead, o' course."

"And that's all that's known?"

"Ain't nothin' known," he corrected her, irritation in his voice. "Rumor, like I said. 'Cept the house where the boy was supposed to live did burn down durin' Civil War fightin'. That's a historical fact. Women say the girl was raped. Had her bein' a virgin. Got to have their little soap operas, women do."

"So there was a daughter?"

"Oh, sure. Name of Mathilda."

"*Mathilda?*"

Joseph's beaky profile went up and down, but the smug smile gave the lie away.

"You don't know her name!"

"Your right name, ain't it? Mathilda? Thought you'd like that."

"I did," Matty said, though why she admitted anything to this awful liar, she couldn't say.

"Rumor has it she died holdin' a new flag she'd just made."

This time, Matty wasn't taken in. The memory of the flag spread out on the couch was too vivid.

"That's a crock!"

"Sure. Thought it was a good touch. No reason not to have a flag in the story if you want one."

The old man's eyes were bright. He was laughing at her inwardly. Matty felt an irresistible urge to take him down a peg.

"Why do you do that, Joseph? Do you lie for entertainment or to get the better of people?"

The eyes narrowed, became more like the eyes Matty remembered at the store. She didn't stop.

"You have quite an imagination. Why don't you write your own poetry instead of lying to your wife? She showed me a poem you said you wrote. It was by William Blake."

"Just as likely to be Edgar Allen Poe. Can you believe that? Nobody around this den of illiteracy recognizes him, either. But Blake is better. Good stuff. I like a literary life. It suits me." The tone was casual, but there was bitter cold in it.

"It serves as an excuse for not working, doesn't it?"

"Sure."

Matty was frustrated.

"Why are you admitting this? Aren't you afraid I'll tell Mary? How would she feel?"

He pulled on his pipe slowly.

"Somethin' to think about. Ashamed or mad? Huh!" He nodded, his mind made up. "Mad." He nodded again and smiled his limited smile. His tone said he didn't care.

"You're a mean man, Joseph Briggsley."

"Sure I am."

It was too much. Matty had never encountered anyone like this before. He was both the worst liar and the most open, honest man she had ever met. And one of the most entertaining. She shook her head, smiled, and the smile turned into laughter.

Joseph wasn't amused. He pointed his pipe stem at her like a weapon.

"Look here, missy. When a man says he's mean, believe him. Don't laugh and think it's a joke. Lots o' mean men in the world. Evil ones, too. Bound to meet one oncet in a while that admits to it. If by shootin' you, I could get aholt of one idea interestin' enough to keep my mind busy the rest of my life, I'd shoot you where you sit."

He sat back, put his pipe back in his mouth and added, calmly, "If I was a hundred percent sure I could get away with it, o' course."

They sat and looked into the trees and the darkening sky until the crickets turned on the night. Nothing more was said. Matty thought she knew people, but she no longer had any idea how to feel about this strange man, much less how to talk to him or when to believe him.

Finally, Joseph finished his pipe, set his cup on the floor, pushed himself out of the rocker and hitched up his worn jeans. There was nothing to hold them up, no belly, no hips or buttocks on this pole of a man. No, not a pole, Matty thought. Not that straight. More like a locust tree, crooked and hard and not a good tree, forever sending out shoots that spoiled everything around it.

In silence, he walked ahead of her back to the station wagon, dull from lack of wax, got in and turned it around. Just before driving off, he looked at the sky and then at Matty and said one word.

"Storm."

It was said with authority, as though he were personally responsible. Then he patted the pocket of his plaid flannel shirt to make sure Matty's money was there and drove off.

She watched his car move into the shadow of the trees, feeling that, for all her years of meeting hundreds of people, perhaps only at this old house had she begun to touch the basic stuff of human nature.

21

It was long past time for dinner. In spite of the fact that the coffee still burned in her stomach, the first thing Matty did after closing the front door was go to the old, yellowed refrigerator, take out the cap-topped bottle and pour herself a glass of Joseph's wine. It wasn't cold yet and was thin and sharp, although neither was the reason it failed to offer the usual small touch of calm, like a soothing hand across her shoulders. The regret that she hadn't opted for Diazepam came immediately. She dropped into the uncomfortable straight-backed chair at the tacky little table, set the disappointing libation on the oilcloth and tried to pull her thoughts into some sort of order.

At this rate, I'm going to get an ulcer. Caffeine, alcohol and worry. Perfect recipe. Worry about it later. Like Scarlett O'Hara. For now, just survive. I won't survive if I don't eat. I don't want to eat. But it's been okay for two days. What do I make of Joseph? Why does he talk like a hick? He knows better. Must know better. He reads. It's home that counts. Home and parents. Mack Thurwell wants a big house, impressive house. Trying for a Vice Presidency. High hopes. Never get it. Bad grammar. Can't tell him, either.

This isn't getting me anywhere.

She took another sip of wine, more conscious than usual of the burn as it went down her throat.

Fix dinner!

The rush of adrenaline Joseph had produced was gone. At lunch, she had kept up a cheerful patter for the sake of the girl, but tonight she was too tired to put on a show. Who knew if she could hear it, anyway? The girl would have to settle for a silent partner.

There was enough food to choose from for a change. Joseph had renewed her supply of yogurt. He hadn't brought the low fat kind she had ordered, but it didn't matter. In spite of two days without incident, eating was a fearful experience. It wouldn't be long before her stomach would reject anything. Meanwhile, enough of yogurt, she decided. A diet should be varied. From the freezer, Matty pulled a block of frozen mixed vegetables that had seemed a healthy thing to order. They would do.

Waiting for the water to boil, Matty pondered the enigma of Joseph.

Putting on an act? Shoot me where I sat? No way! But...Something frightening. Eyes? Voice? Yes. Hard. More than that. Menacing. Yes. Menacing. Wrong about Mary. Mary wouldn't be mad. Betrayed. Humiliated. She worked hard so her talented husband might one day be published. Cruel. Can't tell her. Let her die thinking Joseph was what she thought he was. Does she think he loves her in his own way? Possible. Not a woman to question. Trusting. Can't destroy that. Maybe if they were young, if she hadn't put so many years into it...A son dead. Poor Mary...Why not poor Joseph?

The dented aluminum pot had burned dry. Matty took it to the sink to add water and start over.

Must call Tom. What should I tell him? Car trouble. That would do it. Why not have it fixed and stay?

She shook her head. It was too hard to plan when she was this tired.

Must sleep tonight. More Diazepam. Not good. Not too soon after the wine.

She looked at the clock. It was a little after seven.

Okay. I can stay awake until ten. Then Diazepam will be all right. It's okay to take it. Home soon. Fix things then. Scarlett O'Hara is ruling my life. Tom. What to tell Tom?

The water was boiling. Matty had forgotten to open the package and did so now quickly, ripping the paper off, pulling the box apart. The contents fell into the pot in a solid block which she began to stab with a fork.

Why not fix the car here? Oh, I don't know! I don't know and I don't want to think about it! At least, Tom's no good at cars. He won't offer to fix it.

The vegetables began to simmer. She stirred them with the fork, pale green baby limas, bright green peas, little orange squares of carrot.

Beautiful. Never noticed before. If you're this tired, you have to slow down and then you smell the flowers. No, not smell. Don't trust smelling.

But she did smell them. They gave off an earthy scent.

Odd. Never noticed before.

Someone's coming to get the car! That's it! And when Tom and I come back, it will, of course, be fixed! Inspiration!

Good for me! Ideas just pop into my head. I have a good brain.

No, I don't. Not any more.

She sat down and forced herself to eat.

◆　　　◆　　　◆

Matty was carefully folding the flag when the first crack of lightning startled her upright. She clenched the cloth as if for protection. Joseph had been right about the storm. Out of habit, she went onto the porch to watch as her Mother always had.

It was extraordinary. Being near the top of the mountain put her up in the sky, deep in the storm's ferocity. The knives of lightning were all around and the thunder shivered inside her. The trees protested, tried to wave away the rain that made its own thunder as it beat down on the tin roof. In a way she didn't understand, it suited Matty. In her well-ordered life, she had been rarely short of sleep and the lack of it created a sense of unreality, of things coming apart. The storm was a perfect companion.

◆　　　◆　　　◆

"Tom? Can you hear me? I couldn't wait until this storm was over. It seems as though it will go on forever."

"Re—" snaps and pops "—errible."

"I know. There's a storm," she yelled. It was important to get the message across. "Can you come tomorrow afternoon?"

There was no response.

"Come tomorrow afternoon?" she repeated even more loudly.

The crackling allowed her to hear only "…good…time…Inn?"

"After church. After two or so," she shouted three times before she was sure he understood. "No Inn" finally got across, too. She hadn't the energy to dress up and eat out.

It was too difficult to communicate, too difficult to tell the tale of the car. It was only as she hung up that she realized the story of the car wasn't necessary. All she had to do was get Tom here Sunday. Then would be the right time to tell him about her problems, her need to see Neil. The inspiration about the car problem was—from some unremembered source, memory finished the sentence "—the fruit of a disordered mind." She went back out into the tempest where she seemed to belong.

In time, the storm moved eastward, leaving behind only the crisp smell of ozone and a trail of ragged clouds. Matty got up from her rocker and realized that she was cold. She hadn't minded the gusts blowing rain under the porch's protection, spraying her from time to time. It had seemed cleansing, the storm's fury filling her mind, driving out less comfortable thoughts. Now she badly needed to warm up.

◆　　◆　　◆

Immersed in hot water in the old tub, she decided it had been a pretty good day in spite of a level of fatigue that made her feel ill. Between Evie and Joseph, she was now sure the girl was nothing her imagination had produced. She had never really been able to believe that, anyway. After Neil fixed her, she could come back and learn more. It still seemed that something needed to be done for the girl. Finding out what that was would be the new focus of her search.

Her little visitor was with her now, unseen. It no longer bothered Matty to be in the bath. The girl must have seen her naked many times.

"Did you see the storm from the window? I'm sorry you couldn't come outside. Will I ever find out why you can't come outside? How will I ever find out what you need if you can't tell me? We both need help, don't we? Can you hear me?"

It seemed that she ought to be able to, although there was no reason to think so. Was it possible she could hear but not very well? Something Evelyn had said gave her the impression she was supposed to speak clearly and a little more loudly. Somewhere in the last few days that had been forgotten. Did the girl understand she was going home? She had mentioned going home when talking to Neil, but it had been only a question. How had that ended? She couldn't remember. It was time to get out of the tub. A foot, pink from the hot water, came up out of the water and fell back. It would be much easier just to go to sleep like a baby in a warm, wet womb.

A good day. Exhausting, but exciting. Maybe exhausting because it was exciting, but good because she was going home tomorrow, because of Joseph and Evie, because, although her thinking showed the effects of fatigue, her senses had worked just fine.

That thought had no sooner passed through her mind than she lost awareness of her body. It was the same as when she had been dancing. The warm water was no longer there nor the feel of cool porcelain against her forearms, just like the other time. Only this time it wasn't as brief. There was no doubt it was happening. She told her hands to grip the sides of the tub and squeezed her eyes shut. It was terrifying to see her body when she couldn't feel it. Her eyes flew open again. It was even more terrifying to have no proof that she existed.

She began to sob helplessly.

It was almost as though the tears turned sensation back on.

Matty didn't even count the pills this time, just threw a few down her throat and then lay down, arms stiffly at her sides, to await the few hours of sleep that might eventually come.

22

It was nine fifteen. A recording had told Matty how to find the church and that the service began at ten. She had been up since five. The bran cereal was revolting and she wondered how it had been possible to eat it every morning for so long. Reading on the couch, her head had dropped from time to time, but no real sleep had come. There was no way to determine whether her drowsiness came from too little sleep or too much Diazepam. It seemed physically impossible to do anything but just sit and hope energy would come from somewhere when it was needed. Nothing was packed, but Tom would do that, would be glad to have something to do for her after he had heard her news. The same slacks she had worn to Frederick would have to do, this time with a sweater. It was much too cool this morning to wear the blue skirt and blouse. Or perhaps tiredness made her feel the cold.

Another cup of coffee to stay awake? Her stomach said "No" and that verdict was accepted. Perhaps it wasn't too early to leave.

◆   ◆   ◆

She was grateful the church was near, only those two turns off the main road and there was little traffic on this cool, gray Sunday morning. Towering over its inadequate frill of chrysanthemums, the handsome brick building sat in a sea of crumbling asphalt. The tall steeple had a bell that wasn't ringing. It was probably too early, only nine thirty. Why did so many churches have bright red doors? There were four cars in the parking lot. Deciding she wasn't up to social chatter, Matty parked off to one side and slid down onto the seat for a few more minutes of rest.

A car door slamming jarred her from half-consciousness. Nine fifty. Time to go in. She got out and followed the couple that had just arrived. He was wearing jeans and a flannel shirt, she dark blue slacks and a flowered knit top riding up over ample buttocks. Matty felt better. Jane's pink suit had been a little intimidating, but slacks were apparently acceptable.

Inside the doors a chubby boy handed her a program, his eyes averted. No doubt he was too shy to do his duty and greet her. She slid into the back pew and took stock of the interior.

It was surprisingly elegant for the rural area. Stained glass windows washed the polished mahogany pews with muted color. There were far too few people for the size of the church, mostly clustered down front in the center, heads turning as they talked. Only two people were in her row, women with their hair of mixed white, gray and black twisted into lopsided buns. The older of the two—the mother?—had a dented chrome walker beside her. Up front, Evelyn was impossible to miss, her red hair like fire in a sea of ashes. Jane Goodman's pink suit was easy to spot, too, short, iron-gray cap of hair above it. Mary was harder to find. Most of them were Marys.

Matty hadn't been to church since her mother's funeral almost twenty years ago and didn't look forward to the next hour. In a church this small, how good could the pastor be? Or the music? In spite of Mary's comment that Evelyn was in the choir, there seemed to be none to offer a musical break today and the impressive organ stood abandoned as another gray head hunched over a piano, its owner playing softly and competently. She remembered sermons as endless ordeals. The service was something to get through until the meeting with Jane. The bench felt uncomfortably hard already.

The pastor, pink-faced, white-haired and surely too old to be working, appeared and the chatter yielded slowly to silence as the service began with a short prayer and announcements. Matty tried to make this a time of rest, conserving what little energy she had. It seemed that one of the announcements had been aimed at her, but she hadn't been listening.

There was an unexpected hurdle and Matty decided not to try to jump it. The Lutheran service was highly structured, requiring the congregation to stand, sit and kneel frequently on padded stools that ran the length of the pew and read multiple responses from the books on the back of the pews. Matty left the book in the rack, got up and down when the others did and just listened, often with her eyes closed by tiredness. It was soothing. Many of the phrases were echoes from her childhood, recited with subdued earnestness by the little cluster of mostly women ahead of her and the two in her row. There had been some changes over the years. "Thee" had become "you," no more "eths" on the ends of words. Nothing sounded quite right without them. She could hear Evelyn's strong, clear alto always, especially in the hymns. They were even more familiar than the spoken words and brought back memories of singing them with her mother. Tears filled her eyes and she blinked them back.

The psalm they read together was beautiful. "I lift up mine eyes to the hills…" It would be wonderful to believe there was such help. "Turn it over to God," her mother had always said, especially in the last year. She had been able to do that. How did you do that?

The sermon was based on a Bible verse that initially sounded absurd: "I believe. Help my unbelief." Evelyn's head bobbed in agreement. Matty, having missed the Biblical reference, looked at her bulletin. Mark 9:24. Her father's words, "We are a data-based culture," came back to her as the minister put his finger directly on the problem her father had always had with religion and which he had passed on to her.

"Why should we have unreasoning faith? Faith in what? There is too much to choose from and little proof."

At least the pastor asked the right question. Her father would have liked that. She became more attentive.

"Some are blessed with a lifelong certainty in the existence and loving presence of God and his son Jesus, but most of us have periods of doubt. Such periods are times of struggle and even despair, but for most of us, this testing of our faith is necessary and we come out at the end with a more enduring faith. Thus the man says 'I believe. Help my unbelief,' something which I have said myself many times."

Perhaps this was going to be more than just a waiting period until she and Jane could talk. But how to help unbelief? Just as with her ghost, proof was needed. How was he going to get around that?

The reedy but firm voice seemed to know where it was going.

"Christianity has gone through a time of authority, when believers couldn't read and needed to be told. They believed what they were told because the educated seemed to be the ones who knew. Then the age of science came and we were sure that with it would come the answers. Science has not failed us in all ways, but it has failed us in this one."

Here the preacher paused for a sip of water, the hand that held the glass trembling. The break was clearly more for rest than to ease thirst, but when he continued, his voice was still strong enough to reach the back row.

"Many of the explanations and discoveries of science only opened up more mysteries. Einstein believed in God. Now we are entering an era of a new kind of exploration. Cults abound. Eastern religions attract some of us. More important than a walk on the moon is the discovery that man is a spiritual animal. Something innate drives us to seek God. Or do we hear God seeking us?"

Matty's thoughts took their own path. Did God and her little ghost have anything to do with each other? Another nagging thought that was absurd, but would not go away was closely related to her attitude toward those who believed in God: was something in her creating the ghost? Memories and speculation occupied her for some minutes before she heard the word "proof" and came once more to a labored attention.

"Jesus said, 'I have many things to say to you, but you cannot hear them now.' Most of us still cannot hear them now. Our vision is too limited. We have only glimpses of the great truth of God and so faith is easily lost and we are frustrated by the lack of permanent, universally acknowledged proof. Proof is given to us one by one and sometimes only off and on throughout our lives. We believe in a personal God. It seems that the only external proof is in the efficacy of prayer. Even medical science now acknowledges its healing power. Beyond that, you must look within. Do I mean you must seek God? Not precisely. I mean that God is seeking you.

Always. When your faith fails, remember that it is frail because we are frail. You need only open your mind and your heart. God will speak to you if you just let him. Let us now, in silence, sit and ask God to speak to each of us."

It seemed that the pastor might be giving himself an easy out. Matty was probably the only one who felt such skepticism. The others had followed the instruction and heads were bowed under a deep silence. For the first time, a few outside sounds penetrated the interior, birds, a passing car, the purr of a gentle but persistent wind.

Matty was tempted to give the pastor's suggestion a try. How could she deny there was a God when only a week ago she would have been even more adamant in denying the existence of ghosts? In any case, closing her eyes and dropping her head was the part of the service she was most grateful for. And as long as she had gone that far, she decided to ask, silently, "God, are you there? It would be really nice if you were. Excuse what I'm saying. I don't remember how to pray. Anyway, the preacher said just to listen, so I'm doing that, okay?"

There was no resounding, "Sure, that's fine," from above, but praying was peaceful. She was aware of an unexpected unity with the others in the church. Maybe she'd try this again sometime, just to see…

It was over at last. It had been better than she had expected. She had stumbled through the hymns with a minimum of embarrassment. Perhaps among the many changes were shorter sermons, but, more likely, time was just passing more quickly now that she was older. As the pastor ended his benediction, she rose gratefully and began to plan how to join Jane without attracting attention. The minister would pass her as he went to the front door…

But he didn't. He exited by a door near the altar. A few people followed him, including Evelyn and the parents with the chubby boy and two little girls, but most of them headed straight for Matty, Mary leading the pack.

"Well, you did come! I am pleased! Everbody, this here's Matty what's stayin' in that old log house like I tol' you. I asked her and she came!"

Mary was clearly pleased at her accomplishment.

Nearly a dozen names were thrown at her and Matty nodded, smiled and shook an assortment of hands, some callused, some soft, all gripping hers firmly and at length. From the babble she finally extricated the universal message: She must come for coffee and doughnuts in the kitchen. Was that the announcement the minister had aimed at her?

Mary moved past her. "I can't stay. Good tourist business Sunday. They'll all take good care of you."

Astonishingly, she gave Matty a possessive little hug and hurried out the front door.

Over Mary's shoulder, she had seen Jane, alone up front, unobtrusively moving her head from left to right.

Got it, Jane. Food is out.

There were only three men, standing in the back of the women, saying little but nodding encouragement, joining the women in welcoming her. Was church always this friendly, she wondered? Matty remembered that her Mother talked after church while passing women made an embarrassing fuss over her and Father waited. She had always hated all those pats on the head and was grateful for the six inches she shot up in one year that ended that particular ordeal.

"I'm sorry. It's very nice of you. But I have an appointment. I'd like to come back again."

A chorus of invitations assured her she was welcome and one woman confided, "We're a dying church, you know. All oldsters except for the Clarksons and their kids."

"Well—*Evie!*" objected another.

"Yes...well...Evelyn." It was a reluctant concession. "We like to see young people here. Young people don't seem to know how much support a church can give."

"Well, Josie," a sharp voice corrected her. "You sound like it's got nothin' to do with God."

"Well, of course it does," Josie said mildly. "It's just that God could use us to help some younger people, too, couldn't he?"

"Oh, well, then." The voice was no longer sharp. "We know how hard it is with both parents working." She looked at Matty inquiringly.

"Or when there's only one parent," a third woman offered.

Matty recognized the beginning of a major inquisition and excused her-self again, turned and, following the direction of Jane Goodman's gaze, went back out the bright red doors.

23

As the heavy door closed behind Matty, Jane Goodman appeared around the corner of the church. She was an unattractive figure, all graceless angles. Her skin was unevenly tanned, her salt and pepper, straight hair cut bluntly, chin length. The pink suit belonged on someone else. Matty wondered, not for the first time, why some women never aimed their intelligence at their appearance.

The strong, irregular face didn't even turn in Matty's direction.

"Get into your car and follow me," she said as she passed, just loud enough for Matty to hear.

"I don't mind talking right here," Matty said toward the retreating figure.

"I do," floated back to her, a reminder that Jane didn't want to be associated with the combination of Evelyn's ghosts, grandmother and the old log house.

What interesting tale lay ahead? Matty hurried toward her car as the pink suit folded, disappeared into a faded blue Plymouth. The Plymouth pulled out as soon as the Acura's engine started.

The road seemed endless as Matty's half-closed eyes stayed glued to the flaking blue paint on the rear end of Jane's car. Finally, it pulled onto a weedy area with just enough gravel sprinkled here and there to identify it as a place to park. Matty pulled over, turned the key in the ignition and sat, muscles in her shoulders and arms pulled down by gravity, her head dropping.

A door slammed. Curiosity made it possible to reach for her own door handle.

Jane Goodman was already on the move, her sturdy shoes flattening the tall grass one step at a time on the way up the gradual slope of the hill. It wasn't a welcoming place. A few piled stones indicated that low walls had once offered a more formal entrance to the overgrown expanse that was home to darkened and tilted gravestones. Some sunshine would have helped, but there was a low, continuous cloud cover as though the world were wrapped in wrinkled tissue paper. On the top of the hill, dark slabs silhouetted against the sky seemed to warn her away. Jane stopped and looked back. Matty could feel her impatience and moved forward through the crumbling rock entrance and started to climb, her thighs complaining at every step.

"Here."

Just below the crest of the hill, Jane had stopped in front of five small gravestones, identical except for the angles at which they were leaning. She stuck out a hand.

It took Matty a moment to realize that she was supposed to shake it. The grip was uncomfortably firm.

"The old church site. Nothing left but the graveyard." Jane's eyes swept the desolate field. "We used to keep it up. We're getting too old. Seems like all the young ones are evangelicals now. Or nothing at all. Meet over in—but that's not why we're here." She turned to Matty. "You know anything about the people who used to live in that house?"

"Names. Just some names."

Jane frowned at her. "You're tired. Or is something wrong with you?"

"Right. Both."

"Sit down then. Here. My favorite seat." Jane pointed to a horizontal memorial.

With an ease Matty envied, Jane arranged herself Indian style on a fallen slab opposite with no concern for her pink suit or the large amount of lean thigh the posture exposed. It was a relief to drop her tired body onto the roughened black stone, but it was harder than the Lutheran pews.

"Why are we here?" she demanded more irritably than was diplomatic.

"Sorry. Didn't know you were sick, did I? Couldn't be seen at your house. Didn't want you seen at mine. This just seemed appropriate." An awkward gesture indicated the black and pitted gravestones beside them. They were less than a foot square, an inadequate testimony to a life, however short. "These," she said.

"Yeah. So?" *Patience,* Matty told herself. *I need what this woman knows.* She forced her tired eyes to focus on the absurd, pink stick figure and sat down hard on the nervous laugh that fought to get out. *Control, Matty. This is not the time to fall apart.*

Jane seemed immune to the effect she was having. "This is the family that lived there, in that house," she said. "I rubbed half the tombstones in this graveyard before I found them. These five—all the same last name and date of death. Month and year only. September, 1862. No day. Means they weren't sure. Civil War battle here that month, sort of. Holding action, they call it."

Matty looked at the random indentations on the weather-beaten stone. "You've got to be kidding. They don't say anything." The words that came out of her mouth still surprised her with their rudeness. The sound, too, was not the reassuring tone her job demanded.

Jane gave her a long look. "No one of them, it's true. But they use a pattern when they make tombstones for a family. To make them all look alike. I studied them together. This is the name I was looking for. Schrader."

Matty put her elbows on her knees and cradled her head in her palms. It helped a little. "Yeah. That was one of the names."

Jane showed emotion for the first time. "You already knew that? Their name?"

"Question is, why did you spend all that time doing those—" She squelched the word "silly." "—rubbings if you already had the name. Did you need the date? That would be in the church records."

"No. I had the date, more or less. Church burned down in 1910. Nothing left. The tombstones were a kind of...something tangible, I guess. How did you find the name?"

"Grantee-grantor records in Frederick. Wanting something tangible I can understand. But do we have to stay here? I'm freezing!"

The sweater Matty wore was no barrier against the wind.

"Sorry. Let's go back to the cars. Your car. It's more comfortable than mine."

"Yes. Let's. What else..."

But Jane, as usual, was ahead of her, already marching downhill. A few crows, startled into activity, flew off, their raucous calls both appropriate and offensive. Matty pushed her palms against the gritty stone to help herself up. Standing made her even more vulnerable to the wind. Going down was easier than coming up except for an alarming tendency to slip on the damp grass. At the bottom, Matty took one quick look back. The crows were coming back. It was a Halloween card.

Jane was waiting, not patiently. Apparently she deemed it inappropriate to get in the car before Matty arrived.

Once inside, the two women turned towards each other as much as the car allowed. It wasn't comfortable for Matty to be this close, knees almost touching between the armrest and dashboard. Jane wasn't a comfortable person.

"What does she look like?" Jane asked. "Is she pretty?"

"Pretty? You know there is a girl, then!" Relief flooded Matty.

"Silly thing to ask, first off, wasn't it? But, yes. Was she ugly, scary, or pretty like you?"

"Yes. She is pretty, but not like me," Matty said, changing the verb from past to present. "Is that important?"

"Life is different when you're pretty. I'm not. I look like my father and his mother, my grandmother. Doesn't matter so much for a man. For a woman, your face dictates your life."

Matty was not here to discuss Jane's opportunities for happiness. How had their conversation taken this absurd turn?

"Okay, so it's good to know she's real, you know about her, but what else? You haven't told me anything but her name!" An uncomfortable suspicion was growing that this peculiar woman's testimony might not be any more believable than her own. "You don't even know what she looked like? Are we just here so you can pick my brain?" Tears of disappointment and frustration burned in the back of Matty's eyes.

It didn't seem to matter whether she was polite or angry. Jane maintained the same expression, as unchanging as the carved angels on the hill above them.

"You've been searching for years and you want me to tell you about her?" Matty fought her tears with anger. "We could have covered that over the phone. I don't know anything."

"I think my grandmother knew your girl."

Silence was a third inhabitant in the car. Jane's direct gaze held her while Matty's mind swam with the possibilities that one sentence contained. How could she have forgotten the grandmother?

"Tell me!"

"Something—someone—in that house drove my grandmother insane. She was a school teacher. It was a big deal for a woman to buy a house for herself then, but her father had left her some money. I'm told she was a strong and independent sort. Not when I knew her. She never made much sense. Sometimes rambled on about some girl who was after her—"

"Not my girl," Matty interrupted. "My—" It was hard to use the word. "—ghost is sweet. Silent, shy, sympathetic. She certainly doesn't chase me. Quite the opposite."

"Sweet? Now, that's not what I expected." When Jane frowned, her whole face participated. "Well, I don't see—Mamaw—Grandmother—only stayed in the house a short time. By the time she left, she wasn't so strong any more. Not quite right. Had to quit teaching. Always seemed like this girl she was afraid of must have been in that house."

"So that's why I'm here? To analyze your Grandmother?"

"Sorry. Wanted to see you, see if you were someone I could trust, first off. Then—I want to believe something specific in that house affected Mamaw, that it wasn't just a genetic thing, ramblings with nothing to account for it. Now I know at least this girl was real and I thank you for that. Maybe I'm getting too old to worry about it, but I want to believe I won't ever get like her. Everyone used to say how much I was like her, back when I was young. I know I'm odd. Don't you think I'm odd?"

It certainly was odd to be so embarrassingly forthright and Matty was at a loss to respond. This countryside seemed to be populated with eccentrics.

"Well, I think I'm odd, too," was the best she could do and there was an undeniable element of truth in the statement.

"You? You certainly don't look odd. Do you feel that way just since you were in that house?"

"I don't think looks have anything to do with it and no, the house has nothing to do with it."

Matty leaned her head back against the car window. Disappointment fed her exhaustion. The suspicion was forming that her companion's curiosity resulted from a lack of anything else to do in her life. She had gleaned some small pieces of comfort. Someone else believed in the girl. She had a name. It was time to give in to her body's demands and go home.

"There's more," Jane said, a comment that lifted Matty's head again.

"There has to be more," Matty echoed as a thought rose from her fogged brain. "You knew her name! What else did your grandmother tell you? About the girl?"

"Nothing intelligible. Only what I've told you. Used to cower, call for help and say 'Go away!' Stuff like that. The rest made no sense, not even real words sometimes."

"Then how did you know it was a girl she was afraid of?"

Jane held up an index finger, as though it were a reminder. "Oh yes. That. Mamaw prayed sometimes. Prayed for God to take the girl away."

"But it seems…How did she know the girl's name?"

"Alice."

"Alice," Matty echoed flatly. *I'm supposed to know who Alice is?*

"A friend of Grandmother's. She knew what had happened in that house. Back then."

She knew? My God! Why didn't we start here? Hope and impatience overcame tiredness. "And?"

"Alice didn't believe in ghosts. She thought Mamaw just fed the story into her delusions."

"Story?" Matty's elation began to fade. "A story about a girl engaged to a boy nearby? She hid in the basement and was maybe raped?"

Jane managed an expression this time. Her eyebrows lifted slightly and she tilted her head forward. "Not rape. That wouldn't fit. But, yes. That's the story I mean. How do you know of it?"

"Joseph."

"Oh. That old liar."

"Precisely." Matty's head dropped back again.

"Pre—Oh. I see what you mean. You didn't believe him. Guess I wouldn't, either."

"He was just feeding me what I wanted to hear."

"Not entirely. We all know the story. Probably some of the details are wrong, but we know the house where the boy lived was burned down. That's in historical records. There was a battle here—"

"Yes, yes. I know about that. General Hill."

"Lieutenant General Hill."

Matty shut her eyes. *Get on with it, lady!*

"Very sad. This area was divided, you know."

No. This I didn't know. So what?

"Alice said she and her—They were engaged. On opposite sides. Didn't matter in the end. They both died, didn't they?"

Did they? How the hell am I supposed to know? "Yes? So? The girl. What about the girl? How did she die? Where?"

Jane pursed her thin lips and nodded, as though affirming that her memory was accurate. "Only girl in the family. Mother was dead, you see. Brothers, three of them, and father went off to fight. Girl was hidden in the basement for safety. No other explanation. No doubt told to stay there 'til they came for her and—" Jane paused for effect. "They never did."

"So? So she came up and went—What? I mean, she wouldn't have stayed down there."

"It was a hospital. Would you come up with all those horrifying sounds?"

"Yeah, I would."

"Maybe so. Maybe so." Jane shook her head as if indicating that she, too, might not have been intimidated. "But it would have seemed safe down there. And she could hear them. The Southerners—her family was confederate—didn't win the fight. The Northerners were in charge so she would likely have wanted to wait for them to leave, for her family to come get her. She would have had food and water. It was the kitchen then. Anyway, she did wait for them."

"But they died!"

"Yes."

"Yes, *what*?" Jane seemed to have no sense at all of what Matty needed to know. "She wouldn't have stayed forever!"

"She did, in a manner of speaking. After the war, the house was taken by the County—"

Tax sale. Matty could see the words on the old record.

"—and the new owners found her body. Must have been quite a surprise. Decayed and all."

Jane's lack of concern was offensive. This was her sweet little girl they were talking about!

"That's absurd! Why would she stay down there 'til she died?"

"To hide her, they would have had to hide the entrance. Nail a board over it. Load the closet with heavy junk nobody would bother with. Something. Nobody knows for sure. Anyway, she didn't get out, so must be she couldn't for some reason."

"The window..." But even as Matty said it, both women knew the windows were too small to serve as exits. "Alice said this?"

Jane nodded. "Some of it's speculation, of course. But it seems right."

"I want to talk to her."

"Can't. Maybe through Evelyn."

"Evelyn...Oh. You mean Alice is dead."

"Don't take much stock in those séance things. Can try if you like. What I need to know...What you said before—This has to be the same girl my grandmother talked about. She doesn't scare you? How can a ghost not scare you? Mamaw owned the house. Had a reason to try and stay. But you? You could leave, not wait to go nuts."

"I am nuts."

That seemed to shut Jane down and there was silence in the car as each woman's thoughts took off in the direction that interested her.

Matty began shaking her head in unconscious denial. Vivid in her mind was the dark basement, the smell of damp earth. "No," she murmured, multitudes of thoughts flooding her mind.

Would the girl have dared to light a lamp? Probably not if she feared the men whose voices she heard above. There was no immediate need to leave her sanctuary. Maybe I would have stayed hidden, too. Then...when they left and her brothers, her father, didn't come... Would a light have shown through those two little windows? How tall were the trees then? Did anyone live near enough to see? Probably very few homes in the area. It was a huge property then, no doubt a farm. Description in the old records impossible to follow now. How much food and water was there? Starvation? Illness? September. This same month. Was that significant? Cool, but not cold. Lonely. Oh, dear God, how lonely, how frightening, wondering where her family was, what had become of them, why they didn't come and get her!

If was as if Matty herself were in that basement, listening, waiting, afraid. Matty knew fear. She began rubbing her chin, her mouth, her cheeks, unconsciously. It was not something she normally did.

"No!" The story was not acceptable. "Your grandmother and her friend couldn't know all that! Rumor, just as Joseph said. It was just rumor. It was a long time ago."

"It seems so to you. Grandmother was born in 1872. Alice was, I think, about four years older."

A new kind of pain grew in Matty, a grieving for what a young girl might have suffered, a girl she wanted to help but couldn't. *How can I pity myself for silly psychological problems? I have already lived longer than this child. Please, God, don't let it be true!* She could feel warm tears moving down her cold cheeks.

Jane's voice came to her with a gentleness not heard before.

"You're like Mamaw, aren't you? You feel things too much."

Matty heard the car door open.

Then it shut and Jane Goodman was gone.

24

Matty looked at the intrusive console next to her and longed for an old-fashioned bench seat to stretch out on for a while before driving home. Then she remembered her seat dropped almost all the way down. Stupid to have forgotten, but it was a feature she had never used and her mind wasn't working right. Nor was her stomach, which was supposed to sit there quietly, not lurch and boil like this. Eating less than was required every day had created a persistent hunger. She took a TicTac from her purse. It only made her salivary glands burn and increased the craving for food even more. Sleep must wait. She had to get home and face the ordeal of eating. Why still this fear of eating when there had been no loss of taste for—was it three?—days now. Fear was a huge part of her that never seemed completely to go away. Even now, she was anxious about backing out of this parking area.

She looked right and left four times before entering the highway, afraid to trust her eyesight or her judgment. Now that the stimulation of talking to Jane, the first excitement of hearing a possible explanation for her ghost, was over, Matty was appalled by her weakness. Her eyes didn't want to stay open, her hands hung from the bottom of the steering wheel, limp arms at her sides resenting every necessary movement. Keeping pressure on the accelerator took real effort. After the turn onto the main road, an old pickup truck came up behind and was tailgating, its proximity irritating until Matty realized she was going less than forty in a fifty-five mile zone. At sixty, the truck receded behind her, but sixty felt dangerously fast.

Rejecting the compelling desire to think about Alice's story, Matty forced herself to tend solely to driving. Get home, get food, then flop.

Surely then sleep would come. Tom would be taking her to Neil soon. Very soon. The solace of that thought would help her sleep.

The old driveway had never looked better. There would be no traffic there. It seemed to take an extraordinary amount of pressure on the gas pedal to get up the hill, but Matty could feel herself begin to relax. The final sharp left turn toward the house was just ahead. Her weak arms failed her. The turn lacked the necessary energy and fell short. The car bounced out of the ruts, aimed down the mountain and ran head first into a tree.

Matty started shaking.

How could I do that?

The remembered anxiety from the old accident overwhelmed her. She leaned back and let it have her, knowing it was only temporary. Her breath was shallow, tight, audible. She felt hot. Her pounding heart seemed to be pushing most of her blood to her ears where it resounded with every heartbeat.

It faded slowly. Sanity took over. Below her, the mountain fell away frighteningly. *God bless the tree,* she thought and then wondered at her language. Was church having an influence on her?

My poor car. Have I dented you?

Surprisingly, she didn't much care. It could be fixed. She uttered a small sound that was almost a laugh. It wouldn't be necessary to lie to Tom about the car needing repair!

The overreaction was due to tiredness, hunger and leftover emotional baggage. Rest and food and Tom and doctors who knew what to do would make it all right. In the meantime, she had to take care of herself. She was fragile, vulnerable. That must be respected.

She managed to back the car up and pull very slowly and with more accuracy into the guiding ruts. It took nothing from there, just a slight pressure on the gas pedal and she was home.

Her stomach heaved slightly as she opened the door and Matty spoke to herself as she would to a child.

"It's okay. We're going to eat something. We're going to eat just a little something. It doesn't matter if we don't taste a bite or two. That's okay.

Neil is going to fix that. And Tom is coming soon. How soon is Tom coming?"

The old round clock announced the time, eight past twelve. *Soon. I said two o'clock, didn't I? Or was it one? There was so much static. I don't remember. Something about church people inviting me to lunch? Did I say that or just think it?*

Matty shook her head, discovering in the process that she had a severe headache.

It doesn't matter. Tom will be here soon. Thank God he's been here before and can't get lost. There's that God again. What is it with me?

Knowing it was the wrong thing to do, Matty nevertheless headed straight for the refrigerator and Joseph's awful wine, downing half a glass instantly. It was scalding all the way down but tasted just right, comforting, promising. The quickest foods were yogurt or ice cream. Yogurt sounded sour. Ice cream, neglected since the raspberry disaster, would be better. Much too cold, but acceptable. She took the carton out of the freezer and grabbed the spoon still in the sink from her breakfast cereal. There was no loss of taste.

"See. It's okay," she said, not sure what part of herself she was addressing. "It's just fine. Have some more." She gobbled down a few more spoonfuls. It came then. A bite, a big bite, she couldn't taste or feel. Her stomach churned and she was afraid she was going to vomit.

She leaned over the sink, all her consciousness concentrated on keeping down the food. Her fingers gripped the edge of the stained porcelain. The few bites must stay down. She needed it. *Think about something else*, she ordered, and turned to the window for distraction. On the porch, a squirrel sat on the railing, motionless as a statue.

"Hoo," she called inanely and the squirrel looked toward the window, locking eyes with her for an instant before leaping out of sight.

It had been enough. The food slid slowly back down. She looked down at the carton. A few bites of ice cream were not enough but would have to do for now. Sleep was next. Turning to the stairs, she caught a glimpse of a plump, white arm.

"Hello," she said. "You're there, aren't you? Come to offer me sympathy, have you? I could use it."

Matty turned and the girl stayed in place.

"Good," Matty said. "Don't be shy today. I need to talk to you. I think I learned something about you today."

The girl registered no expression.

Matty didn't know how to start. Jane's horrifying tale needed careful introduction.

"Your name is Schrader, isn't it?"

The girl disappeared.

Matty almost cried. In her condition, it didn't take much.

"Don't go. I want you here when Tom comes. You looked sad, you know. If it's because of me, it's all right. I'm going home for my doctors to fix me and I'll be just fine."

Matty was aware that she sounded like a child, but that probably served the purpose better than clever chatter.

"I want you to be here when Tom comes."

Will you be here when Tom comes? And will you let me take a picture of you?

"I'm going to sleep now. Upstairs. You want to come with me?"

Matty climbed the steps, almost laughing at herself for being so weak and slow. *Old lady. Thirty-four-year-old old lady. This must have been what it was like for Dad before he lost his legs when the blood couldn't get to his muscles.* A sudden wave of understanding and affection flooded her, more than she had felt for her father in a long time. *Why do I spend so little time with him? Why do I prattle on about things that he doesn't care about? There are things that do matter. Things he needs to tell me like he tells Tom. My fault. All my fault. Must fix that.*

Matty dropped onto the bed. The girl hadn't followed her, hadn't taken her position in the chair. That was all right. The only thing that mattered, for the moment, was that, at last, she had a little food and could shut her eyes. It was too much trouble to lift her legs. They hung over the edge. Later, she would lift them and take off her shoes. For now, it was wonderful just to lie there and close her eyes. Some of the feeling of illness began to dissipate. Sleep would surely come.

It didn't. The abandoned cemetery, the leaning slabs of weathered stone under a low hanging sky, the absurd figure of Jane in that improbable pink suit, created a surreal painting behind her eyelids. The basement floated in and out, blessedly empty. Pictures from the story were too painful to imagine, though the words wouldn't go away. Tears slid out from under Matty's eyelids. *The terrible, terrible story that I want to talk about with the girl, my poor little girl. When I have the strength. But even then, will I be able to bring up that subject? Look how the accident affected me. I'm still a mess. What must you be like, child? But you've had longer to heal...Long, long time... Will you talk? No... You'll just disappear again. I can trust Jane. She believes the story. Didn't she?* Matty tried to remember. *No. Jane wasn't sure about anything. She was just collecting information. It was Alice. Alice knew the history, but didn't believe there was a ghost. And Jane tied them together, the history and the ghost with Grandmother. Mamaw. Funny. It was hard to imagine Jane calling anyone Mamaw. Jane's story doesn't work for me. No one could be afraid of this sweet little... Yes, they could. She's a ghost. Probably...*

It was no use. Her eyes stung as she opened them. She wasn't going to be able to sleep and she found these were thoughts she didn't want to deal with right now. The Diazepam was beside her, but she was afraid to take it in her condition and after wine. It might knock her out. What would Tom think? Poor Tom had enough to worry about as it was. "When your body has to sleep, it will sleep," Neil had said, cautioning her as he wrote the first prescription.

Right, Neil. Like I don't need sleep now? At least, I can rest. Just lie here. Feels good. I was going to bake a cake for Tom. Sort of reassure him that things were...somewhat normal. Sure. Climb Mount Everest, too. Fly to the moon...

She could pull her feet up on the bed now. The rest was helping. Or had she dozed off for a few minutes? There seemed to be no reason to take off her shoes. The ice cream had been an appetizer. She was even more hungry now. It was two o'clock. A small bowl of bran, half a glass of wine and a few bites of ice cream were all she had eaten since five this morning.

The cake she was going to bake for Tom sounded wonderful, but there was no way she was going to get up and go all the way downstairs.

Her cell phone tinkled its Mozart.

The phone was downstairs.

She couldn't possibly answer it. If it was Tom, she should. They had a code to let one know when the other was calling. They let the phone ring four times. Then they hung up and dialed back and let it ring only four times again unless it was important. More than four rings meant an answer was necessary. The fourth ring came and then silence before it began again.

One… Two… Three…Four…Five…

Shit! It was Tom and it was important.

She rolled over, the weight of her body pulling against her, and sat up on the bed.

Why is Tom calling? Why isn't he here?

She got up and walked across the room, paused at the doorway, hanging onto the frame, and swung around to the stairs. *Watch for the third step.* Going down wasn't too bad, easier than climbing up. She grabbed the phone on the end table at the bottom of the stairs.

"Tom?"

"Matty! I'm sorry. I may be late." His voice changed, registering concern. "You don't sound well."

"Tired. I was…sleeping." She moved to the couch and dropped onto it.

"Oh. Good. I mean, I'm really sorry to have wakened you. I don't even—Wait a minute—Amoco. This is an Amoco station outside of Frederick. It may be something about the distributor. They're checking it now. If it's just wiring—You know I take good care of my car. Tires are new, fan belts fine, muffler okay, all the usual—"

"Tom, you don't have to explain. Just—When will you get here?"

"I don't know, Matty. I'd probably have to rent a car. There's really no one here to make repairs on a Sunday, just a guy who's kind of into cars. I'll rent a car if they can't fix it in time. If you want me to."

"I do, Tom."

There was a brief silence. She had surprised him. Why would she want him to go to the trouble of renting a car just to see her for half a day? This would not have been her usual response.

"Sure. Sure. I will, Matty. If I can find a rental place. I suppose they're open on Sunday. I can get a taxi to—" He was talking fast, anxious, apologetic. "I should have found out these things before I called you. It could be some time before I get there."

"That's okay." She needed to say something to reassure him. "I'm baking you a chocolate cake."

"Great."

"Don't speed. Just get here when you can."

"Right. I will. Maybe they can fix the car."

"Got the camera?"

"Camera?"

"Yeah. The camera I need."

"You didn't mention a camera, Matty."

His voice told her he was still worried about the way she sounded. Had she forgotten to ask for the camera? There was something about a tape recorder. Was she supposed to get a tape recorder, not a camera? Best to forget it.

"Oh, that's right. Never mind. I'll let you go now."

They said the required good-byes. Matty set the phone on her chest and inhaled once, deeply. It had been good to hear Tom's voice. Why had she said she was baking that damn cake? Now she would have to do it. She pushed herself up and turned reluctantly to the kitchen, her mind already addressing the gigantic challenge of baking. There was a nine by thirteen pan somewhere. That would save some time. No need to make layers, just leave the cake in the pan. The mix was easy.

"We're going to make a cake, little ghost," she announced and it became possible.

Slowly and with great deliberation, Matty took the cake mix off the shelf and twice read the directions that she knew by heart. Then she turned on the oven and laid out a bowl, the pan, eggs, oil and a measuring cup. There was no mixer, but somehow she would find the strength to beat the batter smooth. It didn't have to be her best cake. Tom would understand. *Poor Tom.*

"We're in business, little ghost. Wonderful cake. I make my Grandmother's mocha icing. Easy, but the food of the gods. Gods. Yes. Must check into this God thing. Do you remember cake? I have some other questions for you, too, but I have to think about them for a while. And I need to concentrate. I definitely need to concentrate."

In spite of the directions, she always followed her mother's cake routine, breaking and beating the eggs first. She cracked one against the side of the bowl. Half of it went into the bowl and half onto the counter. This struck her as funny.

"If you wanna make a cake, you gotta break some eggs," she said sententiously. "No, little ghost, that's not right. Wouldn't want to give you a bum steer. That's for omelets, kid. Don't mind me. I'm dopey, see. No sleep does that. Some gas or other builds up in your brain—forget which one—and you get dopey. This seems like too much water. I don't remember this much water. Is this recipe wrong? No. Can't be. Box knows. Box is an expert. Didn't have expert boxes in your day, did you? Much easier now."

The girl was there, in front of the oak table. Matty could see pieces of her as she turned to various ingredients. At one point, reaching for the oil, she could see the whole figure. The light from the window shone through her hair, making a golden halo around the darker, silhouetted face.

"Different, isn't it, my world?"

The idle chatter had begun spontaneously. It was an effort to keep it up, but it seemed the best way to keep the girl with her. Would she ever think of a way to ask her how she had died?

The pan went into the oven.

"Do I look like someone you knew?" Matty ventured. "Are you here to take care of me like the Nanny ghost?" She turned around. "How nice."

Drunk with tiredness, she approached the figure and it disappeared.

"Too fast? Did I move too fast? Couldn't be. Not possible. Not moving fast at all. You're not here now, are you? Maybe you'll come back. I need a timer. Cell phone. Cell phone has an alarm."

Matty went back to her phone, still talking, hoping the girl would come back, but putting little thought into what she was saying.

"Sleep. A little sleep. Can't mess up that icing. Good old couch. Good old beat-up, ugly, scratchy couch."

She dropped onto it, grateful to be prone once more, and set the phone on the coffee table beside her.

Why did the girl run away? How many people had seen her? Was that why the house sold so frequently? There was nothing frightening about her. Maybe it wasn't fear. Who would want to live every day knowing someone was watching? Maybe Jane was wrong about her grandmother. Maybe she wasn't frightened away, just modest. And the girl didn't drive her nuts, she just was all by herself.

Her thoughts blurred. Images of the cemetery, the girl, Tom's car coming down the road, the broken egg, the yolk sliding into the bowl, the brown, bubbly mixture yielding to her spoon overlapped in absurd ways. Not quite asleep, her thoughts and visions drifted to a comfortable distance until her nose told her before the cell phone alarm that she had to get up again.

"Get up, get up, the cake is calling," she crooned as she mustered the energy to rise and turn off the alarm. It wouldn't do to run down the battery now. Hunger helped. Had she remembered to put the butter for the icing out to soften?

She tried to hurry to the kitchen, but speed wasn't possible. On top of the oven, the yellow stick had begun to melt softly into the sides of a small bowl.

"Good for me."

She had no recollection of putting it there.

The cake was done, crisp at the edges and pulling away slightly from the pan.

"See? The nose knows. Knows better than the box."

She grabbed a dish towel and, using it as hot pads, moved the cake from oven to refrigerator as she always did when she was in a hurry to ice a cake. Her stomach cried out for a piece now, before the icing.

"No. We're going to do this properly. It will be even better with icing."

Or am I afraid of losing the taste and never liking chocolate cake again? Go away. Don't like that thought!

Matty dumped the confectioner's sugar and cocoa on top of the butter, added a teaspoon of vanilla and checked to make sure there was coffee left over from breakfast. It would have to be heated and added at the last moment. She had moved slowly. Maybe the cake was cool? She opened the refrigerator, ordering her hand not to go near the wine, but allowing it to linger briefly near the yogurt. Her stomach turned over and her hand moved on. Nothing cold. Nothing with any acid. The cake looked much more acceptable, warm, sweet carbs. One touch of the shining brown surface told her she wasn't thinking straight. Of course it was still hot.

She wandered back into the living room but didn't sit down. It was too hard to get up and smelling the cake had strengthened the gnawing in her stomach. To get away from the aroma that permeated the house, Matty walked out onto the porch and stared into the trees, thinking how often she had done exactly this in the last week.

"I need a house on my own mountain," she whispered to the quiet scene. The sun was low in the sky, gilding everything it could reach and sending long shadows where it couldn't. Just surviving wasn't enough. Making money, climbing steadily up the financial ladder had been exhilarating, but it hadn't been good for her. When trouble came, it offered no strength, no solace. Church had been interesting today. This little girl seemed to offer something. If her problem turned out to be something serious, could she turn to them? Would this place, this peaceful, green place, make it easier to bear? It seemed possible, at this moment.

Familiar tears slid down her cheeks. She ignored them. It was trouble to wipe them away and what was the point? She had a right to cry, anyway. There was a cake cooling that she would be afraid to eat. Would the day come when there would be no more taste of chocolate, when she would never again feel Tom's hands touch her?

Enough! She shook her head as if to throw off such thoughts and went back to the kitchen. Cool or not, the cake was going to be iced and eaten!

She stubbed her toe on the door sill.

"Clumsy," she told herself. "Pick up your feet. And be careful with the cake, for God's sake!"

Lord's name in vain. Is that what I am doing? Never been quite sure what that phrase meant. Maybe I shouldn't do that any more if I'm going to consider Him a possibility.

She had become accustomed to talking and singing in the kitchen and, unconsciously, she began humming "As Time Goes By" and then, dissatisfied with that, switched to "Lazybones," which made her laugh at the appropriateness of the lyrics.

"How you gonna get your day's work done?" she sang weakly and then added her own commentary. "Day's work. Church. Cemetery. Bake a cake. That's my day's work. Big deal. Why am I talking to myself? It takes energy to talk. I don't have any energy."

The lack of a microwave had been irritating. It seemed too much work to pour a small amount of coffee into a pan and warm it over the gas fire. But, finally, the icing was done. She dipped a spatula into the bowl and swirled it over the cake. She always made pretty peaks and neat little arcs. This time, the spatula kept hitting the side of the pan and once dug into the cake. The pattern looked as though it had been made by a drunken cook. She giggled.

"Am I a drunken cook? Who the hell cares? Do you care, child? Nah! Me neither! Anyhow, cake's too hot. Icing is melting. Clears up the mess. No problem. Consuela says that. You don't know Consuela."

Resolutely, she cut an irregular piece and, bypassing plate and fork, stuffed a corner of it into her mouth. The moist richness was barely on her palette when it disappeared. She stuffed the dark square into her mouth further, more angry than frightened now. The taste didn't come. As always, there was not even the feel of the texture in her mouth. Her stomach heaved. She dropped the piece on top of the cake and turned away from it. The girl was there, had been behind her. She was standing, her eyes closed, her jaw moving, a look of rapture on her face. As always, some instinct made Matty swallow even though she could feel nothing and, unbelievably, the girl's throat mirrored her action. Matty stared at the girl's face as the blue eyes slowly opened and the small pink lips parted slightly, revealing the tip of her tongue, and then closed.

The girl looked at her, a questioning look with just the slightest bit of apprehension.

And Matty knew.

The truth hit her with a force that slammed into every nerve in her body. A tornado of realizations swirled through her brain, but one fact was clear in the eye of the storm.

The girl had stolen the taste, the feel, of that cake and all the other tastes and feelings and smells whose losses had driven her towards despair!

Matty screamed. It was a high, harsh cry that threw her pain at the figure before her.

The girl's eyes and mouth went wide in astonishment.

"You!" Matty screamed in a ragged voice. "You've done this! You!"

This girl had nearly driven her mad! All for a few bites of food and the feel of hot water! Her sweet, sympathetic ghost had betrayed her! Anger born of torment grew into fury.

"Out! Get out!" she ordered. "Get down there!" Matty pointed to the basement. "Get down there, you hear? You belong there! You're dead! Good God, you're dead!"

The girl's face was frozen in an expression of dismay, the eyes still wide, the mouth slightly open, like a child helpless before its parent's anger.

Matty had never before known hot, uncontrollable rage. It was not her nature. But all the misery of the past few days, the carefully tamed terror, could not respond to that expression. Fury possessed her utterly.

"Go!" she screamed again. It was the voice of a madwoman.

25

Matty was alone in the kitchen. The girl was gone. The room rang with silence. Only the memory of her own anguished screams and the sound of her pounding heart remained. Leaning back against the sink, eyes shut, Matty fought for control. Her ragged breaths slowed. The birds began to sing again.

Betrayal was a new experience. This girl she had begun almost to love, had wanted to help—This kind of betrayal had never happened to her before. There had been control freaks, rude people, angry people who yelled at her, but no one had ever, day after day, knowingly damaged her like this.

Her eyes opened and focused, unseeing, on the window across the kitchen. Unexpectedly, a new truth hit her, bringing a burst of happiness that swept away the torment.

She was all right. Physically and emotionally exhausted, hungry and sleep deprived, but there was nothing wrong with her senses that leaving this house wouldn't cure. She took a deep breath and let it out with a rough sound. Fury had drained the last bit of strength from her. As anger yielded to relief, she began to shake, turned and sagged against the sink. Were the trembling hands gripping the rounded edge of the porcelain her hands? The chipped polish and broken nails could not belong to the Matty Buhrmann who lived in Rockville, Maryland. Anger, barely subdued, surfaced again.

"How could you do this to me?" she said in a hoarse whisper.

She had to get out. This was a house of torture and the girl was its instrument. Jane's grandmother had known. Had that poor woman doubted herself, too? Had this been the experience that had affected her mind?

Holding onto the counter, Matty managed to get across the kitchen in spite of rubbery knees and shaking thighs and, pulling with her hands on the stair rail, hauled herself to the second floor. She paused at the top to catch her breath. Across from her, the mirror reflected disheveled hair, carelessly applied lipstick and burnt-out eyes. How could Jane have called her beautiful?

"What have you done to me?"

The words were barely audible.

Anger provided the steel needed to throw the suitcases onto the bed and fill them quickly, carelessly. A drawer fell out of the dresser as she yanked too hard. It felt good to leave it on the floor. Tee shirts, nightgowns, shorts and sweats went into one suitcase in a lump, with underwear and socks filling the corners. Into the other went jeans, sweaters, the velour robe. It struck her for the first time that cold, numb fingers were not to blame for the loss of its velvety feel as she lay reading on the couch an eternity ago during that first week. It had been the girl, stealing again. Anger forced an acid burn up her throat.

The few clothes from the wardrobe wouldn't fit without careful arranging. They were left on their hangers and rolled into a bundle.

The bathroom was easy. There was plenty of room in her toiletries case. Tubes of lipstick fell into the sink and a bottle of Alpha Keri oil spilled onto the floor, its lid not sufficiently tightened. There was no change in Matty's expression as she carelessly wiped the floor with a towel and then rolled all the towels into a ball. The sheets and pillowcases went on top of them, the blanket and quilt that belonged in the house left in a separate heap for someone else to deal with. Somewhere there was a big black trash bag for the linens. She didn't try to remember where.

The office was next. The empty cartons were pulled out from their corner and filled quickly with the laptop, pencils, pens, notepads, piles of carefully prepared printouts, office files, bent and mixed and folded over one another. She pushed the boxes into the hall with her foot and went back into the bedroom.

The linens flew down the stairs, over the banister and onto the bookcase where they knocked over the already chipped statue of Joshua Chamberlain and pulled it to the floor. A suitcase in each hand, she tried to pick up the few things on hangers. It didn't work. The clothes took flight, too, landing at the bottom of the stairs.

Matty was sweating now and her arms were shaking along with her legs, but there was enough momentum left to pick up a suitcase in each hand, stagger out of the bedroom and begin an awkward descent. The staircase was narrow and it was difficult to squeeze a suitcase on either side.

She forgot about the third step.

The steep angle of the staircase caused Matty to fall directly to the bottom without touching even one of the narrow stairs. There was no fear or dismay on the way down. Her reactions were too slow. Somewhere along the way, her shoulder bumped the wall and she was turned around. Her right shoulder hit the floor first. Then her spine smashed into the edge of one of the lower steps, her legs splayed across the steps above.

The shock of it knocked the anger from her. She was dazed. The information about her condition came gradually, in pieces.

Her right leg hurt. A suitcase had landed on it.

Her head was pillowed by the clothes she had thrown down.

The cold, sharp metal of a hanger dug into her left arm.

Her shoulder took a while to let her know it was damaged, but, once it started, the message grew in strength quickly.

Anxious to relieve the pressure on it, Matty tried to turn and pull her lower body off the stairs and immediately was pinned down by a bolt of pain in her middle. It was a familiar enemy. The car accident had pinched a nerve in her spine. It had been unbearable. Afraid to move, Matty lived with the ache in her shoulder and leg while she tried to put her mind in order. The effects of being almost upside down were beginning to make her dizzy. This position couldn't be maintained for long.

If she slid very carefully...

She pushed with her left foot, trying to move just a little bit off the stairs and onto the level floor. The hot spear stabbed her in the back again and blackness closed in...

Waking brought an awareness of a new, persistent throbbing in her back. That wasn't good, but at least it was bearable. Doctors had told her that persistent pinching of a nerve could cause permanent damage. That damage had to be stopped.

Silently, she damned Tom's car. She could neither risk waiting for him nor face the pain of moving again. She was too tired to deal with the dilemma. Tom might not even come. He might phone and she couldn't answer. The phone was on the coffee table. It was herself she cursed now. Why hadn't she put it on the end of the little table here at the bottom of the stairs as she usually did? Then perhaps one of the hangers under her could knock it off.

A further threat was coming from her stomach. Nausea. She didn't even know the source. Exhaustion combined with fear and pain? Not enough food in her stomach no doubt contributed. The source didn't matter, but vomiting would force movement and movement would produce intolerable agony. Something had to be done. For the first time it occurred to her that she might not be so lucky this time. Was permanent paralysis a possibility?

Don't move the victim. That's what they said, but did that apply to her situation? Careful movement to the phone would bring help. The attempt had to be made. Would the damage to her shoulder prevent her from using her right arm? She dug in her elbows and pushed herself a few inches away from the stairs.

The demon pain shot up from her back and shoulder to her neck and blackness closed in again…

The darkness had turned to gray when consciousness returned. Then it, too, cleared gradually and, as it went, the realization of what had happened returned more slowly this time, sending the message that she had to find help soon. The throbbing was still in her back, but it wasn't worse. The shoulder was screaming for help. How many times would she have to move a few inches and pass out before she reached the phone that sat tantalizingly ten feet away? Moving shoulders and arms involved back muscles, too, she had found. That was the worst pain, the one that had knocked her out. Bracing herself to expect it, praying no serious damage was being done to her back or shoulder, she hunched herself up and dug her elbows into the rough floor. Shoving her elbows down moved her even a shorter distance this time. It couldn't have been more than an inch or two before anguish drained the strength from her, incapacitated her with nausea. At least, this time she didn't pass out, but how long had she been unconscious already? A quick look at the kitchen clock told her it was now almost two thirty. What time had it been when she fell? She couldn't remember, but two thirty seemed late. She had to keep going. Each time, she would have to stop, build energy and determination before the next small advance. It could take hours to get to the phone. And she would be weaker each time.

Give up? Wait for Tom?

She lay back. It was so easy just to lie there. Her leg, her shoulder, her back hurt, but it was bearable.

Don't move the victim. That recurring echo. For how long? Was it her imagination, or was the pain in her back a little worse after that last move? What if it got as bad as when she moved? How could she lie here and bear that until Tom came? What if he couldn't solve the car problem? How long would it be before he worried enough about her not answering her phone and found some way to get here?

Waiting was not an acceptable answer.

Lifting her shoulders carefully, Matty dug her elbows, now riddled with splinters, into the floor once more and waited for the agonizing explosion that would drive her once more into unconsciousness.

It didn't come.

Emotions came and went with lightning speed. First, a relief that felt like joy. Then fear. Only severe damage could have removed pain completely. There was no feeling—

But there was. Her feet felt normal. Matty wriggled her toes and was sure they responded properly although she was afraid to look and see. Even moving them had been stupid. Her leg and shoulder still hurt along with her now bleeding elbows. The nausea was still in her stomach, reaching into her throat. Something had cut off the feeling in her back.

Don't think about it! Not now! Keep moving!

It was time for the most difficult move, the turn around the couch. It must be done carefully, slowly, with minimum impact on her back, dragging her lower body along. Turn without using her lower body? Previous moves had sent the clear message that this was impossible. Mentally, Matty reviewed the area behind her. Something to pull on would help, perhaps would enable her to move with only the use of her one good arm.

The stacked brick bookcase might fall apart if she pushed on it and the back leg of the couch wasn't within reach.

The rug!

She reached behind with her left arm and found the edge of the braided rag rug. A strong hold would be required to resist her weight. The circles of old cloth would tear away easily. She settled for four of them, dug her nails through the threads, weakened with age, that joined them, curled her fingers tightly around the rough wool strands and pulled as hard as she could, trying to avoid moving anything but the one arm. Tears flowed from the sheer difficulty of the effort, ran down her cheeks and into her ears.

It was hopeless. What made her think she could do the equivalent of a one-handed pull-up even if the rug had held? It hadn't. She both heard and felt the few rope-like strands give way as her body continued to lie immobile on the wooden floor.

Fear threatened to incapacitate her. What had happened to her back? Closing her eyes, she resolved to put the possibility of permanent damage out of her mind and return to using her elbows. Resolutely, she dug them in and pushed, harder this time. The shoulder was getting worse and clouds of gray floated over her eyes, but the back pain stayed away. How frustrating to move slowly when, now, nothing prevented her from crawling rapidly or even walking to the coffee table.

If crippling herself could be called nothing.

Over and over, her elbows propelled her at a frustratingly cautious pace until her body was angled into the living room, her head aimed at the phone.

Matty had been concentrating on the coffee table to her left, but as she paused to rest, her face turned toward the ceiling and, out of the corner of her eye, she saw a splash of familiar color to her right. Startled, she forgot to be careful as her head jerked to see. Under the window was the girl, curled into fetal position, her arms around her knees, her face contorted beyond recognition.

Realization came slowly.

Contorted with pain.

Matty's mind was too overwhelmed to make sense of it immediately. Then she knew there was only one explanation.

With my pain!

The need to think, to pull the multiple realizations together was compelling, but there was no time. Two thoughts overwhelmed all else. *The girl is taking my pain. I must move before she gives it back.*

Speed and care were conflicting needs. *Slowly, slowly,* she told herself as once again the lacerated elbows dug into the floor and moved her a few more inches. The rough orange and brown fabric of the couch brushed her elbow. It was painful, but also a relief to feel it. She couldn't take her eyes off the girl, rigid, bathed in sunshine and the pain that belonged to Matty. Relief, gratitude, sympathy, the fear that the girl wouldn't be able to give her enough time to reach the phone, were all there but subdued by exhaustion. What if her little spirit passed out before the phone was within reach? *Don't think about that,* she ordered herself. Thoughts would have to wait. Nothing was making sense now, but movement toward the coffee table was steady and still the girl was holding onto consciousness.

The girl must be stronger. A healthy ghost. Insane. But this was all insane, wasn't it?

It was harder to move on the rag rug, but the phone was near now.

She reached up, moved her hand around, feeling for it, felt its cool, smooth surface and brushed it onto the floor beside her. How easy to pick it up and push the 911 button!

"Need an ambulance. Fell. Spinal injury. House on South Mountain." She had no other address, only directions. South Mountain was a huge complex. Then she remembered the owner's name. That would do. "John Durham's house. I'll leave my phone on. Maybe you can trace it."

That should be enough. She couldn't leave the girl in agony any longer.

There were words that must be said. It wasn't easy.

"I can take it back now."

She started to add "God bless you," but the iron grip of pain strangled the words, her body went rigid and the world went away.

26

Waking was bearable. That was Matty's first clear thought. The pain was there but at a distance, sending only weak signals. Then the image of a small blue figure curled into a ball mixed with memories of bright lights shining on white and voices telling her that she needed to hold on until...until what? It was like the accident a year ago. She had to tell them things. What had happened. Where it hurt. Could she feel this? A constant longing for the unconsciousness that came and went...

This was different. Softer. Quieter.

"Matty?"

It was Tom's voice. She turned to the one dark spot in the room.

Tom. Nice.

His presence stirred some emotion, but faintly. She opened her mouth to say "Hi," but her tongue was thick. She smiled instead.

He said something else. She heard "Okay." That seemed a good word to hear, but she wasn't sure why. She thought she smiled again. She meant to. Sleep closed in.

◆   ◆   ◆

"She did what, Matty?"

Matty turned her head toward the voice. What was he asking?

"You said she did something."

"Did I?"

"I guess you were dreaming."

"I guess."

She could talk, but her voice didn't sound right. For the first time, Matty noticed that her legs were suspended in the air. It would have been more frightening if they hadn't been there once before. She had recovered nicely from that accident and presumably all would come right again. Still…Adrenaline began to clear her thoughts.

"Am I all right?"

"Yes. Yes!" Tom was anxious to reassure her. "I've been telling you, but I know you haven't—How do you feel?"

"I feel…Umm, yes. I do feel pretty good. I am okay?"

"You need some healing time. You cracked a vertebra and pinched a nerve again. This time in your lower back. The crack will heal."

For a moment, Matty could feel the hard floor beneath her, the agonizing pain in her back drowning out all the lesser ones in her shoulder, leg and arms. The image of the girl returned, her face contorted with pain.

"It was bad," she said, more to herself than to Tom.

"I'm sorry, love. Do you need anything?"

"I don't think so." She looked at the tube taped to the back of her hand. "I.V.," she said. "Feeding me. Not hungry."

Tom leaned over to kiss her forehead. His chin was scratchy. She looked at him closely in the dim light.

"You need a shave. You look tired. How long have you been here?"

As she became more alert, Matty was concerned about her husband, but the memories of the last week were also flooding in, demanding her attention. *The girl—*

"I'm fine." Tom said. "You've been here since yesterday afternoon. It's four now."

"Four. At night. No. I guess that would be morning."

"Yeah. They said I could sleep here."

Matty shut her eyes. *The girl. Crumpled on the floor. Her face—My pain. Beautiful face all contorted. Why had she done that? After what I said. What did I say? Told her she was dead. Oh, God! How could I do that? That was awful! Cruel! How could I? But she—*

A nurse came in.

"Awake now, are we? Good. Feeling all right?"

Matty nodded as the nurse changed the I.V. bag.

"It's beginning to hurt more, though."

"That's all right, honey. I'm Andrea and I'm giving you more morphine right now."

"Good. That's good. Thank you."

"It'll just take a few minutes and you'll feel better. You know how to do this? Push the button when the pain gets bad. It won't let you get too much."

With an approving look at her husband, Andrea left.

"You go home now, Tom."

"To the cabin, I guess. It's closer than home."

"Oh? I don't even know where I am. Frederick?"

"Hagerstown. Apparently you said something about a spinal injury when you called and they brought you here. Only about twelve miles. You were in Frederick County, but the hospital in Frederick was farther away and traffic is worse, too, and they don't mess around with spinal injuries. You're very lucky, honey."

"I am, aren't I?" *Am I? I don't even know for sure. There's all this stuff to figure out and I can't deal with it. Too much—*

I'm okay!

The sudden remembrance that the girl had caused her sensory losses, that there was no tumor, nothing wrong with her brain, brought a surge of happiness. It was hard to control the grin that she couldn't explain to Tom. But the girl had caused such misery, so much fear. No wonder she had been furious. Incredibly furious. Yet…

Tom was still talking. "—would have been better for me. I need to put in some hours at work so I can take care of you when you get out. But Hagerstown was safer for you and that's what counts."

Tom got up and leaned over the bed, took her hand and touched it to his lips and then held it against his bristly cheek.

"Matty," He hesitated. "Are you okay? Other than—"

"You said I was."

"I don't mean that. The cabin. Stuff all over the floor, clothes, sheets—"

"Packing. I was packing."

Tom frowned. She knew there was a lot that needed explaining. The papers in a mess in the carton. And—

"I dropped a piece of cake, didn't I?"

"And an egg and—" He shook his head. "I shouldn't be bothering you with this now. It's just not like you. And I didn't know where you were."

"Oh. You didn't find me?"

"No. I called the police and they located you here. But for a while, it was damn scary. You missing and that mess…"

"Oh, yeah. I remember. I called 911, didn't I? I couldn't do anything more, Tom. There was no way…"

"I know, honey. You must have been going through hell."

"What's this sling on my arm for?"

"A cracked collar bone. Bad bruise there, too. Nasty scratches on your arm and a couple of bruises on your leg. I guess you fell carrying those clothes. Thank God you had your phone with you."

Thank God I had my phone with me? Best to leave it at that for now.

"I would have called you, Tom. At least, I think I would have. I wasn't thinking very clearly. And then I passed out."

Where is she now? Did I even thank her?

"I swear I'll get a new car."

"No need." She was beginning to feel the last dose of morphine. Sleep was irresistible. She thought she was assuring Tom he needn't feel responsible, but Tom was only hearing "Mmm."

She didn't feel him kiss her goodbye.

◆   ◆   ◆

Usually, her first waking thought was of the girl and her need to get back to the house. This time, she remembered Neil. It was daylight. She had an appointment this morning. At eight thirty, wasn't it? Matty pushed the call button. It was surprising how quickly a nurse appeared. Not like the hospital she was in before.

"Good morning, Matty."

That was different, too. First names. Was that a small town thing? No. This wasn't a small town. Not exactly Washington, D.C. area, though.

"Would you hand me my cell phone?"

"I'm sorry. I can't do that. They're not permitted in here. Anyway, I don't think they brought one in with you." The woman frowned. "I don't think they brought anything in with you."

"Oh. Sorry. I'm not thinking clearly. My friend here."

"Your friend?"

"The morphine."

The nurse laughed, walked over to Matty and adjusted her blanket, tucking it in tightly.

"Jeanine," Matty read out loud. The name was on a white badge with petunias in the corner. The petunias echoed the wild assortment of flowers on her coat. Supposed to be more cheerful than white uniforms. They probably were.

"That's right. Is there anything you need?"

"I just need to cancel a doctor's appointment. That's silly, isn't it?"

Matty laughed much too heartily for the joke. It was impossible to explain to this nurse why it made her so happy to cancel this appointment, but Jeannine joined her in laughter anyway.

"Breakfast will be here soon."

Breakfast sounded good. More than good.

"Bring me a lot. I need a huge breakfast."

Jeanine was adjusting the tension on her legs. It felt good to change position, however slightly.

"No problem," Jeanine assured her.

Another Consuela. Matty grinned at the sturdy, gray-haired woman who looked so little like her assistant.

"We're cutting back a little on your morphine. But it's under your control. Just push the button."

"I know. I've done this before."

"How are you feeling?"

"Wonderful!"

"Be nice if all our patients were so happy."

Matty grinned a slightly drug-dopey grin and, as Jeanine left, began to plan.

I'll send the girl some roses. Tell her it's all right, that she can smell them. In a note, I guess. Will that work? I don't think I'm thinking clearly. She can't smell them if I'm not there. Silly. The image of fresh roses crushed in the trash brought a pang of guilt. Tom's roses. Did he find them in the trash? Maybe they would have been faded by then and he would never know she had thrown them away instantly.

Her suspended legs mocked her. She wanted to get up, to go back to the house, to make things right. There was only a very bearable and reassuring ache in her back. Of course, she reminded herself, that was the morphine.

◆   ◆   ◆

"Erica. It's Matty. Matty Buhrmann. Thanks for accepting the charges. Is Neil available?"

"He's not in yet. You're on your way?"

"No. That's why I'm calling. I fell down and I'm—Oh, shoot, I don't even know what hospital I'm in. Oh, yes, I do. Hagerstown. Anyway, I'm in traction and I can't come. But the important thing is to tell Neil that I don't need the appointment. I—" There was no way to explain this to Erica. "Just tell him I'm fine. Emphasize that. That I'm fine. And cancel the appointment for me, of course."

"Shall I make a later appointment for you? If you're fine, I assume you're getting out soon? What happened, Matty?"

"Just a fall. Nothing serious. Just inconvenient. And, no. I don't need another appointment right away. *Really.*" Matty couldn't help but sound happy about it.

"You're sure? He could just call you."

Erica was accustomed to patients who made bad decisions.

Explain this to Neil over the phone? Fat chance!

"I'm absolutely sure. Tell him to trust me on this one. I know for certain I absolutely have no...That the problem we discussed turned out to
be...okay. I'll explain when I see him."

Maybe.

◆　　　◆　　　◆

Not soon enough, the sound of breakfast worked its way up the hall,
remembered sounds of trays sliding off racks, the cheery greetings with
which they were delivered, murmured acceptances and then the sounds
moved one room closer.

"You have some extra things here. You ordered a..."

The young man, short, dark, seemingly Mexican with a strong Indian
cast to his features, looked at his notes. "Didn't order anything. Just got
here, didn't you? They sent double portions. That right?"

"Yep. That's for me."

He glanced at the slim outline under the covers, briefly curled his flexi-
ble face into an expression that was half surprise, half approval and set the
tray on the table in front of her.

"Position okay? I can't do much about it with the traction."

"No problem." Matty grinned broadly, knowing it would make no
sense to this young man. He didn't know Consuela.

"And you can eat with one hand? Scrambled eggs should be okay."

Matty looked at the two pieces of Danish and the pile of fresh grapes
and much of her joy melted away. Yes, she could manage, but every bite
would be laden with guilt. She couldn't share with the girl.

◆　　　◆　　　◆

"Matty, who are all those people? They keep bringing me food, asking
about you and then backing out the door."

Matty laughed at her husband's dumbfounded expression. "I don't
know. They're from church."

"I know. They keep saying that. One of them works here, over in x-ray. Forget his name. Carl something, I think. But how on earth did you make so many friends in a week?"

"They're not friends. I don't even know their names. They're from church."

Tom's expression said that was no explanation.

"People do that here. I went to church Sunday, so they're bringing me into the fold. And you're with me."

Tom shook his head. "Amazing. What am I going to do with all those casseroles? And cookies! Actually, the cookies aren't a real problem," he amended with a grin that was not difficult to interpret. "At least they don't all want to visit you. Only a Mary and, uh…"

"Jane?"

"Right. Jane. Outstandingly homely. And abrupt. Brought an astonishing sauerkraut, potatoes and sausage casserole. Couldn't resist trying that one. Good, actually. Odd woman. You know her?"

"I know her."

Matty's mind moved away from Tom as she wondered what she should tell Jane. That day at the cemetery was a blur. She had told her some things. But the sensory losses? Somehow she thought not.

"Matty?"

"Huh? Oh. Sorry, Tom. This morphine…" Matty controlled a smile as she silently finished the sentence, *is a wonderful excuse for social lapses.* "What were you saying?"

"Mary wanted to visit you, but said you'd understand she had to run the store. Jane was wondering if you felt well enough for visitors."

"No."

Matty wasn't sure why her reaction was immediate and negative. She just knew she didn't want to talk to Jane. Or to anyone else except Tom until her own thoughts were in order.

"Tell her I'm too doped up."

"Okay. She seemed real worried."

Yeah. That scary ghost of her grandmother's. Probably thinks I'm the victim of a supernatural attack. "Just tell her I'm fine."

Tom was still talking, but his voice barely penetrated the fog of drugs and sleepiness. Going to sleep without hunger or fear was nice. So nice...

◆   ◆   ◆

Jane was not to be put off. When the phone rang, waking her, Matty knew who would be on the other end.

"Did she push you?"

"What?"

Jane's greeting was an odd departure from "Hello" and for a moment it didn't make sense.

"No! No! Absolutely not!"

Matty glanced around the room, realizing how this protest would affect Tom, but he wasn't there. Not sure how long he would be gone, Matty decided on a quick explanation.

"She steals senses, Jane. She steals touch and taste and—"

"Possession?"

"Uh, not exactly. Mostly just little bits and pieces. It's frightening. It scared the hell out of me. I thought I was going crazy, losing my mind. It must have done the same to your grandmother. But—"

"Grandmother *was* crazy."

"Well, something else may have been going on with her. But, I'm telling you, this sort of experience, if you don't understand it, could drive you crazy. Your grandmother may never have made the right connection, thought her mind was creating the loss of senses and also the ghost."

"No. The ghost was real to her. She was scared of it. You said you weren't."

Tom had appeared in the doorway with a big smile and at least two dozen yellow roses.

"Tom! I'm talking to Jane. Excuse me, Jane. I hate to cut you off, but—"

"You'd better."

It sounded almost like a threat and Matty realized she shouldn't have used the woman's name.

"Yes, I know. Why don't you—Actually, I'm not sure I'm very coherent with all this morphine. Could you wait till tomorrow? I'll tell Tom and he'll leave us alone to have a nice chat."

Matty thought she probably sounded as phony as her smile looked, but Tom didn't seem to notice.

"You shouldn't have said that. You make it sound like a big deal. He might tell someone. You know I don't want anyone to know about my interest."

"Actually, Tom doesn't know anyone here. He doesn't know what to do about all the food. Would you thank everyone for us?"

"Can't do that."

"Yes, I see."

Of course Jane wouldn't want anyone to know they had any more in common than Matty had with anyone else at church.

"Ten o'clock? That's when visiting hours start," Jane said.

"What?" Matty shook her head. She was slow. And the head shaking hurt and that didn't help. "Yes. Tomorrow. Ten."

"Will your husband be there?"

Matty looked at Tom, now sitting almost close enough to hear Jane's voice on the phone. "Will you be here tomorrow, Tom?"

"No, darlin'. I really have to go to work while they're taking care of you here."

"No. Tom's going to work."

There was silence. Matty could see Jane's dark, asymmetrical face twisted in thought. The woman had no idea how unattractive her exaggerated expressions were.

"You could be my friend," Jane said.

"I…?"

"I can talk to you. I don't put you off, do I?"

"No, of course not." *Liar, liar.* "You're an interesting woman."

"Never was accused of being boring. I can visit you at the hospital. People do that. Anyhow, probably no one would know. If Carl doesn't see me. It might make people curious if I saw you back at the house. We never even spoke at church."

"I understand." Relief created feelings of guilt.

"Right. Goodbye."

"Uh. Yeah. Good—"

But Jane had hung up.

◆   ◆   ◆

"That's wonderful, Doctor."

Matty smiled benignly at the white-coated, gaunt figure who had just told her she could probably go home in another day or two.

"No questions?" he asked. The fingers of one hand came up to cover his mouth and press his lips into a fish-like pucker. Then he caught himself and lowered his hand quickly.

Matty recognized that the man was uncomfortable with this part of practicing medicine and hurried to reassure him.

"Well, I've been through this before, so no, not really. I'll be just fine."

He didn't feel free to dismiss himself. "You'll have a smaller sling for that cracked collar bone," he explained slowly, as though she had difficulty understanding. "You don't have to wear it, but it will remind you not to do too much with that arm for a while. Your back will get gradually better, too, if you're sensible. We will give you some strengthening exercises before you leave to do later. In the meantime, don't overdo." He nodded to emphasize the importance of this piece of advice. "Lie down as much as you can. Keep your knees up."

He lifted one bony knee slightly to illustrate and Matty had to smother a laugh.

"Stretch out your spine. If you're up too much, pressure might begin to pinch the nerve. Or," he added with a somber shake of his head and an earnest tone of voice, "—it may never bother you again. I'm sorry we really can't predict these things. Another day's traction should be adequate. How is the pain right now?"

"It's fine. Just fine. Wonderful."

The doctor looked behind him and, finding a chair, pulled it up, sat down and leaned toward her.

"We've cut down a good bit on your medication." He spoke hesitantly.

"I can tell." She nodded, her expression matching his seriousness.

"Then you do still have some pain."

Matty thought it odd that he should want her to complain, but gave him the assurance he seemed to need.

"Oh, sure."

That clearly was not the response he was looking for.

"What's the problem, Doctor?"

"Your—Shall I say elation?—seems oddly inappropriate. Are you always this happy?"

"Oh, no. Mostly I'm busy. Used to be. Wasn't at all happy last week." She laughed. It came out a silly giggle, not at all reassuring to the doctor, she could see. "I certainly wasn't happy lying on that floor. I was sure I was going to end up paralyzed. Or dead. I can't tell you how relieved I am there will be no permanent damage."

The frown left his face and the thin lips smiled for the first time.

"I see." He nodded. "Yes, of course. Naturally, you're relieved." He hit one knee with the papers he was holding. "You've had us worried, my dear lady. Your husband included. You were altogether too unnaturally happy for a woman who had just taken a bad fall and was in some discomfort."

He pushed himself off the chair and said, almost to himself, "Happiness is perfectly acceptable in a hospital. Just doesn't happen all that often."

He stopped at the door and added, thoughtfully, "Maternity ward excepted, of course."

Maternity ward. That was a nice thought.

Matty went back to sleep.

27

"See, Jane, it's all so clear now. I've had hours to think it through. Would you push that button down there and put my bed up a little farther? Or hand me the control. I can't use my right arm. Cracked a collar bone. I don't know why that thing is on the wrong side of the bed. Yes, I do. Tom was—Never mind. More interesting things to talk about."

Matty took the control from Jane and pushed the button to raise herself to a slightly higher position.

"There. Can't go any higher because of the traction. But now I can see you comfortably."

Jane was wearing an obviously hand made sweater of colors that should never have been put together in an insecure diamond pattern. It was even less flattering than the pink suit she had worn Sunday. Sitting rigidly upright in a straight-back chair, she looked more than ever as though she belonged in her own "American Gothic" painting. Alone. One would never imagine a man beside her.

"See—" Matty leaned toward her and was irritated that her collar bone still hurt a little when she moved. In the short time she had been in the hospital, the gratitude for having sustained only minor damage had dwindled and she now minded the ache in her back, the occasional twinges elsewhere and, more than anything, not being able to get back to the girl. At least with Jane she had someone she could talk to about her experience and her visitor had barely been able to say a word since her arrival.

"See—" she repeated, "There's this pattern that I never recognized. Or, I kind of did, but I was too—I guess the right word would be 'distraught'—to put it together the right way although..." Matty eyes went to the ceiling as she tried to solve this piece of the puzzle. "I'm not sure I'd have gotten it even on my best day. Anyway—" Her eyes went back to Jane. "She never came in the morning. Or maybe she never did anything disturbing in the morning because I didn't tempt her at all. Black coffee, bran cereal and skim milk. My standard breakfast. Don't care about losing weight any more, but it's easy to fix. Then I'd go up and work on the computer." Matty laughed. "That must have astounded her, don't you think? But nothing tempting to steal in the way of sensory...sensory...stuff, you know?"

Matty knew she was rambling on too fast, but it was such a relief to be saying these things. She didn't even need to worry about the inert, elderly woman in the other bed. She was as deaf as a post.

"Then I'd always eat lunch outside. See? It was part of my therapy. Then I took a walk. When I got back, that's when I would have trouble. Apparently, she can't leave the house. I thought it was because I was getting more tired as the day went on. For a while I thought the first thing was the bath. But there was a sandwich and a glass of milk I didn't remember eating—No, tasting—Whatever—as I was working at the computer. I do vaguely remember eating. I think that was first, but I can't be sure. Maybe I really was just concentrating too hard on my work to notice. That was when I first got to the house and hadn't started that 'lunch out' therapy thing. Then there was the bath. I couldn't feel the bath! Only for an instant! I was so startled! I was reading *Realtor* magazine or thinking about something, I forget which. But it was so brief I just passed it off. Isn't it interesting that at first she stole only so briefly I wasn't even sure or she stole what I wasn't aware of? I felt my robe once or, rather, didn't feel it. It's really soft. I thought my fingers were cold, numb, you know? It looks like velvet. Is it possible she had never seen velvet? But I'm not really sure about that one. Maybe they really were cold. Tom sent me roses. That's what really did me in. I *knew* I couldn't smell the roses. Tried twice. Oh, I've tried *so* hard to remember every little detail! Now that *was* in the morning! But dinner always gave me the most trouble. Except—" Matty laughed. "The liver! She didn't want the liver! Or the spinach! Isn't that wonderful? So like a child! And I kept saying 'we.' I realized that only this morning. I kept saying things like 'What shall we have to eat tonight?' I invited her! Can you believe it? The cake was the worst. God! I will never forget the expression on her face! And she actually looked like she was eating. At the last—the cake thing—her mouth was moving. And I guess—" Matty stopped to think. "Yes. I guess she thought it was all right for me to see her because all the time I was baking, I was talking to her, telling her how good it was going to be. So she thought I knew, understood what she wanted. I talked about how good the cake was—would be. Or…" Matty shut her eyes, trying to remember exactly how the scene had looked. "…did I turn suddenly and catch her? I'm not sure. Do you suppose—No, no. She couldn't know what was on my mind. Could she? It has always been a question for me whether or not she could hear. Must have. She stole the sound of the music. Did she need it loud like that? Was sound muted for her? Or was she always kind of inferring what I was saying? No. That wouldn't account for the music. But that would mean all my—No. I really think she heard my invitations. I mean, it has seemed to me, lying here thinking about it all this time, that she…intruded?—when I was concentrating on other things in the beginning and then, after I had seen her, the way I kept sort of inviting her in—But I was such a nervous wreck, crying. That's another thing! When I was really upset, unhappy, she didn't do anything. Does that mean she knew she was causing, or at least adding to, my problem? Did she hear my phone calls to my…" Matty hesitated. Jane didn't seem the kind to approve of psychiatry except in the most extreme cases. "—my doctor?"

Things sounded different when told to another person. In the brief silences in which Jane could have spoken, it became obvious that she wasn't carried away with the same enthusiasm. Her lips were pressed together, making the vertical lines on each side of her mouth even deeper.

"You sound as crazy as my grandmother," she said finally.

Her dark face was twisted by thoughts Matty couldn't discern.

"Exactly!" Matty said "Don't you see? Wouldn't it drive you crazy if you thought you were losing your sensory…whatever? You would suspect you were losing your mind. Couldn't that be what happened to your grandmother?"

"You thought you were losing your mind and now you're fine. Seems to me you always did think straight. Mamaw didn't. There's a difference."

Matty felt deflated. This was the only person who might believe her. "We're different people, your grandmother and I. We brought different backgrounds, information, attitudes to this situation."

Jane chewed her lower lip.

"Look," Matty went on, trying hard to convince this wooden woman. "I'm pretty sure the girl knew she was causing a problem. She was obviously sympathetic. Maybe by the time I came along, she had learned to be more careful. After all, she didn't want people to leave because then she lost her...her—What's the word? Access! That's what I mean. Her access to someone to work through. Then, too, maybe your grandmother knew the girl was doing it, but couldn't afford to leave. She owned the house, you said. And she probably didn't feel free to talk to anyone. And she didn't have the help I did, you and Evelyn and my doctor. Since I already had a problem, I had some help from drugs—"

At this, Jane gave her a questioning look.

"Just a mild tranquilizer, Jane. If anything, it would have helped me, certainly not caused delusions." Matty could hear Neil's voice telling her to limit the Diazepam and wondered if what she said was true.

"Don't trust drugs."

Of course Jane didn't trust drugs. You could tell that by looking at her. Matty forged on.

"I don't know why I didn't realize sooner that nothing happened while I was outside. I assumed the outdoors, the walks, were therapeutic. I was so afraid to drive because of my earlier accident, I suppose. I was really scared to meet you at church and I was probably at my worst in terms of physical and mental condition."

At this, Jane began to nod slowly. "Maybe I'm angry that neither Mother or Grandmother ever told me any of this," she said.

"But why would they? You're afraid to tell anyone for the same reason I am. I don't think I can even tell Tom. It would just worry him."

"Mother should have told me something. The existence of this girl has important implications."

Matty knew what she meant. It had made her have second thoughts about a lot of things.

"Jane? Are you with me on this? You were working on the idea of a ghost before you met me. You thought you knew who she was. You have to believe me. There isn't anyone else I can even talk to."

"No. For sure."

"I guess I'll just have to ask you to believe me."

"No reason not to." It was said in an off-hand, flat tone of voice.

One didn't expect surprises from Jane Goodman, but they came anyway. With no need to win Jane over, Matty found herself suddenly out of words. They sat in silence for a few moments. The patient on the other side of the curtain snored softly.

"Do you think she knew what she was doing?" Matty asked and then realized the absurdity of asking Jane. How would she know? She added, "Has Evelyn ever talked about anything like this?" Mentioning Evelyn made Matty wonder, for the first time, if the girl had made that faded flag. That would explain the energy in it.

"I don't talk to Evelyn about this. This girl—You showed the hurt?"

Sometimes it seemed to Matty they didn't speak the same language. "The hurt?"

"Yes. That you were what you said in the car. Bad nerves."

"Yes. I cried. A lot."

"Then what?"

"Then what? Oh, I see what you mean. How did I deal with it. I put it out of my mind and made myself go about my business. I sang. Yes. She certainly would have had reason to assume I wasn't hurt seriously. I danced. She stole that. The feeling of my entire body." Matty's eyes went to the ceiling again. "I'd had a wonderful weekend with Tom. She probably thought she was entitled to some of my...my joy. It was joy. She didn't bother me when I was clearly, uh, distressed. I hadn't thought of that. She knew, then, that what she was doing could cause problems." For the first time, Matty's guilt lightened a little.

Jane's nodding became more pronounced.

242

"I shouldn't have started by telling you about how I ended up in the hospital. It's probably the hardest thing to believe. But I was just bursting to tell you how she helped me. I owe her! I've got to get back!"

"Don't owe her anything. Like you said, she caused the problem."

Jane would never understand. She had no abundance of happiness to share.

"I know. But I want to do something for her anyway. Not only because I owe her. Maybe it's gratitude for the overwhelming, as you said, implications that she represents."

Now that the first release was over, Matty was beginning to tire.

Again there was silence between the two women for a while as each thought her own thoughts. The sunlight through the window came to rest on Jane's right side. Matty was struck by her immobility. She sat stiffly straight, her knees falling unattractively to each side, like a man. Matty thought how different they were. She could never have thought seriously about a deep problem in that position. She had to be flopped somewhere, on a bed or sofa. Even a bathtub would do, but not upright like that. She would have been leaning on the arm of the chair, chin in hand, her feet on the lower rails of the bed. Jane seemed uncomfortable in the world.

"So there we are," Matty said. "We have a little ghost who wants to taste more of life before finally leaving it? Is that enough? Would chocolate cake keep your soul on earth?"

"No."

"Chocolate cake and the feel of silk and the smell of roses and the sensation of dancing?"

"There's more."

"More?"

"She's still here, isn't she? After her cake and her roses and all?"

"Of course!" Matty had to remind herself not to sit up. "She wants something more! Or she's here for some entirely different reason."

"Those stories, legends, whatever you want to call them. They told her to wait."

"So she waited? She's waiting for her family?"

"Maybe. Or—"

"Yes?"

Jane backed off. "It's all speculation. We don't know."

"But we have to speculate, don't we?"

"Why?"

"It's human nature. And I want to figure it out. How else can I help her?"

"I was thinking maybe she didn't want to die before she had…"

"Yes?" Matty prompted again.

"I'm not sure what I mean. If I say love, you'll think I mean sex."

"Not if you say it that way. You mean she had just fallen in love and she hadn't really had a chance to experience it?"

"Something like that."

"Would that be strong enough to keep her here?"

"Yes."

Matty was surprised. The affirmative had come out with an unexpected certainty.

"Yes?" Matty probed her own feelings. She had had two lovers and then, and still, Tom. "Is love that important to a woman? The love of a man? Many women live without it. They have the love of friends and relatives and they have jobs and lead perfectly good, full lives without romantic love. Or sex. But it's certainly more important than chocolate cake. Do you think that might be the reason?"

Jane's expression didn't change. "Yes," she said again.

It was said without visible emotion, almost curtly, but it was not to be doubted. With a wave of compassion and unexpected humility, Matty realized that, for Jane, this was not entirely speculation.

◆　　◆　　◆

Time passed slowly. The weights on her legs were decreased. Tom had returned to work in Bethesda after apologizing so frequently that she echoed his own words and reiterated the necessity of taking some time off when it was his turn to care for her. She had talked at length to her father, feeling guilty that she had left communication to Tom for so long. Mary had called, anxious to collect news to spread to her friends. She promised to send a box of groceries when Matty got out of the hospital. Evelyn called, too, more anxious about her investigation than about Matty's condition. Matty briefly debated telling her story, then decided privacy was important for what had to be done next and used her injuries as an excuse for indefinite delay. There were a few questions from the office, but very few. It seemed they were getting along fine without her. Or creating some problems she would have to deal with later? It was a little worrisome. By Wednesday afternoon, the shoulder no longer ached, Tylenol had taken the place of the OxyContin that followed the morphine and the longing to repay the girl had become a persistent ache. There had been more than enough time to plan all the pleasures she would offer. It would be like taking a child to the circus. Surprisingly, she missed her little spirit, needed to get back for her own sake. How delightful it would be to give the girl a hug, to brush her long blonde hair and explain all the things that the modern world offered. Dare she hope for a little interaction? Just a smile would be a blessing.

Tom was worried about her recuperating in the old house. It was cold and lacked the comforts they were accustomed to, but he accepted her explanation that she was frightened of crowded highway traffic in her fragile condition. Neil called, more concerned than Tom at the delay in her return, curious about her message that everything was fine now. Matty was uncomfortable, unsure how much to tell him. It seemed necessary to insist her problems had gone away rather than launching into the unlikely story of their cause. It had not been the kind of conversation he was accustomed to having with her.

"What are your plans now? I can't see you while you're up there."

"I don't have any."

"You don't have any? That doesn't sound like you."

"It doesn't, does it?"

She had been left wondering at her own attitude. Neil was right. It wasn't like her not to think beyond a relatively short recuperation time. Looking at the phone after she hung up, the word "magic" crept back into her thinking. There were a lot of things she had left unsaid. Was it possible that was also true of Neil?

Hospital life gave one plenty of time to think. Eventually, she would go back to work on a part time basis, handling the personal contacts, making the major decisions. Meanwhile, it felt wonderfully free to think only of living again in the old log home with the clouds and moonlight outside the bedroom window, less arduous walks through the trees, the ragged flag that had made her reassess time, quiet days with Tom, reading, listening to Brahms and Mozart and, most importantly, finding ways to repay the girl for her astonishing gift.

Funny that Neil had said the house was magic. Her whole life was going to change because of these last two weeks. In a way, that was magic. Just an odd coincidence that he had used that word? And what had happened to his sister? Not the same thing, obviously, or Neil would have made the connection the first time she had called. Maybe just saw the girl? Not something to worry about right now. The days when everything had to fit into reasonable niches were gone.

28

"The flag is up!"

A thorn from the roses on her lap scratched Matty's arm as she pointed to the pale colors moving in front of the house.

"I put it up." Tom stopped the car short of the house so she could see it better and turned to her. "You asked me to, remember?"

"I did?"

The rush of emotion subsided. It wasn't, after all, a supernatural occurrence. It was just Tom.

"One of the first days you were in the hospital. You said to fly the flag when you got back."

"For heaven's sake," Matty said as she sat back in her seat. "I wonder what was on my mind."

"Stay there. I'll come around," Tom said as he drove the last few yards and pulled up outside the door.

"I'm fine."

He threaded a few strands of hair behind her ear and smiled indulgently.

"You're fine as long as you keep that sling on and lie flat on your back most of the day and don't do much of anything the rest of the time."

She made a face at him. Tom laughed and got out to open her door. She handed him the roses and accepted his hand without protest, her heart beating faster than normal. Would the girl be there?

It was cooler inside than she remembered and there was a dank smell that brought back the memory of her first tentative steps into the darkened house. It had been closed up while Tom caught up at work.

The living room was now charged with emotional overtones. It seemed friendly because it was familiar, the sun through the front windows making the motes of dust shine in their dance over the shabby furniture and the pompous little pot bellied stove, but the stairs held a threat and she saw that there was a hole in the rug where she had pulled loose the strands of braided rug trying to reach the phone. The memory of pain has a hurt of its own and Matty couldn't move for a few moments. Then her shoulders dropped and she shook herself loose of the emotional baggage. It was just her nice old house.

"It's a mess," she said, surprised. Magazines and books were strewn on tables and chairs, couch pillows on the floor, shoes by the front and back doors where, presumably, she had stepped out of them as she had entered.

"Matty, I'm sorry. I've spent most of the time you were in the hospital back at work. I unpacked the suitcases and put the clothes back so they wouldn't get wrinkled. Figured I'd get it cleaned up while you're here recuperating."

"It's fine, Tom. I wasn't criticizing. It's my stuff. I just can't believe I was living in this mess."

"You should have seen the kitchen!" Tom backed off that subject quickly. "Listen, you shouldn't stand there. You want to lie down on the couch or upstairs?"

"The couch. No. Upstairs."

Chances of seeing the girl would be better without Tom around. Matty started up the stairs. Tom held her arm from behind and guided her. It was no help, but the thought was nice.

The bedroom, at least, was neat. She had nearly emptied it.

"I made the bed," Tom said.

"Did you? Funny. I assumed I had. I always do." This was a part of her experience she had not dwelt on in the hospital. It came back to her now, the frantic rush, throwing her possessions around. That had been all right. But dumping the blanket and quilt on the floor—They had belonged to someone else and it seemed impossible that she could have been so thoughtless. And the drawer she was going to leave on the floor…No wonder Tom was…confused? Worried? Probably both.

"No. I took the sheets home to wash," Tom said. "They were—Never mind. Down you go."

Tom pulled back the covers and she sat carefully on the edge of the bed, turned and stretched out, enjoying the gradual ebbing away of the ache in her lower back. She slipped the sling off her shoulder and held it out to Tom.

"You're still worried about me, aren't you?" she asked.

His long face was still, the pale blue eyes circled with worry lines.

"I should never have let you go off alone to this place. It's just that you seemed fine the weekend we had together. But—"

"But I didn't stay fine."

"Well, obviously you didn't. I may have something to say to this Neil of yours."

He leaned over, kissed her forehead lightly and brushed the hair away from her face. He had always loved her auburn hair. It was because of him that she put up with its inconvenient length.

"You rest now. I'm going to go build a fire in the stove. I ordered some firewood when you told me you wanted to stay here a while."

He left Matty to her thoughts. This small insight into Tom's viewpoint clarified the decision not to tell him anything about her little spirit. Clothes on the floor, the mess in the kitchen…And what did he think of the boxes of office stuff? Papers thrown in helter skelter. Not something she would ever do in her right mind.

"Poor Tom," she said half-aloud. He was trying so hard not to pry into the reason for the awful mess in the house.

Tom's mention of Neil had prompted new thoughts in that direction. *Magic*. The word lingered from a conversation that seemed worlds away. Was it possible that Neil knew something about the girl? Not all, of course, or he would have known why she was having sensory losses. Perhaps different people had different experiences here. Again the idea arose that only certain women had a special connection to the girl. In the hospital, she had pursued the thought that perhaps September being the month the girl had probably died was relevant.

It wasn't September any more.

"Are you there?" she whispered. "Please be there." Matty lay still, trying to sense the girl's presence. There was nothing, but she went on. "I need to apologize. Explain. I want to thank you. Please come. Tom is a nice man. Did you see how he took care of me? I'm sorry I yelled at you. I was…I didn't understand. And I was overtired. Exhausted. And frightened. I thought—"

She stopped. It seemed fruitless to be talking to an empty room. She was tired. Walking to and from the car, the drive and a climb up the stairs was all it took to use up the strength in her muscles weakened from too much time in bed. There was not enough energy to go on arguing with a ghost. She closed her eyes and whispered one last appeal.

"Please come back so I can explain. And apologize. I was awful, wasn't I? I didn't understand. You did help me, there at the end. And now I'm fine. Or, at least, I'm going to be fine. Now I want to help you, to let you taste things and you can smell the roses. No, you can't. I'm up here and they're down there. But later—" Her voice drifted to a whisper. "Oh please, can't you come back and tell me what you want?"

As she fell asleep, the sunlight through the trees filled the room with shadow patterns. Nothing else moved.

◆　　　◆　　　◆

"You can't bake a cake!"

Tom's order was issued as he blocked the kitchen doorway, his arms akimbo.

"It's just a mix," Matty protested. "Didn't you get the mix I put on the grocery list?"

"That woman, Mary—Talkative, isn't she?—brought it. She said she remembered the things you had bought before and brought up a couple of cartons of stuff yesterday."

"A couple of cartons? What on earth will we do with it all? Did you take some of the church offerings home to eat?"

"All of them and ate the same casserole every night I was home."

"How boring!"

"Nope. Scalloped potatoes, cheese and ham. I was sorry to see it go. The others I transferred to our containers so I could return the dishes to the church. I think they had it in mind for me to take them back when I attended a church service, but I can't do that with you laid up. Mary said she'd see they were returned. The food looks a mess. Bought some of those aluminum containers, but casseroles don't transfer neatly. But everything's edible. I put the stuff in the freezer so you won't have to cook when we get home. Probably for a month. I'll have to be back at work no later than Wednesday."

Matty was impressed. It had never been Tom's job to organize meals. She kissed him awkwardly. The sling was a nuisance.

"Thank you, love. It's nice, being taken care of. It was kind of Mary, too. I wouldn't have credited her with a good memory, but perhaps it's good for certain things."

"Old man, Joseph, came with her, too. Interesting guy. I may sell him my car."

"Your car?"

"Yeah. I told you I'd buy a new one and I'm going to. Works out nicely. Leaves us just your car to get home. Buy one there. Shop around while you recuperate. Forgot. He brought you a poem. It's actually quite good, I think." Tom looked around but refused to move from the doorway.

Matty smiled. "I'm sure it is. Now move."

"If you must have a cake, I'll make it. I can read the directions. I'm very good at reading. But not yet. I have to figure out dinner. For now, hit the couch, babe." He took her good arm and led her into the living room.

"You can't cook!"

"I can bake a potato and grill a steak and I'm sure I can figure out a green salad."

"Raspberries, then, for dessert. With ice cream. Drizzle on some chocolate. Maybe a lot of chocolate. Oh! Did Mary bring raspberries?"

"She did. But since when do you eat dessert?"

"I'm skinny. Need to gain weight." Matty sat down on the couch and carefully removed her sling.

"Can't argue that. Raspberries and ice cream it is. Shouldn't you keep that thing on?"

"My arm's getting stiff. See? I'm getting petulant. Watch out or it'll turn into a full-fledged whine. I'll be careful. No sling when I'm lying down."

"Okay. But keep the arm still. All your books and magazines are piled by the couch so you won't have to get up again."

Books and magazines held no appeal. There had been too much of those at the hospital.

"We ought to plant some of those raspberries," she called out to his retreating figure. "Everlasting, they're called. Last almost until November."

"Right. They'd take over our little yard in no time. Thieves couldn't possibly break in."

"I want a big yard. With a view."

"Really?" He turned in the doorway to look back at her.

"Really."

"I'll be damned. You talked about a house last Sunday. I thought it was just daydreaming." He nodded approvingly. "I'll plant the raspberries. When we get a house."

Tom went back into the kitchen and Matty slid down on the couch, a soothing wave of happiness moving over her aching body.

"Some land, Tom. I want some land."

"That's the yard you're talking about. My job. Don't overwork me."

"No. It can be uncultivated land. Wild vegetation. Pine forest. I don't care. I just want some space."

"At a million dollars or so an acre in our neck of the woods, how much space do you think we can afford?"

"I don't like our neck of the woods any more."

"Do you salt steaks before or after you broil them?"

"After you bake the potatoes. Four hundred fifty degrees. Make it four twenty-five. Oven runs hot."

"Oh. Yeah. No microwave. Okay. Potatoes in. An hour?"

252

"Forty-five minutes after the oven temperature's up. You washed them?"

"Give me some credit!"

"And stabbed them to vent the steam?"

"Four times each. They are definitely dead."

"Then you are well on your way to successfully completing this difficult culinary task."

"Thanks a bunch! Can you have a glass of wine?

"Definitely. Only taking Tylenol. Liked that Oxy stuff, though."

Tom appeared with two glasses and set one beside her.

"Now," he said after swallowing a good-sized mouthful. "What's this all about?"

She knew what he meant. It was time.

"It started with the flag."

"It started with the flag," he repeated dryly.

"It did. It made me think about time. And being here made me examine the way we live."

"And you don't like it?"

"I like it fine." She shook her head, frowning. "No. Not really. I thought I liked it. I felt I was accomplishing."

"You were."

"But it was so frantic it caught me up and...and..."

"You were compulsive. I knew that. I thought you knew it, too. The accident made it worse."

"Much worse. But I never really considered the alternatives."

"Matty, I think—" Tom stopped, frowning.

"Tell me."

"I think you need..." He ran a hand through his hair and avoided Matty's eyes.

"You think I'm bloody well messed up mentally and physically and I need a rest somewhere else and not alone and when I'm better I'll feel differently about all this."

He nodded, still avoiding her eyes. "That's about it, yes."

"Sh—" She stopped herself, remembering the girl. "You're probably right in a way. But I do mean to change my life."

"Maybe you burned out, Matty, but you loved your business, loved creating something. Don't throw that away too easily. You got a charge out of helping people. There were negatives, sure. Like Rosemary. I think you ought to get rid of her. She's a downer."

"She frustrates me."

"She frustrates you because you can't just shrug your shoulders and let her live her own miserable life. You want to rearrange her mind, fix everything for her. So if you're going to feel that way, you've got to get rid of her. She'll have no trouble getting another job with someone who uses her abilities but doesn't give a damn about her personally."

"You sound like Neil. I'll have trouble finding another Rosemary."

"You don't want another Rosemary."

"We're quibbling. We know what we mean. And you're right. Okay. So I find a happier person even if she's not as capable. But Tom!" she wailed. "I do want a house and some trees and some space!"

She waved her arms and then cocked her head and gave Tom a phony smile, hoping he hadn't noticed she had used the arm that should have been held to her side by the sling.

Tom laughed. "Fine. So we'll commute a little. I just hate to see commuting eat up more time. We don't have enough of it together as it is."

"I know. My hours are bad. I'm going to do something about that. It's difficult in this business. People want to see rentals evenings and weekends."

"Stalemate."

"Stalemate."

"What do I do next?"

"Nothing right away, as you said. Good advice. We'll look at houses when I've recovered completely. Maybe we can find some land not too far out."

"Actually, I meant dinner. Should I be doing something?"

"You could wash the greens for the salad."

"Right."

Tom got up and went into the kitchen.

"See?" Matty whispered. "Isn't he nice?" Then, more loudly, "Tom?"

"Yuh?"

"Whistle."

"Whistle? What is this?"

"It's cheery. Haven't heard you whistle enough lately."

"Requests, please."

"Amazing Grace."

"You can have my raspberries and ice cream," Matty whispered to the still empty air. "Please. When we have dessert, I want you to have mine."

"What?"

Tom had stopped whistling.

"Nothing. I'm just singing along. There's something about 'blind and then can see.' Or is it 'blind but now I see?' How does that go?"

"Don't know lyrics. I just whistle."

"Was blind and now I see," she sang along softly. *I was and now I do.*

◆   ◆   ◆

"That was wonderful!"

Matty lay back on the couch and put her hands on over her stomach.

"After hospital food, anything's wonderful. Though I admit you ate like the proverbial horse."

"No, honestly, Tom. Steak was just right."

"Joseph picked them out, he said. Said it was especially for you."

"Really?"

"He got a thing for you?"

"I don't think he has a thing for anyone but himself. Most incredibly egocentric person I have ever met. Worse than egocentric. A liar. Mean."

Tom looked incredulous. This didn't sound like the wife he knew.

"No, I mean it," she insisted. "He said so himself." Matty took her plate off her thighs and set it on the coffee table next to the roses. "He can be a little scary. Makes you think there may be pure evil in the world. Do you believe in opposing forces, good and evil?"

"Sure. Probably inside everyone. But I don't think I believe in an incarnation of pure good or pure evil, except maybe…There are psychopaths. No conscience. Do you believe in pure good and evil?"

"I don't know. I suppose not. Do you believe in souls?"

"Not sure what a soul is."

"I mean something distinct from the physical body. Something that could survive after death."

Tom pushed himself to the front edge of the recliner, put his empty plate on Matty's and leaned his elbows on his knees, studying her for a minute before speaking.

"This vacation has really set you thinking, hasn't it? I thought you went to church because you were lonely. It was more than that, wasn't it? We haven't talked about things like this for years. We used to agree that we just didn't know. Have you changed your mind?"

Tom had her in a trap. If she said "Yes," then he would ask why and where would she go from there? She decided to do Neil's thing and answer a question with a question.

"Have you?" she asked. "You must have some new thoughts on the subject."

"No. No change. I still don't know. What have we experienced in the last few years that would enlighten us? Read your own poems. There's one in there about souls."

"*My* poems?"

"Yeah. Thought you might get inspired to write again if you read some of your old stuff. Give you something quiet and safe to do. Notebook's in that pile somewhere."

"I know the one you mean. The last line was, 'Not just one drop of genius or of madness in my soul?' I was bemoaning my ordinariness. My poetry never quite lifted off the page, never had that magic."

"You don't have to write great poetry. Just write for fun. What's wrong with that?"

"I don't know, Tom. I think you're the word person in this family. I wrote poetry because, when you're young, it seems a romantic thing to do.

Or maybe a kind of entertainment, a game, getting the rhyme and rhythm right and thinking of the right word."

"What's wrong with that?"

"Nothing as long as nobody else reads it."

Tom picked up her hand and looked directly into her eyes.

"I promise never to read your poetry," he said earnestly.

She laughed and pulled her hand away to bat the side of his head.

"Thank you very much!"

◆　　　◆　　　◆

Tom's lips moved across her eyes, her face, brushing, caressing.

Take it, little ghost. Feel it. Don't you want to know what it's like? Shut your eyes and pretend it's that young man of yours.

But the feel of Tom's lips continued to move across her face, now to her mouth, licking ever so lightly.

Tom groaned and lay back on the bed.

"Got to stop that," he said.

"You don't have to."

"Not going to mess around with your back, m'dear. You heal. We'll wait."

"Not for long, Tom."

"As long as it takes, Matty." His tone was firm. "I want you well more than I want you."

Matty rolled on her side and smiled at the jagged shadow of the flagpole on the rough split logs of the wall. It was going to happen sooner than Tom thought. The girl hadn't taken the kiss. Maybe she wasn't quite ready for that. But they would get there. She was still here. Matty had eaten a large bowl of raspberries and ice cream this evening without tasting a single bite.

29

Joseph came the next day to negotiate the purchase of Tom's car. From the couch, Matty heard them, Tom's voice low and easy, Joseph's ragged, abrupt and challenging. He didn't come in, nor did Matty want him to. Their last communication had to be their final one. As her understanding of why he had brought these particular lines grew, so did the certainty that he had too much pride to see her again.

Between the idea
And the reality
Between the motion
And the act
Falls the Shadow

Between the conception
And the creation
Between the emotion
And the response
Falls the Shadow
Life is very long.

Matty knew the poem well. What lit major didn't? They were selected lines from T.S. Eliot's "The Hollow Men." It was a confession of sorts but also a plea for understanding. He wanted her to know he was more than a liar. Joseph was a hollow man and knew it. He was unable to bring any of his ambitions or ideas to fruition. His world would end as the poem did, "Not with a bang but a whimper." That was tragedy enough, but what made it worse was that, in writing these lines to her, a stranger, it was clear that, in all his world, he felt that only Matty would understand the depth of his failure.

It was good that the men had to leave to transfer the title, allowing her a little time alone to grieve for Joseph.

◆   ◆   ◆

Matty woke in the middle of the night with a feeling that something was wrong. The feeling quickly clarified into the certainty that what she was doing was crazy. What made her suppose that she knew anything about the girl's needs? A few sensual experiences—What were they? Merely incidental, surely. It must be the sex-crazed era she was in that made her suppose a spirit couldn't rest for lack of physical love. Or Jane.

Sitting up now, restless, almost angry, she inhaled deeply and tried to come to terms with disappointment. The clouds were outside the window, slow-moving wraiths behind the thrusting flagpole. She had asked Tom to take down the flag to prevent further wear and it sat as it had on that first night, folded in a pile on the little chair opposite, leaving the pole stark and useless outside.

Phallic symbol, she thought ironically. But the symbol remained, holding the focus of her mind. Love, physical and emotional, had been an ongoing part of Matty's adult life. Jane had a different experience. Perhaps her opinion was more valid. People raped, murdered, went crazy because of sex and love. But a young girl? She lay back and sent her mind back to her own teenage years when she had wondered and longed and ached. The hours lying on her bed day-dreaming, pressing her mouth onto her hand, imagining a boy's lips pressing back. It was a powerful drive even then. Those girls in Salem—Look at the havoc they had wreaked! Hadn't she read somewhere that poltergeists were more active when there was a pubescent girl in the house? Maybe emotional or physical need *was* at the bottom of this. But optimism does not rule the night and Matty was sure there was nothing she could do to help the girl who had lost her love. He was probably a young, bunchy-muscled farm boy. How could the girl's dreams be fulfilled by loaning her Tom's forty-two year-old, pale and sedentary body?

Matty turned to her sleeping husband. *I love you,* she thought. But the girl didn't. And that, surely, made all the difference. A few tears slipped from the corners of her eyes. Remembering the girl watching them make love from the house, she had created and been caught up in the excitement of her plan, of her own need to repay the girl for the gift of freedom from pain, her own need to mother this child and…maybe to play God and free the girl's spirit? Was that part of it? Who wouldn't want to do that?

She curled up on her side, adjusting the position of the arm in the sling carefully on top of her ribs. The flagpole sprouted stubbornly out of the window sill, stirring a faint hope.

She could try. It was all she had to give.

30

It took time.

The girl had to be lured back slowly. The raspberries and ice cream were a start, followed by an irresistible chocolate cake Tom baked next day. That evening, Matty ate a piece of cake for the girl and then cut another for herself. This time, the girl watched and let Matty have the second piece. It was strangely social and thoughtful.

The hot baths would have felt wonderful in the cold evenings and Matty missed the feel of them without resenting the loss. She wore every soft, silky, plush piece of clothing she owned and the girl enjoyed them. At least, she took the feel of them. In an inspiration, Matty sat at the old dresser one day and brushed her hair until it shone. That invitation was accepted, too.

The roses were a great success. Evidently the girl loved roses and could see them adequately. It was an ongoing mystery that it seemed the girl didn't need to steal Matty's sight. She surely had to see where she was going or where Matty was or any number of things in order to do what she did. It reinforced Evelyn's theory. Only some ghosts talked, touched, had substance, interacted, could affect their surroundings, and apparently never all of these things. Perhaps all the dead did move on, leaving behind only a limited echo, but sight seemed the most common ability. Why else would the woman object to a change in decor or the nanny see the baby?

Tom teased Matty about being unusually affectionate as she lay on the couch one evening listening to Brahms' violin concerto, her head in his lap as he stroked her arm and played with her hair. *Take it,* Matty told the girl silently. *Take it.*

It didn't happen.

She fluctuated between despairing of ever being able to give the final gift of loving touch and wondering if, perhaps, the girl didn't want it after all. Was her little spirit reluctant to intrude on a personal relationship or uninterested? Or perhaps the outward, physical expressions of love were no substitute for the sight and feel of the boy she had cared for.

As the week neared its end, Matty's attitude went through several shifts. One afternoon, she decided that what she was trying to do was downright disgusting. She was trying to corrupt this young girl who, after all, couldn't have been much more than sixteen. She lay a long time alone on her bed reviewing everything she knew and all that had happened and came to the conclusion that the idea of corrupting a ghost was absurd. In over a hundred years of haunting this house, she must have seen it all. If there was any chance that wanting the physical experience of love was keeping her earthbound, Matty was obligated to offer it. The girl, after all, didn't have to accept it. For the first time, she wished she had never gotten into this situation. Tom had gone to the grocery to get beer and Matty desperately needed to talk to someone.

"Thank God you're in! I'm beginning to think I'm crazy again. And corrupt and immoral and stupid. Among other things."

Jane's reaction to the situation both shocked and reassured her.

"I wish to hell you could do it for me," she said.

Neither had much to add and Jane hung up in her usual abrupt manner.

Matty walked to the middle of the living room.

"Are you there?"

She was and obediently appeared.

"I'm leaving," Matty said.

Did she only imagine the anxious look on the girl's face?

"Not immediately, but you have to know I can't stay much longer. This is the last time I'm going to say this. I don't mind if you take over my body when Tom touches me. I'm glad to give you that if it's what you want. But it must be soon, that's all. It must be soon."

There seemed to be a little fear in the girl's gaze.

She's not sure, Matty thought. *She isn't really sure.*

◆   ◆   ◆

Matty's warning must have had some effect, because the next day the girl began to appear when Tom was around. Had she been afraid before and had managed to overcome it? What had caused the fear? There had never been any response to this oft-repeated question, not the slightest change in the girl's blank expression. Was it something she couldn't face? Had she repressed a memory, but the emotion lingered? Matty despaired of ever knowing. Now the girl was with them all the time. She watched as Tom walked through the house, read, helped with meals. Matty couldn't help but wonder if she observed him in the bathroom, too. It seemed immodest, improper, but it was absurd to expect a ghost to behave according to social norms.

Finally, just two days before they had to leave, the girl appeared and watched intently as Tom held Matty and kissed her, which he did often, gently, still careful of her back, and it seemed that for just an instant, the touch of Tom's lips left her. Or had he moved them away for that split second?

It seemed that the girl's form had more weight, to be more solid now, too. What, exactly, did that mean? Was the plan going to develop in time?

The trouble was, there wasn't much time. She was mending nicely and Tom needed to get back to work.

◆   ◆   ◆

The rest of that day and into the next, Matty had the strangest feeling that they were a family of three. Her little spirit was approaching Tom more and more boldly. It seemed impossible that he couldn't see her. Much of what Matty did now was for the girl. The worry that her behavior would seem peculiar to Tom proved groundless. Rather, he delighted in her increased involvement with the sensual world, sniffing bunches of wild flowers and finding that many of them smelled pretty bad, helping with the cooking, which involved a great deal of appreciative tasting, building fires so they could toast cold toes together and eagerly followed her lead in prolonged fondling. It was a revelation to Matty that the old feeling that her marriage was getting stale, even sour, was gone now that her concern was focused on the girl rather than on her own fears and endless lists of things to do.

"God!" he said as he pulled his hands out from under her sweater and took a deep breath. "It's like high school all over again!"

Matty laughed. It wasn't at all like high school. For one thing, she hadn't met Tom until later, but, more than that, she had felt those high school explorations intensely and now felt nothing most of the time, thanks to the girl.

"I know," she told him. "We'll make love soon."

"We shouldn't. We'll get carried away. Your call," he said, wiping his hand over his damp brow. "Don't trust me."

She smiled, not looking at her husband, and wondered again at how much could remain hidden from someone so close.

◆   ◆   ◆

Matty had fallen asleep on the couch. She woke feeling sensual, heavy.

"Rub my back, Tom" she said as she rolled over, not caring that this was demanding, unusual for her.

Still half asleep, she was aware that he got up from his chair and sat on the floor beside her. She felt his fingers pulling her sweater up, the unhooking of her bra and then nothing. The girl was moving in more quickly each time. It was tempting to look for the figure in blue, but it was better to lie still.

It progressed very slowly. Afraid the girl would back off, Matty dictated the pace and it was nearly half an hour before the slow, easy kisses and caresses led to her slipping out of the sweater and bra. Would the girl panic?

For a split second she felt Tom's long fingers on her breasts. It was strange. On waking, she had felt aroused, probably from an erotic dream.

Now that was gone. She felt nothing. Tom had taken off his shirt and lay alongside her, his mouth on her neck. She wondered if the girl felt the tickle of his chest hairs on her arm and whether Tom was using his tongue or brushing only his lips against her neck. Never before had she been sufficiently free of her own emotions to be aware of how carefully Tom tended to her needs and preferences. Now, as she watched, it was clear that he was more aware of her than she was of him in this situation. Gradually she realized that perhaps the oddest thing was that thoughts and ideas, even those with emotional content like gratitude and love existed in the minds, but without the physical reaction, the knowledge alone was cold and meaningless. What quirk of the body made such separation possible? It was, she thought, rather like being a computer.

What would the girl want her to do? Matty remembered how shy she had been the first few times she herself had made love, wanting to touch, but uncertain of her role. Would the girl want to be passive or would that limit the experience too much?

"Let's go upstairs, Matty. We can be more careful of your back on the bed." Tom's voice was rough.

Matty hesitated. She wasn't sure the girl had left her the ability to speak, but "Yes. All right," came out sounding quite normal.

It was difficult, climbing the stairs without the feel of the tread to reassure her. Matty watched her feet carefully. In the room, Tom insisted on pulling back the covers himself.

"Don't want you to hurt yourself at this point," he said.

He pulled off his slacks and shirt and looked at her, obviously wondering why she hadn't done the same.

"You want help?"

"Yes," she said teasingly.

Tom was willing to play any game. He came over to her and slid his hands under the elastic of her slacks and underpants and pulled her to him. He kissed her like that, his hands on her bare flesh.

Yes. This is just right.

The thought should have been followed by a surge of happiness, but the girl had taken all the physical responses that made that emotion recognizable.

"I love you, Tom."

It was important that this be an act of love, not just sex. She wondered what the boy's name had been and whether the girl had shut out the vision of Tom and was imagining the younger man in his place.

"I love you, too," Tom groaned. "Oh, God, do I love you!"

It was good that Tom was in a serious mood. They were apt to be playful when making love and that wouldn't do today.

They lay down. Matty remembered how cool the sheets should feel. Today, it was eerie to be there and yet not there, as it had been when she was dancing. Again she was a bundle of thoughts, floating.

Would the girl want to touch him, explore his body? Tentatively, Matty reached down for the interesting combination, the hardness with the soft, velvety cap. Usually, she felt her way to it, but this time she had to look down to make sure her hand found its way. Memory told her it was hot.

"Don't do that, Matty. I won't last."

She released the pressure, uncertain, without the reassurance of sensation, just how strong that pressure had been.

"Is your back okay?"

"It's fine." *I hope.*

She wondered if she should lie over Tom and put her breasts in his groin. There was a wonderfully appealing difference in a man's belly and groin and it had been one of the first impulses she had succumbed to in her first days of making love. She decided not to. Better to keep it simple, stay passive. Don't scare her away. Let Tom assume it was her back limiting her. Everything was going fine.

And yet, in a way, it wasn't fine. It was becoming a little scary, this business of not feeling anything. Her sense of smell was gone, too. She had noticed that the aroma of the fresh roses Tom had ordered had disappeared down in the living room and she missed the always pleasant smell of Tom's body. Could she taste? She kissed Tom, putting her tongue in his mouth. No. The bite of his pipe tobacco was gone.

Matty felt a little wave of fear flowing in, but quelled it. This was all planned. It was her gift.

Tom was in her now, moving slowly, cautiously, watching her face for guidance. How protective he was. And she realized that he always was, that her needs always came first. She was the selfish one. No feeling of love swept through her. That, too, was a physical thing. It registered now with no more impact than a printed sentence on a page. How was it on the other side? Surely the girl had her own thoughts. What were they? Was she filling this in with remembrance from the past, shutting her eyes to Tom's image and imagining her long-dead love?

Matty touched Tom's hair, ran her fingers down his cheek and looked at him as she never had before. It was supposed to be a ridiculous posture, but it didn't seem so to Matty. Tom's shoulders looked strong and his arms were swollen with the weight of his own body on them. His skin was clear and clean and altogether beautiful. Sex would never again be quite the same.

Tom could delay no longer. He came with a loud cry, followed immediately by remorse.

"Are you all right?"

"Yes, yes, I'm fine."

"But you didn't—"

"Yeah. I did." *Did I? Did she?* "It was kind of different, but I feel wonderful."

"Did I hurt you? Is that why you were holding back?"

"No." She hoped she was smiling reassuringly. At least, that was the message her brain was sending. Her hands had obeyed and apparently her voice did, too. "You didn't hurt me at all."

It was a little amusing that this, at least, was completely honest.

Tom pulled the sheet and blanket over the two of them, lay back and caressed her hip with light, slow strokes. Soon his fingers stopped moving and Matty heard the heavier, regular breathing that told her he was sleeping. She usually enjoyed the lazy after-sex feeling, Tom's body touching hers, before she, too, dozed off. Sometimes it was only a few inches of an arm or thigh, but it was delicious. Matty supposed the girl was enjoying that now. She waited for the return of feeling to her body.

The minutes passed, marked only by Tom's quiet breathing and a noisy flock of geese heading south. The time grew uncomfortably long. Matty looked for the girl. There was no reason why she shouldn't appear, but there was no sign. The annoying thought grew that, in a peculiar way, the girl was avoiding her. Could the person inhabiting your own body be said to be avoiding you?

The minutes grew longer. Matty sent out a silent message telling the girl that the time was over. At first, it was a friendly message that also asked how the girl was, if that was what she had wanted, if she had enjoyed it. It would be nice to see the look of gratitude in her eyes, perhaps some confirmation that she had received something she had needed.

The word *succubus* floated into her mind. She pushed it away...

The moment came when Matty had to admit that her little ghost was completely in control and that she, Matty, was helpless. The girl could hold her forever if she chose.

It was a stunning realization. Matty waited for the jolt of fear, but, of course, anxiety and fear were felt through the body. There was only the emotionally empty mental notation that this was true.

Possession. This is called possession. This is bad. Could I even survive with no information from my body about what I'm touching, feeling, without the warnings that pain and cold and heat provide? I could punish her by eating bad food and wearing rough clothing. But she could punish me, too, not tell me when I feel ill or have pain. This kind of thinking is crazy. I need to keep my mind under control here, figure out what to do. Could she take over the rest of me, my mind, my ability to control my movements? She moved her fingers and feet, careful not to disturb Tom. *Not yet anyway.*

Matty lay naked on the bed she could not feel, mentally, unemotionally exploring what lay ahead. It seemed a shame that she had discovered again how life should be just before losing the ability to live it.

But she didn't care.

No jolt of electricity in her nerves, no fast heartbeat, no nausea rising from her stomach told her that it mattered.

31

They rode in a dream world. The sunroof of the Acura framed clouds moving in ragged lines across the brilliant blue of an October sky slashed from time to time by the darkness of passing telephone lines, the occasional bird or overhanging trees. She and Tom had agreed long ago that they should each drive their own cars, she the automatic and he the manual shift. They had developed different instinctive reflexes and it was safer that way. But, of course, she couldn't drive now. This was the first time she had tilted back in her own passenger seat and watched what passed overhead.

Tom hummed or whistled a few bars of unidentifiable melody from time to time. A slight smile came and went, crinkling the corners of his eyes. He was taking his wife home. When would the time be right to erase that smile, to tell her story? It seemed no more possible now than it had that night in the restaurant. Maybe when they got home. Maybe then.

Every time Matty looked over at his profile, gratitude caressed her. This was a man who would always love her, would never leave her. The car accident made that clear a year ago and should have created then the gratitude she felt now. It hadn't. Not then. More like her father than her mother, gratitude was not an emotion that came readily to her. Independence felt better.

Neither she nor Tom talked much when driving. It was one of the small things they liked about each other. Now, especially, Matty needed to lie back and let her thoughts flit through all that had happened, picking up a memory here, another there, like randomly plucking wildflowers from a field. But there was no collected bouquet nor any compulsion to arrange and evaluate the total experience yet. The engine that had powered her life, the multitude of worries, had drifted into some abyss of irrelevance. She felt empty, her body drifting through a world as foreign and unfamiliar as Oz in which the colors and shapes overhead provided a mental distraction without emotional content. It was as though she had taken more Diazepam than ever before. The doctor in Hagerstown had recommended it as it had worked best to prevent spasm after her former accident. It had been funny, accepting his prescription. An ample supply already sat on her nightstand at the old house.

Neil knew more than he was saying. She had come to that conclusion based on the one word, "magic," and the fact that he had not insisted she return immediately when the sensory losses were first reported. Neil had planned all this. No. Not all this. His plan had gone wrong. What had he known and not known about the "magic" that caused his judgment to be so flawed? She must have a special connection to the girl, probably like Jane's grandmother, that had made her experience different from the others Neil had known about. He could have had no idea how it would end. They must talk. In person. His earlier reticence was now understandable. He hadn't wanted to begin this important conversation over the phone while she was recuperating in the hospital and he still had no idea what had followed the hospital stay. How much regret was he carrying already over his part in this insane "vacation?" He would want, need, to help her, although she couldn't see exactly how he could. They should tell Tom together. That would be best, the only way Tom would believe her. And then life would go on very differently.

Riding like this with the clouds floating away with her thoughts, she had relived pieces of the last encounter with the girl over and over. Remembrance brought a diluted version of the feelings she would have felt then. It was more like a memory of a dream than of reality...

◆　　　◆　　　◆

Lying in a bed she could not feel, Matty's brain played with the implications of losing control of her body with an astonishing lack of anxiety. Without phys-

ical sensation, there was no recognizable fear, no pounding heart, tingling nerves or sickness in the stomach. She prayed silently, her eyes searching the room, hoping her expression would explain to the girl the necessity of returning her senses. Speaking aloud would waken Tom. It would be cruel to alarm him. In between these appeals, she examined the lovemaking. How nicely her back had played into the necessity to be passive that lack of feeling had imposed on her! Did her back hurt now? Had she done anything to damage it? She didn't think so. As it had so often, her gaze came to the window and remained there. Outside, her familiar flagpole, her phallic symbol, now the symbol of… What, exactly? What lay in her future?

A half hour passed. The clock on her night stand seemed afflicted with some technological ailment that caused the bright red numbers to change at impossibly long intervals. Her mind, done with imagining what life would be like if she remained like this, moved on to an attempt to find a solution. A solution had to be found, for there was a mental facet to fear and it must be erased. Cold logic told her this. The girl's hold had to be broken. It was still hard to believe her sweet spirit could do this to her. Had sex proved to be the final, irresistible temptation?

It was that window, the focus of so many of her thoughts over the last weeks, that offered an answer. The girl had never left the house. Maybe if she went outside, the girl would be left inside. The girl had left her the power of movement. That made sense. What could she experience if Matty couldn't move?

She stood up beside the bed, careful not to wake Tom. Careful, too, to watch her feet so she could set them carefully, quietly, on the floor. With neither kinesthetic feeling nor touch to guide her, it was necessary to hold onto the bedroom door frame before turning and placing one bare foot on the top stair. Leaning over to put the other foot on the next step, she saw her breasts, her feet, and was aware of her nakedness. She didn't feel naked. It was probably cold. Or had Tom's fire warmed the house sufficiently? An attempt to say "Please" to the girl came out an incomprehensible whimper. At least, her voice was still under her control. Perhaps she had to leave that, too, in order for Matty to continue to function on the girl's behalf. Would it be like this forever? Was this Nirvana, leaving her free of physical drives? Would the members of some sects consider her fortunate?

You're going a little mad now, she told herself. She sat down on the step and took a familiar, usually consoling position, arms folded on her knees, head on her arms. It was intolerable. Shutting her eyes took away her last hold on the physical world. She opened them immediately and jerked up her head.

The girl was there, standing at the foot of the stairs with that familiar expression, very faint, just slightly sad and sympathetic, a kind of tightness around the corners of her mouth and a way of looking up out of the tops of her blue eyes.

At the same moment, Matty's back began to hurt and her bare buttocks felt the unfamiliar cool hardness of bare wood. She laughed and felt the muscles of her throat making a hiccuping, stifled sound as she stood.

"Poor child. You couldn't resist, could you? But you're a good child. A dear child. I love you, you know."

Careful of the step that was the cause of this extraordinary situation, Matty moved quickly down the stairs, her arms held out. The girl's arms were out, too, reaching for her. It seemed that this time, they would touch.

"Matty, who are you talking to?"

Tom was at the top of the stairs and the girl was gone.

◆   ◆   ◆

It still sat in her chest like a stone each time this moment was relived. It probably had been an absurd, comic scene to Tom, his wife standing naked on the stairs holding out her arms to the empty air, but it had felt like tragedy to Matty. Could she have embraced the girl who had instantly disappeared? It seemed important, that one touch, the physical exchange of feeling. Knowing that only reinforced how important making love must have been to the girl. The sweet aftermath, too, the warmth of the bed and each other, the kiss of body to body that removed tension and brought a sensual peace.

Would the girl have returned if they had stayed another day or more? The key to that wide plank door was still in her purse. Would she have to give it back to Neil?

Matty became once more aware of the passing scene.

"I'd like a house like that, Tom."

"Like what?"

The house was well behind them now. It was too late for Tom to see. That was all right. There would be lots of houses. Matty opened her window and offered an arm to the cool breeze. The moving air ruffled the pale hairs on her arm. She smiled. Everything felt good to her now.

"Never mind. We'll see what we find. I'll help you plant the garden. I love flowers."

"Roses?"

"I don't think so. They cause too much trouble."

"Cause too much trouble?"

"*Are* too much trouble, I mean. Too much trouble to take care of."

The car lurched over a bump in the road.

"Sorry," Tom said. "I didn't see that. Did it hurt?"

"I'm fine. Not to worry," she said. It had hurt. She wanted to laugh. Hurting was good. Soon she could tell all this to her husband. The urgent need to see Neil rose and then fell back into the well of peace inside her.

They were silent again. Matty went back to her languid dreams of a house and a yard with a child running around, smelling the flowers. Not roses. But something beautiful.

"I want friends, Tom. We've been so busy—*I've* been so busy—we've become unsociable, haven't we? I want to sit out in the back yard and watch the fireflies and talk to people I care about."

"Sounds good to me," he said.

"And maybe really, seriously, think about a child."

"That sounds good, too. We can make love like today more often. Take our time."

Matty smiled.

"I'm not sure it will ever be quite like that again," she said.

32

"I'm sorry. The doctor is out of town for three days." The voice was dripping with regret.

"Erica. It's me. Matty. He's gone again? Wasn't Neil expecting me back?"

"Oh! Matty!" It was a voice with genuine warmth now. "You didn't sound like yourself. You sound great! I'm not supposed to say that. How you sound. Or anybody. But you do." Erica was aware that she had broken from her usual warm, but proper, professionalism.

Had her voice really changed that much, Matty wondered? Perhaps it was—She sought the right word—looser? Someone had once said her voice had "bounce," that it had a wide register. That must have been lost this last year.

Erica regained her usual control. "The vacation must have been helpful. He's only gone for two days, back day after tomorrow. Tight schedule, but he'll want to see you. Shall I book a time?"

Matty blessed Neil's discretion. Erica's tone made it clear that she knew nothing of her troubles in the house on South Mountain.

"Thanks. Yes. Can you get me in as soon as he's back?"

Erica was trained not to argue this point. Matty could see the familiar face that always twisted in concern when Neil's availability was limited.

"Whenever you can fit me in."

It was hard to keep from sounding impatient, but she knew Erica would do her best.

"Wednesday at seven?"

"In the evening?"

"He's really booked when he's away for a few days like this. But I know he'll want to see you."

Something in her voice told Matty that Erica knew Neil's interest was more than professional.

"I'll be there."

Matty was reluctant to set the phone back in its cradle, to relinquish that tie. How could Neil have done this? After what she'd been through! He could at least have told her about taking off for two days. Not that it would have been possible for her to come back earlier. She sat back in the soft, comfortable couch in her own home in Rockville and smiled, impatience quelled, anticipating the coming conversation.

◆   ◆   ◆

Mrs. Grogan was crooning again, her thin voice rising and falling in an anguished protest against what her life had become. Matty stopped at her wheelchair in the corridor and laid a hand on her shoulder.

"It's all right, Mrs. Grogan. It's all right."

The woman looked up briefly, horrors in her milky eyes that Matty never wanted to understand. Then she went back to her song, but it was better this time, a little softer, a little intelligence in the animal sound.

Her father was in his wheelchair watching Wall Street Week on television. It must be a good day.

"Mathilda! Should you be driving?"

"This is the first time since I fell. A short distance is okay."

The nursing home had been selected partially because of its proximity to the office.

He looked pleased. "I was worried about you."

"I was in good hands."

"So you said. But the other accident—"

"I know. I think I can promise you I'll do better this time."

He nodded approvingly.

"Dad, can we turn the TV off? I'd like to talk to you."

"Of course."

He flicked the switch on the bed next to his chair as she sat down.

"Done," he said and looked at her expectantly.

It occurred to Matty that she had never asked this before. That had been a mistake, as though her visits were no more important than the ongoing television and didn't require his complete attention.

"I was doing some reading up there at the cabin," she began. "About ghosts. It was pretty interesting. Do you—Have you had any experiences that would—Do you think it's possible there are ghosts or something like that?"

He smiled at her. "I ought to believe. I'll be one soon enough."

Matty leaned forward.

"You do think that? You believe you'll be one?"

He raised his curly eyebrows and pursed his lips in surprise.

"Well, no. I guess I can't say I do. What's on your mind, Mathilda? Why are you suddenly interested in ghosts? That fall scare you?"

"Maybe."

"I have no idea what's after death, my dear. Nor do I much care. I think it's important to have a good life, one you can lie in bed and think about with some satisfaction. Whether there is more after this...Well, why do we need more? The issue surfaced most strongly for me when your mother died. She believed in God and heaven and the whole kit and caboodle. Totally and completely. For no reason I could ever ascertain. It would be wonderful to see her again. It doesn't seem to matter quite so much as it used to. Death isn't an awful thing, you know. You get tired. Sleeping without waking doesn't seem the worst thing that could happen. It's better than suffering. Sometimes I think it's better than boredom." He gave a snort that was meant to be a laugh, but lacked humor. "If there is an after-life, they damn well better give you back your health and some energy." He smiled as if to reassure her, his teeth darker than the skin pale from lack of sun. "If I can come back and let you know, I will. But Blackstone couldn't do it for his wife."

She laughed. "I remember. No, I wasn't asking because I was scared. It's just...Maybe it's just time for me to think about such things. Did you know—" She pulled an odd fact from one of her real estate magazines

"—that in California and Vermont, sellers are legally required to tell buyers if the house is haunted?"

It was his turn to laugh.

"You think that's silly?" she asked.

"I think it's damn silly. Don't you?"

Matty stared out the window as though her attention had been caught by the familiar sight of more brick blocks like the one they were in. Until Neil and she had their talk with Tom, this conversation was over. United, the issue could be brought up with more credibility.

"Do you think of Mom much?"

"All the time. Haven't much else to do."

This was distressing.

"All the time?"

"No, no. Don't frown. They're happy thoughts. Never expected her to go first, though, almost twenty years younger than I was. But I was lucky to have had her at all. There are damn few good marriages around, you know. Really good ones where you get to caring more about the other person than you do about yourself. You're lucky to have Tom. He feels that way, you know."

"I know."

"You don't."

That hurt. "I know. I know." She couldn't meet his eyes. "He's a better person than I am, isn't he?" She looked at him then. "I'm working on it, Dad. Really. Some things that have happened lately have made me appreciate him more."

"Glad to hear it. A little...maybe...tame for you, is he? But exciting doesn't make the best husbands, in my experience."

"What about you? Mom always thought you were an exciting man. So did I. And you were certainly a good husband."

This time it was her father who couldn't meet her eyes. It caught her by surprise.

"I don't want to know, Dad."

"And I'm not stupid enough to tell you."

"Anyway, I think you must have been a good husband. Mom loved you. Funny that some people think you owe love if you're married. It's the one who is loved, who elicits love, that deserves the credit, don't you think? At least, some of the time. I think you were both lovable."

"I like that." He nodded in approval. "Then you have to take credit for Tom's love for you."

Matty made a face. "Shoot, Dad. I didn't mean that. There are people who are just less self-centered, more loving. He's like that."

"Shoot? What happened to shit?"

"Did I say that in front of you?"

"This last year. Good for letting off steam, isn't it?"

"Maybe." She grimaced. "Yes. Yes, it is. Still, I'm trying to ditch it. By the way, while we're into this relationship stuff, it's time I said you and Mom were good parents. Don't think I ever told you that. Thank you for the way you raised me."

"Thank you?" The eyebrows went up again. "What's this?"

"I don't know. Time alone with little to do lets you evaluate things."

"That's news?"

She smiled back at him. "Sorry. Of course you know that. But I was thinking the other day in the hospital how many people I know with too much baggage left over from the way they were raised. If I have a child—"

"Is that what this is all about?"

That caught Matty by surprise. She had to think a few moments before responding.

"Maybe. Maybe it is. I've been thinking that when—if—I'm a parent, I'm going to try to be like you and Mom. You cared. You watched. You let me know when I was doing wrong or doing well. But you mostly let me be me, didn't push me into a mold, try to make me what you thought I ought to be. Except in the really important things."

"Did we do that well? Funny. I left that pretty much to your Mother. I thought we just enjoyed you."

"Maybe it comes to the same thing. You taught me to enjoy, too. Somewhere along the line, I lost that and, this last week, I think I got it back again. Do you still value soft clothes and nice smells and things like that? Are they important to you now?"

"Sometimes I think that's all you value when you get old. Really old, I mean. Like me."

"You're not that old!"

"Forget years. These legs made me old."

Each knew the other was resisting the impulse to look at the space where his legs should be.

"Losing your mother made me old," he continued without a change in intonation. "Ideas are nice entertainment, but it's too late to do much about them. The body becomes more and more important. Just getting comfortable can take all your energy and ingenuity. Interests contract, geographical boundaries become restricted, names are forgotten, people drift away. Or die. Your own body remains. You can't escape it."

"Would you want to if you could?"

"That's death."

"Yes. I suppose so."

They sat for a few moments in comfortable silence and Matty realized this was another thing they hadn't done before.

"What kind of vacation was that," her father asked, "that sent you back thinking of ghosts and death? What did you do there? Something you read?"

"Not exactly."

Matty wasn't quite sure where to take this.

"I learned that I had moved too far away from…Shoot! Don't know quite how to explain this. It's odd, Dad," she said, sticking her feet on the bottom of the bed's side rail. "I always thought that ideas, intelligence, the…the mental and spiritual aspects of man were his highest nature. The most important. Maybe I still do. But I have relearned the importance of the physical and I'm having a little trouble coming to terms with that."

"Let me tell you how important the physical is!"

At first, Matty assumed her father was referring to the loss of his legs, but it was more than that.

"We are, inescapably, physical beings!" he said. "And we live in a physical world. Your accident should have taught you that. Too much pain or hunger and you can't philosophize worth a damn!"

"I know. I know. But you can't compare eating a steak with the experience of love, for instance."

"Love is very physical."

"I'm not talking about sex."

"Neither am I. Or even a kiss or a touch. I'm talking about a man giving his jacket to a woman who's cold or your mother giving me the last piece of cake when you know she wants it herself. There's no way to show love that isn't physical. Words aren't worth a damn without action!"

He was speaking more emphatically, more loudly, now.

"You could write a poem." Matty smiled, trying to lighten the conversation a little. This conversation had the potential of becoming depressing. Her father had always been stoic. Could she handle an open admission of misery from him?

"Man takes your sandwich from you, throws cold water on you, punches you in the mouth and then gives you a beautiful poem that says he loves you, what's your take on that?"

Matty laughed and the thought of her father crying on her shoulder fled. He would never do that.

"He could write something that gave all his money to her. Those are words."

They were both smiling now.

"Money's not worth anything in itself. Its only importance is what it can buy. Mostly physical stuff."

"You're arguing for the sake of argument. Like we used to do. Right now, you're finding intellectual debate entertaining even while you're telling me it's not important."

Her father's grin brought her a surge of happiness that he could still feel joy and that she could give this gift.

"Golden mean, darlin'. Golden mean."

"Socrates. You're sharp today, Dad. We haven't batted around ideas like this in ages."

"I'm stimulated. And I thank you for that. This is a damn sight more interesting than what you usually talk about."

"Business."

"Well...I want to know what's on your mind. So if it's business, I want you to talk business. But I like this better. It's nice to share thoughts of your Mother. She was wonderful that way, you know. Loving us in a physical way. She took care of us, our clothes, our food, our home and enjoyed doing it. She showed love every time she ironed a shirt and made meat loaf. God, I loved that meat loaf!"

"Is the food bad here, Dad? I thought it was pretty good."

"It's fine. I ate your Mother's food too long."

"I'll make you meat loaf."

He picked up her hand and kissed it.

"Now that's love, Mathilda. I know you don't like to cook the way your Mother did. But you're not entirely well yet and you've got a business to run. This old man can live without meat loaf."

They sat a few minutes thinking separate thoughts. The leaves on the trees outside were warning of rain, turning silver sides up and moving restlessly. The room had a big picture window. The home guaranteed "Every Room Has a View." This room had about one fifth of a maple tree if its resident was sitting up in bed.

"There's a lot we can live without, isn't there? Besides meat loaf, I mean," Matty said finally. "I learned that at the cabin. I'm going to hang on to that simplicity thing. Homes today are overdecorated. Too much to take care of. And I want a yard, some space."

"Do you now? When did that get decided? At this wonderful log house, I suppose."

"Mm." She nodded. "My life was going in the wrong direction. I'm going to fix that."

"Remember the pendulum."

"And Socrates. Why are you grinning at me like that?"

"I never thought I'd be giving you advice again. It's damn nice."

"It is nice. Wouldn't you like to come and live with us when we get settled in a house? We can get a rambler, a single story house or one with a first level bedroom so you wouldn't have to use steps. Guaranteed space and a view of a whole tree."

"No."

"No. Just like that?"

"Just like that. This is my place. I pay to be here. No favors from any-body."

"But do you like it? And, Dad—" She wasn't sure she should say this. "You seem like your old self today. Do you really need a nursing home?"

"Hah! You noticed! Well, of course you did. New meds. Thank God they keep coming up with new stuff. Could probably live on my own. If I learned to maneuver this chair so I could cook and keep house and all that. Don't want to. Don't want to be dependent on you, either. Tell you what, though. I'll visit. Maybe a weekend once in a while."

"Deal."

Both reached out to join hands at the same moment. They looked at each other, recognizing the unity they shared, the absolute indestructibility of their relationship.

"Would you like to take me for a walk?" he asked.

"I'd love to!"

"You've been here nearly an hour."

Matty ducked her head. "Ouch. I'm sorry, Dad."

"No. I'm sorry. I didn't mean it as a criticism. I know you're busy. Yes, I have noticed you always stay exactly an hour, but today I meant you probably shouldn't be abusing your back and with the arthritis in my arm..." He always stopped before admitting to any physical limitations.

"No. I probably can't handle your wheelchair today. Would one of the attendants wheel you out and we could just sit in the garden? It would sort of be like old times at Grandma and Grandpa's. Except the Hortons won't come over."

He laughed, a sharp bark.

"Always wondered if they couldn't stand to be alone together."

♦   ♦   ♦

Only the chrysanthemums were blooming this late in the season, but they were enough, a carefully selected mixture of yellow, white and rusty red. There was a nice variety of foliage on the trees and bushes.

"They need a blue spruce," Matty said.

"Yes, they do," her father agreed.

It seemed important, that blue spruce.

"I notice you don't mind being called Mathilda any more," he said.

"I think I like it."

"Must have been some vacation."

A short, overweight attendant in light blue, breathing heavily, pushed the chair back in when it started to rain, turned the wheelchair into its usual position by the bed and left without a word, only the same shy smile that had been his greeting.

"It's been a good visit, Mathilda."

"It has."

She leaned over to kiss him. Tired now, he looked old and helpless. It would be difficult for him to get through dinner in the dining hall, but he was too proud to ask for meals in his room. In winter, they put a robe across his lap, but now the blue cotton pants were visible, pinned at knee level.

"Dad, death isn't the end."

She had to say it.

"I'm glad you believe that."

"No. Really."

"Maybe some day you'll tell me why you're so sure."

She smiled a promise, turned and walked through the doorway. Behind her, his voice came.

"Don't wait too long."

She was grateful for the note of humor.

33

"Neil!"

Matty burst through the door with her eyes lit and a smile that was carefully contained but ready to become a world class grin as soon as this little man had responded properly to the one word that was half greeting, half accusation.

There was no response at all. It seemed that Neil wasn't sure how to respond. There was no matching laughter in his eyes, no conspiratorial smile, no suggestion on his small, calm face that he had any secret to share.

Matty dropped onto her favorite chair, big enough for her to sit sideways and tuck her feet under her skirt after slipping off her shoes. It was soft brown leather, typical of this room which hid luxury with understatement.

"You look pretty good," Neil said tentatively. "—considering what you've gone through."

Psychiatric fencing, she thought. He doesn't know all that has happened. Has it ever happened before? She could play his game.

"I feel great."

"Good. Good." He sat down in the chair opposite. "No further sensory disturbances?"

She eyed him warily. Who was going to make the first move?

"What do you think?" she asked.

"What do I think?" He looked a little surprised before he replaced the mask. "You're in a playful mood today. That's good. Being back home is good for you." He nodded, approving both his diagnosis and her condition. "Why don't you tell me about your vacation? No. It was hardly that, was it? I'm sorry. Tell me about the last few weeks, then."

Anyone else, she thought, would have leaned forward in anticipation. Not Neil. That might look like pressure. Matty was getting a little impatient. Why couldn't he let down the barriers this time, give something away? He had done it before. Perhaps he regretted that. She tried an indirect approach.

"I read some books on the history of the house."

His eyebrows went up. "I wasn't aware there were any."

"Oh, yes. And some, um, folklore. About the girl."

She paused.

"The girl," he prompted.

"Oh, for heaven's sake, Neil, the girl!" Matty was impatient now.

He nodded, but it was just for encouragement. There was no understanding on his face. She had been leaning forward and now sank back into the chair.

"Psychiatrists!" she moaned. "You're taking all the fun out of this, you know. Tell me you don't know anything about the girl."

She stared at him, daring him.

"I'm sorry, Matty. What girl is this?"

"This—" She paused, turned her head and looked out of the corners of her eyes. "You really don't know?"

"No."

"None of the other people you sent there ever had, uh, let's say, unusual experiences?"

"Such as…?"

Matty rubbed her forehead. It didn't help. Neil was her psychiatrist, bound by legal obligations not to tell what she said. She would have to be the one to begin this conversation. Why did a ghost on South Mountain seem so far away, so unlikely in this responsible-looking office? How to begin?

"I met your ghost."

Neil's hands steepled, his elbows on his chair arms. That was a bad sign. "Ghost?"

There was no trace of emotion in that one word, certainly none of the confirmation she was looking for.

"Oh, shit—shoot! No one told you about her? The girl?"

The top of the steeple parted and reformed.

"Was this before or after your fall, Matty?"

"All the time, Neil, for heaven's sake…" She realized what he was getting at. "I didn't hit my head, Neil! Oh, well, yes, I did, but she was there before that. All the time. She lives there. Or lived…" Matty stopped. "You're not buying this. Well, of course, you wouldn't if you hadn't heard if from anyone else. But *she* took the smell of the roses that time I called you. *She* did it. And you didn't insist I come back. So you must have known…" She waved her hands in frustration. "…something! You've got to give me something here! It wasn't me. I was okay. Give me that much, at least. Say you know that!"

"All right. I know that." The tone was reassuring. "You're okay."

Matty dropped her head back against the expensive leather and shut her eyes. *Finally! Thank God. Of course Neil had to be careful. Who would go to a psychiatrist who believed in ghosts? We can talk now.* Relief poured through her, melting the muscles in a downward pattern, starting with her shoulders. She closed her eyes and pictured her little spirit.

"Well, I'll accept that you didn't know it was a 'she.' A young 'she,' just a girl. And I never caught on. Thought she was just being sympathetic. I don't know how I managed as long as I did. Looking back, I can't believe I stayed there when I was such a mess! I was—You wouldn't believe how incredibly exhausted I was! Those sensory losses…Fear kept me from sleeping and I had to force myself to eat. I was always hungry! And then—Oh, this gets too—"

Neil's part in this hit her suddenly and she sat up to stare at him accusingly.

"Why? Why did you let this go on? Why did you put me through this misery?"

There was no response, only a blank look impossible to read.

"Neil? Neil, I really need you to tell me—Well, damn it, you owe me an apology! That was Hell! Part was Heaven, I grant you, and I'm going to check into that. Start going to church and reading. But…"

She stopped. It was his turn now. Measurable seconds passed. Finally, Neil spoke.

"I'm listening, Matty."

The anxiety that had gone away only a few moments ago began to prick at her again.

"No! That's not good enough! I need to hear *you* now. You said you believed…What was it I said?" She rubbed her forehead, trying to remember exactly what it was he had agreed to.

"Yes!" She dropped her hand and glared at him. "That I was okay. That means I wasn't responsible for those sensory losses. That was it. You said that." She paused, trying to read his face. "You were lying. You didn't believe I was all right, did you?" Matty's voice was low and tight, each word a separately and emphatically enunciated accusation.

"No. Not exactly. You said to say you were okay and I did that. I *do* agree with that. This is, as I said before, something we can fix. I was, perhaps, a little misleading. I didn't want you to stop. I think it's important that you tell me about this experience."

"You just don't want me talking about a psychiatrist who uses a ghost for therapy! It would make you look nuts!"

Matty was sitting up straight now, leaning toward him. Neil hadn't moved from his carefully maintained, relaxed posture but the ends of his steepled fingers rubbed together, agitated.

"No, Matty. I wouldn't manipulate you that way."

It was impossible not to believe that gentle, caring voice, but that voice was his stock in trade. Did it mean anything?

"You said it was magic!" she said almost triumphantly, stabbing a finger at him. "Before I left! You gave yourself away!"

"I meant that in a poetic way. The magic of nature's healing powers. They seem almost magic sometimes." He was leaning towards her now, speaking earnestly, the mask gone. "We're a part of the earth. I have found that those who garden, who walk, who knit or work with wood, people who keep in touch with the physical world, who are alive to its smells, its tastes, its feel, are more at peace with themselves. That's what I wanted you to experience. That's all."

It was a long speech for Neil. Matty felt the weight of his belief in what he was saying. She had just learned this lesson herself.

"Well, that was eloquent! Then you do think I'm nuts."

"Of course not," he said, leaning back again, encouraging her to do the same. "Why don't we talk about it and see what we come up with."

He started to steeple his hands again, then caught himself, rubbed his fingertips together one final time and then set them carefully on his thighs and waited for her to give in. But Matty knew the power of silence, too. The game was going to be played her way from now on or she wasn't going to play.

She pulled her feet out from under her and her toes felt for her shoes. He gave in.

"All right, Matty. Let's discuss an idea just as a possibility, all right? You were under considerable strain and had lost touch with a part of your life that was important to you. Is important to all of us. You were living in your head and not in a particularly creative way, planning, worrying. Sex had become a brief, programmed encounter. You had ceased to enjoy things like improving the appearance of your environment. You rushed through simple meals or fast food. You weren't social any more. The people you dealt with at work were problems, not companions. You were insulating yourself from life in a misguided attempt to avoid overstimulation. We've agreed to all that in past sessions."

It was a litany she knew all too well. Matty nodded her head impatiently.

"But that's why I needed her! That's why she made me really see, feel!"

"That's what was going on before you left and we know why," he concluded as though she had not spoken.

"The accident."

"Precisely. And you were coping well, considering your personality—"

"I know. I'm one of those exceptionally sensitive people. Too much imagination. I remember asking you if those were the kind of people who went nuts—"

"I never—"

"I know. Of course you didn't say 'nuts.' Anyway, you meant they go 'round the bend more easily. This is all old news, Neil. And if you're implying this is all my imagination, I have to tell you you're the one who's nuts!"

Matty shoved her feet into her pumps, reached for her purse and sat staring at her doctor in an unblinking defiance that clearly indicated imminent departure.

Neil pursed his lips and moved them around in different positions before he spoke again.

"Your imagination might play into that but that's not what I'm getting at."

"So what else in my personality is such a problem?"

"Your tendency to feel responsible for everyone. Your need to fix things."

"We know that. That's old news, too. What's that got to do with this?"

"I think I underestimated how much guilt you were still carrying."

"I'm not guilty! The accident wasn't my fault!"

Matty was angry now, an anger she would later realize was born of disappointment. She and Neil were supposed to be sharing stories, the excitement of her incredible experience.

"Mentally, of course, you know the facts that came out at the trial proved your innocence. But until then, you weren't sure. Everything had happened too fast for you to be certain you had responded appropriately. Emotionally, you were still holding on to that guilt. You weren't responsible for killing that woman, but it feels as though you are, doesn't it?"

This wasn't going at all the way she wanted it to. Neil had scored a point.

"Sometimes. Yes, sometimes. But I always talk myself out of it."

"That you need to do this tells me that what I said is true, that you haven't let go of the guilt."

289

"Who says?"

"What has happened to you says that. I can't tell you how sorry I am that I missed the depth of this problem before. We need to dig more deeply to explore why you haven't begun to shed this burden. And, of course, I am, to some extent, making an assumption here. An assumption I believe is warranted, but needs to be reinforced by finding out more about your current state. That's what we need to talk about. This hallucination—"

"Ghost. She was a ghost. A spirit. A...a..." Matty tried to think of the many words she had used to describe the girl, but they wouldn't come.

"All right. The ghost. In all probability a part of you—"

"A girl from Civil War times?"

"The environment, the house, could have suggested the times, couldn't it? The girl was you as you once were. She represented a time of guiltless innocence, pleasures you had abandoned."

"Then why would she take them from me? All those pleasures?"

"Punishment. Guilt requires punishment, does it not? How old did she appear to be?"

"I don't know. About sixteen, seventeen."

"About your age when your Mother died. In your mind, the last time you were truly able to be a child, then, free from responsibility and therefore from guilt."

"She was too real. Vivid. The blue of her skirt—"

"Your favorite color."

"Okay. Okay. Her blonde hair."

"Blonde is sometimes a symbol of youth and innocence."

"It was ongoing! She was always there and always the same!"

Although the anger was still there, Matty was leaning back in the chair now, subdued by the logic of Neil's unhesitating, confident responses. He knew her. Knew she would respond to reason.

"That would be appropriate," he said in his frustratingly calm voice that made her sound all the more irrational.

Neil hesitated before adding, very softly, almost apologetically, "Did Tom see her?"

That was too much.

"You know damn well he didn't or you wouldn't have asked!" She sat up again, rigid, ready for confrontation. He couldn't win this argument. The ramifications were unthinkable. "Just why would I conjure up a girl who would drive me crazy? Why would I want to scare myself to death? I got hurt. Badly hurt!"

"Pain is necessary for punishment."

"You're totally out of your gourd, herr doktor! Why didn't anything like this happen before?" She smiled in triumph. This was one he couldn't have an answer for. "It only happened at the house! Where *she* was!"

"I mentioned this the first time you called." Neil was speaking even more softly now, comfortingly. "You had lost the restricting routine, the familiar environment, supportive people that held this in check." He shook his head and his round face crumpled. "It's my fault. I should have foreseen the possibility of a psychotic break."

"Psychotic?" It was a scream of protest.

"Please, Matty." The professional voice was gone. He leaned toward her, entreating. "Didn't we discuss this before?" He was clearly distressed. "No. No, perhaps not. I wouldn't have wanted to…Not on the phone. Forgive me. This was not the time, perhaps, yet I can assure you, since the incidents have gone since your return, that you are well on your way to recovery already. A psychotic break is often misunderstood. It does not imply ongoing insanity. Not at all. In your situation it is completely understandable. These breaks often occur well after the incidents that cause them, even years later. They can be controlled and in time will go away. A simple routine of medications will be of immediate help. Please do not be overly distressed. We can deal with this."

"Deal with this," she said flatly.

"Yes. Yes. Before you leave I'll give you a prescription for Zytrexa and Prozac. And I have some in the office. We can begin—"

"Prozac. That's for depression."

"Yes."

"I'm not depressed. I'm angry. Frustrated. But I am not—I am *not* depressed!"

His hands fluttered. Matty had never seen him like this before. Was the distress due to what he believed to be her condition or his mishandling of her?

"You did seem fine when you entered, but there are other factors."

"Like?"

She felt in charge again, challenging him.

He leaned toward her and Matty feared he would take her hand. That touch would not have been welcome just now.

"Matty." His voice was even softer now. "You have been taking Diazepam?" He paused briefly, reading admission in her lack of response. "You will, of course, stop that, as I asked you to before. Prozac will take its place. Diazepam has been known to cause hallucinations. Although in larger doses. But you are very sensitive to drugs of all kinds. Other factors that may have contributed to this new problem are the sleeplessness and hunger you've just told me about, both of which led to exhaustion and this alone could make you hallucinate."

"I wasn't always hungry!" How easily he put her on the defensive! "Only moderate amounts of wine and Diazepam." This last wasn't true, so she added, "Almost none this last week. Just enough to keep my back relaxed. And I've had trouble sleeping ever since the accident a year ago. That wasn't new."

"Perhaps it was a little more difficult to sleep alone in a strange house?"

That first night, the excursion into the back yard to haul down the tattered flag...Of course it was more difficult to sleep there at first. Later...How could a comparison be made? Sensory problems were not something she had had to deal with at home.

Anger was gone now and it was necessary to fight back tears. *I will not cry! I will not cry!* echoed from her walk over the mountain weeks ago. This had all gone wrong, fallen apart, this interview looked forward to with such eagerness. That she was beginning to give some credence to Neil's arguments was frightening. She needed to get away, out of this office and sort things out.

"Not significantly worse." She didn't sound convincing, even to herself. "I had some good days there. This last week there were no problems at all."

"When Tom was there."

"When Tom was there," she echoed in a voice quiet with resignation. Clearly, it was impossible to tell him why the sensory losses had ceased to be "problems." Neil would never believe that her girl was real. Everything he said was unarguably reasonable. Sadness began to grow, replacing anger. Was Tom never coming to this office to hear and believe what had happened? Could her father never be told?

"It is sometimes difficult for people to accept these breaks initially." Neil's voice revealed relief at her acceptance of his words, the little edge of anxiousness gone. "You recognized the sensory losses were abnormal. In time, you would have come to realize that the same was true of this hallucination. Do you really believe in ghosts?"

Matty pressed her palms against her eyes, trying to hold on to what she knew, what she absolutely *knew*, had to be true.

"There was a whole story going on, Neil. Not just the occasional appearance! She was with me all the time after I got out of the hospital!"

"What did they give you for your back pain?"

"Morphine. Then OxyContin. Stuck with the Diazepam to prevent spasm."

"Then there is that, too, to be considered. You see why we must talk more frequently. I'd like—"

"But only Tylenol when we made love!"

Neil couldn't prevent his eyebrows from rising a little.

Matty waved a hand as if to brush her words away.

"Forget it. I made love to Tom. Forget it. You'll never believe me." There was a kind of anguish in that statement. He never would believe her. Neil could no longer be a useful part of her life. She gave up trying to convince him and her tone was dismissive as she said, "There's too much you don't know. Her history. Courthouse records. Tombstones. Other people's experiences with her. I haven't told you any of that."

"Tell me."

Her imagination heard it all through Neil's ears and she knew there was no point in going on. Her own belief had diminished, receded to a distant part of her mind. Neil didn't trust her and what proof was there outside of her own experiences? An old man who told her what she wanted to hear, records of the existence of the house during the Civil War, a spinster whose Grandmother had fled the house, a tombstone with no discernible name on it.

34

For days Matty wandered around in a confused state unlike anything she had ever experienced. Nothing crystallized, not anger at Neil or frustration at her inability to completely trust herself. Certainly she was unable to make any important decisions. The seed of doubt Neil had planted, though rejected over and over, clouded her mind. Each time she dismissed the notion that she had imagined all this, some odd fact made her doubt again, like the awful mess the house had been in when she returned from the hospital. How could she not have seen that?

Consuela welcomed her back at the office with a shriek of joy, Rosemary with a guarded smile that made Matty wonder what had been going on while she was gone, immediately followed by guilt for being suspicious. Tom was right. Rosemary was bad for her.

Often, she sat at the battered oak desk and stared into space, trying to pull together some certainty from the last few weeks, but here, in a property management office in Rockville, the old log house and everything that had happened there seemed unreal. All she had to do was imagine herself telling Tom or Rosemary or Consuela about her ghost and that seed of Neil's blossomed into a gigantic plant. In a lunatic moment, she even had created a label for it, *mathildus insanus giganticus.* By the time she had been back to work for three days, she no longer was sure of anything. It was impossible not to contrast the way she felt now, confused but oddly happy off and on in spite of her mental fuzziness, with the bundle of nerves that had first entered that cabin and launched her into a week of, as Neil had pointed out, hunger, wine, tranquilizers and sleeplessness. Neil's theory sounded more and more probable, a conclusion that was insulting to her intelligence and contrary to her instincts, but undeniably reasonable. Initially, she had cursed Neil and reassured herself that she was neither sleep deprived nor hungry after leaving the hospital and at the end was taking only Tylenol and a measured amount of Diazepam to prevent back spasm. Then she remembered she had hit her head at the bottom of the stairs when she fell. That hadn't amounted to anything. Or had it? Should she go back to Neil and try to sort this out?

Slowly, there formed in the midst of confusion and the dismay of opening her mind to the possibility that Neil might be right, a kernel of truth that she cherished. Whatever the circumstances, whatever the means, she had found something at that house that was changing her life for the better. She had regained something lost years ago and she wasn't going to lose it again: the sense of being fully alive.

One week after returning to the office, she turned on the answering machine, called Consuela and Rosemary around her and announced changes.

"We will no longer be open on Saturdays."

That didn't affect Consuela, who stayed home with her son on Saturdays anyway.

"Or Thursday evenings. We will mail a notice to that effect to all our clients and tenants."

Rosemary looked both cynical and superior. "And how are working people—" Somehow "working people" excluded Matty "—supposed to sign leases? And when do we show them houses and apartments?"

Matty had foreseen this objection and had the words ready.

"Most people take off work to look at our properties because they're anxious to get to them before someone else does. They can take off work to complete the job and sign leases, too. Housing is important. People don't move that often. We can use more faxes or even ordinary mail if they can't get in here. No more routinely hanging around after closing hours, either, to take care of them after they get off work. If they're off work, why shouldn't we be?"

"That's great!" Consuela clapped her slim hands.

Rosemary gave Consuela a hard look. "That means no more overtime." The look moved to Matty. "If you're so keen to save money, why don't you give me a day off during the week and I'll keep the office open Thursday night and Saturday morning?"

This was said in a tone that indicated great self-sacrifice. Matty had anticipated this, too. She had left Rosemary alone with the business for almost four weeks, knowing that she would do a competent job of getting the paperwork done promptly and accurately. Knowing, too, that she would snoop into all the clients' files and probably offend a number of people. Rosemary wasn't going to be left alone any more. Rosemary might not even be here for long.

She had decided simply to say, "No," without the explanations that would have been offered apologetically a month ago.

The corners of Rosemary's mouth twitched, but she said nothing.

"Also, we are changing the off-hours message on the answering machine. It will ask callers to indicate the nature of their business. I will no longer return all calls promptly from home, only those from our clients and tenants that are really emergencies."

"Like a broken hot water heater," Rosemary explained to Consuela.

Matty corrected her with a firmness that felt good. "Actually, lack of hot water is not an emergency. From now on, the tenants can wait until morning for a plumber like any homeowner would do. No more overtime rates for repairmen. I've thought for some time that we owe that to our owners. After all, they're our clients."

"You're saving a lot of money," Rosemary said.

That was easy to translate. Rosemary wanted some of it.

"I hope to pay those savings to someone who is good at computers. Most of our files are on disk now but it was a real struggle for me. I need someone who knows how to manipulate them better. He or she can train us all."

"Anyone who knows computers that well will be expensive."

Matty thought back. Did Rosemary ever say anything positive?

"I won't need anyone full time. I'm hoping to get some mother who will work a few hours during the school day."

"Summer will be a problem."

"We have eight months until summer. By then, we should have learned what we need to know."

A pause to look at each of them and a decisive nod ended the meeting. Later, when Rosemary was in the rest room, Consuela came over to say Rosemary had told her that, if the new employee worked out, the computer expert would stay and Consuela would go. With the computer, they would need less help.

"You know I no can' miss no paycheck. You give plenty notice, okay?"

Matty shook her head. How often and in how many ways did Rosemary find ways to spread her unhappiness? It was a relief to find that her response was sympathy rather than anger.

"I can't get rid of you, Consuela. Our tenants wouldn't pay their rent till I got you back."

As the light came back in the dark eyes, Matty was more than ever aware of how much she had depended on this wiry Spanish woman during the last, miserable year. At the same time, it became apparent that she had also been suppressing any expression of her dislike for Rosemary, placating her instead of correcting her or standing up to her. It was incredible how much she had been suppressing emotions until…until what? Until whatever it was that happened, happened. She put a hand over Consuela's.

"You're like family. I couldn't fire you."

The dark eyes turned thoughtful. "Rosemary—She no like family."

"No." Matty shook her head. "But I don't think it's time to say anything yet. I'm not sure what I'm going to do."

"She kind of nee' me, you know."

"Yes, I know, Consuela. We both kind of need you. About Rosemary needing you—I'll take that into consideration."

Matty watched the slight figure settle in behind her desk and thought that what she had just said applied to too much of her life. She wasn't entirely sure what she was going to do about several things. Yes, the office was going to change. Yes, she was going to enjoy herself more. Larry and Wendy Helms were coming over for a barbecue Saturday. The computer had cranked out the few houses with a half acre or more that she and Tom could afford and they had spent an enjoyable evening going over the print-outs and planning. They had stopped taking precautions, too. The house would have to be big enough for at least one child. But would a child arrive? If so, would she keep on working? The need to tell Tom about her extraordinary experience was a constant pressure. Could she ever tell him? This question couldn't be resolved until she answered the most haunting question of all.

Could Neil be right?

◆   ◆   ◆

Only inch-high, glowing red numbers intruded on otherwise complete blackness when Matty woke. It was 4:14 in the morning. Across from her side of the bed was a wide, three-sectioned window completely invisible now in the room where she and Tom slept, a room warmed by central heating and almost adequately insulated from sound by triple paned glass and heavy drapes. It was a perfect environment for sleeping. But it felt all wrong now. It was lifeless, a bland, meaningless cocoon. There were no night birds calling, no wind rustling in the trees, no clouds playing with the moonlight, no shadows on the wall to animate dreams.

◆   ◆   ◆

"Neil, I need the key to the cabin again."

Matty sat at her desk. Rosemary had taken the postage meter to the Post Office and Consuela was busy on the phone getting to know their latest tenant.

Neil always picked his words carefully but usually quickly. He was having trouble this time.

"Why don't you come in and we'll talk about it?"

The tone of his voice made Matty feel guilty. The pain in his round eyes as she had left his office that last time had not been for her but for himself.

"It wouldn't do any good to talk about it. You don't believe me and now I have to find out if I believe myself. I need to go back."

Emergency calls had interrupted their sessions a few times and she could picture him now. His hands were busy, fingers rubbing his chin or pulling his hair.

"Neil?"

"Yes. I'm sorry. How are you feeling?"

She recognized the delaying tactics. That was all right. He needed reassurance.

"Wonderful. I've shortened the office hours, interviewed a couple of computer-savvy people and Tom and I are ready to look at some houses. I'm happy. Relaxed. No more tranquilizers." That wasn't entirely true. Dependence needed to be broken gradually. "Have a new, fresh slant on life. Honestly. Now can I have the key? To use just for a day? Or maybe one overnight?"

"Any more…"

"No more ghosts. All gone."

"Good. Good." The relief in his voice was unmistakable. "Tom will go with you?"

"No."

"I think it would be a good idea to take Tom."

It wouldn't work that way. But Neil would never understand.

"Okay. Probably a good idea." *But I didn't say I would do it.*

"Then you will come in and we can discuss what you found."

"We could. Yes." That was no lie. She could, but she was pretty sure she wouldn't. Still…"Yes. We might need to discuss it."

He liked that.

Two hours later, Matty picked up the key from a smiling and unaware Erica, glad that Neil was behind his heavy walnut door.

35

October light was mellower than September's. The trees were different, too, just hinting at the color variations that would become a vivid autumn, a little gold on the maples mixed with the green. Brick-red sumac bushes ornamented the roadside.

There had been a greater change in her than in the light. The first time, she had ridden these driveway ruts still in the clutches of the madness of rush hour, tense, frightened and hungry, the last time as a passenger reclining to appease a bad back, dreamy, grateful, but confused almost to the point of disorientation. Anticipation was a big part of her emotions now. And just a drop of anxiety. She was like a child at Christmas. Would she get the present she wanted? How would she deal with disappointment if Christmas didn't come?

The house was as stark and uncompromising as she remembered. It was only five o'clock, but the sun was setting and the golden light came over the trees, aiming straight at the front of the house. It glanced along the side, picking out the rough texture of the logs, leaving the back entrance in shadow. She missed the flag.

A small animal, a squirrel or chipmunk, moved through the dry underbrush beside the stopped car. Squirrels gathering nuts and birds shook leaves in the trees and somewhere in the woods a small branch or pine cone fell. Soon the crickets would start. Matty smiled, remembering how silent the place had seemed the first time she had pulled up to this door. Only the shrill crickets had intruded on her awareness. She knew all the sounds, individual and meaningful, now.

She knew, too, just how to get the key to open the stiff lock but stood unmoving for a few minutes, reluctant to push the rude door open and find no reassurance.

Tom had done a good job. The place looked neat, nothing out of place, the broken pieces of Chamberlain's bust sitting on top of the fifty dollars Tom had assumed would more than cover its replacement. The setting sun shone through the windows, filling the air with the gold dust she remembered. Her hand still on the knob, Matty waited, breathing with controlled quietness.

"Hello," she said softly. "I came back to see you."

◆　　　◆　　　◆

By six o'clock, the small suitcase was unpacked, its meager contents in familiar places in the bedroom and bath. Groceries, only enough for one dinner and breakfast, were stashed in the refrigerator or arranged neatly on the counter. There was no point in putting them away. She had brought fancy food from Sutton Place Gourmet, small portions of turkey and green grape salad, tortellini and vegetables in alfredo sauce, croissants and, of course, a single slice of incredibly rich chocolate cake. No bran cereal or skim milk. Instead, there would be apple strudel and raspberries in the morning.

The kitchen table and the battered coffee table in the living room each held an old milk bottle with a dozen yellow roses.

Memories were everywhere and she walked through clouds of past emotions.

Humming a hymn, its melody but not its words, remembered from her childhood, she put the tortellini and vegetables on to heat over a low fire, both the music and the food calling up memories of her mother and her little spirit. They blended well together.

Tom had left some wood and Matty built a fire with the same slow enjoyment with which she had unpacked and begun preparations for her meal. Never very good at lighting fires, two of the owners' magazines were sacrificed to get it started. The burning covers prodded her memory. She and her brothers used to burn Christmas cards in the open fireplace, crowing with delight as unexpected colors flamed and died and Mom and Dad sat together and smiled, made happy by their children's happiness.

Matty sat down on the rough fabric of the couch with a peaceful feeling of having returned home and began to talk quietly to the companion she hoped would hear.

The sun set magnificently before the pasta mixture was hot. Instead of turning on the lamp, Matty lit a pair of candles. It seemed more appropriate. By their light, she ate slowly, inviting the girl to taste each bite. It seemed important to enjoy the food herself, too, but it took effort. She kept picturing her little spirit, as though seeing her in imagination might prompt her appearance.

Inevitably, the moment came when the plate was empty. It was time to take the dishes to the sink, time to pour a glass of milk and put it, with the cake, on the table's worn oilcloth. There had been not one glimpse of any part of the small form in a blue dress, no loss of taste or the scent of the roses, not even a sense of the girl's presence.

The cake, so richly chocolate it was almost black, so moist it glistened, lay invitingly on a chipped crockery dish. Matty didn't want it. She wanted *her* to have it. It was important at least to see the girl. No one could accuse her of being drugged, tired or suffering from sleeplessness tonight.

Consuming the cake in impossibly small bites, it disappeared slowly. Then it was gone. She scraped the side of the fork over the bottom, collecting the last crumbs. Matty had tasted every bite. She felt the irony of having wanted what had been feared before.

Washing the dishes, Neil's explanation pressed on her. Could any delusion have been so complete, ongoing, predictable, consistent? The adjectives could go on and on. What Neil called an hallucination had been a huge part of her life this last month. Realizing that she had forgotten to sing, Matty began her truncated version of "Amazing Grace," but it was hard to maintain the tune when her mind was busy evaluating the evidence pro and con with, if possible, even more intensity than she had before. Surely Jane's grandmother's ramblings, however vague, combined with Alice's Civil War tale and Matty's own experience, created a cohesive story. Neil was wrong. This had all happened, although the message was clear that she was a different person on this second visit.

The dishes were done. The kitchen was lit with the lamp and the bare bulb over the sink now. It had seemed pointless to wash dishes by candlelight. It was an empty kitchen. Not even a particularly nice empty kitchen. She had become immune to its imperfections by the time she had left. Now they struck her as they had the first day. It seemed a place of magic no longer.

Should it all be dismissed as a meaningless delusion as Neil had done? Was it wrong to believe what our bodies told us? To believe our own eyes, our own minds? Some people couldn't trust them, she knew. There were such things as psychotic breaks. Neil knew what he was talking about. She needed a courtroom, a judge and jury. A jury of people who knew more than she did about the human mind. Here, ladies and gentlemen, is the evidence of history and my senses and on this side, the evidence of reason. What is your verdict? There was no question what their verdict would be.

How could she be sure of her own?

◆   ◆   ◆

It was dark. Matty wasn't sure where she was when she woke. This was no bed beneath her. She sat up and felt the rough texture with her fingers. Shapes moved out of the darkness and identified themselves. It was the living room and she had fallen asleep on the couch. When had she turned off the floor lamp over her head?

Memory brought a smile. Weeks before, she had needed a tranquilizer to sleep. This night, sleep had come easily and early and was dreamless.

She reached up and turned on the lamp. On the coffee table lay what she had been reading before falling asleep, a book of her own poems, one of the ones Tom had brought to inspire her to write again. He hadn't been so organized after all, had left them among the old magazines that lived here.

The bed upstairs was all made up, ready for her. Her watch told her it was just after five in the morning. Was it too late to catch another hour's sleep? Was it necessary? Last night, after dinner, had come one final bath in the old tub before making up the bed and laying out her nightgown and then a trip downstairs to find something to read. The poems had been a surprise. Most of them had been written when she was very young and she had read a few aloud, hoping they might interest the girl, although she knew by then there was no longer any girl. It was impossible to have invited her to taste the slowly eaten, tempting meal, to enjoy the scent of the roses, to have begged her to appear one last time, and yet have seen, felt nothing.

Her little spirit wasn't here.

An emery board, her usual bookmark, indicated where she had both started and stopped reading to the empty air. Near the end of the white and black, spiral notebook, it seemed a curious coincidence that her attention should have been directed to this small verse written in her careful high school hand. It had no title. Matty remembered she had cried so hard she had given up trying to find a title, for these few lines were based on some words her mother had said shortly before she died, her sunken eyes pleading with her sixteen-year-old daughter not to mourn too much, to move on with some pain, of course, but only a little and only for a while. It wasn't a good poem, but it was oddly appropriate.

> Clouds form within my failing eyes,
> Shadows not of sun and skies.
> God pulls me from your tears.
> Is it enough? Sixteen years?
> Let go. Your hand, in its own time
> Will feel the touch, once more, of mine.
> Trust that your tears, my child, will dry.
> Now say it as we always did:
> Goodbye,
> God bless
> And thank you.

Matty had cried as she had read it over and over, wanting to believe that the childish poem written many years ago had something to do with now, wanting to believe that the emery board was not there by accident, proving that some day Matty would see her mother and the strange young girl again, finally knowing that it didn't matter what was sensible or logical or even what was true in the hard, scientific sense. Last night, she had come to terms with all of it, including the final little mystery of the poem. *Don't deny a gift because you don't understand it,* she had told herself. That was going to be the end of this story. Tom could never be told. Neil would never believe her. As for herself, she was going to believe because she wanted to believe, because belief was the best resolution, because it felt right and good, because, at a certain point, not believing was the true madness. It was this final decision that made it possible to set the notebook aside and drift gradually and easily into a peaceful sleep.

Now she wandered slowly through the old log house, collecting her few possessions, her mind examining, without anxiety or need, but only with curiosity, the lines of the poem. Though written from her Mother's viewpoint then, which of them was the teacher and which the pupil now? Was she free, the little spirit? As free as she, Matty, was?

Affirmation rang like church bells.

The small overnight case sat by the front door, her linens, purse and a small paper bag containing her breakfast on top of it. Raspberries and strudel now were pleasures only for herself and it was too early to eat. Perhaps she would stop and get a cup of coffee to go with them somewhere along the road.

Matty picked up her belongings, set them on the porch and turned the key in the lock for the last time. She stood with her hand pressed against the rough planks for a long time. Finally, she was ready.

"Farewell," she said. "God bless. And thank you."

978-0-595-37544-
0-595-37544-8

Printed in the United States
66379LVS00014B/18

AFTER THE FEELING

7-10

AFTER THE FEELING

T.N. WILLIAMS

www.urbanchristianonline.net

Urban Books
1199 Straight Path
West Babylon, NY 11704

After the Feeling copyright © 2009 T.N. Williams

ISBN- 13: 978-1-60162-988-3
ISBN- 10: 1-60162-988-5

First Printing May 2009
Printed in the United States of America

10 9 8 7 6 5 4 3 2 1

*This is a work of fiction. Any references or similarities to actual events, real
people, living, or dead, or to real locales are intended to give the novel a sense of
reality. Any similarity in other names, characters, places, and incidents is entirely coincidental.*

Distributed by Kensington Corp.
Submit Wholesale Orders to:
Kensington Publishing Corp.
C/O Penguin Group (USA) Inc.
Attention: Order Processing
405 Murray Hill Parkway
East Rutherford, NJ 07073-2316
Phone: 1-800-526-0275
Fax: 1-800-227-9604

DEDICATION

In loving memory of my grandfather, George Williams, who
was the first man I loved unconditionally.
I hope you're looking down on me with pride.

ACKNOWLEDGMENTS

I first have to give God honor for being the head of my life. There are not enough words in the vocabulary to give you due praise.

To Jackie, Zay and Jordan, I thank you for giving me space to complete this book, and for understanding that your momma still believes you are a priority. To my momma, Cynthia Phillips, I love you and thank you for encouraging my gift. To my grand-mothers, Elvira Green and Alma Williams, although two vastly different women, I've discovered that God designed me to be an individual, but growth came from what I learned from you. I honor your strengths and knowledge. I definitely have to thank May Furlough for reading my manuscripts, giving me advice and loving me when you didn't have to. I appreciate you more than you could ever know.

To my husband, Shun, I thank you for always trying to grow and teaching me in the process. I need to thank my brother, Antonio DeShawn Williams, for being an incredible hard working family man. Helping to raise all daughters can't be an easy task. I love you for being you and I apologize publicly for not putting your name in the last book. To my other brothers, Broderick, Little Larry and Evander, I love you all separately, yet the same. This world likes to stereotype black men, but each of you has unique characteristics that you carry on your own. Keep pressing forward and stay true to yourselves. To all my siblings, nieces, nephews, aunts, uncles, cousins and ex-tended family that I didn't mention by name, I love all of you and pray that you prosper in your many gifts.

This story forced me to look at life from two perspectives, feminine and masculine. I have to thank every man that touched my life and made me see things through the eyes of men. That includes my father, Greg Williams, and the man who helped raise me, Larry Davis, as well as, my grandfathers, Travis McBride and Louis Green. To all the men, from childhood until now, I want to thank those that stepped up to the plate and took care of their families despite obstacles, struggles, temptations and frustrations. You are appreciated.

To Allen Pontarelli, a former co-worker and great person, who introduced me to porn help resources that I would have never discovered on my own, thank you so very much. I hope you continue to be an example as a youth and community leader.

I want to thank my new pastor and first lady, Bryan and Debra Pierce of Bethel Baptist Church in Kannapolis, North Carolina. I love your unity and honesty. You both have beautiful spirits. To Pastor Nathaniel Moody and First Lady Laura Moody of Brown and Hutcherson Ministries in Grand Rapids, Michigan, I will never forget you.

To the Urban Christian authors, I thank you for your encouraging words and suggestions in fine-tuning my skill and marketing my stories. To my executive editor, Joylynn Jossel, thank you for pushing me to challenge myself. To each and every person involved in my writing process, I sincerely thank you for dealing with me.

Lastly, to all the readers, reviewers and book clubs, I hope you are enlightened by the words I captured on paper. Please email me with your responses to the story at *tn.williams@yahoo.com*. I would love to hear from you. Be Blessed!

PROLOGUE

GERMANI

October 11, 2007
9:58 P.M.

The fateful call came in.

The credits to a re-run episode of *Grey's Anatomy* had begun to play.

I didn't answer on the first ring.

I was too busy wallowing in aggravation and exhaustion as I devoured a plate full of grease-laden buffalo wings and mozzarella sticks.

My husband, Scott's, porn obsession was wearying me out. Nothing I said or did seemed to matter. My feelings of confusion, shame, loneliness and rejection were ignored by the man I vowed to love unconditionally; wasted on deaf ears like a bruised apple tumbling from a windblown tree.

Scott's attention was consumed by sexual images on his computer from the Internet, DVDs from the local sex shops, and those videos from Pay-Per-View. It was more than I could handle. More than I knew how to deal with. Maybe if he acknowledged how bad things were, we wouldn't be at odds. Maybe. But he kept making excuses; justifying his actions at the expense of our family.

There's only so much understanding that a woman can give before . . . enough becomes enough.

It brought to mind a colorful logo I saw on the bumper sticker of a Yugo parked at the grocery store that read, *SEX SELLS*. Made me think it was too bad that same statement didn't come with a warning.

Sex kills too.

The phone's ringing interrupted my sulking.

I was willing to let that call go to voicemail, but curiosity compelled me to answer just from the phone number flashing across my television.

"Germani?" an anguished voice cracked after I answered.

The caller on the other end of the line was familiar, but sounded in worse condition than I felt. I couldn't put my finger on it. There was no other definition to describe the conversation beyond peculiar. When the caller made a shocking confession I saw warning signs and red flags go up all around me.

I put the caller on hold while I went to the bathroom to wash the remnants of my meal from my greasy hands. The caller needed better advice than I could give. I was clueless on how I'd help 'em when my own thoughts were all messed up. But I knew I had to do something. On the way back to the family room, I grabbed a New King James Version of the Bible off the bookshelf near the computer center and flipped through as I walked. I tried to find the right words amongst the pages as my mind drew blanks. By the time I made it back to the phone with Bible in clean hands, a busy signal blared through and the caller was gone.

My heart quickened as I thought about what to do next.

10:41 p.m.

Blood.

There was blood everywhere when I made it to the caller's home. Deep crimson streaks that saturated vanilla satin sheets and rained burgundy droplets onto the Persian area rug beneath the bed.

I stood planted against the door frame like a wisteria vine attached to aluminum siding. I was too afraid to step in the room and too disturbed to walk away.

Music was playing. The eighties song, "Real Love" by a group named Skyy ended. An eerie silence penetrated the air for just a few seconds. The song began to play again. Somebody had put it on repeat.

Don't be afraid of the way you feel.

Fear came quickly. I was too late.

I couldn't think as my eyes stayed locked on the crimson streaks, mesmerized like a teenager on an acid trip. Dazed and stunned, my lips slowly opened as my brain processed. I was in the middle of a gory crime scene and somebody was dead . . . murdered. Suddenly, terror filled the once irritated space of my abdomen where aggravation was devoured by panic, and I screamed at the top of my lungs.

CHAPTER ONE

GERMANI

June 16, 2007

"Lord, I can't believe I agreed to this," I muttered with irritation. Rings of smoke blew my way as the three men at the table behind me whistled obscene remarks and cat calls at the stage performer.

I glanced back to match the voice to the owner of its lewdness as I tried to cough away the singe of my throat. I wanted to tell him to show a little respect, but my comment would be contrary to my environment. Instead, I sized him up. Gray sports coat, navy blue and gray stripped silk tie, white button down shirt, simple mustache on pale skin, short auburn hair, professionally cut, every bit the representation of the all-American white male. A thick gold band adorned his ring finger, on his left hand, the same hand he smacked the waitress' behind with when she set a glass in front of him. I wondered if his wife knew he frequented black stripper joints with his co-workers, or if she was even slightly aware that he had a taste for chocolate. More than likely, it was a secret obsession. The allure of the forbidden could be an aphrodisiac, and he looked like he was high on something.

I diverted my eyes back to the table where I was sitting. I was trying to contain my growing annoyance, but it was becoming more difficult by the minute as I observed my surroundings. Most importantly, my husband was just as much a part of the sexual utopia as the other horny men in the club. I watched the pleasure and glee play across Scott's face, from the smile straining the corners of his lips to the smoldering gaze of undivided attention as he sat in the chair on the left of me. Attention that should have belonged to me instead of the stage before us. My only response was to let the anger and embarrassment simmer inside as I gritted my teeth.

I had no business sitting in the Playa's Lounge gnawing away at my enamel. My husband had no business foaming at the mouth over a stripper named Satin, and we, for sure, had no business being there together.

My skin crawled with each penance glance around the room. Shame mingled with irritation, slowly rising to full blown anger as I thought again about what I agreed to by coming to the Playa's Lounge.

Scott looked my way and the smile disappeared. He could sense my displeasure instantly. "Hey, are you okay?" He leaned toward me with concern in his eyes. He rubbed my back as I choked when another ring of smoke assaulted my already sensitive throat.

"Yes, I'm fine," I forced from my lips.

I had agreed to come. In fact, I was the one who insisted that I come. Even suggested that Damon and Cherish ride with us to the Playa's Lounge. Thought it would be better to indulge in his fantasy, instead of arguing about why he couldn't enjoy his evening the way he wanted to. It was his thirty-fifth birthday and I didn't want to ruin the night for him by acting uptight. I thought if I could handle the porn videos we watched regularly, then one night in a strip club couldn't be all that bad. As long as we were together, the environment shouldn't matter. That's what I kept trying to rationalize. But no matter how I tried to convince myself to relax, my mind and body wouldn't cooperate.

Scott smiled with relief and captured my lips, not recognizing that my words and my body language weren't in sync. "Good," he replied.

I leaned my head down toward my chest and coughed again.

Scott went back to drooling over Satin, who was removing the flimsy material that rendered her topless.

I watched Satin sashay across the stage and bend down. A short rotund man tucked a fifty dollar bill down the front of Satin's gold costume bottom. His chubby fingers held languid on the fabric beneath her belly button. A bulked up bouncer moved forward and the stripper's bottom was quickly released.

Things were far from good.

My fingers tightened around the silver links of my purse strap. I could feel the metal press an indention into my palm. I glanced at Cherish to gauge how she was taking in the scene, but to my disappointment, she was hugged up with her husband, and Scott's best friend, Damon, smiling just as hard as the men. I felt entirely out of place. Evidently I was the only one in the whole club that didn't think pole dancing was a suitable activity for married couples to be watching.

My co-worker, Daphne, had sent me an email that Walter Beasley was playing at the Jazz Café for the weekend. Scott and I both could have enjoyed the smooth melody of a saxophone extraordinaire. Or if my husband needed hot and spicy excitement, we could have gone salsa dancing at Latorres.

Just about anything would have been better than us at the Playa's Lounge.

"Hey, man, check out that female over there. She must be new. I haven't seen her in here before. Now that is what I call a fine specimen. All that definition . . . " Damon's tongue hung from his mouth like a dog in heat as he gestured toward a caramel sister with black and burgundy streaked hair that hung to the middle of her bare back in loose waves.

I tried not to grunt with disgust as my eyes roamed in the direction he pointed to near the bar. The girl had on two silver dollars covering her chest and a neon green thong. I could do nothing but close my eyes and shake my head. This was what I agreed to, taking my husband to lust over other women. I must have been completely out of my mind. I knew better.

Knots of guilt formed in my abdomen.

I cast my eyes on the Missoni lace stitch dress I got on clearance from Nordstrom for seventy-five percent off. When I picked up the sleeveless cowl neck little outfit, I thought it was extremely sexy. I was convinced that me in it, would drop Scott's mouth to the ground and I'd have to help him get his jaw back in place. When I first put it on and strutted in front of him, he slid his hands down the soft wool from Italy as I twirled to give him a full view. He acted like I was the finest thing alive. How quickly that changed.

"You know who she reminds me of?" Damon asked Scott like wives weren't present.

Scott scrunched his eyebrows and squinted like he was trying hard to figure it out.

Damon licked his lips and grinned devilishly, "Tandy. That's who she favors . . . that girl from high school. You remember her. I know you do, because you had a hardcore crush on that girl back in the day. You drooled and stuff every single time she walked by smelling like peaches and cream from Vicki's Secret. I wouldn't be surprised if it was her. She seemed like she had a little freak in her back then. That female even sways those jumbo hips like Tandy."

Scott tilted his head slightly and looked the girl up and down before disagreeing. "I don't see it."

Damon stood up and pulled his wallet from his back pocket. "You're crazy. We just need to see her up close." He was intent upon proving his point. "I'll tell you what I'm going to do. Thirty-five only rolls around once. You deserve a birthday lap dance to make it memorable."

I was appalled. I bore my eyes into Cherish and willed her to check her husband. Once again, I faced disappointment. Cherish was staring absently into her glass of mandarin flavored Absolut vodka as if being disrespected was a normal thing. I understood being open. I came to the Playa's Lounge with the full intent of being open, but it wasn't that much openness in the plains of the Maharia Desert. I wasn't about to sit back and get humiliated, birthday or no birthday. Damon was out of line, and if I had to end this fiasco, then the ugly might come out of me.

Damon waved three crisp hundred dollar bills in the air and the dancer approached the table.

Money exchanged hands. Scott scooted his chair back in anticipation of her gyrating thick hips between his legs.

"It is not going to happen," I blurted out loudly, so insulted I couldn't contain it anymore.

"What?" Scott blinked twice at me like he had seen an apparition.

"Scott, I'm ready to go. This is not my type of thing. I tried to get into this for your sake, because I thought . . . I don't know what I thought. I don't know what I thought at all, but I'm not feeling this." I chuckled sarcastically as I waved the dancer away from the table. I rose from my chair, snatched my purse off the table and put the chain strap on my shoulder. "This whole raunchy, sordid little scene is more than I can take."

My husband rose too, obviously disappointed. He nodded his head. "Alright, baby, we can go. It's no problem." There was no point in arguing about it in the middle of the club. Eyes had already diverted toward us.

Damon objected. "Whatcha mean, it's no problem? I just

spent three hundred bones for a lap dance. It is a problem. That ain't refundable. I don't have money to be throwing away like that."

"Well, I suggest you call her back over here and let her grind on you, because my husband and I are leaving!" I snapped at Damon. I had to maintain my composure and act like the lady I was raised to be. Then again, if that were the case, I wouldn't be here in the first place.

"Somebody must be feeling insecure," Damon snapped back.

"Look, man, we're leaving," Scott cut in to diffuse the conversation before it became more heated. "Are you riding with us or catching a cab?"

"Oh, it's like that?" Damon asked, holding his hands in the air like he was the one offended.

I turned on my heels and walked out of the club. How Damon got home was of no concern. He was a real piece of work, but I didn't have to put up with him. That kind of ignorance belonged to Cherish.

I walked to the car in a parking lot across Davidson Street, barely waiting for traffic to clear. I didn't know what had come over me, whether it was purely irritation or something stronger. But like flies on mess, I had to get it off me.

CHAPTER
TWO

SCOTT

My eyes deviated from I-77 to my wife. Germani had a wicked scowl on her bronze-toned face. Creases etched a map across her forehead. She looked like the Olmec stone sculpture we had seen on a trip to a little town in Veracruz, Mexico. The expression pinched her features. Made a fine woman look ugly, act ugly. I had never seen her veer from sophistication in public, rarely caught drama in private either.

"What is with you?" I asked as I reached over the armrest and clasped my fingers around Germani's left hand. It lay limply in her lap. I looked her in the face and squeezed her fingers, trying to get her attention. She glanced at me out of the corner of her eye. She then removed her hand from beneath mine. The hand went to the back of her neck where she rubbed like she had a painful crick.

I didn't understand the problem. Germani asked to go to the Playa's Lounge with me. We went. She asked to leave the club. We left. So, why was she blowing a cold drift through my 300C like a Siberian winter in June?

Giggles reverberated from the backseat. I looked up into my rear view mirror. Damon was whispering into Cherish's ear. It must have been something good to make Cherish cup Damon's cheek and pull his head closer to her face. I watched him whisper, her giggle.

If I was a lesser man, I would be envious. I'd covet the intimacy that should have belonged to me. My wife didn't even want me touching her, yet, the two lovebirds behind me were acting like they were on a backseat rendezvous. That was supposed to be me hugged up with Germani, buzzing sweet nothings against her lobe.

"Happy birthday to me," I mumbled under my breath as I pulled into the Ballantyne subdivision.

Damon and Cherish's place was a three-story brick front with an immaculate lawn on a corner lot. I often wondered why he needed that entire house with just the two of them. I kinda figured it was a trophy palace for the business partners he entertained. It definitely wasn't for accommodating his estranged family. His mother, two sisters and brother weren't allowed within two hundred feet of him.

I turned into the driveway and said, "Alright, man, it's been real. Thanks for coming out to celebrate my day with me."

"For sure. We need to get together again and do something with just me and you. Hang like we used to do. Manly stuff; uninterrupted." Damon patted my shoulder as he got out of my vehicle. I chuckled, remembering the trouble we got ourselves into doing manly stuff before I changed my lifestyle.

Germani snapped her head our way. She evil mugged him and then me. Damon didn't notice, and more than likely didn't care. The comment was yet another reason for Germani to be mad at me. A brotha can't win for losing. I can't even laugh without it being a problem. Some things shouldn't be that serious.

The ride home was silent and I was cool with it. If she wanted to be mad, let her. She would calm down if I didn't feed into her attitude. When we made it to our modest bi-level home, she jumped out of the car and stalked up the front entrance before the garage door could go all the way up.

"What the . . . ," I said to myself, baffled as I cruised the car into the garage. "Oh, she is seriously trippin'." I cut the car off and sat there for a minute. I didn't do anything wrong.

When I made it into the house and up the stairs, Germani had her arm twisted up behind her back, wrestling with the zipper.

"Here." I walked behind her and gently pulled the zipper to the middle of her back. The bareness of her back, with its creamy soft skin, made my masculine impulse kick in. I brushed my lips against her shoulder as the garment fell to floor.

Germani mumbled, "Thanks." She picked up the dress that poodled at her feet and walked around me like I was a piece of the furniture.

I watched her stiff movements as she walked around the room like a lost sheep. She was working overtime to show her peevishness. I sat on the bed and began unbuttoning my black silk shirt. I was waiting for her aimless quick strides to cease.

She opened the closet door and hung up the dress. Then she pulled that same dress back out of the closet and tossed it over the chair with the hanger still on it. Germani opened drawers and pulled nothing out, and then she slammed them closed. She scuffled through another set of drawers. A light blue lace nightie appeared as she snatched it out and tossed it over her head. She closed the drawers and stood, making circular motions with her hands like it was some kind of yoga self therapy. I had seen her do the same moves to a video she watched before she went to work each morning.

"We are not going to be like this, Germani. Let's clear the air and discuss this before we go to bed," I stated calmly as I stripped down to my boxers while I was still on the edge of the bed.

Suddenly, she stopped and pivoted around to look at me. Her frown was prominent. "Do you feel the least little bit of guilt?"

"Guilty about what?" I asked incredulously.

She popped her tongue against the roof of her mouth. "Yeah,

that's what I thought. We . . ." Germani swung her index finger between the both of us like an out of control clock pendulum. Her head matched the stride of her finger, ". . . . don't have anything to discuss." She stomped to the bed, snatched the covers back and jumped in. She bumped against me with her feet until I was on my side of the bed. The comforter rose up to her chin as she wiggled to get comfortable.

"Whoa. Wait," I said as I noticed the corner of the comforter that was left for me to sleep under. I couldn't let the night end that way. Besides, it was my birthday and I deserved some tender affection. I rose from the bed to turn off the bedroom light. My wife was still beneath the covers as I looked over at her before darkness covered the room. I slipped back into the bed next to Germani. I tugged at the covers until the barrier she created was gone. I nestled my body against hers and placed my hand on her thigh.

'No!" she snapped like I was trying to steal her loving.

"Fine." I removed my hands and lay on my back. She was about to take me to her side of anger. I was too tired to be mad about nothing.

I stared at the ceiling and took myself to an earlier portion of the evening. I had taken the day off and spent the morning with our three-year-old son, Elijah. After dropping him off at my sister, Sharon's house to spend the night, I picked Germani up and we went to enjoy a Gullah Island cuisine at a restaurant called Mert's Heart and Soul on North College.

Sharon was due in August with her first child and wanted some hands on training with our son before hers got here. She never really wanted kids, but her husband, Corbin, convinced her to have one baby. He came from a big family and wanted at least one child of his own. He told her that he would do most of the work. I think Sharon was testing Corbin to see how true to the word he really was. Personally, I thought she should have done her parent testing before she got pregnant, but I guess we would have to see how all that worked out.

It was at Mert's that the discussion about the Playa's Lounge came up. I was waiting for the right time to mention it, because I hadn't been to that strip joint since we got married over four years ago. Damon talked constantly about how the spot had gone through a major renovation. New management had hooked the place up and I wanted to see the improvements with my best friend. I knew Germani wouldn't see it that way. She would think I had ungodly intentions. I was surprised when she said she was all right with me going. That is, as long as she went with me. At first, I was apprehensive about the idea of my wife sitting in the Playa's Lounge with me, but I knew Cherish went with Damon all the time and I had seen other couples there. But boy, oh boy, if I would have known she would get to acting the way she had, the topic would never have came up. I drifted asleep with regret on my mind.

"Scott." I could hear her voice, but my sleep induced coma wouldn't let me respond. "Scott!" The voice came more firmly as I felt my shoulder being nudged.

"Yeah," I responded as I lingered between slumber and consciousness.

"We need to talk," Germani said.

Talk. Talk. My body didn't feel like cooperating with a conversation, but I could tell from her determined voice that she needed to be heard. If it would bring peace and a conclusion to her irritation, then talking is what we would have to do.

I sighed as I pulled my eyelids up and reached for my watch on the nightstand. My pupils needed to adjust to the lack of light as I tried to see the time. It took a minute for my vision to come into focus, but I still had to squint to see the hands of the watch. The big hand was on the four and the little hand sat above the ten. Seconds ticked by and it was still too early in the morning for me to think.

"Can we have this conversation in a couple more hours?" I asked as I turned on my back and tried to stretch away the fatigue. I glanced over at Germani who was sitting with her back against the headboard. "We are getting up for church at eight. I can set the clock back to seven thirty if need be. Baby, I'm tired and I'd be more coherent in the morning."

"You were going to let her grind on you, weren't you?" Germani asked. She still had an attitude.

"What are you talking about? Who? What?" I was tired, clueless and trying not to be irritated.

"Tandy or Tandy's look-a-like. Whichever way you want to call it."

"Tandy? You mean that stripper?" I arched myself up on my elbows and became fully alert.

Germani sighed like I was automatically supposed to know what she was talking about. "Scott, don't play like you don't know what I'm talking about. Of course, I'm talking about the stripper. You certainly didn't mind when Damon shelled out money on your behalf. I'm kind of glad I went. Now I know what after hour activities you're really into. God only knows how far that sexual exchange would have progressed if I hadn't been there to intervene."

I waited for her to pause as I let her words sink in. Her interpretation of the night was all wrong. "Germani, I was not going to take a lap dance with my wife sitting right next to me."

"Oh, so you would have taken the lap dance if I wasn't there?"

There she goes, trying to twist my words all up. "No. I didn't ask for a lap dance and I didn't want a lap dance. It all happened so fast. I didn't think that Damon was serious about paying that girl. I would have called his bluff."

"Money exchanged hands, Scott. There was no bluff."

"Damon and I joke around like that. It didn't have to go that far."

"Once again, money exchanged hands. I thought you had more respect for me than that. Heck, I thought you had more respect for women period. Do you know how that made me feel? I've never felt so devalued. Like we . . . like we didn't have morals." Germani sounded hurt as her voice cracked.

I sat all the way up and reached over. She allowed me to embrace her. I needed to calm the storm. "Oh, baby, I'm sorry you feel that way. I didn't intend for it to be that way. You shouldn't have gone."

I could feel her pull a little away from me, but I held her within my arms. "*We* shouldn't have gone," Germani stated as the acid in her voice disintegrated.

"We shouldn't have gone," I agreed. I still didn't see it her way, but I cared more about getting some peace and some sleep more than I cared about being right. Especially about something that went on in a strip joint. I was hoping this would be the end of the conversation.

"I need to feel respected by you, Scott . . . all the time. That whole scene was jacked. We're supposed to be Christians. What kind of mess is that for us to go to a strip club on Saturday and then go to church the next morning? Didn't you feel the least bit out of place? Why did you need to go to a strip club anyway?"

"But, Germani, you wanted to go to the strip club."

"No, I wanted to be with my husband on his birthday. Clearly, I wasn't thinking when I agreed to the rest." She adjusted the covers before continuing. "Am I not enough? Are you going to take Elijah to those places when he grows up—"

"Germani, I said I was sorry we went to the Playa's Lounge." I had to cut her off, because she was taking the conversation to a whole other level. It wasn't that serious.

"But I want you to understand how I felt."

"You already told me how you felt. Can't we just kiss and make up? Maybe make love?" I said, kissing her neck as I stroked her arm. I wanted a repeat of the lovemaking we shared the night before.

She wiggled like she was fighting the feeling. "I don't want to make love right now. Can we pray?"

I lifted my mouth from a comfortable place. "Yes. We can do that. You want to do it or you want me to say something?"

Germani sighed. "You go."

I didn't know what to say. Her thoughts weren't the same as mine. I prayed for what I wanted all night. "Lord, Father in heaven. I ask that you restore peace in my home and our hearts. My wife is troubled and I don't want to be the cause of her frustration. Mend what is broken and give us strength. Lord, I want to thank you for bringing some resolution on this night so we don't carry discord into tomorrow. In your Son's name, I pray. Amen."

It was short and sweet, but I know the big man heard me. My wife finally relaxed and we spooned as we fell asleep.

CHAPTER
THREE

GERMANI

I didn't sleep a wink last night and it was becoming increasingly difficult to hear what Pastor Mackenzie was preaching about.

After our pre-dawn discussion, I had laid awake and listened to the hum of slumber coming from my husband's lips. I couldn't get comfortable. My mind had stayed conscious as I remained in his arms. Scott made the conversation last night seem simplistic. He completely disconnected my words and the emotions attached to them. First, he devalued me and every other woman in that raunchy club, and then he disregarded me in our own bed.

I wanted to let it go like he said. I wanted to settle into our closeness like our night wasn't scarred and the cove of his arms was my shelter. But I couldn't. He allowed me to vent just enough to appear like he wasn't completely self-absorbed. That wasn't acceptable. All of last night's activities were unacceptable.

I redirected my attention back to Pastor Mackenzie. His voice boomed across the room. "Unification is necessary for the body of Christ." He paused. "Church, I don't think you heard me. Unification is necessary for the body of Christ." Pastor Mackenzie strained 'necessary' like its four syllables were separate words.

Deliverance Temple was a small church by today's standards. A white building on the Eastside of Charlotte only housing about three hundred seats, it made the church more of a family atmosphere. Everybody knew who was a member and who wasn't. The pastor also knew who all his members were and didn't hesitate to make himself available whenever necessary. Pastor Mackenzie was a man who knew the Word and taught it with fervor.

I nodded my head and tried to focus with both hands occupied; highlighter in right and ballpoint pen in left. My instruments of learning were angled in preparation and my notebook lay flat in my lap beneath my Bible. I waited for the pastor to instruct the congregation on which chapters the message was coming from. When he spoke, I put the bottom of my highlighter in my mouth while I flipped pages of my Bible to the New Testament. I had to keep blinking. Every time I looked down at the Bible, my eyes became heavy. I took the highlighter out of my mouth and put it back in my hand after finding the page I needed. I suppressed the urge to yawn and rolled my neck from side to side. Scott briefly glanced at me. He had his arm resting against my back on the pew.

Pastor Mackenzie further stated, "In Ephesians four, verses thirteen through sixteen, the Word says, *'til we all come to the unity of the faith and of the knowledge of the Son of God, to a perfect man, to the measure of the stature of the fullness of Christ; that we should no longer be children, tossed to and from and carried about with every wind of doctrine, by the trickery of men, in the cunning craftiness of deceitful plotting, but speaking the truth in love, may grow up in all things into Him . . .*"

I could hear those words as my head drooped and I drifted into unconsciousness. Sleep felt so good I didn't even try to fight it. It wasn't until my mouth dropped open, a sliver of

drool left my lips and descended to my Bible that Scott tapped
me on my back. My head jerked up and eyes popped open.
The highlighter fell to the floor. I reached under the pew in
front of me to grab it. I sat back up and wiped at the wet spot
soaking my page, but didn't bother looking at Scott.

Pastor Mackenzie was still preaching. "Just because this
chapter says '*speaking the truth in love*' doesn't mean you have a
license to gossip, congregation. You see, we like to get things
twisted and dog out people when they're down. The first thing
we want to say is, 'I'm just telling the truth.'" He perched his
lips, rolled his head and put his hand on one hip like he was
imitating somebody he knew personally.

I was trying hard to stay awake. When Pastor Mackenzie
moved across the pulpit, my eyes followed. I knew if he stood
still I would be gone; my eyes would drop back down.

He scanned the church like he was seeking out the gos-
sipers. He waved his Bible as he walked the full length of the
pulpit. "People, we have got to learn that the words that we
speak from our mouths can be lethal. We can break somebody's spirit with these lips. Love in truth is saying to your fel-
low sista or brotha that you don't agree with their lifestyle and
know a God that can meet all the needs they seek out in the
street, but you will love them where they are in the meantime.
It is by showing them how good our God is to us even when
we are going through."

My eyes became heavier and heavier.

Scott whispered in my ear, "Maybe you should go to the
bathroom and try to walk it off."

He was right. I needed to get my blood circulating. I handed
him all my stuff and stood. Luckily we were on the end of the
row. I wouldn't have to interrupt anybody who was sitting
down.

I walked into the lavender and sage bathroom with its array
of colorful plants that would put a greenhouse to shame. The
space looked like it would infuse energy, but it did nothing to

make me less tired. I went into a stall, closed the door and laid my head against the cold steel partition. I could hear several other women come and go, but I didn't move. My mind kept going back to how disrespected I felt the night before.

I didn't realize how uninhibited Scott was until after we were married. I should have put a halt to the direction our sex life was taking the first time he asked to watch a sex tape. It was our wedding night; one of many nights I would make a compromise to please my husband. Submission. I thought I was doing my part in our marital contract. Scott explained that he just wanted to enhance our sensual union. He convinced me that anything we did in the privacy of our room was well . . . our business.

The experience at the Playa's Lounge was an eye opener for me. Watching a pornographic video was one thing. The movies didn't have the same effect as being at the Playa's Lounge. Maybe it was easier to be desensitized by a television. But watching the gyration of naked female bodies and lewd participation from men. . . . seeing that up close and in person was a bit much. A wake up call.

That one experience let me know that things in my marriage needed to change. I couldn't keep accepting what I knew wasn't right. I couldn't keep allowing Scott to use porn as foreplay to our intimacy, and we definitely wouldn't be going to anymore strip clubs. That was a first and last time for me.

As I finally left the bathroom, I had my mind set. I would just have to get Scott to see things my way.

I didn't know how long I was in the ladies room, but benediction was ending as I approached the sanctuary doors. I waited outside for Scott to appear in the crowd. When he saw me, an awkward expression crossed his face. "Did you fall asleep in there?"

"Hardy ha ha. What time am I picking up Elijah?" I asked as I took my Bible, notebook and purse from his hand.

"My sister probably won't be out of church until around three o'clock. As long as you call her first, I don't think it matters."

Scott headed to his car and I walked to my Cougar. We had driven to church separately because he had to be at work at two o'clock. His job as manager at Car Care was eight miles from the church, but also in the opposite direction of where we lived. He wanted to transfer to a location closer to our house than the forty-five minute commute, but the request was denied. He worked in a high crime area and the boys in charge didn't want to let him go.

My phone began to vibrate in my purse.

I shoveled it out and checked the caller ID. *Private*. I was inclined to not answer with all the hang-up calls I had been receiving from private lines. Couldn't nobody be calling private and want something good from me.

"Hello," I answered.

"Hey, Germani," the man said pleasantly, but I wasn't pleased as I recognized the voice. I could hear hollering of profanities in the background.

"Who's that?" Scott questioned as he watched my apprehension in answering. We were almost to our cars, but I had stopped short in the parking lot when I saw the screen.

"Mekhi," I stated dryly.

"Yeah?" my cousin asked, hearing me call his name while I talked to Scott.

"I was talking to Scott. He asked who was on the phone. You know I just got out of church, right?" Mekhi found the most inopportune times to contact somebody.

"Look at this mess. What is wrong with you? Don't ignore me. Look at what you did, Mekhi," the voice screamed in the background from Mekhi's line.

"What's going on, Mekhi?" I didn't really want to know, but the sooner the problem was revealed, the sooner I would be able to get off the phone. I was sure that his girlfriend was the one going off like a siren at the fire department. I was also sure that Mekhi had done something to make her that mad.

"I need you to come get me," Mekhi said without answering the question.

Getting him was not a good thing. There was no telling what I would be walking into.

I spoke loudly into the phone to combat the hollering on the other end. "I said what is going on?"

Scott furrowed his eyebrows with concern as we began walking again and approached his 300C. My car was on the other side of his. I used my remote starter keyless entry, while I debated whether I should go get Mekhi.

"'Shell is over here clownin'. I need you to come scoop me before something pop off." Mekhi must have gone into a different room. I could finally hear him clearly.

"I'm on my way," I reluctantly told Mekhi before ending the call. I then explained to Scott, "They're having a crisis over at his place. I'm going to swing over that way and see what's up."

"They always got something going on over there," he groaned disapprovingly. "You need me to go with you? Mishelle can get a little wild."

I looked at the time on my phone. It was a quarter to two. "Yes, she can. I'll be alright though. Mishelle is probably kicking him out again."

"You sure?" he asked, like he needed to protect me.

I smiled at my husband gratefully. "You better get to work before you're late."

Scott was neurotic about punctuality. To him, late meant fired. He didn't feel he could ask his employees to be on time if he wasn't leading by example. That was probably another reason the company heads didn't want to transfer him. He didn't abuse his position and his employees respected him.

Scott checked his watch and nodded his head as he jumped

into his car. I got into mine as well. Scott rolled down his window before pulling off. "Call me if you need me."

"Have a good evening at work, I will see you tonight." His concern warmed my heart and made me want to set aside my irritation about our disagreement.

I turned on my car and drove out of the parking lot behind Scott. He went left. I veered right. I headed toward Sugar Creek, not knowing what to expect once I got there.

CHAPTER
FOUR

SCOTT

Car Care was running a sales promotion to stay in line with the competition. For the month of June each store was giving various discounts for repairs with any of the automobile repair shops working with the store. Business was booming.

The only problem arose when my employees decided to take unscheduled extra days off for their own recreation. Granted, I considered myself to be a lenient family-oriented boss, but some of the excuses I had been hearing were on the ridiculous side. When I came into work this afternoon, three people had called in sick. One from the morning shift and two from the evening, which put me in a bind, because I only had one other person, Craig, in the building with me to handle the crowd of customers standing before me. Anybody in retail would know that customers didn't care if you were short staffed. They wanted to get their purchase and get gone.

"I need to return this." A short pudgy man with baby dreadlocks in gray dirty overalls stood before me and plopped his bag on the counter.

I pulled the item out of his Best Buy plastic bag and examined the product. Besides a few smudges from a finger imprint, the part seemed to be in good condition. I looked inside the bag for the receipt to go with the product. When I didn't find it, I set the bag aside and asked kindly, "Do you have the receipt on you for this item, sir?"

The man patted his overalls and then dug his hands inside the pockets. When his hands came from his pockets, they were empty. He took the bag and shook it upside down as if expecting the receipt to appear. A scowl came across his face and he frowned. "I must have lost it."

"Okay, give me just a second," I said as I ran the item number etched into the metal. I had to make sure that it was our product. After clicking the numbers into the system, the verification popped up.

"This is a Crankshaft Position Sensor for a 2004 Kia Sorrento with four wheel drive. Priced at $127.50 with tax. It has a one year warranty."

The man nodded his head as confirmation. "Yeah, that's it. I got the wrong part. It was supposed to be for a 2003 Sorrento. That one won't fit."

"Well, because you don't have your receipt I can't give you a refund, but I can do an exchange for you and get the sensor for a 2003."

"I just bought that sensor two days ago. Can't I get my money back?"

I hated when people acted like they didn't know the store's policy. NO RECEIPT, NO REFUND was in big bold letters on both sides of the glass entrance door. I pointed at it and he briefly glanced that way. "I'm sorry, sir. If you want to go and see if you can find the receipt, I would be more than willing to give you your money back, or as I said before, I can give you a sensor to match the 2003 Kia Sorrento."

The man appeared to be getting irritated as his lips above a nappy goatee formed a straight line. "Man, I was just here. Torrance helped me out. I'm a regular customer. I know you ain't gonna make me go through all that. Plus, I called a junkyard and they have one of these available for $45, but I can't get it if you don't give me my money back. How about you let me talk to your store manager?"

He had named one of the employees who called in sick and we had a lot of regular customers. I knew I didn't recognize him and there was a growing line of other irritated customers standing behind him. Craig was ringing people up as fast as he could from his line, but there was only so much that two workers could do.

We needed to wrap this up before customers started leaving and giving Car Care a bad reputation for poor customer service. "I am the store manager. Torrance is not here today, and even if he was, I would still need a receipt because of the amount of the purchase. If you don't want to exchange the item, then I can put your item back into its bag. I have more customers to assist."

"Fine." He snatched the sensor and the bag off the counter. He crammed the sensor back into the Best Buy bag.

Once again, I apologized. "I'm sorry I couldn't be of more assistance, but if you find that receipt, please come back and get your refund."

The man huffed as he shoved the glass door open.

It took close to an hour to help the remaining customers. Thankfully, only a few left, even with the long wait.

Customers came in spurts and there were a few browsers. I left Craig to take care of them while I went to call my missing employees. Craig came in at seven that morning and besides a half an hour lunch, worked straight through. It was almost six-thirty in the evening. I didn't like any of my staff working more than twelve hours. I would prefer them to not work over seven hours a day, because Car Care didn't want to pay for benefits. As long as I kept my employees at under thirty-two hours a week, the company wouldn't breathe down my back.

I decided to call my supposedly ill employees and see if I

could convince one of them to come in to relieve Craig of his duties.

I went to the back office, sat in the mesh office chair and flipped through the employee log. Sara was the first person I dialed. Craig told me she said that she twisted her ankle and needed to stay off her feet for a day or two. A nineteen-year-old vocational training student, who aspired to be a mechanic, Sara primarily worked weekends. I think she took the job to meet men. I found her flirting with the customers on more than one occasion. As long as her persuasions weren't overt or offensive, I left her alone. She memorized the product lines and worked well with all the guys.

The phone rang five times before going to voicemail. I left a message and went on to the next employee.

I then spoke with Richard who stated that he had a stomach virus, everything that he ate kept coming back up. He sounded genuinely ill.

Lastly, I called Torrance. He answered on the third ring. "Hello," he said with his strong Brooklyn accent.

He didn't sound sick. "What's going on with you, Torrance? Craig said you called in sick, but he didn't say what was wrong."

"I didn't tell Craig I was sick. I told him that my mom wasn't feeling well. Her and my aunt took the car to the emergency room. She said her head was hurting. She has high blood pressure and diabetes. She needed to be checked out. They still haven't got back. I'm stranded."

"Why didn't you catch a cab or bus?"

"Man, I don't have any money like that. I'm broke. I've got one dime and one quarter in my pocket right now. You know Car Care ain't paying me enough to keep my pockets lined. I help my mom out with whatever I got. In fact, I just filled up the tank yesterday, so I thought I was good to go. Scott, man, you know I don't be missing work on purpose. Them chicken heads be chasing me for child support." Torrance, a twenty-two-year-old with a hard edge, had four kids mothered by three women.

"Torrance, didn't we already talk about your terminology for the women you have children with. You know how I feel about that."

"I remember, but you're not able to see it through my eyes. If it walks like a chicken head, talks like a chicken head and hits my pocket like a chicken head, then I got to call it like it is. There are worse things I could call them."

That boy was still young and I hoped his perception would change. I was determined to help him out with that as time went on. He was the newest hire working a little over four months.

"I'm going to leave my cell number with you. Next time you get stranded, call me. If we are working the same shift, I will come pick you. Alright?"

"That's cool," Torrance responded.

I proceeded to give him the number quickly. I hung up the phone and went back on the floor to help Craig. Another crowd was forming. People love sales. I mentally prepared myself. It was going to be a long night.

CHAPTER
FIVE

GERMANI

Some things were just uncalled for.

I tried to explain to Momma that Mekhi was a product of his own misery and maybe he would stop the madness if we weren't enabling him. Momma didn't want to hear my opinion or objections, because we were the only family he had to depend on.

I got what Momma was saying, but I didn't agree with her. Ever since him and Mishelle have been together, I haven't wanted to be bothered with him. I still loved my cousin, but the predicaments he puts himself in were just plain stupid.

Mekhi reminded me of Uncle Frank, his daddy and my father's older brother. Uncle Frank was evil and ornery. I used to hate holidays at Uncle Frank's house, because of how bad he treated Aunt Pat. He once threw a whole pan of cornbread dressing in the garbage on Thanksgiving and cursed Aunt Pat out in front of all their guests. He had said the dressing was dry and bitter. He made Aunt Pat cook another one from scratch before anybody could touch the rest of the holiday meal. Momma helped cut up the bell pepper, onions and celery, while Aunt Pat cried herself through another batch of cornbread. I remember wishing that somebody would make Uncle Frank be nice to Aunt Pat; that people shouldn't act that evil.

Aunt Pat, Mekhi's mother, passed away of pancreatic cancer that next year. Uncle Frank took it hard. I thought Aunt Pat died so quickly because she gave up on life, didn't want to live with ornery Uncle Frank anymore. Uncle Frank never remarried. After Aunt Pat's death, Daddy would send for Mekhi during the summer months no matter where we were stationed. That was, until my father was declared missing-in-action during an assignment in the Air Force. Then everything in our family changed.

Mekhi and I were close back when we were younger, both united by a loss of a parent. I didn't realize that the sins of his father would be passed down to Mekhi.

The front door was wide open as I made it to the house. Mishelle's high pitched vocals were bouncing off the walls like an opera singer in Mezzo Soprano. I was expecting a glass to shatter. I followed the shriek into the front room. The closer I got to her voice, I could smell mildew.

Mekhi was sitting on the blue loveseat with a calm façade. Mishelle's tiny frame leaned imposingly over him, her acrylic nail pressed against his forehead.

"You're so stupid, I can't stand you. I don't even know why I'm with your sorry tail." Mishelle's breathing was heavy as she yelled. "You ain't a man. You're a weak little boy perpetrating like a man. A real man would take care of business."

"Move your hand, Mishelle," said Mekhi as he tilted his head to the side.

Her hand moved right along with his head as she continued to spit out insults. "You are a waste of oxygen and space. I should have made you a one-night stand. Somebody more important should be dwelling up in here. At least then I wouldn't have to deal with your sorry tail."

I could see the anger rising in Mekhi. His nostrils flared. "Get your finger off my forehead, girl."

"Or what?" Mishelle pressed into him harder. "What are you going to do?"

His hands balled into fists at his sides. "I'm not playing with you, 'Shell."

She removed her finger and lowered her face to his. "What? You want to hit me? Come on and hit me. Do I look scared? You can jump stupid if you want to. There's some numbers at Forsyth Correctional Center waiting for you to come back and claim them," Mishelle dared him.

Mekhi became volcanic. His body vibrated with anger. He rose up 6'4 with 270 pounds and Mishelle's 5'2, 120 pounds stood against him. Her midget rivaled his mammoth build. She may have been little, but she didn't believe in backing down.

As I looked on, I didn't want to become debris left after their explosion. "Alright, ya'll need to calm down," I said, making my presence known.

They both looked at me like I had walked out of a foreign film.

"Do you see what this fool did to my house?" Mishelle ranted as she pointed to a large hole in the ceiling. Clumps of plaster lay on the carpet directly beneath the hole.

I saw the result, but didn't know the cause.

As if reading my mind she said, "This fool broke my water pipes, let water rain down on all my furniture, and then he left the house. Didn't bother to call me at work and tell me what happened or nothing. I come home and there are wet towels every dang on where." Mishelle had her hand on her hip as she flayed the other hand toward a pile of towels brimming over the top of a laundry hamper.

"I didn't break the pipes, they burst on their own," Mekhi interjected.

"That's what your mouth says, but you still the reason I have a big hole in my ceiling. How am I going to explain that to Section 8 housing?" Mishelle asked Mekhi as he looked at the pile of rubble dumbfounded. She snapped her hand like she was dismissing him. It looked like her rage was waning; her fuse dying out. "Don't answer that. You don't care. I already know that."

"Where are Camry and Lexus?" I didn't mean to sound insensitive, but my concern was with the kids, who were too often witnesses to their parents' blow-ups.

"They next door at Twanda's," Mishelle responded before turning her attention back to Mekhi. "I pay the bills. I clean the house. I do everything. All you do is watch the kids. You're just a glorified babysitter."

Mekhi threw his eyes up at the hole. "And all you do is guilt trip me. I shut the water off as soon as I heard the pipe blow. I had nothing to do with your old broken down walls falling apart. I told you I was handling it."

The fuse reignited. Mishelle hollered with attitude rolling from her head. She stomped across the room to the basket sitting against a wall. "Oh, you handled it. Yeah, right. Then you kick down my crib and you haven't put three pennies on rent."

"You don't pay rent either, Section 8 does. You only work part-time at Family Dollar."

"So what if I only work part time. At least I have a job. I'm one up on you."

"You can't clown me about not paying rent. I help out around here. I was handling. I don't care what you say," Mekhi said as he picked up a leather duffel bag like he was ready to go.

"You have got some nerve." She reached into the laundry hamper and pulled out a dripping wet flowered hand towel. "This is handling it?" Mishelle threw the towel at Mekhi, hitting him in the face. Before the towel could hit the floor, another towel went flying into the air and then another. All aimed at Mekhi's head.

I watched Mekhi drop the bag and take incensed steps toward Mishelle. I rushed over to him before he could get to her. The air became still. I stood directly in front of him like the rock of Gibraltar, praying that my spirit woman would block Mekhi taking a chunk out of Mishelle's behind.

"You wanted me to come get you. Don't do anything stupid," I warned.

The crease left his forehead as his face went blank. "You're right. I've been in enough trouble anyway."

"Yeah, get gone, troublemaker. You're not welcome here anymore," Mishelle said tauntingly as she came up behind me and swung a towel at his face. It hit him right below the eye. Water splashed on us both.

Mekhi's nose flared as he gave Mishelle an angry stare. He shoved me aside and rushed into her. I fell against the rectangular coffee table as I tried to brace my fall. By the time I got up and turned around, he had Mishelle penned against the wall. His hand held her by the jaw as she dangled several feet off the ground at eye level with him.

"Oh, Lord, Mekhi. Please let her go," I pleaded with him as I used both of my hands and pulled at his thick unmovable arm. The veins in his lifted right arm bulged against his skin as he stared into Mishelle's teary eyes.

I used all my strength to try and remove his arm, but he was too strong. "Dang it. Mekhi, stop it. We've been down this road before. It's not worth some more prison time. You can't raise your kids from inside a block cell."

His teeth gritted, but he slowly lowered his arm with Mishelle's head sliding down the wall. He let go of her jaw as her feet touched the ground.

"One day your mouth is going to get you killed," he told Mishelle as he grabbed his duffel bag.

"I hate you, Mekhi," she cried.

Mekhi backed out the front room with his eyes intent on Mishelle. I followed. He walked out and I was grateful to God that things weren't worse.

Mekhi muttered to me when we were both outside after leaving Mishelle's house, "Thanks for coming to get me. I'll get the rest of my stuff while she's at work tomorrow. Mishelle's liable to throw my clothes in a plastic bag on the front stairs."

If he was looking for understanding, he wasn't going to get it. My right arm hurt from where I fell against the coffee table when he pushed me.

"Do not call me anymore for your junk. You two got way too many issues." I checked my sore arm for bruising. "I'm not going to keep dealing with your mess, if you don't find a better way to deal with it yourself," I warned as soon as Mekhi got into my car.

He didn't have anywhere else to go and he wasn't staying with me. Recently, Momma sold the three-bedroom house on East John Street to downgrade to a two-bedroom loft off Gleneagles Road. She had only lived in the new place for two and a half months and was enjoying her empty nest. I had to take him over to Momma's condo. Even with less space, she wouldn't mind him being there. Mekhi had a way of making Momma feel sorry for him since Uncle Frank was in a nursing home with multiple sclerosis.

Mekhi looked ahead with a mean mug on his face. "You just don't know."

"I know it don't make any sense to be acting like that. Why didn't you leave before things got crazy?"

"That's why I called you. I was trying to get out of there before I lost my temper. I tried to ignore her until she calmed down, but she wouldn't shut up. Now, you were there and you saw I was trying to be civilized while I waited for you to come get me. But Mishelle likes to push things to the limit." Mekhi looked out the back window like he expected Mishelle to be coming down the street.

Excuses. He knew he could have avoided the drama.

"Mekhi, you weren't forced to stay. It's not like you didn't have your cell phone on you. You should have started walking out the house when she started cussing you out. You knew nothing good was going to come from your sticking around. In fact, you should have been down the block before you dialed my number. I can't keep rescuing you, for you to turn around and go right back into it. You aren't married to Mishelle. It's not like you're obligated to be with her. You haven't been out of prison five months yet for domestic assault and already there have been two big blow-ups between you and Mishelle. Only five months of freedom." I put my hand up and flashed five fingers at Mekhi representing his time on parole.

He looked at me and shook his head.

"I don't care about no marriage papers. We have kids together. I just want to be around to watch them grow up."

"Camry and Lexus are not gaining anything positive from seeing you and Mishelle acting crazy. You won't get a chance to see them grow up if you keep doing what y'all been doing. You're going to end up locked up permanently."

Mekhi rubbed his bald head. "I really have tried to do better since I got out. I thought because I got saved in prison and started living for Christ that Mishelle wouldn't get under my skin like before. All them times she was visiting me things were nice. We talked about all the things we were going to do different after I got out. I thought the time apart did some good for the both of us."

"Well, you were wrong." I glanced at him sideways. Mekhi was delusional if he thought Mishelle changed that quickly and once he got delivered from his anger like he claimed, then he wouldn't go back to the one person who provoked him.

I sighed. "Being around you and Mishelle is dangerous. You pushed me down trying to get at that girl."

He winced. "Oh, dang . . . Germani, I didn't mean to do that. I just was so mad at the way she was treating me that all I saw was red."

"Yeah, uh-huh," I mumbled as I drove down Independence past the sign for Steve and Barry's. I grabbed my phone, which sat in the cup holder, then went to Momma's number on my cell and pressed the button of my Bluetooth.

I didn't want to get all the way over there and find out she wasn't at home. Momma was supposed to give me a spare key, but the front locks frequently jammed and she still needed to get somebody out there to replace them.

She didn't answer when I first called. I hung up before the voicemail could come on. Momma wasn't always the most expedient in answering her phone. I dialed the number again. It seemed like it took her forever to answer, but she finally did.

"Mom, Mekhi got kicked out again. He needs some place to stay." I was exasperated as I got within a couple blocks of her house.

Mekhi mumbled something to himself.

Momma was quiet.

"Hello. Are you still there?" I said into the phone.

"Is he with you right now?" she asked.

"Yes. I'm on the way to your house as we speak."

"I'll be waiting," Momma replied warmly.

I rolled my eyes as I pressed a finger to my ear and turned off my Bluetooth.

Mishelle could kick him out every other day and Momma would make sure he had somewhere to lay his head.

Instead of constantly being rescued, Mekhi needed to get his life together. His emotions were out of control. He needed to do something constructive with his time. Let that girl go before his temper and excuses got him into trouble that neither Momma nor I could get him out of.

CHAPTER
SIX

SCOTT

"I wish you would let me die. Please, just let me die," my niece, Alexis cried, knocking an empty water pitcher to the ground as a nurse tried to stick the IV needle in her skinny arm.

"Don't talk like that. You don't really want to die. That's the pain talking. The nurse is going to give you some relief, but you have got to stay still," her mother and my sister, Beverly said, patting Alexis on the thigh while she sat in a chair alongside the bed.

Beverly, Sharon and I had come to the hospital three hours ago after Alexis complained of chest pain. It was the first Monday I had off in weeks and I thought I was going to get to spend some time with my wife after our bad weekend and Mekhi calling her with his drama.

"I don't think Matthew likes all this noise. I hate when he gets under my rib like this." Sharon leaned on the chair arm and rubbed her eight-month pregnant belly. She and Corbin had already named their unborn son.

"Nurse Coleman, no disrespect, but you're going to have to hurry up and do something. Alexis has been poked for the last fifteen minutes and the IV still isn't in. We've never had this much trouble getting her hooked up before," Beverly explained.

The more the nurse tried to hold her arm steady, Alexis pulled away in resistance. Her peach-toned complexion turned bright plum as she used all her strength to fasten her arm against her side, the injection site hidden from the nurse.

"Leave me alone," Alexis said defiantly.

At twelve years old, people assumed she was three or four years younger due to her squeaky voice and thin frame. The sickle cell disease delayed her growth.

The nurse apologized as she slowly poked at Alexis' skin. "I'm sorry this is taking so long," she explained to Beverly, "but your daughter has small rolling veins. Every time I think I have it, the vein moves." She turned her attention to my niece. "Alexis, I realize you are uncomfortable, but you're going to have to keep this arm in one place."

"Can't you sedate her and then put the IV in after she falls asleep?" I suggested, wishing I could do something to bring my niece relief. Her face was soaked in tears. I grabbed a box of Kleenex from a table by the closet and handed it to Beverly.

The nurse shook her head, while a brown ponytail swung against her neck. "No. Dr. Sanchez needs her to be awake for an MRI and some other additional tests. We have to make sure she doesn't have pneumonia from her sickle cell crisis. That's the biggest concern. I can't get it."

"Lexie, stay still," Sharon demanded as she waddled over to the top of the bed behind Beverly. She grabbed Alexis' flailing arm and held it against the white sheet. "You are acting a fool. Stop twitching and let this nice nurse help you."

Sharon had the patience of a jackrabbit. On occasion, she could handle Elijah because he was a quiet child, but Alexis had a strong personality that irked Sharon.

"Uh-uh, I just want the pain to stop. I don't want—," Alexis' voice ceased as she lost consciousness. Her body suddenly and violently began to spasm. The brown of her eyes rolled back as her head jerked on the pillow.

Sharon stepped back from the force.

Beverly and I both stood up saying simultaneously, "What's going on?"

Nurse Coleman pressed a call button. "I need some assistance in here. This patient is having a seizure. Stat." She abruptly shifted the pillow from beneath Alexis' head and pushed the bed down until Alexis lay flat. We watched her body rise and fall. The vibrations shook the whole bed. Seizures weren't uncommon for Alexis, but we had never seen one this bad.

A doctor, along with three other people from the medical staff, rushed into the room. Sharon came and stood with us. Beverly grasped my arm as she looked at her daughter.

"We're going to have to get this under control. I need for you three to step out of the room," the doctor said as the small space became overcrowded with people.

We knew the routine and walked into the hall. Beverly threw her head up to the ceiling and wailed, "I shouldn't be her only parent dealing with this."

Sharon and I exchanged looks.

Bad choices breed bad results.

Alexis didn't know her father even though she was his namesake. At seventeen, Beverly had thought Alex Haworth was the 'one' just like every other young woman with high expectations of love. But I should have known what that brotha was up to when she introduced him to me at an A & T frat party. Back then, Beverly and Germani were dorm roommates. I had taken them with me to the party. I didn't want my sister going to frat parties by herself. I also liked being around Germani. She had a boyfriend and didn't see me as anything other than Beverly's big brother. I wanted to be more to her and found how easy conversation came between us. Germani and I were sitting against a wall talking when Beverly brought Alex over by us. My mind was on Germani and not where it needed to be.

I'll give it to him; Alex stuck around longer than I expected. Two years longer than any of us expected; even was there through Beverly's entire pregnancy. Alex vanished out of her life when Beverly told him his child was sick and Beverly needed him to add Alexis to his health insurance policy. Her Medicaid physician kept misdiagnosing Alexis, and Beverly wasn't going to let her child get passed over because they didn't have good medical coverage.

We all carried the sickle cell anemia trait. Our mother had it and it was passed down to her from her father. The trait in itself was harmless, but when two people with the same trait had a child, it could be detrimental to that child's health. Beverly didn't realize that both her and Alex were carriers of the sickle cell trait until the test results came in after routine testing during Alexis' birth. For some reason, there were no signs, but it seemed that the disease took a seriously hard toll on Alexis' body. She had been in and out of hospitals since she was eight months old.

"Did you call Mom or Daddy and let one of them know that Alexis is back in the hospital?" I asked.

Our parents had gone back to Baton Rouge, Louisiana, where they grew up, to take care of Grandma Edna after her stroke. Daddy was trying to convince his mother to move to Charlotte, but Grandma didn't want to leave Louisiana. She wasn't giving up her house.

Beverly responded, "Not yet. I wanted to wait and see what all is wrong. Her doctor was talking about all the long-term complications and how we may need to take a more aggressive approach. And you know what that means."

Levine Children's Hospital was a state-of-the-art facility dedicated to the health and well-being of small sickly kids. Yet, I didn't have a whole lot of confidence in their ability, because they couldn't cure Alexis. All they could do was drug her until she didn't realize the pain was there.

The medical team rolled Alexis out of the room and stopped in front of us.

The doctor was a short, chunky man with dark hair that was balding in the middle and a contrast to his young face. "We've got her stabilized, but I'm going to take her down for the test now to see if there is a reason for the grand mal seizure she just had. We'll give her regular physician a call for further orders. You can go back in her room and wait for us to finish."

As we all walked back into the room and sat down in the cushioned chairs surrounding Alexis' empty bed, Beverly confessed "I finally saw him."

I knew who she was talking about as soon as she said *him*. I remarked in shock. "You were able to get in touch with Alex? I thought you said he moved away to some part of Minnesota and his family acted like they didn't know where he was at."

"That's true. Most of his family isn't even from here and the only people I knew were his cousins that stayed near the Microtel Inn. They don't care about Alexis, so I wasn't going to waste my time contacting them anymore."

Sharon frowned at Beverly, filling a cup with ice from Alexis' pitcher on the side table. "How did you end up seeing him? Was he in town recently or something?"

"Because I am desperate to help my child, I found his information through the public records office in the City of St. Paul. He bought a house there. They have the deed on file for the mortgage company. Alex owes twelve thousand dollars on the house. I checked the market for his area in Macalester-Groveland. Those houses go for between $250,000 and $400,000 now. Amazing that his house is almost paid for, yet I can't get the $54,657.88 he owes me in back child support."

She shouldn't be keeping track of what he owed. If he didn't want to pay, no calculation on paper would make the money appear.

Sharon asked as she chewed on chipped ice, "Why would you waste your money flying all the way out there on some wild goose chase for him and he has never done a thing for Alexis?"

"I went to St. Paul after Alexis' physician first told me she may need that bone marrow transplant. He said that a family member could be a good match and he asked me all kind of questions about her paternal background. I don't know squat-ditty about Alex's side of the family. Therefore, I had to go find out."

Beverly continued talking. "Anyway, I showed up on his door-steps. Saw his wife, Selma, the two kids, both boys, and his dog. One of their boys answered the door. I think I scared the heck out of Alex when he saw me standing there." She chuckled thinking about it. "He was scared stiff. I didn't give him time to deny Alexis. I took a picture of Alexis with me and showed it to his wife, and explained what was going on. Right there in front of Selma he told me that Alexis wasn't his problem and he wouldn't be paying for a mistake from twelve years ago. Once I explained that I knew about the worth of his home and I was more than willing to take my cut of child support in a lump sum out of his property value if he wanted to be a butt about it, he changed his tune."

"He was a butt back then too. You shouldn't expect that to change," Sharon said as she tipped the cup of ice up into her mouth again.

"And that's the man I chose to make a baby with." Beverly let out a despaired yak. Her misery for present circumstances and disgust with the former relationship only deepened with her daughter's illness.

Withholding my opinion of Alex, I had to know. "So I take it he is willing to be tested as a match for Alexis."

"Yes he is. It's a shame that I have to bribe Alex to man up to his responsibility. I wasn't thinking at all when I got with him, and now, our daughter is paying for it."

I wasn't going to let her wallow. "Beverly, you can't keep beating up on yourself. You didn't do this to Alexis."

She shook her head, "I'm not in denial, Scott. This is my fault. I knew we had the trait. I just didn't believe it could happen to me or my child; like I was invincible or something."

Sharon rose from the chair and gestured toward the room with a toilet. "I got to use the bathroom. Do you think they will let me go in here?"

"There's nobody here to stop you," I told her as she wobbled to the bathroom holding her bladder.

I turned back to Beverly. "Alexis is going to be okay. You have got to stay prayed up about God healing her. Especially with the way she has been talking lately about dying."

Beverly began to tear up. "Scott, she is always saying that she doesn't want to live anymore. I don't know how much fight she got left. I really don't."

"It's going to be all right. If we have to be her strength and hold her up when she can't hold herself, then we will," I assured Beverly.

The orderly wheeled Alexis back into the room. "We're all done. This young lady was a real trooper." As he put Alexis into the bed, I moved the covers back. Beverly quickly wiped her own face.

I could tell some medicine was working from the glazed serenity in Alexis' eyes.

"Swiss Miss stirred up," I told her in the phrase we created when she was six years old to describe the doctors trying to treat the oddly shaped blood cells flowing through her veins. It meant her system had to be mixed and shaken to get it right, just like the hot chocolate milk she drank all the time.

"Yeah, Uncle Scott, Swiss Miss stirred up." She gave me a slight smile as the orderly lifted the rail on her bed.

I knew my niece and she had enough fight in her to get through, and with God's help, she would.

CHAPTER
SEVEN

GERMANI

I searched through the bathroom pantry for the scented body oil. It had been a while since I used the bottle.

"Ah-ha." I found the Ocean Body and Bath oil behind Elijah's bubble bath. I pulled it out, took the cap off and inhaled the intoxicating fragrance of watermelon and cucumber mixed with lavender and rosemary. The smell always did something to me. Made bad days seem tolerable.

I discovered the brand while searching online for a gift collection to give my mom for Mother's Day. The company, *Carol's Daughter*, popped up in the search engine. I recalled seeing an article about that line of products in a magazine. Jada Pickett Smith and Mary J. Blige adorned the pages of the website as obvious endorsers for its credibility.

I purchased Mango Melange Shining Star for my mother and the Ocean Collection for myself. I must admit, I was impressed. It kept my skin silky smooth, plus the body oil had multiple intriguing uses.

Pattering barefoot from the bathroom after my shower, I quickly maneuvered around the bedroom to make the environment sensual before Scott came home from work. Scott and I hadn't spent any time making up with me having to go rescue Mekhi on Sunday and Scott getting called to the hospital for Alexis yesterday. He usually made it in by 10:30 P.M. when he worked the evening shift.

I folded the bedspread and lay it on the floor next to the bed. I removed the burgundy and cream striped sheet set and replaced it with a white, more durable cotton one. I then sprinkled lavender talc from the headboard to the bottom bedpost for a pinch of extra freshness.

Scott's favorite lingerie on me was a sheer deep red negligee that flowed to my ankles and split up both sides to my hip bone. I slinked into the nice little number that covered my pear shape and confidently twirled in the mirror. I turned to look at my backside. My definition wasn't as well formed as that stripper Damon had paid, nor were my breasts as large as the pole dancer's, but I could hold my own. That was all physicality anyway. What Scott and I had was much deeper than that.

I heard the door close and slowly walked out of the bedroom to meet Scott on the stairs. The split level design of our home placed merely four steps between the upper and lower level. The distance was short, but I expected the effect to permeate his mind indefinitely.

A moment of delight coursed through my veins when I saw his weary frown turn upside down. That was the look I needed.

I took his hand and guided him to the bedroom as I seductively unbuttoned his pants. "I want you to stand here and follow my direction," I instructed. "First, remove every . . . single . . . thought that's not centered on me in this moment. We are going to have a special night free of anger, sadness, discord and negativism." I pulled his polo shirt over his head while he stood as prostrate as a mannequin on display in a department store.

After his lithe beige colored skin was free of clothing, I instructed him to lie face down on the middle of the bed, while I

hiked up my negligee and kneeled on the bed over him. I proceeded to give him a massage that started with his scalp. My
fingertips gently pressed in circular motions against his buzz
cut. Extra attention was given to tension areas like his temples,
the muscles in his neck and above his shoulder blades. Slow
movements gravitated downward until I covered every inch of
his anatomy. I trickled a small dollop of oil in my palm once I
got to the soles of his feet and began to knead my way back up
again.

"What brought this on?" Scott asked from his now relaxed
position as I stroked lines on his spine.

"Without going into too much detail, I was reflecting on
Mekhi and Mishelle. Their version of love is crazy. Scott,
every time I leave their house I am drained. It's like my energy
is sucked dry by that drama. I can't imagine us being that way.
Three days ago was your birthday and I agreed to something I
knew I wouldn't like and it snowballed on me. I felt I needed
to rectify the situation. Let it go. It's not worth the effort to
stay angry. Life's too precious to stay angry unnecessarily. I
truly was hurt about the other night."

"Baby, you shouldn't have been hurt—"

I cut him off. "Maybe not, but I was."

"I'm sorry you felt that way."

"It's over and done with. We need to focus on the now.
When you walk through those doors downstairs, you should
always feel welcome. I prefer to feel good and flow in the positive." I had stopped working my magic and continued to
kneel next to Scott with my elbows perked on his back while I
spoke.

Scott turned on his back and pulled me on top of him. "I'm
the lucky one, Germani. Believe that you are a special kind of
lady." A smile formed on his face. "Maybe you should meet me
at the door with lingerie on every night. I could get used to
this."

I smiled back. "I bet you could. I'll see what I can do to ful-fill that request."

"Yeah, you do that." His gaze became smoky as he pressed his lips against mine. He pulled the lingerie off me, letting it drop alongside the bed. Our lips reunited like a lovers' return after a long hiatus. I found myself falling deeper into the feel-ing of him. We slipped into a seductive world composed of just us two.

"Want to put in a video?" he asked as his hands made me weak.

"I don't want the sex tapes this time. I want to focus on me and you without any other distractions. We don't need those props for our pleasure. We should be enough," I said against his ear, determined to be the center of his attention. I slid my hands up his arms until our fingers became intertwined, allow-ing my husband to take us to the next level.

My eyes opened when what should have happened didn't. "What's wrong?"

Scott looked just as mystified. A scowl formed as he pressed his hand between the middle of us. "I don't know."

He opened his mouth like he planned to talk. He closed it and wrapped his arms tightly around my waist.

I could feel a repetitive request brewing in his mind, but as long as it didn't come from his mouth, I continued to work my womanly magic and dissipate the option. That is until I looked into his face.

Frustration glimmered in his eyes. "Baby, I need the visual stimulation."

His comment doused me like a car crashing into a water hy-drate. My sexual confidence clipped into shreds like carrots through a food processor.

I repeated what I said earlier. "I don't want to watch a porn video." My words were curt, even though I wasn't trying to have an attitude. My stand on the subject had to be clear though.

"Why not? We've been watching videos as foreplay to our intimacy." His voice was pleading, "You know that's what I'm used to doing. It's a big part of our arousal."

He made our intimacy sound cheap, fleeting and worldly. "No, Scott, it is a big part of your arousal. I just went along for the ride. I don't need to see other people in action to feel connected to my husband." I knew my words sounded crude, but he needed to understand my point. I flounced against my pillow, dejected. My desire for intimacy lost.

Scott uttered inaudible words under his breathe.

I softened my voice. "I don't have to be entertained by movies or books or stage plays for that matter, to make love to you. We could be in a cave in the middle of Timbuktu and all I'd need is you."

"You're upset that I asked to do what we've been doing?" Scott questioned. His inquisition was flat. Scott acted like I didn't make sense.

"Change is good for a healthy relationship"

"Baby, if it works, why change course now?" he reasoned. "If this were an airplane, me the pilot and you the copilot, we wouldn't dismiss the flight plan before we reached our destination. We would discuss it after landing." He jokingly cupped my chin and kissed me. Him and his corny interpretations.

I took that to mean I interrupted the flow of the night, which was probably true, but I felt how I felt. "No, I need us to be one without the over-the-top additions."

"Our making love is over-the-top?" Scott asked, astonished.

"No, not the loving making. The foreplay is a bit much and I sometimes feel guilty after we do what we do."

"There is nothing wrong with two married people finding creative ways to enjoy each other. Your guilt is self imposed and unnecessary torture. The videos only heighten the adventure we already have in us." He placed his leg atop mine and caressed my chest.

The realization sickened me. He didn't want me. His desire

revolved around a fantasy on a television screen or in a stripper's club.

I refused Scott's advances as his lips moved across my body. My arm went up as a barrier, pushing him to his side of the bed. I picked up my red negligee off the floor and clothed my nakedness. Thoughts of Eve in that garden flashed through my mind. I wondered if she felt my kind of shame when truth met her on the ground of Eden.

"Where are you going?" Scott asked. I could hear a touch of aggravation in his voice.

"Downstairs. I'm sleeping on the couch," I replied as I once again clutched emotions I didn't want to feel. My frustration controlled me.

"What happened to removing all negativism, anger, sadness and discord? We're supposed to be basking in the blessing of our union."

My words sounded fake coming from his mouth. "Too late," I grumbled, my tone sated with sorrow. I walked to the hall closet and removed a thin tattered brown blanket to sleep under. Maybe my perceived notion of a blessed union was an illusion. The Bible said dwell with those equally yoked. If that was true, then I was going to need more than prayer.

CHAPTER
EIGHT

SCOTT

The humidity steamed my skin like an outdoor sauna. Sweat circles formed from my armpits all over my teal Rocawear shirt. I could barely think, let alone tee off on the eleventh hole of the driving range at The Golf Village. Damon bought time at the golf course during one of the hottest months of the year. August had 90-degree weather that felt more like 110. I wiped wet beads from my forehead and leaned on my club. My 64-ounce icy Gatorade bottle was down to a corner of liquid. We had been out on the course for over two hours and the heat was making a brotha tired.

Damon didn't seem bothered by the smoldering heat as he swung his club into the golf ball and it flew high up across the green. We both watched that ball until it hit the ground several feet from its intended hole. The flag on the metal pole swayed, giving the impression that there really was a breeze. But if that was the case, I sure wished the breeze would come touch me. We began walking toward the flag pole. I surveyed the surrounding area for shades of color. Damon and I were it. Specks of brown in a sea of white.

"Nice," I said, realizing how skilled Damon was becoming as we eyed his golf ball.

He looked down at the ball then smiled at his near triumph. "How do you do it, man? Swinging like that in this heat? I'm about to pass out myself. I don't know where you get your tolerance, but shoot." That's all I could say. Breathing was becoming a problem. I felt like an asthma patient without an inhaler.

Damon bent over with his club held firm. He appeared to be studying the golf ball as he aligned the iron behind it. "Determination. It's all about the drive and determination. Anything can be accomplished if you want it bad enough and you mentally prepare to get it. Like in Darwinism. Only the strong survive. The weak whither away like dust into the ground, quickly forgotten. I am where I am today because I don't allow weakness to emanate my mind. I focus on a goal, research the methodology of pursuit and gain what I want. Let's discuss this game for a moment. I don't like golf, but it has the perfect advantage." He stood and shrugged like it was an obvious fact. His expression was one of indifference.

He could have fooled me about not liking the game. Damon had been on a golf course every Saturday morning for the past nine weeks. I only came to see the allure because he seemed so devoted to the craft. And considering how hot it was and my dislike for the game, we could have found an equally displeasing sport to play indoors. One that didn't shrink my lungs like I was smoking three packs of cigarettes a day.

I wasn't about to pick up golf as the new black man hobby.

"I play golf for the networking opportunities. The majority of the physicians I deal with enjoy this sport. In order to develop a rapport with my clientele, I have to become equipped in what they know. It's just as much about *what* you know as it is *who* you know. I have to be seen as an equal in order to develop the trust factor. Maybe manipulate a few things in my favor. Once I gain someone's trust, everything else is easy."

It sounded like a waste of energy. "Oh. Different strokes for different folks. Impressions mean a great deal more to you than to me. I'm not going to fabricate me to impress somebody just for financial gain. Manipulation for equality. Nah, I'm not interested. "

"Negro, pul-lease. Who you fooling? Don't hate my game because you can't play it. Besides, I like making money, and connecting with all the physicians for other activities generates a significant amount of funds to play with." Damon popped his shirt like he was fanning his chest. I could see sweat drip down his neck. It was a surprise that he hadn't called it quits. Damon wasn't one to allow himself to get funky; for no amount of money.

"Don't you think it's time for us to resign the clubs for the day? This heat is killing me."

"State of mind. Partner, it's your state of mind. Let me just finish this hole." Damon practiced swinging the club without actually hitting the ball.

"You already have a significant clientele. You're covering all of the Mecklenburg region and the surrounding areas, visiting doctor offices seven hours a day, Monday to Friday, selling prescription drugs and giving away samples. Burnout is going to creep up on you and knock you flat on your butt."

"I've had to get through harder times than balancing my work schedule. I got too much fortitude to go down. That is the main thing the hood taught me. If you stay where you're at, you'll never go anywhere. Just like Darwin's theory, I was smart enough to learn from my environment. If you want to be poor, stay around poor people. They don't mind having somebody to stay lazy, unfocused and stupid with. If you want to be rich, you got to step up your game and get connected to people with the right means. The best way to get somewhere is to step on or over the less inspired to get what you want. Pursuit. Position. Possession." Damon lightly tapped the golf ball and it rolled into the hole.

"I hear you, man. Do your thing. I can't be mad at you for doing you." I wiped at more sweat dripping on my forehead. "Since meeting Germani, my family became a priority. I like money, but I love my wife and son. I'm blessed without all that you talking about."

"Blessed is what you call it. Broke is what I call it. I guess that's why you are living check to check. Waiting on your blessing from God." He chuckled sarcastically.

He didn't used to be overtly egotistical. When Damon became the top performing sales representative for Pharm Access, his life perception altered. All of a sudden, acquiring money became his main focus. The more he got, the more he obsessed about having more.

"Don't hate on me, and I won't hate on you. I'm out." I put my iron back into the golf bag I had rented from the golf course shop. "You coming or are you giving me your car keys?" I said. It was too hot to be talking trash. Damon was my boy, but he could work a nerve when he put himself on an invisible pedestal. I tried not to take it personal. It wasn't like I was slumming. Germani and I did alright financially. Our combined incomes allowed us to do what we needed to provide for our family, plus have a little extra for entertainment. We traveled to countries throughout the world when the budget allowed for it. That was more than some could say.

Damon may be living high class now, but I remember back in the day when we sat on his front porch, eating Spam sandwiches and drinking grape Kool-aid out of mayonnaise jars.

"Alright. I'm done," Damon picked up his equipment and he sniffed himself as he followed me off the course. "You want to go by my crib and get a quick shower, then maybe hit Outerbounds Sports Bar and grab some eats?"

"We can do that." Until he mentioned it, I didn't realize how hungry I was. Germani stopped cooking after our last argument two weeks ago. She went grocery shopping every other week on a Friday. Yesterday, I noticed that all the fresh meats and produce for meal preparations were replaced with microwavable garbage. She knew I stayed away from processed food. My momma didn't raise us on TV dinners and I wasn't going to start eating them now. I could tell my wife was trying to make some kind of crazy point, but she didn't have to do it at the expense of my stomach. It was bad enough that she had taken the sex away. Depriving a man of his food, too, was unnecessary torture.

On the ride to the house, Damon played a recent CD by Brian McKnight. "She Used To Be My Girl" blared from the speakers as we turned off Polk Street in Pineville. The air conditioner came on. It soothed my hot flesh like ice on a sunburn.

I pulled my cell phone off my hip and looked at the blank screen. Germani hadn't called. Not even once. I probably should have expected it, but I was hoping that one day, she would wake up and throw away her attitude problem. Each time I tried to smooth things over, she gave me the cold shoulder. Even walked around me like I didn't exist a couple times. I resigned myself to let her stew alone over whatever issue she had. She and Elijah were already gone this morning when I woke up. She didn't leave me a note to tell me where they were going or nothing. Another reminder that bliss wasn't living at the Wilson residence.

I placed the phone back on my clip and sighed. "Women."

Damon glanced over at me. "Trouble at home?"

I hesitated about how much I wanted to tell Damon. "Little bit," I replied. Germani was wearing me out with her hostile demeanor. It'd be different if I understood the problem. Then I could rectify the situation; but psychic ability didn't run in my family.

"What's going on?" he asked.

"I'd rather not say," I paused. "You know how you get about women."

"What you trying to say, I can't be a sympathetic ear?"

Damon looked offended, but I knew better. My friend had many qualities, but sympathetic wasn't one of them. His logic was hard-edged and unemotional.

"You couldn't find sympathy on a crossword puzzle."

"We boys, though. I've never said anything that wasn't true."

"I know, but I don't know." I was in a state of conflict. I was learning in church to take things to God, but His response time was challenging. Some answers I needed quickly and God didn't work on people time.

"Talk man," said Damon. He slowed the car and moved toward the side of the road as an ambulance zoomed by, sirens screaming.

We pulled back onto the road.

"Does Cherish ever take you through drama just 'cause she can?" I had a vague idea about Germani's issue with me; I just didn't know what to do about it.

"I must admit, I can't complain. Cherish is a dime piece. She doesn't give me any kind of grief. My wife knows what boundaries not to cross. I rule. She follows. It's that simple." Damon was gloating.

I shook my head. "It's not that simple. Not for me. Germani wants to change me and I think she is upset that I have things that aren't up for change. Namely, sex. She knew I was a freak when she married me. I've been watching porn since I was ten years old. Germani watched it with me. Even incorporated some of the positions into our love making. Now, all of a sudden, after five years of doing it, the good stuff is off limits. Ungodly is what she called it. Ain't that a trip!"

Damon's eyebrows crunched together. He looked just as shocked as I felt. He used his palm to turn the steering wheel, placing us onto Mallard Creek Church Road. One side of his mouth twitched. His disapproval was obvious. "That's messed up, Scott. Over some movies?" he questioned like he couldn't believe it.

"Over some movies," I confirmed as we pulled into his driveway. "And now she has cut me off from the goodies. She might as well have put a pillowcase over my head and cut off my air supply." It was nice to get the frustration off my chest. Only a man could relate to another man about a subject like sex. Men are physical creatures. I don't care how saved a man becomes, sex is still important.

Damon took the keys out of the ignition and sat for a minute. "Wow. You are dealing with some stuff."

We got out of the car and removed the golf bags. "You wearing panties now . . . Hanes Her Way?" he joked. Damon was having a field day with my problem. "Seriously, aren't you the head of your household?" he asked as we entered his house and walked through his entryway, stopping at the carpet to take his tennis shoes off.

"Suppose to be," I responded.

"See, I told you to be careful with all that religion and niceties. Church will have you acting like a little punk. You need to get your manhood out of Germani's purse and attach it back where it belongs."

We headed up the spiral staircase and into his master bedroom. A 60-inch flat screen television was on the wall directly across from the king size Mahogany four-column bed that Damon threw his car keys on. The room was massive with twenty-seven feet of professionally decorated space. Damon strolled into his walk-in closet.

I stood at the bay window and looked down on the patio and in-ground pool.

Damon came out of the closet and handed me a folded beige Lacoste polo shirt. "Your wife running you because you let her. Get a grip on your emotions and show Germani who's in charge. Cherish knows her place and she can be replaced if she crosses the line of respect."

Damon made Cherish expendable. Germani was my heart. Another woman couldn't step into her shoes.

I unfolded the shirt and checked the size. Damon was only

maybe ten or fifteen pounds heavier than me, but my shoulders were broader. "This is not football. I'm not trying to trade up. I want a solution for my current problem, in my current relationship. Thanks for looking out, but I'll find a way to fix things with my wife."

"Do what you got to do." Damon shrugged and went to his attached bathroom. I went to the guest bathroom down the hall thinking up a resolution. Whatever was done, Germani would have to meet me halfway.

CHAPTER NINE

GERMANI

The balls of my feet were aching like I'd walked barefoot down a beach on ridgy stone. The warm bubbling water of the foot spa soothed the sharp pain caused by wearing too many uncomfortable but fashionable high heels. I needed to invest in shoes with supportive soles.

"Don't you get tired of being around dead people?" I asked my best friend as she sat in the chair next to me talking about her latest autopsy.

Autumn practically lived in the morgue as an Assistant Medical Examiner. She had graduated from medical school only a year ago and was still morbidly fascinated by the causes of death.

"I just can't get over how diabolical people are. The killer bonded that seventy-five-year-old lady's mouth and nose shut with super glue. He probably stood there and watched her suffocate to death after he raped her. He's probably a serial killer, because his method is signature. It was too precise to be the first time he'd done something like that."

I cringed at the image she put in my head as I watched a technician skillfully paint the long awkwardly curled nails of a young lady at the nearby nail station in blue topaz as a first coat. A yellow triangular pattern was airbrushed on top of the blue. It made for an interesting flashy design. The girl looked to be in her late teens or early twenties. Just the right age for daring self expression.

I wondered how she drove her car, cooked, cleaned or answered her phone with nails that extended at least seven inches. It seemed that nails like that would disable a person from their daily function. Then again, determination had no bounds.

Yousei, one of the female nail technicians, finished with another customer and came over. She pulled Autumn's feet from the thermal basin and patted them dry with a cloth. She gently massaged foot cream onto Autumn's skin.

We came to Ming's Nail Salon twice a month for a spa treatment. I had discovered the location after receiving a coupon packet in the mail with a few of their promotions. I clipped out the duo special, where we purchased a pedicure and the manicure was free.

They had me as a lifetime customer from the first time I stepped into the serene Asian-style environment. Not only did Ming's have excellent interior design with the accents of bamboo lamps, silk shoji screens, copper vases and natural looking grayish green and bronze color scheme, but the nail technicians specialized in outstanding customer service. I felt special each time I came back. The whole staff of eight knew me and Autumn by first name.

I decided to change the subject before Autumn went deeper into detail. "Have you ever felt like you blocked your blessing or stifled your anointing?"

I was trying to stand by my convictions, but it was harder than I thought it would be. The days seemed longer since I declined watching sex tapes with Scott. I dreaded interaction with my husband because I knew what he really wanted to do. If I remained aloof, he wouldn't approach me sexually. On the flip side, the longer we walked around each other like immigrants at U.S. border patrol, the harder it was going to become to successfully live together.

"You know . . . trying to undo some garbage that you created, but the efforts seem in vain when you work to make things right? Get caught in the cusps of wrong, even when it is obvious that wrong is wrong?" I asked Autumn while Yousei airbrushed her toes with French tips. My heart felt heavy with indecisiveness. I looked down the row and another technician was finishing up. I would be next for my pedicure. I needed to be pampered.

Autumn stared at me, "What's going on? You're sounding real philosophical."

"I went to the Playa's Lounge with Scott on his birthday," I confessed.

As her eyebrows rose, her mouth formed a circle. She was clearly shocked by my admission.

I should have allowed my embarrassment to be enough to shut my mouth, but I kept talking anyway. "It was the most degrading experience of my life. I felt spiritually out of order and physically out of place. My skin crawled and there wasn't a bug in sight. There were plenty of snakes in that spot, but no bugs."

"And your husband was one of them?" Autumn asked the question slowly as if she feared insulting me with the truth. I couldn't be mad at her for speaking what we both knew. Honesty could destroy just as quickly as it could build. I just had to discover where my reality was taking me.

"Don't get me wrong. I agreed to go to the Playa's Lounge. So I can't act like I was forced to be there. I had no idea Scott would show his all natural that way though. The straw that broke the camel's back was the lap dance. Can you believe he was going to take a lap dance from some half naked hoochie, while I was sitting right next to him?" I paused while waiting for her reaction. I expected her to be just as appalled as I had been when it happened. I wanted her to co-sign my frustration.

Instead, her eyes cast downward. Instead, her lips merged together into a singular railroad track. Her effectual silence neglected the confirmation I needed because of my suffering, my irritation and my continued angst.

Autumn must have scrolled through a dozen thoughts in her head. The silence got larger and longer, extending a mile.

My technician, Oaku, had come during our conversation and was painting my toes a vibrant color of red as she tried to act like she wasn't listening.

When Autumn finally acknowledged my question she said, "So, what are you going to do now?" She put the ball back in my court without answering, like I felt she would.

I didn't know what I was going to do. That was the problem. If I had my own resolution, then I would've never mentioned the subject to her.

I stated as much. "That's why I asked you. I need advice."

"You don't want my advice," Autumn stated in a matter-of-fact tone.

She had been my prayer partner since before I was married, even before I knew Scott existed. Prayed for me back before I was saved and prayed with me after I discovered how awesome God really was. Autumn was there when I trusted no one else in my business. Her unbiased straight-to-the-point commentary always made me feel she had a direct connection to the Higher Power.

Autumn hadn't given me significant advice since I married Scott. Although she thought Scott's nose was wide open for me, she was opposed to my less-than-honorable reason for our nuptials. I had an ulterior motive for wanting the marriage. My best friend was certain that I'd regret my decision to go forward with the wedding. Until now, I'd proved her wrong.

"What you allow is what will be expected. That's the problem women have. We lower our standards and then get mad about the lack of respect. If you set a firm foundation in the beginning, one not built from deceit I might add," Autumn gave her I-told-you-so look, "you don't have to worry about things crumbling at your feet later. You've known the power of God for quite some time. You are familiar with the ability to discern demonic forces, especially if they are in you. I'm not married, but I'm sure God wouldn't want you to willingly let your husband stray you from the love of Christ. The enemy will use those closest to you, who are weaker in their Christian walk, to lure you away from God."

"Nothing can separate me from the love of God. I may lose favor, but not His love," I said confidently. "My concern is pleasing God and pleasing Scott simultaneously."

Yousei finished with Autumn's feet. The salon was still packed, so Yousei moved on to the next customer. Autumn thanked her before she stood up, admiring her pedicure, and slipped her feet into her sandals. She placed the magazine on the spa chair "If your husband's not living right, you have to spend less time pleasing Scott and more time pleasing God. If you focus on God, pray about the lust demon ruling in your marriage, God will work out the rest."

I knew she was right. I had to get my mind focused. Scott would have to take a backseat to God. The Lord said He would never forsake me. He also said to meditate on His Word day and night. If I gave God His due, then maybe Scott would start to see things my way.

"Maybe that's all I need, improvement of my prayer life." I pondered that thought and instantly felt my load of frustration lifted.

I reached down and rubbed the smoothness of my soles. Oaku had done an amazing job on my feet. She had the magic touch in those fingers of hers. The sharp pain was gone. They felt like satin. I slipped my feet into a pair of blue denim low heel mules. Autumn and I walked to the cash register to pay for our manicures and pedicures.

"That and get some blessed oil. Cover every surface that may be tainted, including your door frames, the televisions, and—" Autumn handed the salon hostess her MasterCard, "rub oil on Scott's forehead while you pray for his deliverance."

She was trying to give me a death wish. "Scott's not going to let me do that." That decision was as far from wise as one person could get.

Scott thought that my former church was a cult and it was the same one Autumn still attended. He got spooked all three times that he visited with me. Scott declared apostolic shouting to be chanting and Holy Ghost dancing to be voodoo. His Catholic upbringing skewed his perception of the Holy Spirit. He said it didn't take all that for God to hear you.

It was one of very few arguments that we had. I wasn't happy about leaving the church that I'd grown spiritually in because it challenged his belief system. It wasn't until my former pastor suggested that I go with my husband to a church we could both be comfortable in, but for us to pray about the decision. I didn't know what I was praying for. My husband wasn't going to be happy with any church I picked, and I doubted my spiritual hunger would be fed at a synagogue. Out of obedience to my pastor and self-sacrifice for my husband, I prayed anyway.

It took a while, but eventually, we ended up at our current church. The non-denominational fellowship center catered to both my and Scott's interests. It wasn't as live as my former church and we didn't use blessed oil, but when the Spirit of the Lord showed up, He showed out. Plus I saw a change in Scott. But was that change enough? That was the million dollar question.

CHAPTER
TEN

SCOTT

The desire awoke me in the middle of the night. It surged through me intensely as I dreamed. Sexual images emerged that were as real as Germani who slept on her side next to me; ones in which pleasure sated my need. I delicately touched my wife's soft skin as I pressed my lips to her neck. I inhaled the sweet smell of her. My eyes closed while I pressed against her curves and thought about us making love. Yet, I couldn't get completely aroused, just like the last time we tried to be intimate.

I didn't want to chance the development of an argument if I woke her up and asked for porn foreplay again. Instead, I slipped from the bed, needing a release. Just because she decided to give up our sexual ritual didn't mean I had to. If only she could allow things to go back to the way they used to be.

Of the things I could do wrong in our relationship, watching porn with my wife should have been minor. I didn't smoke, drink, cuss, hang out all night nor cheat on Germani. Damon kept suggesting that I get a mistress, but as far as I was concerned, one relationship required enough work. I wasn't the cheating type anyway. I just wanted to be with my wife and enjoy sex-heightening movies together.

Obviously, what I wanted was of no importance to Germani.

I tiptoed down the hall to the computer room. I had an extensive adult DVD collection, but could watch nothing in the living room. That television faced the stairs and I didn't want to take the chance of Elijah coming down while my movies were playing. The one in the bedroom would surely wake up Germani and she didn't need to know what I was doing.

I closed the door of the computer room and rushed to the desk like a kid after the ice cream man. I pushed the button to turn the computer on and my giddiness escalated as the Internet browser appeared. I hadn't skimmed an online porn site in years. With a sex life as active as ours had been, who needed a computer? Germani had been more than willing to entertain all my fantasies. Even created a few of her own.

I tried to recall the sites I used to explore, but my mind drew a blank.

I glanced to my right as I tried to jog my memory and there was a Bible sitting on the desk. I looked at the Bible, and then looked at the computer screen. I could feel guilt creeping up inside of me.

Bible . . . Computer.

Computer . . . Bible.

The brown leather bound book felt heavy as I slid it across the desk and palmed it. I wondered how Jesus resisted that temptation in the desert. He had to be a seriously disciplined man. "Lord, forgive me," I muttered as I tossed the Bible in a drawer and quickly shut it.

My sexual desire won out. Compared to all the drive-by shootings, car jackings, parents drowning their children, spouses decapitating their mates, the ridiculous and unnecessary travesty of war in Iraq, my little sin was inconsequential. If Germani wasn't trippin', it wouldn't be a sin at all.

I clicked from one porn site to the next, fascinated by all the new virtual reality options. My senses almost overdosed on the visual stimulation. Reminded me of my introduction to adult entertainment.

We were two rambunctious twelve-year-olds, Damon and I. Damon brought over a couple of movies from his mother's stash. I thought he was going to get in trouble, but he assured me that his mother wouldn't mind that the movies were gone. Damon said that his mother let him see adult movies whenever he wanted to. She would rather he learned about sex watching it at home instead of experimenting out in the streets. If it was anybody else, I would bet money that they were lying. Most parents I knew, including mine, weren't that liberated. But I knew Damon's mom, because she was dating my Uncle Gabe. He was the fun uncle that would let us get away with just about anything. Damon's mom also had a different parenting perception.

My parents bought a new VCR and let me get the old one from the family room. It made loud whizzing noises, especially when the rewind or fast forward buttons were pressed. The picture quality appeared grainy as if dust had settled inside the component and it had no remote control. To a ten-year-old, it was prime electronic equipment. None of the other kids in the neighborhood had the luxury of their own VCR in their bedrooms. My house became the hanging spot. We snuck in all kinds of stuff we had no business watching. Once I got a hold to those porn movies two years later, I graduated myself to adulthood.

Traded Disney for Del Rio.

From then on, I was hooked—a habit I formed over twenty-two years ago.

I remembered the frustration and hurt I saw in my wife's eyes the last time we tried to have sex. When I couldn't rise to the occasion. Maybe I could give it up. Maybe I needed to pray about it. Reopen that drawer and pull the Bible back out.

Maybe . . . just maybe. But not tonight.

CHAPTER
ELEVEN

GERMANI

The verse for the day on my Christian calendar had a saying that perplexed me. It read: *The sluggard will not plow by reason of the cold; therefore he shall beg in harvest and have nothing*. I wondered if that applied to me. Probably. I felt convicted. A different version of that meant a lazy man doesn't eat. I hadn't cooked in weeks. Not out of malicious defiance, as Scott would like to believe, but more out of weariness. My doubts about my marriage were wreaking havoc on my ability to perform basic household duties. I cleaned regularly and made sure Elijah was fed. The least Scott could do was cook a few meals once in a while. If I wasn't appreciated, why put forth the extra effort? Okay, maybe I was exuding a little defiance. I wasn't perfect, but I wasn't lazy either. Maybe that verse wasn't applicable.

I chewed on the straw from my Dairy Queen mocha latte as I visually scanned the application for the second time. The words jumbled together. Name melting with address, employment history becoming abstract print. I shuffled the papers, widened my eyes and tried again.

Focus . . . Germani . . . Focus

Abraham and Sons needed to fill a machine maintenance technician position; preferably, by the end of the day on Friday. If the company I worked for, Job Track, weren't able to come through, they would post the position in the jobs section of the Sunday newspaper, costing us a significant residual from their contract and jeopardizing a working relationship. Abraham and Sons expected us to follow through, and usually, we did. We hired the majority of their industrial and clerical staff. I was fast running out of decent candidates to fill the position though.

Mitchell Camden's qualifications matched the company's profile from our database. He was the first one I called because of his twelve years of experience in the industry, but after relocating from New Orleans following Hurricane Katrina, he was still having a tough time finding something that suited him. When Mitchell came in for dexterity testing, I pitched the benefits. The job sounded promising. A long-term position would close his gap of non-employment. An eight-month contract. What more could he ask for? Money. Mitchell asked for a higher wage. He thought he had room for negotiations as he requested five dollars an hour more than offered by the company.

I warned him that he may want to rethink his demanding stand. We weren't a permanent placement agency. Job Track specialized in temporary employment and he hadn't worked in close to a year. Mitchell didn't take the hint. The company said no. Now I had to keep looking for other applicants and the options were thinning like an eighty-year-old man's receding hairline.

Daphne, our petite freckle-faced administrative assistant, appeared in the doorway of my cubicle. "There's a man here to see you."

Couldn't be for me.

I leafed through my black date binder.

Tuesday, July 5th at 11 A.M. was blank.

A scowl formed on my face. "I don't have anybody sched-uled with me this morning. Did he give you a name?"

"No. He said you would know him."

People always try to front like they have connections that don't exist. "He is mistaken."

We exchanged knowing glances.

"Get a resume from him and tell him that I will call him if I find a position to match his skills." I removed a business card from the holder on my desk. I handed one to Daphne, then thumbed through the stack of cards. It was getting low. I needed to order more.

Daphne took the card and nodded her head. Auburn curls bounced against her shoulders. She was used to walk-in clients claiming to have interviews with the agency. The trend was predictable. People will lie their way through just about any-thing. Misconstrue a situation to meet their purposes.

Within minutes, Daphne waltzed right back in my area. "He doesn't have a resume and he won't leave." One eyebrow arched as she looked at me suspiciously.

"What do you mean he won't leave? He has no choice. This is a professional environment, not some free hangout spot. See, that's why we need security." I picked up the phone to dial John's extension. He was our staffing manager and everybody looked to him when clients clowned, which didn't happen often, but it did happen. A former marine with combat mili-tary training, he retired after twenty years of service. John's charming, yet aggressive personality commanded attention and demanded respect.

"John's on vacation," Daphne said.

My hand slowed as I punched the third of four digits.

"He won't be back for two weeks. He went to Mackinaw Is-land in Michigan." She finished as she watched me with a cu-rious stare. "The guy out there doesn't look dangerous, just determined."

I sighed, "I guess I'll have to take care of this myself. Is he out in the lobby or in a testing room?" I jaunted around my desk and stood next to Daphne. I couldn't be sure of his location and wanted to handle things accordingly. Preparation, if there was a scene. We didn't need commotion in the lobby. That's bad business. Seeing that Daphne didn't fear our intruder or the possibility of him going Virginia Tech crazy, it was probably safe to take him into one of the testing rooms.

"Lobby," Daphne replied as we strolled down the hall and around a corner.

Daphne fingered him as he pulled a "Tips to Employment" brochure from the floor spindle. His bald head bowed as he read.

My erect professional posture immediately eased. A relieved breath escaped my lips. "Mekhi?" I asked, although it was more of a what-are-you-doing-in-my-place-of-business statement rather than a question.

My cousin looked up from the brochure innocently smiling.

He was too big to be playing coy.

"It's about time. Your gatekeeper refused to let me walk back on my own. She was posted up like this is Homeland Security." He placed the brochure back on the spindle.

"This is my cousin, Mekhi," I said as Daphne stood by waiting for an introduction. "Well, maybe if you had told her your name, some of your time would have been shaved off your unexpected arrival. Next time, call before you show," I told Mekhi as I escorted him back to my cubicle

He stopped at the entrance. "You don't have your own office. With a door?"

"No."

Mekhi bit the inside of his cheek as he looked up and down the row of cubicles. "These things don't have any privacy."

What did he need privacy for? My co-workers didn't care about his conversation. He had nothing to worry about.

"State your business," I said as he sank into my client chair. I sat back in my chair and rolled in close to the desk.

"I need to borrow your car."

I had automatically assumed he was already in a vehicle. "How did you get down here?"

"Bus. Route Eight. Took me fifty minutes to get here," he complained.

"Why do you need my car?" He had used it before, but loaning out my car wasn't habitual.

"I got to pick up something."

"Something like what?" His game of mystery, annoying me when my temperament was already compromised, didn't work in his favor. Mekhi only beat around the bush when he doubted my understanding of his need or situation.

He leaned closer to my desk. His voice dipped several octaves. "I got to go pick up my replacement food stamp card."

My pitch rose like a Ferris wheel on the upswing at an amusement park. "Food stamps? What are you doing getting food stamps? Boy, what is wrong with you?" I scolded. "Your feet should have never stepped in a welfare building. You are not that deprived."

I eyeballed his white, red and black Rocawear jersey, the nicely pressed matching black jeans, and Mark Ecko Crest Watch. Clean white Nike tennis shoes peeked out from the other side of my desk.

Mekhi glanced down, ashamed. He rubbed his hands across his jeans. "Things are kinda tight for me right now," he explained. "I'm trying to make due. You know how hard it is for a black man out here."

I cocked my head to the side and pursed my lips. Once again, no reason would justify a healthy able-bodied man standing in line for a hand-out.

He further explained, "Mishelle hipped me to it. When I got out of prison, she took me to fill out the application so we'd have more food in the house until I could get back on my feet.

"Uh-huh." I wanted to run down the laundry list of other things Mishelle had him doing that weren't in his best interest.

"Mekhi, you could have used that time to find employment. I don't know about you, but to me, application means job and work. Your applying for food stamps should have never been an option. A lazy man is supposed to be hungry." I referred back to the verse I learned earlier. I felt a sense of pride from being able to share the scripture I learned.

His nettled gaze told me he didn't like my comment.

"Donate your plasma at the Red Cross or somewhere, they pay for blood. An even exchange. You give, you get in return. That is more dignified than taking your overgrown behind through a welfare line."

"You act like I want to live this way. Ain't nobody hiring felons." He clapped his hands in sync with his measured words. "Believe me, I've been looking. I stay on the hunt. Both you and Scott work in management and neither of you can hook a brotha up. Now can you?"

"I . . . well, um," I stuttered, knowing he was right. Our company had a strict policy about criminal backgrounds. I could barely get a person with a misdemeanor employed, let alone someone with felony assault charges.

"But I do know a guy who is looking for some part-time help unloading trucks. He called last week. We don't really specialize in that type of thing, but he may still be hiring. Here is the address. Go check it out." I scribbled on a piece of yellow tablet paper, opened a top drawer and pulled out my car keys. "Have my car back here before this building closes at five."

He smiled as he jumped from his chair. "I promise."

He tried to pull the keys, but I held on with fingers looped around the ring. "Mekhi, you deserve better than hand-outs from the welfare system and you might want to stop taking advice from Mishelle. You feel me?"

"I feel you," he said, nodding in agreement as I released the key ring.

I hoped he did. I sure hoped he did.

CHAPTER
TWELVE

SCOTT

The undeniable smell of food greeted me as I entered the threshold of my house. A home-cooked meal appeased my appetite. Chicken pot pies don't give off that aroma. I followed the smell like an obedient servant to hunger. The house had been void of anything remotely requiring preparation beyond the removal of plastic or compression of microwave buttons. Food fixed in five minutes or less. I'd forgotten what it felt like to eat the real deal.

Germani stirred a pot on the back burner of our electric stove, already dressed for bed in a hot pink short pajama set. She didn't turn as I walked into the kitchen; probably didn't hear me come into the house. She was completely engrossed in her cooking as she dipped a serving spoon into the pot and tasted the contents. She picked up the salt shaker, sprinkled a dash in the concoction and slowly stirred clockwise.

"What's this, a special occasion?" I asked as I stood next to her and lifted a lid. A steamy cloud rose from the low simmering pan of smothered chicken with brown gravy and Vidalia onions.

"Not really. Eating garbage everyday gets old after a while."

She strolled over to the refrigerator and reached inside to get a stick of butter. I could see juice, milk, eggs and what looked like a fully stocked refrigerator from my view. A welcome change.

I took that to mean she was no longer on a silent war path. The caustic environment changed. I could relax a little.

"Are you going to eat with me?" I lifted the lid of another smaller pot. French style green beans.

She turned off all the burners and opened the oven. "I'm not all that hungry, but I'll eat a little something with you. Can you hand me the pot holders?"

"Sure," I walked to the far edge of the 'L' shaped countertop and slid the flowered mittens we used for kitchen towels off the shelf. I put the mittens on my thick hands and removed the tin baking pan from its rack.

"Thanks." She continued to give me minimal conversation as she rubbed over the top of a dozen golden dinner rolls. I didn't know what kind of mood she was in. No smiles, but on the upside, she wasn't frowning either. The vibe didn't feel negative. She'd cooked, so I wasn't going to question her mood.

I watched her fill each of our plates with food. Mine was stacked, while hers had a single chicken drumstick, three tablespoons of mashed potatoes and a dab of string beans.

"That's all you're gonna eat?" I asked, pointing at her plate atop a placemat. We sat down at the glass round table and Germani lowered her head to pray. I followed suit.

Raising her head she responded, "I ate a ham sandwich and a bowl of grapes with Elijah."

Elijah had to be sleep. It was well after ten at night.

She propped her elbow on the table and placed her chin in her palm. "How was your day?"

"It was okay." I dug my fork into the mountain of potatoes and swirled my utensil in gravy before bringing it to my mouth. I took in a couple more forkfuls, grateful for the meal. "The inventory numbers are off. Totally inaccurate. The calculations don't add up on paper. Our system usually computes the product line minus the amount of items purchased. Takes me a couple of hours to add the bottom line."

"Merchandise doesn't disappear into thin air. Think it could be a computer glitch?" Germani asked, poking her drumstick with her fork.

"That's my hope. It's going to be a headache to scan every item in the back room of the store and break down the numbers by manual application. Shoot, I've only had to do that two other times, and both times, the calculations were off because something was placed in the wrong location and not counted."

"Hummmm"

"If our company had more updated registers and tracking equipment, this wouldn't be a problem. It could take months to get this figured out."

The miscalculation made me edgy. Several hundreds of dollars in car parts had vanished. I didn't want to startle Germani by confiding my fears.

"This is delicious, baby. After working fourteen hours, this was exactly what I needed to come home to. Thank you. Thank you. Thank you." I took another bite and let my expression say it all. I truly was grateful, and if I could keep this momentum going, our relationship may be in a much better place.

Her lips extended slightly, but then she got a far away look. The kind when something has been on the brain all day. I didn't ask what it might be. If she wanted to talk about it, she would tell me. And to be quite honest, I didn't want to hear about anything that was going to change the element.

"I went to Bible study this evening." She watched me like I was supposed to respond to that.

"What did you learn," I asked.

"Pastor Mackenzie came from the Book of Proverbs."

"Proverbs. That's the one mainly written by King Solomon."

"Yeah. That's right." She acted shocked, like she didn't expect me to know that.

I might not be a theologian with an advanced degree in the subject, but I knew a little something about the Bible.

"In fact, Pastor said that there was much debate over whether the son of David, King Solomon, had penned the whole book or just pieces of it. Pastor Mackenzie's lesson was based on Proverbs 12:4 which read: *An excellent wife is the crown of her husband, but she who causes shame is like rottenness in his bones.* He told us that our actions and words have more power than we realize. If God gave woman the ability to bring forth life, wouldn't we also have just as much power to bring forth death? In today's society women are honored for being strong and independent, but sometimes, independence can breed spitefulness or indifference. Women have the ability to build a man up or tear him down. Women like to be right and we tend to do things or withhold things to prove our point.

"Pastor can't stand to hear women say they don't need a man for nothing, because it was God's design for us to need each other. Woman was created from a rib to be a helpmeet, which basically means for women to help men meet God's plan for life. Pastor clarified that he wasn't talking about women allowing themselves to be used by beaters, leeches, or cheaters. Men in those categories haven't reached manhood yet. He spoke for all the men trying to do the right thing. On no occasion is belittling a man acceptable in God's eyes. Shame brings about destruction." Germani summarized her version.

"It sounds like Bible study got real deep," I replied.

"It did, but the whole point of Bible study is to go more in depth into a biblical perspective. He made all of us women in class think about the reason we do the things we do. If the purpose of doing is because of what we gain by our actions, we end up losing anyway. We are to revel in our men's accomplishments; encourage them despite their failures."

While Germani talked, I polished off my meal and sucked fragments of chicken off the bones. I wasn't leaving a smidgen behind, nothing but gristle remained. After close to a month without a decent meal, I savored every last morsel.

She paused as I got up from the table and placed my plate in the sink. I poured a tall glass of sweet tea from the refrigerator.

"I forgot to get you a beverage," she apologized.

"Don't worry about it. I was so hungry I didn't think to get myself something to drink." I gulped the cool liquid.

Germani was still picking at her food.

"Do you mind?" I asked before taking her plate from the table. She shook her head.

I began to rinse the dishes and put them in the dishwasher while Germani sat in the chair quietly watching. "Continue telling me what you learned," I encouraged.

She got up from the table, pushed both our seats in and removed Tupperware from the kitchen cabinets on the side of the refrigerator.

"We haven't exactly been enjoying life lately. The lesson taught me to do things in kindness despite what I may be going through mentally. I must admit my actions were a little spiteful. Just a little bit." She pinched her fingers close together.

At least she admitted her angst. Obviously, her attitude was more than a figment of my imagination. I kept to myself and let the storm ride out. I didn't like walking through my house waiting for Hurricane Germani to pass over.

"I'll try not to take you on a roller coaster of my emotions, but I don't like feeling like a piece of tail. There is a difference between sensual intimacy and straight raunchiness. We need to find a way to work through this whole porn loving thing."

"We only have a problem because you're making it into one," I remarked as I dried my hands and playfully snapped the waistband of her cute little shorts while she was bent over in the refrigerator rotating items around to make room for the Tupperware.

She stood up and turned around. One container still in hand, her eyes slanted as she frowned. The frustration was on the rise again, but she kept it at a reasonable level. "It's deeper than that. I need you to take this seriously. I'm not going to keep doing what I've been doing when I know how wrong it is."

I felt like Keith Sweat, whining in a love song. "I'm sorry. I'm so very sorry. If you don't ever want to watch another pornographic movie and experiment together again, then we don't have to. I promise you that we will never have to watch or do anything that makes you uncomfortable."

I didn't know how I was going to hold to that promise, but I loved her enough to try.

CHAPTER THIRTEEN

GERMANI

"You know Richard was blowing smoke up our rear end," Stewart, my recruitment partner, said with his strong Southern accent after we left our meeting at Plas-tech. They were in the middle of a merger with an unknown corporation and we went out to discuss plans for the ninety temps we had placed there. Richard, Contract Divisional Manager, assured us that our temps wouldn't be affected by the upcoming changes, but we knew better. Whenever there was an acquisition, somebody lost their job.

Stewart wanted to make a stop at The Grape Wine Bar and Bistro to pick up something to drink for a date who was cooking for him that night.

As we pressed through throngs of weekend shoppers at the Northlake Mall, I thought of Scott. He had just promised that we would both stop watching porn last week. I didn't even know that he was into the Internet porn until a few days ago when I did a search for a gumbo recipe. Once I saw the first porn pop-ups, it wasn't hard to pull up URL entries on the computer we shared. There were thirty odd viewings listed before he made the promise to stop; five viewings after. What was the point in him making a promise that he wouldn't keep? How reliable was his word? Why did Scott pick porn over me? Question after question that wouldn't have resolved anything. I guess a little piece of me had given up on the subject. I didn't know what else to say to Scott that hadn't been said already. The porn pop-ups jabbed at my sexuality as a reminder that my husband didn't want to be intimate with me . . . with only me. My womanly pride was wounded. I missed being touched and caressed by my husband. I missed us making love. Scott wasn't the only one with needs and desires.

"I shouldn't be long. Meet you back at the Macy's entrance in about half an hour?" Stewart asked, looking at his watch.

"Works for me," I agreed.

I went to Borders Books and perused the aisles for a title that would catch my attention. Strolled from Biographies down to Christian Fiction around the corner to the Inspirational section. My attention was caught by a book about the discovery of a divine plan for sexual and emotional fulfillment. The title . . . *Every Woman's Battle*.

"Germani?" a voice as familiar as ice cream floats on a hot summer day called my name.

I instantly felt buried emotions revive themselves as I looked into hazel eyes that once captured every essence of me. A smile grew across my face, one that shouldn't have been there.

"Tre." I wanted to be enraged, but my smile remained intact. I conjured up hurt, but the pain of old wounds stayed buried.

I placed the book back on its rack as I soaked in his appearance. The stone-washed jeans and tan t-shirt hung loosely on Tre's medium frame. His simplistic style of dress hadn't changed.

He hugged me. As my chin touched his neck, I inhaled the scent of his cologne: Perry Ellis 18. The same brand he wore back when.

"How have you been?" he asked with a wide grin on smooth mocha skin. He'd cut his goatee off since the last time I'd seen him.

I wanted to tell him that it was none of his business how I was doing, but I couldn't deny my joy at his presence. He always had that effect on me; could make my heart do double-dutch. Somehow, marriage didn't change that or maybe it was the state of my marriage that was the problem. Maybe if Scott and I were on better terms, I'd be able to block the feeling rising in me.

"I'm doing well. Life is good, better than it ever has been." I embellished a little, but hoped I sounded convincing. I wanted him to think I was okay even if I wasn't. I couldn't have the first man I ever loved, an ex-boyfriend, realizing my life didn't turn out as well as I expected.

"I heard you were married," Tre said as his eyes locked with mine.

Tre's and my relationship had ended six years ago when he joined the Peace Corps for a three-year assignment. It dissolved on a bad note, one that took a serious toll on me. I started seeing Scott one year later and married him six months after that. It was easy to do. His sister, Beverly, was my college roommate and Scott used to come visit her every other weekend. Scott and I became close friends and he stuck around when Tre left me. I knew I wasn't over Tre, but Scott soothed the rejection I was feeling at the time.

A woman with a double stroller came down the aisle and tried to get past us blocking the way.

"Excuse us," Tre said as he instinctually pulled me to him as she went by. Being that close to him felt too familiar. I took several steps back as soon as the aisle cleared.

"Scott is his name. We have one son, Elijah. What about you? What have you been up to?" I asked, controlling that slight tremor in my voice.

"Well, I can't say that I have the pleasure of sharing my life with a mate, but I've been busy. The organization I work for is still focused on relief efforts in Darfur. I just recently came back to stay for awhile."

His peace work was a point of contention for us. I didn't comment because I didn't want to sound bitter.

"Found anything interesting to read?" I asked.

Tre read avidly. He was so many firsts for me. Tre introduced me to the biographies of Coltrane in Jazz and Nietzsche in Philosophy. He gave me a lot of knowledge from the books he used to pick up.

His hands were empty. "No. At least not what I was looking for. I just wanted to say hello when I saw you standing in this section. I'm going to get out of here."

I said hesitantly, "Oh, okay. It was good seeing you."

"You too." He headed toward an exit and I wished he had stayed to talk just a little longer.

CHAPTER
FOURTEEN

SCOTT

Cut-N-Up barber shop on Eastway Drive was packed with brothers on Friday. I brought Elijah with me so we could get hooked up at the same time on either Wednesday evenings or Friday mornings, based upon my time off.

There were five barbers on hand and all of them were busy.

Deon handled the heads of young boys and placed a booster seat in the chair as I lifted Elijah up. "Want the usual?" he asked me as he picked up a set of clippers.

"Can you taper the sides a little more this time and curve the line by his ears." I pointed to Elijah's head as I gave Deon instructions.

Steve, the owner of the shop, turned the television volume up on *ESPN* as a picture of Michael Vick flashed across the screen.

"Why they messing with Mike? They know that ain't necessary. Don't nobody care about dogs fighting like that," Steve said as I sat down to wait for the next available barber.

The Vick coverage had been all over the news stations since the dog fighting story first broke.

Joe responded, "Well, you know what it is. Discrimination.

Michael Vick is popular. He was the first African American quarterback pick taken number one in the NFL Draft back in '04. The Atlanta Falcons signed that boy on a $130 million dollar deal, plus $37 million just as the sign on bonus. Nobody's ever been offered that much money to play football before. And they gave the deal to a black man. You know that somebody was going to start looking for some dirt on that brotha."

The customer sitting in Joe's chair added to the conversation. "Yeah, somebody was mad he had all that money. They brought the Feds into it too. What do the Feds have to do with dog fighting? Nothing until Michael Vick. He didn't even live in that house."

Steve responded, "Evidently, he didn't have to live there. Mike admitted to funding the gambling ring for the dog fights. He kind of set himself up for the rest when he started talking. The NFL said they want their money back for signing him on. They said he knew he was into some illegal stuff when he signed that contract. He's supposed to give back twenty million of the thirty-seven he got for the sign-on. And he lost all his endorsements."

Joe pointed his clippers at Steve. "No. What happened was he got bad legal advice. He might as well have had a public defender instead of that attorney of his for all the stuff he lost. That cat wouldn't have got paid if he was my lawyer."

"Too bad Cochran is gone," the customer added.

Joe placed his clippers on the stand behind him and brushed off his customer's cape. "He needs R. Kelly's lawyer. Those sexual charges have been pending since 2002. Now that's what I call some good legal defense. Whoever he has is seriously earning his pay to keep R. out of jail."

"It's not too late. Mike better call Robert and get the hook up," Steve joked.

Everybody in the shop laughed.

Next to my chair was a table full of reading material:

Maxim, swimsuit edition of *Sports Illustrated* and *King* magazines. I looked over at Elijah who had his head bent while
Deon trimmed the back of his hair. I picked up a *King* magazine with Kim Kardasain in a bikini on the cover, but I wasn't
all that interested in reading it.

There was such a steady stream of people coming through
that I didn't notice when Doug, from church, sat down next to
me.

"Hey, Scott. I didn't know you got your hair cut here," he
said as he glanced at the *King* I was holding.

I tossed the magazine back on the table. "Yeah, my son and
I come here every couple of weeks. You know how it is. Got to
keep a fresh cut."

"True. Taylor is at the shop up the street getting her hair together too. Me and the wife are going to the Comedy Zone in
Greensboro tonight. She keeps complaining that I don't take
her anywhere. She sees me everyday at home, but evidently,
that's not enough. I hope they funny, since we driving an hour
and a half to see this comedian she heard about. Have you
been to the Comedy Zone before?"

"No. Germani and I haven't been getting out too much
lately, because of our work schedules. Not a whole lot of quality time in the evenings."

Doug opened a folder and pulled out a flyer. "I don't know
if you heard the church announcement, but we're starting services for Angel Food Ministries next weekend. We are desperately in need of volunteers if you can spare a couple of hours
on that Saturday morning."

I was hesitant. "I don't know. It's not going to be an all-day
thing is it?"

I didn't want to get locked into an ongoing obligation that I
knew I wouldn't commit to. I knew some of those people who
spent every day of the week doing church stuff. That wasn't
my type of thing.

"No. We are just trying to increase our community support.

Let people know about the positive things we got going on at the church. I think Pastor Mackenzie is expanding outreach for the Church Without Walls programs. We don't have enough men representing the good things we are capable of doing. Let the media tell it, black men aren't doing anything positive. We can't let that continue to be the perception. The children's center will be open if you want to bring your son." Doug smiled as he gestured toward Elijah, who was almost finished.

I took the flyer from him. Volunteering for one Saturday sounded doable. I made the schedule at work, so I could take that day off and Germani could probably go with me to lend a hand. "I'll be there. What time we need to be at the church?"

Doug gave me all the details.

A couple of hours at church couldn't be all that bad, now could it?

CHAPTER
FIFTEEN
GERMANI

Momma called me over to look through some kids' clothes she picked up at the Salvation Army. I had already created three piles. The 'yes' pile, the 'absolutely not' pile and a hill of clothes that were in good condition, but not adequate for my son. Her bedroom was a nice size space, but she had it cluttered with things she didn't need. An old record player that hadn't worked since 1975, hat boxes stacked underneath the bed and in two corners of the room, and a portable wardrobe closet full of her church coats and dresses that wouldn't fit into her regular already overstuffed closet, took up the whole wall next to her Bombay dresser and mirror.

Thin streaks of gray were beginning to show through the hard green rollers of her black hair rinse as she leaned over me to grab something. Momma didn't like to go to the hair salon; instead, once every two weeks, she would press and curl her own hair. She also had a cabinet full of Dark and Lovely jet black hair color products she used.

"What's wrong with this?" Momma asked as she held up a gray overall set. The white shirt attached had little dancing panda bears covering the ribbed material. She couldn't just let me pick out what I liked; she had to rummage through all the discards.

"Maybe you didn't notice the awkward shaped hole in the buttock." I took the outfit from her hands and showed her the gaping hole.

"Oh, child, that's nothing some thread and a needle won't fix. The outfit only cost me fifty cents and it's good material for the winter months. Didn't I buy you a sewing kit?"

She knew I didn't like craft projects, especially ones that required me to stitch something without the aid of a sewing machine.

I stuck three fingers through the hole and waved at my mom. "Yes, mother, I still have the sewing kit at home. It's going to take more than thread and a needle to get me to put this on Elijah." I threw the overalls back into the absolutely not pile where they landed atop a pair of faded navy blue corduroys.

"I'll sew it myself. You just so . . . ugh sometimes." Momma grabbed the panda outfit from the discarded pile again. Her nose rose in the air like she was too through with me. "I bet if you add up all the money you spent at Carter's and Kid's Depot in comparison to the deals at the thrift store, you would see how much you're wasting. The clothes you buy aren't new any longer after you wear them once."

I endured the same lecture regularly. It was like clock work. She would find something she thought was ideal for Elijah, I'd reject her selection and she'd go on a tangent about my spending habits. My respect ranked too high to tell her to mind her business. Instead, I had gotten skilled enough to listen and tune her out at the same time. She had bought so many clothes from discount stores over the years, that I no longer had room for them. It just meant that I got rid of the clothes I didn't want at a later date.

My mother wasn't broke, she was frugal. Money came slow after dad went missing. She'd pinched pennies ever since they brought that American flag in place of Daddy. The military compensation for my father's honor couldn't cover all the bills. From her job on base as a civilian office worker, Momma scraped money together for us to maintain.

Thinking about the military made me think about Daddy as well. I wondered where we'd be if Daddy were here. The longing never left me. I always hear people say boys need fathers, but girls do too. I had only a few significant times with my father that I could recall. For two years, Daddy was stationed in Colorado Springs when we were able to enjoy him like never before. That's where I gained my most memorable experience with my father.

I was seven years old. A city surrounded with winding cliffs and picturesque mountains pocketed in crisp clean air, we snow sled in the winter and went swimming in the warm months. On the coldest days, I often fell asleep on a recliner snuggled up with Daddy next to the roaring fireplace. Daddy had taken a position as a Military Recruiter so he could come home at night. He loved us, but he was never happy doing that sort of job. The thrill of foreign land and challenging assignments lured him back into Special Forces.

My fore long memories froze the expression on my face. I caught myself staring across the room at an eight by ten brass polished frame with the picture of a youthful, but stern William Beckford in his uniform with his radiant bride posed at his side under an archway. The photographer's powder blue background didn't do justice to the glowing couple.

"I still miss him too," mom said, reaching into my thoughts.

My father was a Senior Master Sergeant in the United States Air Force on special assignment in the Hashemite Kingdom of Jordan. Reportedly, his plane disappeared in the desert on route to Sinai. The radar picked up no sign of the aircraft. Eight crew members and the pilot were missing. Daddy wasn't coming home.

"Do you think Daddy would have liked being a granddaddy?" I asked as I stuffed the discarded pile of clothing back into a white tall kitchen bag and looked at Elijah rolling his toy truck around on the carpet.

"I'm sure that he would have loved being a granddaddy. He would have loved all three little ones, regardless of whether they were his own. Now that Camry, I don't think he'd be as devilish as he is now if William were alive. The other day, I came out of the bathroom and I heard him cuss at Lexus. Nearly burned my ears right off my head. They were playing in the TV room and Lexus was screaming, 'Stop, Cam-Cam.' I guess she and Camry were tug-a-warring over some toy.

"I got to the room right when he called her the "B" word and demanded she give him his toy. Then I witnessed him snatch the thing out of her hand. I tore his little behind up and made him gargle his filthy mouth out with undiluted vinegar. And yes, I know I taught you and Mekhi to never hit kids while you mad, but that great-nephew of mine is going to have me catch a child abuse case." She whispered the last part of the sentence so that Elijah wouldn't hear.

"Oh, Mom." My mouth dropped open. "He gets it from his parents. If Mekhi hadn't called Mishelle that word, Camry would never have known the word existed. Or he may have known what the word was, but he wouldn't be able to get away with using it. Cussing is a regular activity over in their home."

"Don't get me started on that. I'm just glad that Mekhi changed his vocabulary and attitude when he came from prison." Momma pointed her finger at me and exclaimed, "I'll tell you what, if Mekhi and Mishelle don't get a grip on that little boy right now, they are going to have heck to pay when he's older. Your daddy would have had that child strictly disciplined. Camry would have been scared to talk without being told, let alone cuss. Y'all knew better. Lord knows I wished he were here." Mom's voice seemed to wail as anguish covered her face and she waved one hand in the air with closed eyes.

Elijah stopped playing with his truck and looked up at Momma like she'd lost her mind. I shuffled through the other clothes on her bed to keep the evening from becoming a crying fest.

"Whew. I had to get that out. I reconciled long ago that God must have had reason to take my William away, but when I've seen his brother deteriorate from multiple sclerosis, watch Mekhi on his own destructive warpath and Camry acting downright disrespectful . . ." She took a deep breath, but didn't finish her thought.

Momma stood from the bed and smiled. "Mekhi is on the right path. I guess I need patience for this situation and for my great-nephew. Camry will be all right. This family will make sure of that."

Momma tried to be the mother Mekhi no longer had and the father he didn't see.

"That reminds me, I want to take Camry and Lexus to the church carnival on Friday. Is Mekhi over at 'Shelle's, so I can see if they already have plans?" I asked.

"No, he only goes over there to pick up the kids. He's in the room." Momma gestured toward the room across the hall. She checked the time on her nightstand. "Has a foul mood too. 'Shelle probably said something to get under his skin. I don't say nothing to him when he gets reclusive. You can go talk to him if you want. It's time for *Deal or no Deal*."

The world stopped on its axis when her show came on. No matter what was going on around her, she was going to watch the bald headed Howie Mandel. The apparition of winning a million dollars made tangible.

"Mom, can you get Elijah some juice and take him into the living room with you?"

She grinned at my little man and held her hand out. "Come on, baby, let's go get us a quick snack."

I went across the hall as they walked toward the kitchen. I knocked, but Mekhi didn't answer. Instead of knocking louder, I let myself into the room. Mekhi lay on a weight bench in the corner of the bedroom. His arms were in mid lift of a set of dumbbells.

"Can I come in?" I asked as I eased the door closed.

"I don't care." His tenor voice grunted as he brought the weights back down to his chest.

"Having a rough day?"

"A little like."

"'Shelle?"

"'Shelle," he confirmed dryly.

I didn't want to ask what happened because it was usually the same story on a different day. Mishelle pissed Mekhi off. Mekhi clicked out on Mishelle. Or visa versa. The attitudes would be gone by morning and they'd be blissfully reunited all over again.

"We're having a carnival at the church on August tenth. Do you think that Camry and Lexus can come with me? I'm sure they will have a fun time. Last year, I took Elijah, but he was too little to really appreciate it. I think the clowns scared him."

"They don't live over there anymore. Mishelle moved out yesterday." He sounded like he didn't have any say in the decision.

Mishelle's parents had bought that house for below market value when Camry was born. It was a foreclosure property the bank was desperate to get rid of. When Mishelle applied for the housing voucher program, her parents received a Section 8 check for rent and gave her half the money back for living expenses. Her rent was less than my phone bill. Due to her having a different last name than her mother and stepfather, she was able to get away with the arrangement. I was surprised that she was leaving her nice little set up. "Where did she move to?"

Mishelle had only put him out two weeks ago. I didn't know how she could have planned to move so quickly.

"She moved in with some cat she barely knows. Said she

met him at the Groove Club a few months back. I have limited knowledge about the cat and she's got my kids in the house of some stranger blowing promises in her ear."

I didn't know if I was relieved, shocked or disgusted. They had been on the bad side of love for so long that I didn't expect for it to change. Even when Mekhi was locked up, Mishelle was there to visit him every weekend. Mishelle had unexpectedly moved on awfully fast.

Mekhi sucked on his teeth. "Talking about she finally got a real man. She knows that stuff gets to me. I've been spending every day since they opened that prison gate trying to get it right. Trying to make up for all the wrongs. I haven't hit her one time. As bad as I've wanted to, I've kept control of myself. And she dogs me. What am I supposed to do with that?"

I could feel vibrations on the floor as he dropped the weights on the rack above his head. He grabbed a towel and wiped the sweat from his brow.

I sighed as I searched for my tact. Needed to speak with an unbiased view, but I couldn't. "You're trying to stay in the wrong place with the wrong woman." I let the words fall from my lips, knowing he wouldn't be receptive.

Mishelle wasn't the problem. Mekhi not letting go was.

"She said since I couldn't take care of my children, maybe I need to relinquish my parental rights. I'm a man, Germani. I have no problem hustling to take care of mine. Before I got these aggravated assault charges on my record, I had no problem getting a job. 'Shelle was deep in my corner when I kept money in her pocket. Then I hit a bad stroke of luck with this criminal record, and she has no love at all. Nags me when I'm there and complains when I'm not. Now she's trying to use the kids like they pawns. All I want to do is be there for my family."

"You can't make her want you. Camry and Lexus will be your family whether Mishelle is your woman or not."

"It won't last. We're still in love with each other. Eventually, 'Shelle and I will be back together," Mekhi said confidently.

I didn't say anything else. My cousin was so far gone over Mishelle that he couldn't think straight. Whether he acknowledged it or not, I had an irksome feeling that things were bound to get worse with their situation.

CHAPTER
SIXTEEN

SCOTT

My employee from work, Torrance, called me this morning at home. He needed a ride to work; said his car wouldn't start. He thought it was the battery, but his cousin had already tried to jump it and the engine still wouldn't turn over. I told him that he could use one of the mechanics we worked with to take a look at it, but he said he already had somebody to work on it.

I pulled up to the address in Charlotte's housing project off Tryon. I had his house number on a slip of paper I ripped off an envelope. I thought I had passed his address and slowed down in search for his number.

A flash of red passed by my eyes as I looked up from the paper. Suddenly, a crunching sound exploded under my tires. My wheels screeched to a halt. I didn't know if I should put the car in reverse and see what I had run over or stay still.

My tongue felt like paste. I jumped from the car and ran in front of my vehicle to check and see what damage was done.

Two small children were nearby. There was a turned over tricycle on the ground. A little boy, that looked to be about two years old, lay beside it. The other, a girl with two long ponytails dangling on each side of her face, who looked to be in kindergarten, had her arm wrapped around the little boy's arm as she picked him up from the ground.

"Is he okay?" I asked the little girl about the whimpering boy. A steady line of tears flowed from his eyes, skin darkened by his flushed face.

Oh, my God; did I hit him without realizing it?

"He fell," the little girl told me as she consoled the boy, who must have been her brother.

A sigh of relief escaped me as I saw that my car was at least two feet from where the bike lay with a crushed two-liter Sundrop plastic bottle beneath the wheel.

"Dominic, knee hurt?" she asked as we noticed his skinned leg. The boy stood up and walked with a limp.

I set the bike upright then held my arms out to see if he would let me pick him up. The little boy reached up to touch my outstretched hand and I lifted his lightweight compact body into my arms.

His sister stared at me with doe eyes. A cross between suspicion and uncertainty played on her chubby face as she eyed me up and down.

I held my free hand out for her to grasp, but she simply stared at it like I had fungus growing.

"My momma told me that we're not supposed to talk to strangers." Her voice was loud and clear as she watched me.

I searched the area for a distracted parent. An elderly woman sat in a lawn chair placed in front of her door. Her gaze followed me as I stepped over a small patch of grass between the parking lot and the sidewalk. Five teenage boys bumped against each other as they threw a basketball around a makeshift hoop and court.

"Where's your momma at?" I stopped on the sidewalk and sought direction from the little girl.

Her index finger pointed at the apartment three doors down. I looked back at my awkwardly parked car and hoped a police officer didn't come by and give me a citation while I took the children to their mother. Between my front end and the bumper of my car, I was blocking three other vehicles. I had to make it quick.

The little girl opened her front door and trotted in. I stood at the door, the screen slapped against my backside. Dominic, as she called him, remained in my arm. Dry streaks of tears covered light brown skin. He looked comfortable, so I let him stay where he was. I also felt guilty that the little man had hurt his leg.

A woman with black naturally curly hair pulled back into a clip, high cheek bones, full pouty lips, green eyes and skin the color of smooth sandstone stomped toward me with an angry scowl. She was so fine I had to stop myself from staring.

"Who are you and what are you doing in my house? With my child?" she demanded. The glare of a protective woman slammed into me as she snatched her son from my arms. The little girl crept up behind her and peeked at me.

I automatically stiffened.

All I could do was defend my reason for being there. "I almost hit your son. I was driving down the lot." I paused. "I was looking for an address when your son and daughter came from behind a parked car on their bicycles right past my car. Fortunately, I was able to stop in time, but—" I held my hand up and out. I tilted my head letting my body language tell her that stuff like that got kids run over.

Her angry glare went from me to Dominic and the sister I had no name for. Her attention set on her daughter. "You know I told you to stay on the sidewalk. All I asked was for you to watch your brother for a little while. What were you doing in the middle of the parking lot? You . . . know . . . better." She verbally chastised her daughter as she jotted her index finger at the child. "Do you realize how dangerous that is? You know better than that, don't you? Don't you? Answer me, Cheyenne."

Cheyenne quickly shook her head as tears spilled and her lips quivered. "Yes," her small voice said.

The air seemed to thicken.

"Stop all that crying and go to your room. Stay there until I come get you." Her voice roared as she held Dominic against her chest. He had begun to cry again.

I knew I needed to get out of there.

"I'm not sure what you were doing while they were outside, but . . . um . . . they really need an adult to supervise them. You can't expect children as young as yours to be responsible. Maybe you can entrust one of your neighbors to look out for them when you're busy," I advised.

She rocked as she talked. "I don't trust everybody with my kids. Besides, Cheyenne is not your average six-year-old. She is smart enough to know right from wrong."

People took too much for granted. Assumed safety was an automatic. If somebody snatched up both of those kids, she would feel differently. Unsupervised children went missing all the time. I guess my face must have said something because she went hard on the defensive.

"Don't look at me like that. I am a good mother. I take care of my kids. You come in here trying to tell me how to parent and you don't know a thing about me. While you talking, you probably have a bunch of your own kids you're not taking care of. You can't judge me."

"Whoa, lady, all I wanted to do was let you know what was going on with your kids. I'm sorry if you took it the wrong way." I started walking toward the door. I wasn't expecting all the angry commentary when I stepped in, and was definitely ready to go by then.

Her emotions changed yet again, from anger to guilt. Women kill me with that.

She said before I touched the doorknob, "My name is Lisa. I was only busy for a minute. I tried to put together her bedroom unit and didn't want the kids running back and forth through the room. I should have waited until they went to bed to complete the chifferobe."

She seemed more like an overwhelmed mother instead of an unfit parent. Something inside urged me to lend a hand. I didn't know why. I couldn't explain it. I guess I felt sorry for her. Thought about my sister and what Beverly had to go through as a single mother.

"I'm Scott. Do you need help putting the chifferobe together? Two people work better than one."

Her face brightened.

"It would have to wait until I got off work this evening, but at least then you wouldn't have to do the job by yourself," I offered.

She paused to think, and the rocking ceased. "I don't know; it's not like you know us or anything. What do you get out of it?"

"Nothing. It appears that you need help and I would hope somebody would look out for my wife under similar circumstances."

Just as she agreed to accept the help, I heard a car horn blowing.

"I did leave my car blocking some other vehicles in," I said hurriedly as I opened the door. "I got to go. I'll stop by later."

She placed Dominic on the floor as she followed me.

"No strings?" It looked like she was still trying to decide if I was trustworthy.

"No strings," I assured her as I walked outside and glanced toward the vicinity where my car was parked.

Torrance was sitting in my driver's seat. He pressed his hand to the horn one more time before he saw me coming his way.

"Scott, man, I didn't know where you were. I was about to have an Amber Alert put out on you." Torrance had the seat tilted back with one hand on the top of the steering wheel like it was his car.

"What are you doing?" I pointed to his comfortable position in my seat.

"Let me get your whip?" Torrance asked without even attempting to budge.

I responded as I opened the driver's side door and waited for Torrance to move from my seat and go to the other side of the car. Lisa stood in her doorway and waved at me like we were old friends.

Torrance watched Lisa go back into her home. He chuckled a little. "So that's why you had the 300 parked like you running something over here. You kicking it with the sexiest thing on the block?" Torrance nodded his head without waiting for me to confirm or deny. He seemed to be proud of me.

I drove out to the street. "It's not what you think. I'm happily married."

Torrance pushed out his lips. He didn't believe me. "Everybody tryna holla at her fine self. I heard she was from Cuba. Is it true? Cuban women into that kinky kinda loving."

Torrance's mind stayed in the gutter.

All I could do was shake my head at the boy. "I already told you that I don't see every woman as a conquest. Lisa seems like she's going through a lot."

"I heard from Lemon, who's kicking it with a girl who works in housing, that Ms. Fine's man got busted on some Federal charges. They repossessed the house they were living in and all the furniture. They wouldn't even let her get her kids' clothes out the crib. Then they deported her man back to Mexico."

"See what I'm saying. Even if I didn't have a wife, what I look like trying to use her when she already having a hard time? Plus, she's got two kids. I don't roll like that."

Torrance ignored my point. "She's vulnerable. She should be easy booty."

"I have more respect for women than that. I grew up in a house with sisters. I would hurt a man over any one of them. Dogging women don't make you a man. That stuff ain't cool."

"You make it sound like a bad thing. If she's consenting,

then it shouldn't be nothing but pleasure. Women know whassup if you holla at them."

"I can respect that she's not trying to listen to somebody who just wants to get in her panties."

Torrance rolled down the window as we passed three girls on the sidewalk. "I like them shorts you got on," he shouted out.

I could hear the girls giggle as I kept driving.

CHAPTER SEVENTEEN

GERMANI

"Mommy, can we watch *Ratatouille*?" Elijah came into the kitchen and asked.

"Do you remember which button to push?" I replied as I scraped out the hardening grits from breakfast. The children wolfed down the pancakes and country ham, but picked over the little bit of grits I had put on their plates. I thought everybody liked grits.

"Yes, ma'am"

"Okay. Go ahead."

Elijah went back into the room with Josiah, Lexus and Camry. I had the children overnight after taking them to the church carnival. Mekhi's kids had spent the night on several occasions, but it was the first time Josiah got to stay. Nicole had attachment issues and didn't trust her son with just about nobody after a recent divorce. Elijah and Josiah often played together in the toddler room at church, in which I spent two Sundays a month monitoring the children's care. I had been around Nicole enough to gain her trust. She knew I was just as protective over Elijah. Compared to the twenty to twenty-five children that were regulars in the toddler's room, watching the four was like a cake walk.

Elijah broke my concentration when he walked back into the kitchen and patted my leg while I rinsed plastic cups. "Mommy, Camry won't help me find *Ratatouille*. My movie is missing."

His eyes began to water. Camry was always being mischievous. The oldest of the bunch, he liked to be the bully.

"Is Cam in there being mean to you?" I wiped Elijah's face after drying my hand on the front of my robe.

"He won't let me watch *Ratatouille*," he repeated. "I don't like the naked people. They're making scary noises and hurting each other."

"Naked people? What naked people?" I went from the kitchen into the family room where the children lay on blanket pallets made for them the night before.

Josiah and Lexus were lying on their stomach with legs fanning the air. Camry sat up close to the television on Scott's ottoman. His cheeks were about to burst from the grin spread across his little face.

My mouth dropped as I realized what he was fixated on. Actually, the sound of sensual moaning caught me first, and then I looked at the screen. Two women and a man were performing erotic acts on each other.

I don't know which one was bigger, my mouth or my eyes as I realized what they were watching. I rushed across the room and turned the DVD Player off. The *Ratatouille* disc sat on top of the black box.

I turned to look at Camry, who was no longer smiling. "What do you think you were doing? Didn't nobody tell you to put that movie in there. I should whip your little mannish behind."

The adult movies should have been in a box on the top rack of the storage room where I had placed them to get them out of our bedroom and far out of reach from little prying hands. Yet, I knew Camry had a knack for getting into unusual places;

messing with stuff he had no business touching. I couldn't figure out how he got to the box without my knowing it. Especially considering he would have to pass by me in the kitchen
in order to even make it to the storage room. I was pretty certain none of the children were out of my sight for more than a
few minutes this morning, and I had slept on the couch in the
same room as them last night. But somehow, he got his hands
on that box.

"Aunt Germani, I didn't put it in. It was already in there. I
didn't want to watch *Ratatouille*. I already saw that movie at
home. I wanted to watch something different." He batted his
eyes innocently.

I slid the disc from the player and stared at the cover. The
front of the disc read *Latina Caliente* and had to be new. I didn't
recognize the title from the collection I had stored.

Scott must have recently bought and watched it. How irresponsible of him. He knew Elijah liked to watch his movies in
the family room. The least Scott could have done was watch
his sex flicks in our bedroom if it was that serious for him.
After all, he acted like he was going to quit watching the stuff.
I couldn't believe him.

Scott wasn't at home. He had gone to the pharmacy to pick
up a prescription of Codeine for his niece. Beverly had called
early this morning because Alexis was up all night crying in
pain and there was little else they could do until the pharmacy
opened at eight. I would have to address his obsession with
pornography yet again, and after he told me that things would
be better. Foolish me. Now I had to go tell Mishelle and Nicole
how their children accidentally got a hold of a sex movie while
they were supposed to be watching a cartoon. I didn't like being
put in that position to explain at all.

I looked up to see all four children staring at me. I snapped
the disc in two.

"What you saw was a very, very bad movie. You are to never
watch anything like that again. We are all going to get dressed

so I can take you home. Camry," I pointed to the bathroom around the corner, "you go first. Lexus, I'll take you upstairs with me. Josiah and Elijah, when Camry comes out of the bathroom, you two go brush your teeth. I will help you get washed up and dressed in a little bit."

As I drove the children home I rehearsed different ways to tell Mishelle and Nicole about their kids' accidental exposure to Scott's sex flicks. In one scenario, I could explain how remorseful I was about my husband's lack of discretion and they could be assured that it would never happen again. In another scenario, I could play down the incident as if they flipped past national geographic and saw some bushmen running through African fields instead of the kinky lust triangle. I knew my conscience wouldn't let me go with the second scenario, but it sounded easier to explain.

Mekhi's children lived closer to me than Nicole, whose home was going toward South Charlotte, but I dropped off Josiah first anyway. After I told Nicole about the movie being left in the video player, she hugged me and said I couldn't be held responsible for my husband's actions. She knew I was upset about it and prayed with me over the issue. I felt a little better when I left her house, but the nagging guilt lingered.

Mishelle's new residence sat in the middle of a new development off Oak Drive. When I first picked up Camry and Lexus from the brick front two-story home, I wondered if she gave up her Section 8 or had it transferred, but it wasn't my business so I didn't ask her about it.

I rationalized that maybe Mishelle wouldn't be bothered by her children watching a little nudity. She was a round-the-way kind of female. Considering that she let Camry cuss like a sailor in front of her and laughingly remarked, "Kids say the darnedest things;" or when she had Lexus hump the floor to the music video *Laffy Taffy* so her girlfriend could see her baby's dance moves. I doubted that she took offense all that easily.

After I pulled up to her house, I got out to unstrap all the children. My Cougar was loaded down with car and booster seats. I wondered how people managed more than three small children without a minivan.

"Take you and your sister's bag up to the house," I told Camry who had the small luggage on rollers between his legs in the backseat.

Camry was at the steps by the time the other kids' feet hit the pavement. In my haste to bring them home, I forgot to call and let Mishelle know that I was bringing them back early. When she opened the door in silk pajamas, she looked surprised to see us.

"Good morning," she said with a raised eyebrow, standing to the side as Camry rolled the bag inside.

Lexus trailed in on Camry's heel. Elijah stood by my side.

"Lexus, get your thumb out your mouth," Mishelle told her daughter, who was sucking away, before closing the door behind us.

"Mind if I talk with you for a moment?" I requested, still not knowing how Mishelle would respond. So often when I was around her, she was going off on Mekhi.

Mishelle looked down at Elijah. "You can go play with Camry," she told him.

He followed Camry and Lexus up the stairs.

We walked down to her living room which was adjoined to an eating area where her boyfriend, Cyrus, was drinking from a mug while he read a newspaper on a barstool.

"Uh-oh, what did Camry do?" Mishelle sat on the couch placed diagonal to the kitchen opening.

I stood by the overstuffed chair explaining what happened. "Actually, Camry wasn't the one who did something wrong. It was my husband. Scott left a little flick of his inside the DVD

player and I didn't know it. The kids were supposed to watch
Ratatouille while I cleaned up after breakfast, but it turned out
that they ended up seeing something they didn't need to see."

"So my kids saw a dirty movie?" Mishelle's posture shifted.
She wasn't going to make this easy.

"They only saw a little bit. As I said before, I thought a cartoon was in the player and I encourage Elijah to be independent, so I didn't think anything about it when he asked to
watch his movie, because it's his favorite and we usually leave
it in the DVD for him. Believe me, I feel awful about this and
I don't know what Scott was thinking. Well okay, I knew what
he was thinking, but it was still inappropriate. You have my
deepest apologies. I guarantee that it won't happen again."

The whole time I talked, Cyrus, whom, I didn't know from
a can of Dutch Boy house paint, shook his head between slurp-
ing his coffee. I only saw him in passing the other day, but up
close, his features were defined. He appeared to be at least fifteen years her senior, his mustache slightly graying, forehead
wrinkled; not a man I pictured with her. Mishelle's demeanor
remained reserved, almost too pleasant. Nothing like I was
used to with her. I could not have felt more awkward.

Mishelle looked over at Cyrus again from her position on
the couch. I was certain that he gave a nod before she said,
"My kids won't be going back over to your house."

When she saw how stunned I was she decided to elaborate.
"Listen Germani, I don't think you are a bad person over all,
but I'm trying to make some changes in my life. Doing things
for the better. And to be real honest, I thought you and your
husband had different morals than that. No, let me rephrase
that. I know you go to church and it seems like a contradic-
tion."

I pulled out a chair and sat down. Even though Scott had a
lapse in good judgment, I didn't expect for her to take it the
way she did. It wasn't like her kids hadn't been to my house
many times over without incident, and Camry could be outra-

geous in his behavior, but I hadn't banned him from my house. We were family.

Mishelle continued on. "No offense to you, but I'm tired of church people faking. Talking it ain't the same as walking it. You go to church just because it's the thing to do, but then you look down on people who aren't interested in being phony. I'm not raising hypocrites and I don't want them around perpetrators confusing them about life."

I thought it was big of me to admit that my husband was at fault. Her personal assault on my religion was unnecessary. "I don't know what's up with the church bashing. I came over here to talk to you mother to mother because I didn't want you getting the wrong information if Camry or Lexus mentioned seeing naked people over at my house. I didn't want any confusion."

Cyrus set his newspaper down while he gave complete attention to our conversation.

"It's nothing new that I don't go to some uniform fellowship, but I do watch the news. I see priests molesting little boys." Mishelle started jabbing the counter with her fingers. "Then you have those mega church pastors soliciting their members to fund their personal planes and multi-million dollar mansions. Explain to me how a church leader can afford thousand dollar suits, but most of his members are living raggedy. We were just talking about that last night. What did you call it?" she asked Cyrus.

Cyrus answered, "Hyped up emotionalism. The feel good services."

So Mishelle finally found somebody that thought like her.

"Yeah, that's it . . . playing off people's troubles," she stated.

He got off the barstool, placed his mug in the sink and walked past us saying, "I'm going to Home Depot before it gets too crowded." He seemed to want to leave rather quickly and probably didn't want to be a part of our conversation.

She waved at him before finishing her talk with me. "Case

in point, Mekhi came over here talking about he was going to enroll in the Minister-in-Training program at your mom's church. Like I was supposed to be impressed. I don't know who he thinks he's fooling with the way he used to smack me upside my head." She threw back her head and laughed like his efforts to get his life right was the best joke she ever heard. She wiped a tear from her eye, her chest heaved as if she was trying to keep from cackling again. "The only reason he's trying to be all holy is so that he can pimp the church. Mekhi hasn't had a job since Lexus was born. He doesn't want to work. I'm so glad we're through."

She made him sound terrible, like she wasn't dishing out slaps, kicks and punches, as much as she was taking it. There were plenty of times that Mishelle was the one going upside Mekhi's head too. Couldn't neither one of them call themselves a victim. I had no idea that Mekhi was thinking about joining a ministry, but I thought it was a great idea.

I needed to get out of her house before I said something I regretted. "I'm happy you broke up too. If you don't want your kids at my house, then that's your business. I know I've taken good care of Camry and Lexus. I guess I will have to see them when their father has them."

"Oh, they won't be seeing him either. Even if I have to take out another restraining order to keep him from here. Cyrus and I are going to get married and I plan on petitioning the courts to have Mekhi's paternal rights terminated. He's not bringing anything to the table to be calling himself Daddy. Cyrus wants to take care of me. My man will adopt Camry and Lexus. Give them his last name. He would make a great father to them," Mishelle said boisterously.

They barely knew enough about each other to be taking the relationship seriously, yet Mishelle was talking about marriage. I wondered if Cyrus knew about all her plans.

Instead of saying anything else, I walked back toward the stairs and called out to Elijah that it was time to go.

"I don't want you to take this decision personal. I have to look out for my family and get rid of bad influences." Mishelle crossed her arms over her chest.

Elijah must not have heard me calling him. I went upstairs to get my child, blocking out the rest of her conversation before she ticked me off.

Of all the things Mishelle had said, only one stuck out in my mind as I put Elijah back into his car seat. *"Talking it ain't walking it."* My Christianity meant something special, and if Scott and I wanted to eliminate some of the temptation and frustration in our lives, we would have to spend more time walking in our blessing. I would need to do everything necessary to get Scott to understand.

CHAPTER EIGHTEEN

SCOTT

Germani hit me in the chest with a Bible as I entered the living room.

"What's this for?" I asked, holding the leather bound book in my hand.

"I think we need to do more Bible study and there's no better time than the present."

"For what? I just walked in the house. And since when did we start needing Bible study at home? That's what Wednesday night service is for." I might not make it there every week like her because of my work schedule, but I did go. She didn't used to be so argumentative or demanding. It was a new thing. A new thing I didn't like and didn't know if I would get used to. "What is going on with you lately? You keep changing things around here without discussing them with me first."

I didn't want to read my Bible, I wanted to sit down and chill for a little while. Alexis had cried the entire time I was over at Beverly's house. It took two hours for the Codeine to take effect and put her to sleep. She wouldn't let me leave her side and I was worried about her having another seizure. Her mother couldn't handle her when that disease was at its worst.

"Have a seat. Let's talk," Germani said, patting the cushion next to her. A pink leather bound Bible rested in her lap. "You already know that I have been reading a scripture a day for life application and I think I'm getting better in my Christian walk, but some stuff got me to thinking maybe this should be a family affair."

Elijah sat at a little blue table set we had in the family room. Even his thick children's Bible was open as it leaned against his ten-piece robot collection.

I eased onto the couch, wondering what had caused the new revelation.

"You know, Scott, I'm teaching Elijah that if he buries God in his heart at an early age, then maybe he won't have many battles with trials and tribulations as an adult. In order for that to happen, he must understand the difference between light and darkness. Tell Daddy what verse you read," Germani instructed Elijah.

"E-feet-some five." He grinned showing all his front baby teeth.

"Good job, Elijah," she said as she picked up her Bible and opened it to a marked page. "Ephesians, chapter five, verses eight through thirteen. *For you were once darkness, but now you are light in the Lord. Walk as children of light, for the fruit of the Spirit is in all goodness, righteousness and truth. Finding out what is acceptable to the Lord.*" She paused, turning the page. "And this is the most important part of this passage. *Have no fellowship with the unfruitful works of darkness, but rather expose them. For it is shameful even to speak of those things which are done by them in secret.*" She closed the Bible, stood up and stared at Elijah. "Scott, once something is exposed, a manifestation occurs. What is hidden becomes magnified by light. Dirt can't bury itself in the sun."

She went from staring at Elijah to watching me. Her mouth clinched into an angered perch.

I wanted her to get to the point. "Are you mad at me about something?"

Germani folded her arms and continued staring at me with a blank face. "Mad wouldn't be the word to describe me right now."

"You want to tell me what's going on?" I unlaced my shoes so I could get comfortable.

Germani dropped a broken CD on the couch next to me. "You left your movie in the DVD player and the kids got a hold of it. They watched a nice portion of it too."

I had forgotten all about that movie. "*Latina Caliente*. Who broke my movie?"

She groaned before shaking her head. "You don't care about nothing I just said, do you? The kids watched your movie."

Elijah stared at us with wide eyes as he clashed two robotic toys together.

"Little man, go to your room for a minute. I want to talk with your momma," I told my son. I waited for him to gather his robots and leave the room before I said anything else. If there was going to be a scene, Elijah wasn't going to be a part of it.

"Of course, I care. I didn't purposely leave the flick in there." I picked up the two jaded pieces of my movie. "I'm human. I made a mistake."

"I thought you said that we wouldn't be doing the porn thing anymore. You're not living up to your part of the deal. You haven't given up porn at all. How are we going to get better if you keep doing the same ole thing? Do you know that Camry and Lexus can't come over anymore behind you watching a sick flick? Mishelle thinks we are bad influences on her children. She said that we are church faking and she didn't want her children confused by mixed messages of phony people. Scott, we are supposed to set the standard. If people can't see God through us, then we aren't living right."

Since when did she begin listening to Mishelle? Mishelle couldn't talk about nobody and I wouldn't waste my time talking about her. But it wasn't Mishelle's jabber that stuck out, the first part of what Germani said caught me. "Sick flick! You're talking like I was watching men having sex with animals or child pornography. They weren't sick flicks when you were watching them with me. You didn't used to complain. And in regard to Mishelle . . . all I have to say is consider the source. Don't start spewing Bible verses at me because I have a weakness." I bent down and took off my shoes.

She squinted at me before standing up. Germani reached around the side of the couch and shoved a box up next to me. "They are movies. What's so hard about giving up movies? Especially when it's affecting our marriage, our child and other people's children too."

I got up and looked inside the box. She had broken all my movies, even the VHS tapes. She was messing with me. "What did my movies do to you? You are taking it over the top now."

"Just movies. You didn't answer the question. Why can't you give them up?" Germani had her arms folded like she was trying to make me choose between her and my weakness, but she didn't understand that choosing wasn't that simple.

She didn't realize how hard it was for me to give up those movies. How I felt pulled by a strong desire and nothing else seemed to satisfy my need for gratification. It drove me crazy that I made a promise to her that I couldn't bring myself to keep. I had been frustrated that I couldn't rise to the occasion when we did try to be intimate without the video foreplay. Every time I sat at the computer desk and logged on, I wanted to stop myself. Every time I pushed a movie into the player, I told myself that it would be the last time I watched a porn flick without my wife.

There weren't words to explain it to her. "I don't know why? There's no science to it. It's a habit that I have a hard time breaking. Do you need me to call Mishelle and apologize for my evil ways?" I joked as I tried to cut some of the tension thickening in the air.

"See, now you're trying to be funny." Germani had such disappointment in her eyes that I couldn't help but feel remorseful that I left the video in the DVD player.

I stood up, pulled her toward me and wrapped my arms around her waist. "No, I just don't think it's as big a deal as you are making it into. Besides, when I watch those movies I'm thinking of you. Wishing we were doing some of those things."

She removed my hands from around her waist and hissed. "*Latina Caliente* . . . Don't insult my intelligence. I'm not Mexican and I don't do threesomes. You could not be thinking about me. Guess you married into the wrong ethnic group."

I had enough with the dramatizing. "If I wanted a Mexican wife, I would have married a Mexican woman. *Latina Caliente* is a movie."

"Scott, I'm trying real hard to be a supportive spouse, but you aren't making this easy." Germani took the broken disk still sitting on the couch and tossed it in the box. "All I'm saying is we need to do better for ourselves and our son. He shouldn't even know what porn is."

"I got what you're saying. I promise you it won't happen again. Now, let it go."

"Fine. I'll let it go."

She said it, but I didn't believe her.

CHAPTER NINETEEN

GERMANI

"Has anybody seen the pre-registration sheets?" I shouted out as I searched the community room where eight volunteers went setting up the space for food distribution. Our church was a new host site and was assigned to Angel Food Ministries duty for the first time, in which we gave out boxes of pre-packed meals that were ordered and paid for by families within the community. The organization was national and offered economical prices, especially for those on low or fixed incomes.

Scott and I bought the meals ourselves because of the inexpensive cost and had already placed the box in the trunk of his car.

"I saw the list taped to the top of a box in the storage room," the church coordinator, Harmony, said as she and some of the other members of Deliverance Temple organized the area. Taylor, Cliff and Doug pulled rectangular tables from the wall and set them up side by side.

I walked toward the refrigerated storage room to grab the sheet. We were opening the doors in less than an hour, and I didn't want to be unprepared. Nobody could get their food until I verified what they had ordered.

Scott and Jose walked past me in the church hallway. Jose was a short Mexican with brown skin and straight short black hair. They were carrying two boxes each and I stopped them momentarily.

While holding a door open for them, I looked on top of the box Scott held. "You guys don't have a sheet of paper on either of your boxes, do you?"

"No. What are you looking for?" Scott asked, shifting the weight of the box as he locked his fingers underneath it.

"Pre-registration sheet with the list of names on it," I responded as I walked around them.

"I thought I saw a paper on one of the boxes I already set in the community room," Jose said as he paused in the doorway.

"That might have been the shipping order. I saw that in there. Don't worry about it. I will find it." I checked my watch and hurried on.

I shivered as I stepped into the cold freezer area. Seven boxes were stacked in the middle of the room. I placed each one on the floor until I got to the fifth box. Ripping the tape off, I removed the sheets. I could hear footsteps approaching.

"Scott, when are you going to let me take you down on the court? Doug asked my husband as they came into the freezer to retrieve the last boxes.

"Yeah, Scott, we never see you outside these church walls. What's up with that?" Jose asked as he picked up the box I had ripped the tag off of and stacked it on top of another box to carry.

Scott's eyes fell on me. "Well, you know . . . me and the wife have family obligations."

I interjected as I shook my head while again holding the door open for the men before leaving the cold room. "Oh no, don't put me into that. I am not a ball and chain type of wife. You are free to hang out with these fellas anytime you choose."

In fact, I would be overjoyed if Scott spent more time with other Christians. Maybe a change in associations would improve our relationship. Scott sometimes acted like befriending someone new would be a betrayal to Damon.

"See. You can't use your wife as an excuse," Doug said as they all walked in front of me back to the community room.

"Yeah, man; stop acting like we stink or something," Jose remarked jokingly. "We get together and have a lot of fun."

Scott said, "I'll see what I can do. Do you have a game planned soon?"

Ahmad piped in, "I'm having a fellowship barbecue at my house next Saturday if you want to come by. We try to do something once or twice a month. It's always something different. Bowling, fishing or whatever."

"These brothas keep me in line, because I was acting a fool before I got connected. Ain't that right, Taylor?" Doug pulled on the hem of his wife's blue t-shirt.

"Yeah, it was pretty bad. We were at divorce's door and I was ready to kick it down. I had already separated our bank accounts and paid down my credit cards. If he hadn't stopped 'acting a fool,' like he said, I was prepared to get out of the marriage with minimal combined debt." Taylor pushed back a chair to sit in.

I glanced at Taylor in her candid description of her plan to leave Doug. As bad as things were getting between Scott and me, I hoped I never got to the point I'd have to secretly plot to leave the relationship.

Jose said, "You didn't tell us about all that, but I could feel the tension rolling off of you when you started coming to men's fellowship. Things must have been real bad in your home if Taylor was about to divorce you."

Doug shrugged as he leaned against a table. "She was well

within her rights. I wanted to be married and single at the same time. I straddled the fence. I needed to change my focus."

"Being married is hard enough, but being a married Christian is seriously extra hard work. People assume we have fewer problems because we're saved," Ahmad stated. He and his wife were veterans of the group, being married for twenty-three years.

"I wouldn't even have y'all in my business if it wasn't a testimony to how good my God is. He brought these men into our lives right on time."

Jose spoke as he sat facing the back end of a chair. "I may not be married, but I still look forward to the stress relief of good male fun. Working for airport security will make anybody go crazy if they don't have a grounding source. This man was going to fight me because I told him to take his shoes off and put them on the conveyor belt. I was sure he was cursing me out in French, literally. He was screaming 'L'idiot viole mes droits.' The only thing I understood was the word idiot. That word is universal. After we took him back for a strip search because he refused to remove those shoes, we had to call a translator over before I took his insults personally."

"What was up with that? Everybody has to be prepared to take off their shoes for airport security," Scott balked as he came and stood next to me.

"Evidently not over there in Marseille. Foreign airports must be letting anybody on a plane. That man thought we were trying to keep his shoes. Why would we want to keep his shoes? People are mental," Jose said as he frowned.

"What does l'idiot viole mes droits mean?" Taylor asked. She mouthed the words to herself as if she were trying to memorize them while she waited for Jose's response.

"The idiot violates my rights," Jose said as if the entire incident was beyond his understanding.

"The idiot violates my rights," I said. "They were just shoes. You would think he was asked to strip down naked."

Taylor, Doug, Ahmad and Scott all nodded their heads in agreement.

"Different culture means different value system," Ahmad stated.

Ahmad's son, Quinn, a tall lanky young man, cocoa brown with acne spots covering his face, came into the community room. "We should probably open the doors. It's starting to rain out there and I saw a lot of people standing by the door waiting to get in here."

"And they say black people don't know how to be on time for anything," Doug remarked as we all began to stand in preparation for the crowd to filter the community room.

For the next several hours, we stayed busy in spurts. I kept track of who needed what. There seemed to be either a line full of people, or no one at all waiting to get their box of goods or school supplies as they prepared for the new semester, two weeks away, at the end of August. We talked amongst ourselves during the lag time and tried to keep busy to make time go quicker.

By two-thirty in the afternoon, only a few names remained on the pre-registration list for the Angel food boxes. We still had several containers full of donated back packs, pencils, notebooks and pens. I took items from an almost empty bin and tossed them into a full container.

Scott came and sat next to me after taking several boxes of food and school supplies to a family of seven. The mother had a set of twins that were five years old and four other children younger than the twins. They were four, three, two and eight months of age. The mother looked tired even though the children were well behaved. The children walked together, hand-in-hand, wearing matching blue jean Osh Gosh short sets as she pushed a stroller.

I had to exhale on her behalf at the thought of that responsibility. Elijah was enough work; multiply his need times six and you have me sitting in the city psych ward waiting for my daily medication.

"Baby, if I ever ask for more kids, you have my permission to slap me dead in my mouth." Scott huffed as if he had just run track in the Olympics.

"Wow, dead in the mouth, huh? I don't think I've ever heard you talk like that, Mr. Wilson." I put my fingers to my lips in fake shock.

"Probably because you haven't, Mrs. Wilson." He leaned back in the chair and stretched his legs. His expression was one of horror. "I don't never, ever, ever want my own self-made baseball, basketball or hockey team. That's more responsibility than I can handle."

"Oh, come on. You want a few more children." I poked at his side.

"No, can't say that I do. One is plenty." He poked me back in the ribs as I playfully pushed his hands away.

"Mommy. Mommy, that's Mr. Scott from over at our house," a little voice squealed.

I turned to see a beautiful little girl with long French braids standing at our table. Hazel eyes stared at me. Right between her was an adult version of herself and next to the little girl stood a toddler. His 49ers basketball cap swallowed his small head. I didn't recognize any of them. I was surprised that they knew Scott. I wondered when he had been at their house, and more importantly, why.

"Hey, Cheyenne." Scott leaned forward in his chair and grinned.

Curiosity had my interest piqued. A look crossed his face of glee mixed with familiarity and I didn't like it. I didn't like it in the least.

"What are you doing here?" he asked the child's mother as his voice seemed to change octaves, soften slightly.

"I came to pick up school supplies for Cheyenne. She's going to the second grade at Shamrock Gardens Elementary. That's a magnet school. You know this is her first year there since we moved from Yonkers." The mother had a tinge of rouge as white even teeth appeared. She was blushing at my husband.

I waited for an introduction, be it formal, informal, or even respectably polite. Their eyes stayed fixated on each other as they made conversation. It didn't feel like casual acquaintances struck by happenstance.

I waited . . . and waited . . . and . . . waited.

"Excuse me," I exclaimed in irritation by Scott's rudeness. "I'm Germani, Scott's wife, and you are?"

She took my hand and I wasn't sure if it was an attempt at maintenance of pleasantries or a nemesis challenge, as if she were saying "I know your husband just as well as you do, now what?"

"Oh, I'm sorry. I didn't mean to be rude. My name is Lisa. Lisa Guarillo."

Scott finally decided to acknowledge my presence. "Lisa, uh, this is my wife, Germani. The one I told you about."

I believe she heard me say I was his wife. It was unnecessary for him to repeat my words. The fumbling from his mouth bothered me just as much as knowing he was in some strange woman's home recently and he didn't tell me.

"Are you set up for Angel Food Ministries?" he asked Lisa as he rolled his fingers down the pre-registration list in search for her name.

Lisa frowned with confusion as she scrunched her eyebrows. "Never heard of Angel Food Ministries. What is it exactly?" She glanced at the sheet he had his hand on.

"Well, it's too late to order anything for August and we don't have any flyers left to explain the dates or menu selection for September, but for twenty-five dollars you get a huge box of food that should last awhile. For example, this month we had four pounds of leg quarters, a pound of ground beef, a pound of ground turkey, a bag of chicken tenders, some pork chops, smoked sausage, seasoned potatoes, green beans, baby carrots . . . Ummm, what am I forgetting?" Scott looked at me for answers.

I was too miffed to speak, so I just looked back at him like I didn't know what he was talking about.

"Of yeah, rice, pinto beans, onions, waffles and some dessert stuff." He was pleased with his memory.

I listened to Scott sounding like a salesman at a discount food store and wondered what other information he was holding out on me. How come certain knowledge escaped me; bypassed my view like a broke down minivan on Hwy 601.

Maybe he found somebody to do the things I no longer chose to do. Perhaps he decided my spiritual renewal was an insult to his sexual libido; one in which my role as wife wasn't nearly as valuable as I presumed. Husbands cheat for far less. I read somewhere that more than half the men who attend church creep out on their wives. Although statistics aren't always reliable, those numbers were still staggering.

It didn't say much for the sanctity of marital vows or family union. God's plan for His people gone awry. Skeletons in closets wearing gold crosses. Dirty business kept on the hush.

My thoughts must have distracted me for a while because Ms. Lisa and her two children had walked away. They were headed toward the exit doors when I snapped back into reality.

Scott was no longer sitting at my side. I looked around to see him breaking a table down with Ahmad.

I wondered if it would be crass for me to chase after her and ask what the nature of her relationship with my husband was, whether currently or previously.

The Holy Spirit had to hold me in my seat as the desire for answers gained strength. Momentum rushed through me like a surge of adrenalin during a 50-yard dash. I wanted to say something so bad to Lisa that it felt as though my emotions were jumping in anticipation.

I prayed for a calm to come over me and take the ugly feeling away. I couldn't question that woman about her sex life in front of her children. That would take tacky behavior up a notch to straight ghetto. Yet, the battle was raging in me to do exactly what I shouldn't and say what I shouldn't.

I stood, and my feet moved in the direction they walked.

"Hey, Germani, can you help me take some of these supplies back to the teen center? I'm thinking that some of what's left can be given out after service," Taylor asked.

"We have a lot of kids, but I don't think we have that many." I allowed my mind to step back into a positive place.

"My sister works at Shady Oaks Elementary. I know she wouldn't mind taking some supplies off our hands. Schools can never have enough pens and paper."

"That is a good idea. I think we should do that."

We completed the task at hand and I tried to keep my mind busy, but Scott had some answers to give and they better be good.

CHAPTER
TWENTY

SCOTT

Bellowing clouds dusted the sky as heavy raindrops pelted the car while we made our way down Davidson Street in the No Da District. A man with a paper bag atop his head tried to battle the elements as he waited for the light to turn green on the corner of 36th. His teal shirt darkened in color as it absorbed water.

I paused in spite of traffic to let him run across. His hand went up as a gesture of thanks while the wilted paper bag came down. The makeshift umbrella was useless against the raging storm.

I nodded my head to acknowledge his gratitude as I began to tap the gas pedal and roll by him.

The day was purposeful. I felt like I accomplished plenty in the hours spent for community outreach. There was a sense of gratification from the event that I didn't receive selling car parts. Which reminded me that I needed to stop by the store after I dropped Germani and Elijah off at home. I left Craig in charge, but I held the responsibility for anything that went wrong.

The previous Thursday, I called my entire staff into the store to discuss the missing inventory. They all acted baffled, perplexed or dumbfounded. The optimism of one of them admitting to the removal of parts for personal reasons or discounted from our inventory for friends or family quickly died as I surveyed their faces. Although the cash amount wasn't very large, charges could still be pursued.

It added unwanted stress to my life, not that anybody ever desired to be stressed. I had my job and integrity on the line. As a manager, I had a certain expectation for my employees; trusted their ability to do the job accurately and honestly. The coldhanded slap was that one of my staff disrespected that expectation and put all our jobs in jeopardy.

"Are you sleeping with her?"

Germani's blunt question caught me off guard, causing me to swerve onto the median, in an effort to avoid smacking the left side of a blue Dodge Neon, while I merged into traffic.

"What?" I said, agitated as the owner of the car moved into the passing lane and laid his hand on the horn.

"You heard every word that came from my mouth." Germani's attitude expanded to astronomical proportions as if she were oblivious to the accident we almost caused.

"Say what?" I didn't know why her words didn't make sense as they penetrated my brain. The implication wouldn't logically click in my head.

"You . . . her . . . intimate." Her eyes drilled into me like she was searching for some kind of admission.

"Say what?" I repeated. "No . . . better yet, who are you talking about me sleeping with besides you?" I knew the only sheets I had laid beneath in the past five years were ours. Who she thought I was sleeping with was a whole other matter.

"That woman at the church, you know, the one in the community room. I believe her name was Lisa. I also believe that you were at her house and I know that *you* didn't tell me nothing about her or being at her house before this afternoon when I met her myself. So stop acting clueless and tell me whether she's your lover, or ex-girlfriend or whatever."

"You are trippin'. Since when did you stop trusting me?" I asked Germani as I soaked in her disposition. I glanced back at a sleeping Elijah. His head was bent to the side, mouth wide open. His little body secured by a booster seat. I was glad he couldn't hear the conversation.

"Since when did you give me reason to not trust you?" Germani countered.

"I am not nor have I ever slept with Lisa. I don't know her like that at all," I stated as calmly as I could. Germani was acting emotional. The gestures, remarks and attitude challenged my ability to react reasonably.

"So you don't know her well?"

"No."

"What were you doing at her house?"

"Putting together her daughter's chifferobe."

Germani spoke in a condescending voice as she squinted at me. "How sweet of you, offering a helping hand to put furniture together for a stranger; mind you, a beautiful woman, but a stranger nonetheless."

"Don't patronize me, Germani. I almost ran one of her kids over while I was picking up Torrance. They were outside by themselves and I just wanted to make sure they got home safely. We talked and I realized the reason she wasn't out with the children was because she was trying to assemble the chifferobe by herself. I offered to help. That's it." Justification shouldn't have been necessary.

"Oh, really?" Germani's eyes became oval slivers.

"Yes, really. If you don't believe me, then that's on you, but I can assure you that I have never nor will I ever sleep with Lisa," I replied.

I made my way down Tryon past a Compare Foods store. A man with tousled black hair and wrinkled clothes carrying a

'Will Work for Food' sign limped up and down the sidewalk. The rain had ceased and left a wet sheen on the ground. Not too far from him, a cappuccino-colored woman stood pensively against a transit bus pole.

I caught a glimpse of her face as I drove past.

Her short yellow flowered sundress made her look twenty years younger than her actual age; up close, small wrinkles formulated on direct areas of her face, around her lips, and at her eyelids. Fine elegant lines that disguised the hard life she lived.

"That's Ms. Ilene, Damon's mom," I said as I made the block to turn around.

Germani turned to look in the direction I was referring to. The distraction seemed to end the uncomfortable conversation about Lisa. "Damon's mom, are you sure?"

"Positive. I'll see if she needs a ride." I pulled into the Compare Foods parking lot and looped around toward the street.

"Going somewhere?" I asked as I pressed the automatic power button on my window and spoke outside as the glass went down.

Ms. Ilene squinted at me. "Hamhock, is that you?" she called me by a childhood nickname I long ago stopped answering to.

"Yes, ma'am."

She edged a little closer to the car.

"Boy, well, aren't you a sight for these eyes. It is wet out here. Can you drop me off on the east side near the big university?"

I got out of the car and opened the back door. "Which one, UNCC or Johnson C. Smith?"

"Johnson." She looked to Germani. "Hey suga, you must be Hamhock's girlfriend," she said as she slid on the tan leather seats.

I shut her door and got back behind the wheel.

"Wife, I'm Hamhock's . . . Scott's wife." Germani corrected herself as she turned to briefly talk with the new car passenger.

I noticed Germani trying to keep her attitude at bay as she spoke.

The man with the sign came up to my window as I closed my door. "Can I get a couple dollars? I haven't eaten all day. All I need is five, no two dollars."

I thought about giving him something out of the Angel Food box, but I didn't want the man pawing through our personal food. I reached into my back pocket for my wallet and stopped at Ms. Ilene's abrupt shrill.

"Uh-uh. Don't give him no money. He's a crackhead. Only thing he's going to feed is his habit. He ain't slick. Tried to get me for some money too. Get on out of here begging. Get, get, get." Ms. Ilene leaned toward my headrest and shooed the man away with her hand.

The man looked offended as he began to stutter, "I . . . I . . . Imna . . . I'm no crackhead."

"Stop lying. Go get a job and get away from this car. You can't wait to smoke up somebody else's hard earned money. Like I said, get gone. Hamhock, roll your window up," Ms. Ilene demanded.

I obliged.

The man frowned, but turned on his worn heels and limped back to the sidewalk.

I felt a slap on the back of my neck as Ms. Ilene popped me. "Boy, you too old to be acting naive. Don't be pulling your wallet out like that unless you want it stolen. You got to be more careful," she scolded me.

Germani looked fascinated. She was probably getting a kick out of seeing me disciplined like a child.

Ms. Ilene continued to talk. "I thought I was going to die in this summer heat. I can't stand waiting for the bus when it's humid. My son, Devon, normally would have picked me up, but he was in a car accident and totaled out his girlfriend's car. His license was already suspended, so he ended going to jail and the car had to be junked. My kids and I are going to combine money and buy a newer car when income tax time comes."

Ms. Ilene scooted back in her seat next to a woken Elijah and buckled her seatbelt. I looked in the rearview mirror and watched her pinch Elijah's cheek. My son cocked his head to the side and stared at the stranger touching his face.

"I didn't know you were married and with the cutest little boy too," Ms. Ilene stated. "He has got some long eyelashes. He almost looks like a girl, he so pretty. Um, um, um. Time sure does fly. I remember when you were a small boy. I didn't know you at his age, but you were young. It's been some years. Um, um, um." Ms. Ilene dozed into a temporary reminiscent gaze.

"Where to, Ms. Ilene?" I glanced in the rear view mirror one more time as I waited for traffic to thin.

"542 Bacon Avenue, off of Trade Street. Suga, what's your name?" Ms. Ilene asked my wife.

"Germani," she responded pleasantly.

"Like that country with Hitler?"

Germani seemed a little surprised to hear her name merged with a reference to a Nazi. She furrowed her eyebrows and jerked her head slightly. "Uh. Well. It's spelled with an 'i' instead of a 'y,' but same country."

"Chile, why on God's green earth would your momma name you after that crazy killing fool? I could never figure out why people would follow such a nut job. Murdered millions of Jewish families, and for what? To stroke his crazy ego. You know he killed women and children too. I watched a documentary on the Holocaust and saw this room with nothing but shoes in it. Big shoes, little shoes and baby shoes. Imagine that. Baby shoes. The babies hadn't done a thing to be murdered like that. I had to change the channel because it was making me mad." Ms. Ilene rambled on with her criticism.

Germani turned to look at Ms. Ilene explaining, "My father was stationed at the Ramstein military base in Germany when

I was born. Both my parents named me after our home. I also spent the majority of my childhood there. Germany isn't a bad country. It had bad people in a position of power that caused great harm to a multitude of people. Just like ours does now. Bush does what he does because we let him do it, and just like some people hold all of Germany accountable for what Hitler did, other countries outside of the United States hold us accountable for what Bush does," Germani made subtle references to the Iraq war. Although she was raised in the military, she didn't have a fondness for the current government and would quickly comment on the subject any given chance.

"Oh, my; you sound like an intelligent young lady. Scott, I think you got yourself a good one. You better treat her right."

Germani grew silent.

"He is treating you right?" Ms. Ilene inquired.

"Why are you talking about me like I'm not sitting here? Of course I'm treating my wife well. That's my responsibility," I chuckled nervously as I stole glances at Germani.

"You were always a good guy; would give somebody the shirt off your back."

Germani smirked.

Ms. Ilene asked, "Why don't I see you anymore? You know I still live at the same address. Just because my son don't come around doesn't mean you need to be a stranger."

"You're right, Ms. Ilene." I couldn't argue with her. Damon's resentment toward his mother had no relevance to me. He kicked her to the curb like she was a butt ugly ex-girlfriend. I couldn't dismiss my mother the way he had. Some ties deserved to be severed, but mom is mom no matter how imperfect.

I didn't want to delve into an unpleasant subject, so I decided not to even remark on anything about Damon.

"Do you still make those chicken and dumplings?" I asked Ms. Ilene, smiling. "Germani, Ms. Ilene could create a mean chicken and dumplings. Have your tongue kissing the bottom of the bowl." I tapped Germani's arm to get her attention as she stared out the passenger window.

She didn't look at me as she nodded her head. Germani was showing me no love. If it wasn't apparent that we were having problems before, it had become blaringly obvious. I was embarrassed at how she was acting in front of Ms. Ilene. I decided I better leave Germani alone and just drive.

I turned off Trade onto Bacon Avenue, stopping in front of a chipped white house with green awning. The porch appeared to be tilted to the right where a crumbling foundation of bricks protruded from the exterior. Two men sat on the top steps, drinking forty ounces covered by paper bags; one looked to be in his early twenties while the other could have been a father or uncle. They watched as I got out of my car to open the door for Ms. Ilene. The younger one with a black and gray urban wear hoodie atop some black jeans threw his head up at me as I glanced their way.

I did the same.

Ms. Ilene got out of the car and kissed me on the cheek. She embraced me in a tight hug. "My phone number is still the same too. Call me sometime and I will make that chicken and dumplings. Bring the family with you."

She leaned down, waving her hand at Germani and Elijah. Germani waved back, while Elijah just looked. He didn't respond very well when he was sleepy.

Ms. Ilene stood back erect and clutched her purse under her arm. "Tell my son I still love him." Sadness clouded her eyes. It didn't match the broad smile she dressed up to appear happy.

"I'll let him know," I responded as I shut the back door.

Her yellow sundress swished against her wide hips as she ascended the porch steps. She stopped to say something to the older man before they both went into the house.

I got back in my vehicle. "Ms. Ilene invited us to dinner. She didn't give a specific date, but I didn't know how you would feel about going over to her house."

Germani shrugged. "Is that what you want to do, Hamhock? Ham . . . hock." The corners of her mouth twitched like she wanted to laugh.

"Ha-ha. I used to sneak and eat all the hamhocks out of the pot of mustard and turnip greens. I got a many whuppins' over it. Now you know my childhood shame. Laugh it up if you want to."

A rumble burst from her mouth as she did exactly that. "How could you be ashamed of such an endearing name like Hamhock?"

I embraced her relaxed mood and smiled as we got back onto Trade Street and headed home.

CHAPTER
TWENTY-ONE

GERMANI

As I ventured through cyberspace on my office break, I found women just like me. Wives married to men obsessed with porn. There was a sense of camaraderie amongst that newly found distinction: Wives of Porn Addicts.

As I read each story, I felt sympathy for the women placing their frustrations on the Internet for the world to see. Sade knew her husband watched dirty movies, but she didn't realize how bad his addiction was until after a gynecological exam that confirmed that she had the sexually transmitted disease, Human Papillomavirus, otherwise known as HPV. He admitted to picking up random women for the duration of their marriage. Joy accidentally found an animal bondage tape while trying to sneak a love note into her husband's briefcase. Katrina investigated a money transfer on a joint charge account and discovered the funds were going to a massage spa for extra services. Just like in Sade's situation, her husband confessed after getting caught in something else. Watching porn for those men seemed to not be enough to fulfill their fantasies. They had to up the thrill by sleeping with strangers.

I continued reading real life depictions of deception, denial, rejection and regret, well past my lunch break.

Story after story broke my heart just a little more; touched my soul just a little deeper. Many of the couples had some kind of church affiliation and attended service regularly. They weren't that much different than Scott and me. Nothing I read made my family exempt. I thought about Scott's need to go to a strip club after almost five years of marriage in which he never mentioned that desire. Maybe there was more to his actions.

Later that night, I found myself scrolling through Scott's recent calls on his cell phone; searched through forty-six outgoing and fifty incoming. I didn't find any incriminating evidence that he was cheating on me, but the thoughts still lingered that something was up, or rather not on the up and up. Let Scott tell it, I had no reason to be suspicious. He lived to love me. If that were true, I wouldn't be competing with high definition, extended version sex movies.

It wasn't that I planned to be snooping through the pants pocket of his Levi jeans. My intention was to get Elijah up and to the bathroom. My son had several accidents, and it's much easier to program myself to wake in the middle of the night instead of spending my mornings spraying my four year old's toddler mattress down with my concoction of hydrogen peroxide and baking soda.

"Wakey, wakey up my tired, little man. You got to get up," I said as I shook the mattress of his engine red toddler bed.

Elijah grunted, but didn't budge an inch.

"Elijah, you need to go to the bathroom."

He yawned and stretched with his eyes squeezed shut. "Mommy, I'm *sheeping*," Elijah complained in a little voice.

"Well, you can go back to *sheeping* after you go to the bathroom. Come on, you know the drill." I lifted him by his arms out of the bed, placed his bare feet on the ground and patted his behind gently. "Scootch."

He slipped into his Spiderman slippers and shuffled to the bathroom. I waited outside the door until I heard the toilet flush. It was a new habit I was forming to give him some independence.

The knob to the bathroom door turned and I stated loudly, "Wash those hands." I saw the knob released and immediately heard the faucet water running.

Elijah came out and I followed him to his room where I tucked him into bed and kissed his forehead. My little man was an angel.

The beep of a low battery drew me in after I put Elijah back to bed. At first I didn't distinguish the sound. I stood in our darkened bedroom fine-tuning my hearing. I kept holding my breath like the hiss of air through my lungs would impede my ability to listen. Each beep brought me closer to the pile of clothes thrown haphazardly on the closet floor. Once I shifted through each garment, I found the phone in Scott's back pocket. I planned to turn it off and set it on the dresser, but the screen was flashing two missed calls.

I couldn't very well be expected to ignore that. I investigated like a regular wife holding her husband's phone. Some women trust blindly and probably would have shut off the phone with no hesitation. I didn't fit into that category of women. Four days ago, after our discussion about Scott's friend-but-not-really, Lisa, I became a little more conscious of where he was, what he was doing and with whom. And once I read the stories about what other women in my situation go through, I realized that I needed to be concerned. So searching through his phone was just a precaution.

I must admit to a sense of disappointment mingled with relief at not finding an unusual number or questionable text messages, especially considering that I took his phone back into the bathroom with me and turned on the shower full blast to muffle the pressing of digits. Then the guilt came. The guilt of mistrust. The guilt of letting my thoughts assume my hus-

band was a trifling, two-timing ho. The guilt of wasting
shower water to play Detective Wifey.

Right there on the tile floor I got on my knees and prayed.
Well, I started to pray, but my knees were hurting on the cold
Formica. I grabbed the baby pink thick cotton bath towel off
the towel rack and folded it three times into a nice rectangle
against the tub and placed my knees centered in cushion. Then
I prayed.

"Lord, I need to hear a word from you to know whether I
am tripping and jumping to unnecessary conclusions. I'm having a hard time dealing with the porn thing and I don't know if
I could take it if Scott cheated on me. You probably already
know that because of how I'm acting. My flesh won't let me
rest on the subject. You said to flee from sexual immorality and
I have done that. It's my husband that doesn't want to follow
your will."

I paused, thinking about my frustration with the whole situation of my husband not wanting only me. My heart overflowed with sorrow, so I poured it out to a higher power.

"Lord, I need you in a mighty, mighty way. Help my husband get through his wicked ways. If you could cleanse his
mind and purify his heart, I would be forever grateful. If I
must be blunt, Lord, I'm asking you to fix him. Demonic
forces are trying to devour my home and I know you don't
want that. I stand in prayer on behalf of my husband's soul.
Give him strength to conquer the lust demon. The devil can't
have what's mine and he dang sure can't have what's yours.
Bind those unholy spirits that taint his mind. Govern his walk
in you that it may be righteous."

Whenever I prayed, I took a minute to absorb His presence.
Nobody could put me in check like God could. Hopefully, the
same move would reign in Scott.

As I turned off the shower head, water splashed on my bare
arm. It dripped from my wrist to my elbow. An idea culmi-
nated in my mind.

Scott needed to be blessed.

I wiped my arm off with the towel I had prayed on. I put it back on the rack and opened the cabinet door under the sink. Inside a white metal medicine kit was a vile of Abramelin anointing oil I had saved when we first bought the house. I got it from my old church and intended to bless the house, but never got around to it.

It seemed like an appropriate, safe place for storage, next to Ace band-aids, packets of Ibuprofen, hydrocortisone cream and other methods of healing wounds.

I palmed the clear vile and turned the oblong sphere upside down, watching the liquids move from one end to the next. I wondered how long blessing oil stayed good. Could it spoil like raw Angus beef, or rather, did it get better with age like Pinot Gris wine? I didn't know, but I prayed for the latter as I shut the medicine kit and carried the cell phone and the vile down the hall to my bedroom.

I crept to the chest where I laid Scott's cell phone next to the jewelry box, tiptoed to my side of the bed and slid in softly. As I lowered my body to the mattress, I placed the vile in my other hand.

Scott was sound asleep facing me. I kept expecting his eyelids to pop open, but just like Elijah, Scott was hard to awaken. He could sleep restfully through a tornado, hurricane or tsunami.

I watched my husband with peace on his face. I guessed demons needed rest too. I lay on my side and twisted the cap off the vile. Dousing my fingers with the Abramelin anointing oil, the liquid felt like silk. Moistened fingers pressed against Scott's forehead, I silently whispered the only thing that made sense after my earlier long conversation with God.

"In the name of the Father, Son, and Holy Ghost, I bless you. Let God's will be done."

CHAPTER
TWENTY-TWO

SCOTT

"He will be here," Beverly said optimistically, as we sat in the pre-op room before Alexis' scheduled surgery.

They had taken her down an hour earlier to see how her blood was reacting to a conditioning regimen of chemotherapy that was supposed to destroy some of the diseased cells and suppress immune reactions prior to the bone marrow transplant.

The entire family was waiting for Alex to show up.

"What time was his flight supposed to get in?" Momma asked Beverly.

"I'm not sure. When I called him this morning he was leaving for the airport. If he took a connecting flight, then he may be stuck in a layover. I'll go call him again and see what's taking him so long. He also said that they were having a hailstorm in Minnesota. Maybe his flight was delayed." Beverly got up with her cell phone in hand and left to go make her call outside the hospital lobby.

"That Negro is lying. He ain't coming here," Daddy said as soon as Beverly stepped out of the room. He knew it was a sensitive subject for Beverly, but Daddy had no faith in Alex following through on anything that pertained to Alexis.

"We don't know that yet. Alex might just have a conscience and decide to go ahead and do the right thing. Beverly said he bought his ticket a week ago," Sharon explained as she let Elijah get out of her lap and go to my mom who had a box of animal crackers.

"Didn't he have tests done there to make sure his bone marrow matched?" Corbin, Sharon's husband, asked as he leaned against the wall behind Sharon.

"Yeah. They shipped his test results here. That had to be done before a surgery could be scheduled," I explained.

Germani shook her head as she sat in a chair next to me, but she didn't share her thoughts.

From what Beverly had told me, Alex had been calling regularly to check up on Alexis. He even told Alexis that next summer he would see about sending for her so that she could spend some time with her younger brothers. He seemed to have made a complete 360-degree turn in attitude.

Daddy replied, "Well let's just hope Alex is on the up and up this time around. Took him long enough to become a real man."

"Better late than never. Some people have to grow at their own pace to become responsible," Mom said, taking a handful of cookies out of the box and handing them to Elijah.

Beverly came back into the room with a long face. "His flight was canceled."

"Yeah, right," responded Daddy, unconvinced.

"He said they got a heavy hailstorm. All flights leaving out were canceled and the incoming flights were delayed."

Momma tried to be optimistic. "Stuff happens. At least he's coming. Alexis is still in pre-op. You need to find out when the doctor can reschedule the surgery. Maybe they can do it tomorrow."

"It wouldn't matter when they could do the surgery. He's not coming at all," Beverly told us, disappointed.

"What? Why not?" I was pissed.

"Alex said that he spoke with his wife and has some concerns that the transplantation might be too dangerous for him. He apologized for Alexis being sick, but said he has to think about his sons too. They need their father around."

"There is no more risk to him than if he were going to the dentist for a root canal. If anything, Alexis has to worry about the risk, because she's already fragile. What is he talking about?" Sharon asked as she angrily tapped her foot on the tile floor.

Beverly sat down in a chair like she had the weight of the world on her shoulders. "I tried to explain the percentage of successful transplants, but he had a rebuttal for my every word. He had been on the Internet reading about how a man went into cardiac arrest while giving bone marrow to his sister, and during the process, he died on the table. And I don't know. He kept talking."

Beverly was too emotional to finish.

I was even more pissed after hearing that. Alex had been playing with Beverly's emotions for too many years.

"That's a cop-out. He never wanted to help Alexis in the first place," remarked Daddy as he put the magazine back on an office table. He said exactly what I was thinking.

Momma put her hand over her heart. "Alexis needs that transplant. He must not realize how serious this is for her."

"Alex told me that the flight cancellation was confirmation by God that he had to look at the bigger picture. Alexis isn't the only person he's responsible for."

"Confirmation by God? The God I know doesn't confirm stupid. That Negro is ignorant and his family is ignorant for not putting him in check. If he were responsible like he's claiming to be, we wouldn't be having this conversation. Alexis has been sick all of her life, and only recently, has he acted like he cared. God should strike his lying tail down. Give him some real confirmation." Daddy wagged his finger at Beverly like he did when we were little and got caught in something dumb.

"There's a torture chamber in hell for people like him." Germani folded her arms.

Sharon suggested, "You should go ahead and take him to child support court. At least sue him for half the doctor bills you've had to pay. If he can't be a man about this, then take it out of his pockets."

"I don't want to go through all that trouble. If he doesn't want to act like her father, I can't make him. I'd rather leave well enough alone. Besides, he might change his mind about the surgery later on and I don't want to make him upset." Beverly waved her hand like inconveniencing Alex wasn't an option.

"Don't none of us care about Alex getting upset. Stop letting him run over you," Daddy drilled into Beverly. "I don't know what kind of backward bayou voodoo magic that fool has done on you, but you better wake up. I didn't raise you to be a doormat."

Beverly put her hands over her eyes. She shook her head, looking ashamed and defeated. "I don't know how I'm going to explain this to Alexis."

My heart sank for Alexis. She deserved a better father. If Alex was in front of me at that moment, I would have beaten him within an inch of his life and then watched him cry for mercy.

Alex obviously cared about his two sons' well being, but not Alexis. I remember when she was born how disappointed he was that she wasn't a boy. There was nothing on this earth that would allow me to let my child, regardless of her sex, get near death and not do something about it.

I wanted Alex to feel his air composed to the point he couldn't breathe or have his body paralyzed by pain. I wanted him to feel a little of what Alexis felt on a regular basis.

I asked, "Beverly, how much does it cost for a plane ticket to St. Paul? If he won't come on his own, then I will go get him and bring him back for you."

Beverly shook her head. "Stop talking crazy. You don't need to go get Alex. What goes around comes around. He will get his due. If not here on earth, than in the afterlife."

Germani agreed. "Beverly's right. We need to pray for Alex and every man like him."

Words coming from the same woman that hacked up my DVD's because my son got a thirty-second viewing. Germani wouldn't allow me to disregard our son the way Alex was disregarding Alexis. They could talk about divine intervention if they wanted to. Alex needed a rude awakening about how he treated my sister and niece. I didn't want to wait for an afterlife for him to give them the respect they deserved. "Pray for him? I think we are past praying for Alex."

"At this point, we need to stick with the treatments she has been getting. Maybe take Alexis out to the Mayo Clinic for testing there." Beverly tried to think of alternative solutions.

I looked over at Germani and thought to myself, I would never take our family for granted. Not on purpose. Not after seeing what my sister had to go through. As a man, I planned to always do right by my family.

I didn't realize that soon enough, my obligation would be put to the test.

CHAPTER TWENTY-THREE

GERMANI

I pulled the zipper up on the straight angle sequined silver floor length dress. I stuck my leg out to check the view of my right calf in the slit rising above my knee. Turning in the three way mirror one more time, I took a deep breath before exiting the Group USA dressing room.

Kira was engrossed in text messaging as she sat on a cushioned chair.

I stood in front of her waiting for her to notice the dress.

"It looks very nice on you," said an older man sitting a couple seats down with a purse in his lap. He was probably waiting for his wife or girlfriend. I gave him a slight smile.

I had no idea who Kira was vigorously typing to, but I coughed to get her attention.

Kira glanced up. "Turn around." She twirled her finger.

I slowly shuffled in a circle.

"I don't like it." Kira began typing on her cell phone again.

I had already tried on four dresses and none of them seemed right.

"I know. It definitely looks better on the hanger. I was hoping to find something that would . . . I don't know," I sighed.

"I think you should go with the first one. It fit you nice without looking sleazy."

"Yeah." I wasn't totally convinced, but I was tired of trying dresses on. "Who are you texting like that?"

Kira looked up at me and grinned like a smitten teenager. "My husband."

"Oh." Jayat had been Kira's second skin since we all went to their wedding in his homeland on Huahine Island three years ago. He seemed to be with her even when he wasn't physically present. I hadn't felt that kind of love with a man in a long time.

"He has tickets to the Actor's Theatre and he's hinting at some other special plans he has for the evening."

Kira stared at her phone and kept smiling. Kira had been my best friend since transferring as a foreign exchange student from Barcelona to South Mecklenburg High School in the tenth grade. She tutored me in Spanish and soon, we were going to all the cultural events held at the school together, soaking in as much international information as we possibly could.

She and Autumn had come with me to pick out a dress for an event that Scott had me going to with Damon and Cherish. I initially declined, but he said it was a research fund raiser, so I figured it couldn't be too bad. Boring, but not seedy. I enlisted their help because I was getting more and more self-conscious about Scott's lack of attraction to me.

"Where is Autumn?" I asked.

"She went to get a Cinnabon. She said you were taking too long trying to make up your mind."

The man who complimented me got up and left with a girl from the dressing room.

"I haven't been that bad. You act like we've been here all day long."

"No, we're acting like we've been here over two hours, watching you be indecisive no matter what we say. You didn't like the ones we did. Not the wildfire red Charmeuse that I picked out nor the peach satin dress with the shawl that Autumn picked. Stop making this so hard."

I saw Autumn coming our way as she squeezed between racks with both hands in the air. A piece of gooey icing dipped bread in one hand and the Cinnabon container in the other. She took quick nibbles as she made her way over to the dressing room.

"Ain't that right, Autumn?" Kira tried to get a co-sign on her comment.

"It's just a matter of what I'm agreeing to. Did you see the sale down at Perfumania? I found a small bottle of Feminine by Dolce and Gabbana for $38. See . . . smell." Autumn waved her wrist in front of Kira.

"That smells good," Kira agreed. "You have to be careful about buying perfume on sale for too cheap, because you don't know how long they've had it sitting on the shelf."

Autumn smelled her own wrist again. "True, but I just dabbed a little on and it's pretty strong. I think it will last for awhile."

I placed a hand on my hip. "Excuse me, but is this a keeper or not? If you were Scott, would you love me in this?"

"I already told you what I think. That dress you have on right now doesn't flatter your figure. Go with the eggplant colored dress you first tried on," Kira responded.

"And I definitely don't think like Scott to even answer that question." Autumn gave me an if-you-know-what-I-mean look.

Kira caught the non-verbal exchange between me and Autumn. "Uh-uh, hon-nee. Spill it."

Kira wasn't the most religious person I knew. I generally shied away from her relationship advice. Loved her to death, but she would give me an entire avaricious response. It wasn't that her advice was bad, but sometimes it turned out that way.

"I'm going to get out of this dress and pay for the other

gown before I change my mind again." It was safe to say that Autumn wouldn't say anything while I put my clothes back on.

When I came back out of the dressing room, both Autumn and Kira were already standing near checkout. I got my purchase and draped the long plastic dress bag over one arm.

As we left the store I explained in a low voice to Kira what was going on in my marriage. "I had told Autumn that Scott and I were having sex problems."

"I assume you are still having the same problems." Autumn took the last bite of her Cinnabon.

It had been over two months since I told Autumn about the strip club fiasco. I hadn't told her about Scott's new friend, Lisa, who I met last week. Things were looking bad enough already.

"Things had been going good, but certain aspects still aren't right. We're still having issues. No more strip clubs, but he's on this porn kick. He wants to watch and I don't." Neither Kira nor Autumn knew, until recently, that we had been watching porn movies for years. I was too embarrassed to mention my part.

"Okay, I agree with that. Jayat and I aren't into watching other people do it for our own personal pleasure. There are too many ways to satisfy each other without needing porn. How about toys? You and Scott should go to Kinky Ways and get you some spice for your life."

"I don't think that Kinky Ways is my solution."

Autumn shook her head in complete disagreement with Kira. "Nowhere in the Bible does it say sex toys are allowable."

Kira rolled her eyes. "Where in the Bible does it say they aren't allowed? As long as you aren't idolizing, it shouldn't be a problem."

I silently listened as we passed Victoria's Secret where a salesperson was holding a sample bottle of Very Sexy II right outside the entrance way. She was a short, perky blonde with a bright smile trying her best to persuade evening shoppers.

We politely declined the test spray.

"What it does say is 'Be not conformed to the ways of the world, but transformed by the renewal of your mind'. Worldliness can lead to destruction," Autumn said as she threw the empty Cinnabon container in the trash bin.

"If that is the case, then you shouldn't have bought that Cinnabon or perfume because they come from this world too. Autumn, you bought what you wanted because it felt good to get it. It is human nature, whether you are holy or not, to want to feel good," Kira stated.

Autumn responded, "Dolce and Gabbana doesn't lead me to sin like a vibrator would."

"No, but if your body's a temple, you wouldn't be putting Cinnabon's with all those 840 calories of sugar and fat in your system." Kira pointed back at the trash bin. She then playfully shoved Autumn. "And you aren't married, so this isn't your subject."

"I don't have to be married to have an opinion." Autumn gave Kira a sour glance.

"Ssshh," I said as we walked into a crowd of teenagers. Kira had parked outside of TJ Maxx at the mall and I didn't need a group of kids listening to my life story.

"Where did we park?" Kira asked as we entered the dry tepid night air.

"Two rows over. That orange Geek Squad Beetle is still sitting there." I pointed in that direction.

"Oh, I see it. As I was saying, we all like to feel good, and a man's libido is universal regardless of race, creed or religion. For me and Jayat, sex toys enhance our relationship and keep us close. And I'm not talking about vibrators. There are a slew of tasteful things to keep lovemaking interesting between married couples, such as motion lotions, rings and massagers.

If you want, we can stop at Kinky Ways before I drop you off. I can show you some of the things that Jayat and I use."

It felt like Kira had parked a mile away. Autumn stopped one car before we got to her Passat, like she wasn't with us. "Oh, no. Drop me off first. I don't want to know what you and Jayat do behind closed doors."

"Don't worry. We won't be going to a sex shop," I said as I got into the car. We were all close, but we weren't that kind of close.

Kira looked at us and rolled her eyes again. "Oh, my goodness. We don't have to go together, but I seriously suggest that you and Scott find the time to go. I'm telling you, it can be a marriage saver."

"Listening to you is how I ended up married in the first place," I replied.

"How are you blaming me for that decision?" Kira asked as she started the car.

"You told me to get with Scott to take my mind off of Tre."

"No, no, no, hon-nee. *Get with* and *marry* are not the same thing." Kira's straight black hair swayed on her shoulders as she objected.

Those months after Tre left were dark times. I was vulnerable to any advice that would stop the heartache. Autumn came to my defense. "You were determined to keep her from moping. I remember that too."

"What! I am not taking credit for that. I didn't make you marry Scott. I told you he would be an easy distraction. We all knew how much he wanted to be with you. Now, you decided to do the rest and make him your husband. Scott was the rebound guy. Nobody marries the rebound guy. You weren't even over Tre when you went down that aisle. Autumn and I both told you that."

I wasn't receptive to their words during that time. Scott's attentiveness made my life brighter and I clamped on to him like a giant lobster. "Yeah, well, I did and now I have to deal with my repercussions."

Autumn must have noticed my downcast expression. "Scott isn't a bad guy. Prayer changes things. You know that. It's not always about how something starts, it's more important about how it ends. God can make the wrongs of the past right for the future. Plus, the blessed oil can ward off those demonic forces he got on him."

Kira interjected. "You don't need any blessed oil. There is nothing wrong with Scott that the right loving won't cure. Karma Sutra is your answer."

I didn't admit that I had already tried the blessing oil and it hadn't worked yet; instead, I listened to all their advice as they discussed how to fix my marriage. My thoughts drifted like hay in a Nevada desert storm. God couldn't want this for me. He just couldn't.

CHAPTER
TWENTY-FOUR
SCOTT

Phony airs combined with pretentious dialogue; a personal pet peeve of mine.

I observed the round table discussion and remained aloof. Chatter just to be heard never impressed me. Sometimes observation beat out the relevance of shallow conversation. At least, it did for me.

Eight people sat in that particular dining area. Damon invited us to the fundraiser after garnishing extra tickets from a physician friend of his. I accepted because it was free and I wanted to take Germani somewhere nice. We hadn't been anywhere as a couple since my birthday turned into a fiasco. Damon also said there would be research information to help with Alexis' sickle cell anemia.

One of the four other people seated with us was Roland Hill, a biological scientist from a research company in Raleigh. He spoke briefly of having a patent on a hormone supplement. His wife, Carmen, accompanied him. The third was Omar Jennings, a dermatologist with two practices, one in Matthews and the satellite office in Ballantyne. Then there was a very vocal

Sophie Duran, heiress to the *Her Naturals* hair care dynasty. She wore obnoxious vibes like a chinchilla wore its fur.

Her conversation sounded like gloating. "My husband just purchased a fifty-foot yacht for our Lake Norman property. I must admit that I was a little miffed at first. It is nearing fall, for goodness sake. I didn't think we would get to enjoy the yacht like we should at this late time of year. Last year, the waters were choppy from the brisk winds. But nonetheless, I am throwing a Harvest Soiree. Roland, I know you and Carmen aren't from the area, but you should consider coming down to enjoy the event. Damon and Cherish can attest to the efforts I put forth in the extravaganza. They were at my Luau in July Soiree held at the Country Club for the Fourth of July last year." She looked to her left for confirmation.

Damon responded, making eye contact with all the occupants of the table. "I loved the pomegranate ice sculpture in the shape of a volcano. It was an extremely unique idea. The successions of fireworks off the middle of the golf course were also a treat."

Cherish listened, but she was unusually quiet and distant. Almost like she was there in body, but not mind.

Damon's arm rested on the back of Cherish's chair as he spoke. "My personal favorite was the hula dancers. Their routine personified upbeat, fun and sexy. I'm telling you that you haven't partied until you attend a Duran Soiree. I've never seen anything like it."

"It sounds fascinating," Carmen said. "What date will that be?"

"Oh, I apologize. How could I forget that tidbit of information?" Sophie's coy smile seemed artificial, or maybe it was the cost of marriage to a plastic surgeon. Too much Botox. "October thirteenth. The soirée will be on the second weekend in the month. Leave me your address and I will have an invitation mailed to you. I'm sort of old fashioned when it comes to that.

Email invitations are so impersonal and rushed. I like to take a personal touch on anything that will represent the Duran name."

A waiter came around to fill the wine glasses.

Roland took a sip of Cabernet Sauvignon before saying, "We look forward to it. I'm always amazed at the connections created by attending these functions."

"It used to be the only money was old money. Now I find that people are quite creative in the pursuit of wealth. Do you not agree?" Sophie geared her question to no one in particular.

Damon answered. Always eager to impress. "Technology opened the doors for greater wealth. Capitalism is the capstone of American culture. The larger the desire for materialism, the greater there is the opportunity to advance. Plus, knowing the right people always helps."

His hand wrapped around a glass like he was making a toast to Sophie. I could imagine the imprint of his face on her behind from all the kissing up he was doing.

"But of course." Sophie lifted her glass to him before taking a sip herself.

Maybe it was because I was seated next to Damon that unwanted attention was drawn my way.

"Scott, you're so quiet. I never did ask. What do you do for a living?" Sophie intently watched me.

I wasn't surprised by the question. That's what people ask at functions such as this.

"Sell car parts," I replied dryly.

"Oh." Her interest in me waned as she turned her head to adjust the pendant on her right shoulder.

Damon spoke up like I needed defending. "My friend here is modest. He's been in management for years."

There was no need to hype my position. I couldn't care less about Sophie's opinion of my mediocre status quo.

"I just sell car parts." I rubbed the crevice behind my ear where a nagging pulse developed.

Applause vibrated throughout the room as the mistress of ceremony, Paulette, a petite ebony female in a blue and silver evening gown, introduced Dr. Javir Cavella, the renowned neurosurgeon from Brazil. I'd seen pictures of him from browsing through his *Gene Relations* book on a shelf at Damon's place.

A distinguished aura followed the guest speaker as he approached the podium. Dr. Cavella nodded his head as he exchanged places with Paulette. She stepped out of the spotlight and became a shadow in the background.

He lifted the microphone to accommodate his size. "Good evening, Charlotte family." He smiled into the crowd. "It is my honor to stand before you today." Dr. Cavella took a sip of water from a bottle placed on the podium. "There have been miraculous advances in medicine within the last century. Medical professionals pioneered research that was unheard of. For example, Dr. Christaan Bernard performed the first open heart transplant back in 1967. His perseverance enabled thousands with cardiac problems to now have a new lease on life. By the same token, Dr. Charles Drew discovered that plasma could be separated from red blood cells, thereby allowing blood to be stored for transfusions."

"Many lives are saved because blood donations are available. Due to studies by researchers at Kyoto University, stem cell cloning has developed a new meaning. The ethical controversy behind human embryonic stem cell use will be no more with a new technique the Kyoto team used skin cells to insert essential genes into viruses that infect the cell and become active as the virus replicated. The skin cell's own copies of the gene were repressed due to their interference with functioning. Quite remarkably, those four genes were sufficient to reprogram skin cells."

I listened to Dr. Cavella break down the stem cell process and wondered if some of what he was talking about was foreign to anybody else besides me. I got the gist of his presentation, but the information seemed drawn out and over analytical. During times such as this, I found my mind wandering. The subject didn't captivate me. I surveyed the table where everyone else seemed to be listening intently.

Dr. Cavella continued his speech. "Funding has been limited. A bill for more research that went to the House of Representatives in June was approved, although it is expected to be vetoed by the president."

Damon leaned over to me and whispered, "Hey, come on. I want to show you something."

I knew it must have been what his persuasion in inviting me was about.

"Germani, I'll be back shortly," I said as I removed the cloth napkin from my lap and set it on the table before excusing myself.

She gave me an inquisitive glance, but then turned her head back to the speaker.

I followed Damon out of the conference room and to the elevator. He spoke as we passed several hotel guests that appeared to be checking in. Damon seemed to be exceptionally giddy, a rarity I'd seen. There were only two other times that Damon shared overweening delight. The first time was when we saw the *Del Rio* video. On the second occasion, Damon received a generous gift from an Economics professor at A&T that paid for his entire academic program, plus an electric blue T-top Thunderbird to flash around campus. The dream of all cars made real. I remember the way Ms. Ilene boasted about her son's jazzy automobile more than she did about his academic career.

"Man, I forgot to tell you that I saw your mom last Saturday," I stated.

I had no intention on souring his mood, but any sign of a

smile disappeared from his face. He looked at me like I had socked him in the mouth.

"So?" Damon said with disdain in his voice.

"She wanted me to give you a message." I paused as we stepped off the elevator and took a right down the hall. "She asked me to tell you that she loves you."

"The mother I knew died when Brandon took a bullet. Garbage needs to stay in the ghetto." The acid in his voice only got thicker.

His youngest brother, Brandon, had passed away five years ago, right before I met Germani. Stray bullets pelted his body as he went up for a jump shot on the basketball court at a park near their home.

Before it happened, Damon had begged his mother to move from the high crime West Corridor area she lived in. He was even willing to pay her rent at a nice place near him in Ballantyne. Ms. Ilene was loyal to her hood. She refused to accept his offer to become 'uppity black folks' as she called it. Damon blamed Ms. Ilene for Brandon's death. Brandon was the only one of his siblings doing anything productive with his life. A multi-gifted honor student, the boy had planned to start college at Howard University that fall where a full academic scholarship awaited him.

Damon had stopped talking to all his siblings, but Brandon, after some of his prescription samples went missing during a party he had at his first house. He accused his brother, Devon, of stealing his stuff and his sisters verbally jumped on him for making the accusation. That was when he banned all of them, but Brandon and his mother. When Brandon died, Ms. Ilene got kicked to the curb too.

It seemed trivial to me that five years later, Damon would still be mad at his mother about something she didn't directly do. "You should let the past go. Mend the relationship between you and your mom," I advised. "How would you feel if she died and you were still holding a grudge?"

He responded with no emotion as he pushed the door open. "Relieved."

I paused for a minute. Damon couldn't be that cold blooded. He was just bitter. I didn't have anything else to say about it.

As we stepped into the lavish aqua and chocolate decorum, I wondered why. I didn't know where I thought we were going, but I didn't expect it to be a room.

"Damon, what's with the hotel suite," I asked as he tucked the key card back into his wallet.

"This isn't my room. It's a business associate's, Dr. Cavella, the presenter of the night rented this room. I have something I need to show you." He gestured toward a table in the sitting area.

On a mahogany and marble oval coffee table there was a tier of champagne glasses next to a bowl of ice with a bottle of cognac. I moved over a chocolate throw pillow and sat next to an engrossed Damon. His mind twirled. I could see from the way he shifted the glass of liquid how the gears of his brain were churning.

"So what is it?" I asked.

"I got something I know you'll enjoy."

All I saw was a remote control that Damon picked up. He pressed a button and music began playing. It sounded like Charlie Wilson from the Gap Band.

"Man, what are you doing?" I asked.

Damon glanced over at me. "Sit back and watch."

A door from an adjoining room slid open and a woman in a black lace short top that stopped at her belly button with a matching thong slowly moved forward. Her hips swayed to the beat of the song.

She had her eyes on me as she bit her bottom lip and performed a seductive dance.

Damon sipped on his drink with a devilish smile.

"My wife is downstairs," I told Damon, quickly becoming uncomfortable with the heat rising in me.

"Yes, she is, and she's not giving you any. I know you're frustrated and your wife is causing you way too much grief. *Pleasure* here is willing to give you a little excitement. If you don't remember, I paid her that night we were at the club and she was nice enough to let me get a rain check. She will be here all night long for some other activities we got going on later this evening, but I wanted you to get a taste of how it's supposed to feel." Damon pointed to the woman who had her top unbuttoned as she shrugged the material off and threw it on me.

I didn't know when strippers started giving rain checks, but I didn't want to get caught up in the thunder storm.

CHAPTER TWENTY-FIVE

GERMANI

I couldn't believe they left us sitting at that table for half an hour. I expected them to be gone five or ten minutes. Fifteen tops.

Cherish had gone to the bathroom to powder her nose. Carmen and her scientist husband had relocated to a table across the room with some business associates they knew. And the very sophisticated Sophie had cut loose on the dance floor. Her hips thrust in awkward gyrations. The partnerless moves didn't match the music, but she lip-synced the beat of "Brick House" while her head swayed.

I was left alone with Omar who looked even more bored than I felt. A sigh escaped as he drummed his fingers against the tabletop. A few times, our eyes met as they roamed around the European designed Pomodoro banquet room set for four hundred guests with its crystal chandeliers, cream table clothes, black tie wrapped chairs and exquisite yellow orchid flower arrangements throughout. We'd shared polite smiles, but no words.

If my boss, Peter, were here, he'd reprimand me for not taking the opportunity to network. *"There's never an inappropriate time to market Job Track. You can meet an employer in the grocery store, your doctor's office or at the utility company."* I could hear his hyper, full-blooded Irishman voice as if he were sitting in a chair next to me.

"What are you doing sitting there like a wart on a witch? Get up and mingle. Show that outstanding and friendly personality we brought on staff. Always be prepared to talk about the great people we have for hire through Job Track. Even when you're not in the office, you are still working; and you're sitting in a room full of medical professionals. It doesn't matter if their business is small or large. If they have a business, then they may be hiring. It's perfect timing for one of our recruiters to make a connection. They aren't going to contact you if you haven't shown yourself worth the call. Or worse yet, you didn't let anyone know what you have to offer."

It was boredom, more than Peter's voice, playing in my head that made me decide to engage Omar in a conversation. Time would keep dragging if I didn't smooze.

"Omar, you said you operate two practices. How many people do you staff at each location?" I asked the dermatologist who looked startled that I was speaking to him as he turned toward my upbeat voice. He probably was surprised that the boredom had left my face as I sipped from a glass of lemon water and waited for him to tell me all about his company.

"Our Matthews office houses seventeen staff members," he answered, "including myself and two other dermatologists. There are two registered nurses, five medical assistants, three receptionists, one of which is part time, two medical transcriptionists, an insurance biller and our office manager. The satellite location in University City is much smaller due to that office only being open two days a week and one weekend per month."

"Do you find a great need for adequate ethnic sensitive laser treatment and skincare products?" I knew Charlotte was an ever growing diverse city that demanded services to fit the needs of people with various hues of color.

"Actually, we are finding ways to expand our operations as we speak because of the rapid interest in repair and preventative treatment. I think we will need a couple more doctors to make that happen. Myself and the partners are in the interviewing stages for associates who've applied to us through Carolina Medical."

I knew we weren't in the business of finding doctors; physicians didn't need help with placement. The office staff was a definite possibility though. "Sounds like a wise choice for your practice. The firm I work for may be an asset to your operations. We specialize in high quality staffing. Job Track confers with our employers to discover what path to take for your specific need. Our applicants go through rigorous skill testing, as well as an extensive background and criminal check. The business journal cited us as a top placement agency with one of the highest success rates in the city."

I wanted to sound confident, not boisterous. I paid close attention to his body language, which would tell me his level of interest in a possible business relationship. Much could be communicated by physical response. His chair was at a side angle, but his leg faced inward. One under the table and one not. That alone would give me the impression that he was apprehensive, but his consistent nods told me that he was, at least, listening.

"I usually leave staffing for the office up to our Human Resources Manager, Sheila. She's pretty good at picking people that fit into our work environment," Omar responded almost apologetic.

"I completely understand. How about you give Sheila my business card? I would love to hear what she's doing to keep the office operation afloat." I smiled brightly as I reached into my satchel and pulled out a card. "You wouldn't mind that, would you?"

He took the card and placed it in the inner pocket of his suit. "Not at all."

I logged Sheila's name in my memory. If I didn't hear from her in a week, I would call to set up a meeting. As I closed the clutch of my bag I noticed the time on my watch read 10:30 P.M. Another half hour had passed with both Scott and Damon absent. I slid my satchel off the table and straightened the hem of my teal floor-length silk evening gown as I stood.

I walked down several halls of the Omni Charlotte Hotel. I got to the exit where the outdoor pool lay before I decided to go back to the banquet and wait.

I rounded the corner near the front desk, and down a hallway near the elevators I saw Cherish's back. I recognized her coral backless designer Vera Wang as she spoke with Dr. Cavella. Her body language was off. The stiff posture seemed defensive like she didn't want to be near him. He stroked her folded arms which she allowed, but the act seemed obtrusive. He stood too close. Invaded personal space. It looked like she needed to be rescued from unwanted company.

As I approached, I could only hear the tail end of their verbiage.

"Your hesitation concerns me. I'm willing to give you luxuries beyond this if you'd allow me." His gray eyes bore seductively into Cherish. Dr. Cavella was easy on the eyes with black tapered hair and smooth olive skin. He had an athletic build, but not super muscular.

The doctor's lips pursed as he saw me. Cherish turned her head to see what drew his attention. Surprise, then what I thought was relief, crossed her face.

"Cherish, I came out here to find our husbands. Is everything all right?" I emphasized her marital status to a man who seemed to have less than honorable intentions.

Cherish blinked rapidly before responding, "Yes, everything is fine. We were just talking."

It certainly didn't sound as innocent as she made it to be, but maybe I was reading more into it than I should. It wouldn't be the first time I was wrong. I had accused Scott of cheating on me and still hadn't found evidence to back it up.

Dr. Cavella extended his hand. "I don't think I've had the pleasure."

"I don't think you have," I responded, taking his greeting for a quick handshake. He put my hand to his lips and kissed the back of it gently before I abruptly pulled it from his grasp.

All that overly affectionate touching might have been a Brazilian thing, but I wasn't from Brazil.

"Were you going back to the conference room?" I asked Cherish as I pointed down the hall.

"Yes, we can go back," Cherish said as she began walking away from the elevators.

Although his attempt at charm didn't persuade me, I did find his speech to be interesting and wanted more details.

I complimented Dr. Cavella as we all headed back toward the conference room. "Your speech was fascinating. I didn't realize all the benefits to stem cell research or that there was an alternative method to performing tests that might counter-act the controversy behind embryonic destruction and human cloning."

Dr. Cavella nodded his head. "Many people don't. Not until it directly affects them, like someone in their family becoming ill. I'm trying to spread the word of its usefulness. That is the only way to get the global private funding that we need."

"What brought about your interest in this particular study?"

We walked back into the Pomodoro room to a jazz rendition of "Endless Love." The banquet floor was filled with slow dancers, swaying to the Diana Ross and Lionel Richie classic love song.

Dr. Cavella stood in the door entrance to allow us in first. "I see long-term illnesses and genetic disorders killing people for no other reason than political fear and public ignorance. For the amount of money used to treat chronic diseases, stem cell research could be paid for one hundred times over." He paused as the mistress of ceremony gestured for him toward a small group she was talking with. "I'm being summoned. Cherish, I'll talk to you later." He stroked her arm before going off to join the mistress of ceremony.

Dr. Cavella had no qualms about showing feelings for Cherish, and as much as I didn't like Damon, a family divided didn't sit well with me.

"Cherish, are you sure everything is okay?" I asked with serious concern. Close up, her skin appeared ashen under artful make-up and false eyelashes.

She didn't respond.

We weren't close enough for her to tell me her problems. That was mostly my fault due to my ill feelings toward her husband. She'd asked me to go shopping or out to lunch and I'd made up an excuse every time. I didn't like the way Damon treated her; as if she were for beautiful display only, with no feelings of her own. An extension meant entirely for his personal use and pleasure. I thought she was a doormat and I could never respect people who allowed themselves to be walked all over.

I felt bad for my judgment. There was no telling what she was dealing with while I was acting like I was better than her. Like I was incapable of having drama in my marriage. God had a funny way of showing me who I really was by the way I dealt with others. Once again, I was convicted on my ego.

Cherish and I sat down at the now completely empty table we'd left. I rested my hands on the cream cloth and turned toward Cherish, who sat on my left-hand side. "Listen. I know me and your husband bump heads on a regular basis, but that doesn't mean we can't be friends. If you need to get some stuff off your chest, please know that I will keep the conversation in the strictest of confidence." I spoke from the heart with as much sincerity as I could muster. Even with our husbands being best friends, there were some boundaries that need not be blurred.

"Thank you, Germani." Before her eyes dropped down I was sure I saw the glint of a tear.

I was being pushy, but I couldn't help it. "If you don't want to talk now, I understand. The door is open for you to call me at anytime. You have my house and cell numbers."

Cherish nodded her head as she wiped the outer corners of her eyes.

The uneasiness that tapped at my soul like a fleet of African dancers told me there were some skeletons wreaking havoc in the Spears' home, ones about to come out. Considering my past judgments, I hoped I was ready to be the kind of friend Cherish needed.

CHAPTER
TWENTY-SIX

SCOTT

Sara was on one register and Torrance on the other. Craig had come on for the evening shift and was scheduled to relieve Torrance.

Craig stopped me as I passed him while he stocked a shelf. "There are two boxes of hubcaps that won't fit on the shelf, and since you rearranged everything back there due to inventory, I'm not sure where you want me to put the extras."

"It's all still arranged by manufacturer. You just have to look on the labels to see what goes where," I explained to Craig before turning my attention to Torrance.

"Torrance, I need to speak with you." I pulled him from the register. Craig and Sara exchanged glances as we walked to the back room. The space was used for an office.

I wanted to keep the conversation light, play it by ear as I pushed the door closed.

"I'm straight." Torrance tugged at his sagging black pants. The waist was three inches lower than it should have been.

"Maybe that belt you're wearing needs to be tightened." I stood against the desk with my arms folded against my chest in business mode.

Torrance grimaced as he looked up at the ceiling, but tucked his dangling green button-down shirt with the black Car Care logo into his pants. He stretched the belt into another hole and lapped it around his waist. His hands slapped against his waist.

I pulled the ledger off the desk and handed it to him. "I ran some reports for inventory, and although your drawer was never short, per se, it appears that our accounts don't match the inventory. Corporate office requested an audit. I probably wouldn't have noticed for another few months otherwise."

I didn't want to automatically assume he was running game on me. Misuse of my kindness. The numbers didn't lie.

"That's all your cashier transactions. For the past month and a half, you've been giving fifty percent off for things that shouldn't have discounts."

Torrance gave me a look of sheer confusion. "I thought you told me I could do fifty percent off for my friends and family?"

"No, I'm pretty sure I said fifteen for a select few and not to make it a habit." Torrance played with the inside of his pants pocket as I tapped a pen against the ledger. "You also took back three items without bothering to get a receipt for the initial purchase. Do you recognize this?" I put the pen and ledger down, reached behind the desk and picked up a large metallic red object. It landed on top of the desk with a thug sound.

"Cam Shaft Rocker Stud for a Dodge Intrepid made in 1997," Torrance responded with scrunched eyebrows.

I was certain of one thing. The boy knew his car parts and had a great memory. "Exactly. And you notice anything else?" I inquired.

Torrance examined the cam shaft; walked around it like a student studying a class project.

I twirled the part around so he could see the serial number. "It's not ours."

"It's not our product?" he asked with bulging eyes like he didn't believe me.

"Oh, I'm sure. The question is why didn't you get a receipt

before you gave that person their money back, or at the very least, run the serial numbers in our system? That's almost a five hundred dollar lost for one item." I held up my index finger as irritation bounced from my voice. For as long as I'd worked at Car Care, I hadn't been responsible for that kind of loss. I had let my supervising duties slip.

Any explanation Torrance gave wouldn't be acceptable, no excuse sufficient for corporate office. Once Sid Matthews, our District Manager, got wind of what happened, it would be grounds for Torrance's automatic dismissal.

I had to be honest and let Torrance know the implication behind his actions. "You might need to start seeking other employment. Maybe retail isn't the place for you."

"Scott, man, don't let me go," Torrance pleaded with a pitiful look on his face. "I need to help my moms with the bills. It's not like I stole parts and sold them on the street. I misunderstood policy while trying to look out for the peeps I'm cool with. You know our people can't afford some of these outrageous prices. Made in Korea for ten cents, sold in America for a hundred dollars. Sh- . . . I mean, shoot. Now you know, you know, you know."

Torrance came at me like we were boys representing the hood instead of a boss and his employee discussing irresponsibility and negligence. I had to take the credit for minimizing my role as his superior. When I hired Torrance, he had just moved from New York, where he was a street vendor who sold name brand tennis shoes in Brooklyn; a kid with a filthy mouth, but a good work ethic. He had a habit of cussing whenever he got frustrated. As he got acclimated to the job, he learned to keep his language under his breath where nobody else could hear him. It was my encouragement that got him to change some of his bad habits. Maybe I crossed the line of professionalism when I started giving him advice on how to treat women and picking Torrance up for work during the whole month he didn't have transportation to get back and forth.

I had to nip his 'we boyz' attitude in the bud.

"Torrance, what I know is we are not buddies. You work here. Furthermore, Car Care has lost too much money since you came on board. That's a serious problem for the big bosses and a serious problem for me. I don't think you understand that when the heat comes down through the ranks . . ." I jabbed my finger in my chest. The lines of my forehead stretched long and wide as I vented my own frustration. "I'm the one that gets burned. I look bad and so does this store. Corporate office already has this location at a different standard because it's in a high crime area. I can't afford for my store to take any more criticism. If it comes between you keeping your job and me keeping mine, we already know how it's going down."

Torrance stood there and blinked at me. Several long seconds ticked by before he responded. "Why you coming at me like that? I know I messed up, but you don't have to treat me like I'm a flunkie. If you didn't want me here any more, all you had to say was, 'Torrance you messed up big and we can't keep you any longer.' I can comprehend being fired. Instead, you're talking to me like I got one testicle. You supposed to be big on respect and righteousness, but when push comes to shove, I can't tell you know jack about those words." Torrance began to walk backward as he eyed me with contempt. "It's all good. We ain't got to be cool."

I wielded my power hard, thinking he needed to recognize me as an authority figure. I didn't mean for it to come out the way it did.

"Torrance, we are cool, but you are my employee first. I can't cut you anymore slack than the rest of the staff. I would give this same lecture to Craig, Sara or anybody else working for me."

Torrance threw his hand up in a waving gesture, like he wasn't trying to hear me. "Man, Scott, man. You keep your lectures. I don't need them if you gonna fire me. A lecture is for somebody that's staying in a position. No, I'm good on that. As a matter of fact, I'm glad you and corporate office are letting me go. That way, I can collect my unemployment. Peace out!" Torrance threw up two fingers and rammed the door against the wall as he exited the tiny office space.

My nerves had remained on edge since Torrance stormed out of the building. Sometimes we get this sense that things are about to go wrong, but we ignore the feeling. I didn't think things could get any worse.

"Car Care," I quickly answered the phone in the backroom after Craig had hollered that it was for me.

"Scott, we have a shut off notice from Duke Power." Germani paused, and when I didn't say anything quick enough, she continued talking. "What's going on that you didn't pay the light bill?"

"I did pay the bill. I think I paid the lights." My speech slowed as I tried to remember which bills I had paid at the beginning of the month. I knew there was one of them that I said I would pay later because it wasn't due yet.

"No, the light bill didn't get paid because I am staring at the notice right now." I could hear Germani rustling the paper through her connection.

"Oh, that's right. I forgot all about paying that," I admitted.

"How could you forget to pay the light bill? We pay all the same bills at the same time of the month? We haven't been getting shut off notices before today. What are we going to do?" Germani was breathing hard into the phone piece. There was panic in her voice.

My thoughts were still on the blow-up with Torrance and the heat from the corporate office. Even with Torrance being let go, I still was accountable for the things he did while under my watch. When I called James, our District Manager, to tell him about Torrance's actions and his firing, James explained that there may be an investigation into my store operations.

"I've got stuff on my mind. Don't stress. I'll take care of it,"

I said calmly as I walked over to the office chair and sat down. I shoved sheets of paper off the middle of my desk and propped my elbows up on the wooden desktop. It was decided when we were married that I would handle the finances. Germani said, at the time, that she knew I would take care of us and that she trusted me. I majored in business management in college and felt well equipped to budget for our household.

"You've been awfully forgetful lately, Scott. What's going on that has your memory all twisted up that you can't remember to pay our bills?" Germani's irritation came through the phone line like thunder and lightning.

All I could do was sigh as I swiveled back and forth in the chair. My memory wasn't that bad. Her only other example of my so called forgetfulness was when I didn't tell her about being at Lisa's house and that was over a month ago.

I had already told her that I'd take care of it. I would be getting paid on Friday; I would just pay it then.

As if reading my mind she said, "You don't get your check deposited into our account until Friday. The disconnection is on or before Thursday. This Thursday."

"Well, I guess I will make a payment arrangement or something." It wasn't like we were the first family to ever be behind on our bills.

"Are there any other bills that haven't gotten paid?"

"No. Everything else is taken care of. I paid the water, telephone and cable bill on the first."

"So you paid the cable bill before you paid for the lights to stay on?" I hoped she was hormonal because that would only last a few days. If we were back to not trusting me again, then we had real problems.

I had to sigh again to keep from getting mad.

"You put the cable before our utilities. Omigosh. I can't believe this. Since when did the cable become so important to you, Scott?" Her words sounded judgmental as if I fell off as a responsible person. My wife questioned me about how to handle things, just like corporate office.

It got under my skin that I had to defend my management ability. I could hear Damon's words rigging my ears. *"Get your manhood out of your wife's purse."*

I'd had enough. "I'm a grown man, Germani. Don't call my place of employment nagging me. I said I would take care of it and I will. Furthermore, what I watch on television is my business as long as I pay the bills. If you don't like what I do or how I do it, then you need to get over it."

"But—"

I didn't let her finish. "I don't want to hear anything else from you. I am hanging up before you get on my last nerve. Bye." I slammed the phone down.

She picked the wrong day to trip out on me.

CHAPTER
TWENTY-SEVEN

GERMANI

I couldn't believe his nerve. He hung up on me. Now, he was the one in the wrong, but I got hung up on. He had some nerve.

To say I was furious would be putting it lightly. My anger smoldered like a Girl Scout camp fire; beneath the smoke lay a whole lot of hot flames. When I got pissed—and I do mean really pissed—one of two things occurred. I either prayed or I paced. The latter fit the bill for my mood.

I started talking to the flat screen television as I walked back and forth across the floor with the light bill still in my hand. "Just when I try to be civilized and call my husband to discuss an unpaid bill, instead of degrading his manhood by paying the stupid bill myself, I get graced with a dial tone. How does that make sense?"

My day had been going fine before that. I'd met with Omar's Human Resources Manager. He came through and gave me the contract for their new employees. Plus, when I got to the office, another company called me because they were so pleased with the twenty temps we sent them that they wanted to bring on thirty-five more for seasonal contract jobs. I spent the entire afternoon scheduling interviews for those positions. It was a lot of work, but well worth it. My boss told me that I would be getting a bonus check from the additional revenue I'd brought to the company that month.

For me to have my joy dashed at the sight of a shut off notice was like a camel in the midst of a haystack filled with straw. My hope in calling Scott was for him to say there must have been some mistake at the light company; that they'd lost the payment and he had a confirmation number in his wallet to verify he had paid the bill. Or, at the very least, I expected him to say the ordeal would be handled by morning. I honestly didn't expect him to basically tell me to mind my business, like the bills weren't supposed to be my concern. I also didn't expect him to pay all the other bills but that one. All that said to me was that the water, telephone and cable were more important than the lights. The lights could wait for another payday. Who cares if they get cut off? That's what candles are sold for. Who needs a working hot water heater when you can boil water on the stove to take a shower or bath? Oh, wait . . . we need power for the electric stove too. Go figure.

I couldn't help but feel sarcastic and condescending about his actions.

I searched through the drawer where we kept bills and grabbed an outdated cable invoice from June. The cable cost half as much as the electric bill and should have been the last thing paid if something had to go. It didn't add up.

From Scott's response to me, I felt he might have lied to me about where our money was going.

I picked up the phone fully acknowledging that I was about to make myself even more upset than I already was. I traipsed across Berber carpeting, waiting for customer service at Dish Network. After waiting for too many prompts and pressing too many buttons, a guy named Colby answered the call.

"How can I be of assistance?" he asked.

"I can't seem to find my current cable bill. Would you be able to tell me my outstanding balance?"

"Sure, I should be able to help you with that. Do you have your account number?"

"I do." I repeated numbers from the shut-off notice I held.

"Please give me the last four digits of your social."

"It's in my husband's name. His last four digits are 4133."

"And the address on this account is at 621 Harris Oak Avenue for Scott Wilson. Is that correct?"

"Yes." I tilted my head side to side, trying to control my mood. *Was all that necessary to get a bill balance?* I had to force myself to be pleasant.

Colby finally said, "The bill was paid in full on October 1st."

I knew that already. "Okay and what was the amount paid." I hoped that Colby couldn't detect my irritation.

"Three hundred and forty-eight dollars and fifty-two cents."

Anger and disbelief didn't work well together. I had to repeat what I heard. "Three hundred and forty-eight dollars and fifty-two cents? No, you must be mistaken. Our bill couldn't possibly be that high," I spoke with confidence. Our monthly bill only averaged about seventy-five dollars."

"Well, Ms. Wilson, the bill *was* paid in full." I guess I was supposed to feel better about that, but Colby didn't know what I knew.

"My husband paid that bill and I'm not sure he realized that much would be taken out of our checking account."

"The payment was called in. We don't have your account set up for automatic pay," Colby hesitated. "Although that is an option if you'd like."

I specifically remember having the conversation about the convenience of our bill payments being automatically deducted from our joint checking account. We were putting the bill dates on a calendar to merge both our incomes. Originally, I paid the lights, water, my car insurance and half the rent, and Scott paid the other half of the rent, cable, telephone and his car insurance. When Elijah was born, which added an enormous debt for daycare and we decided to buy a house, it just seemed logical to merge our finances and pay the bills from one pot.

"Mrs. Wilson, are you still there?"

"Yes, I am. I don't want to change our service at this time. Could you give me a break down of where that amount came from?" My voice sounded hollow, kind of similar to how my heart felt. My feet took me from the living room to the kitchen back to the living room. Non-stop motion. Rapidly going nowhere, but my legs couldn't rest and my sense of deceit wouldn't cease.

"Two hundred seventy-three dollars and forty-nine cents is for pay-per-view movies."

That halted my pace. "Pay-per-view movies don't cost that much. Your systems most have a computer glitch."

"No, Ms. Wilson; that was the amount for pay-per-view at your address."

"Give me dates, times, titles and individual cost for each movie." I pulled a date book and pen from my purse and waited to write on a tasks-to_do page. If any of the movies were during our work hours, Dish Network was giving us a refund.

"*Wet Dreams 4 U* was ordered on August 10th at 1:45 A.M.; *Sex Sandwich Sluts* on August 16th at 11:30 P.M.; *Ghetto Girls Get Nasty* on August 16th at 2:50 A.M.," Colby continued down the list and my disbelief deepened.

Embarrassment warmed my face. I couldn't handle it anymore. "You know what, Colby; I think I've had enough . . . um . . . information. Thanks for the help."

"Sorry for the confusion, Ms. Wilson. I hope you have a nice night."

The night was going to be anything but nice.

"You do the same, Colby," I said pleasantly. It wasn't his

fault that my husband's brain cells had slipped from his head down to other parts of his anatomy. No. That was Scott's fault.

That call ended and I wanted to hurt my husband so bad I could taste my bitter rage. I could understand the reason Mekhi slapped the stank out of Mishelle for her blatant disrespect. Sometimes, the anger became an unstoppable catalyst and a person snapped.

All the love I had to give physically, mentally and intimately was cast aside by Scott's compulsion, and for what? A fantasy I'd never be able to compete with.

I was back to being that camel in a haystack of straw. And I had to do something . . . to get my mind in a different place.

CHAPTER TWENTY-EIGHT

SCOTT

"Time to close shop," I said wearily to myself as I stacked bundles of ones, fives, tens, twenties, fifties and the three hundred dollar bills on top of each other in the office. I had to go home to that woman I hung up on.

The day had been unusually slow with customers trickling through in small numbers. It made my job easier since I had all those boxes to put back into the storage room after the inventory audit.

At the end of the evening, there were only Sara and myself left to cash out. I shut down one register at nine after Craig cashed out, and it only took forty minutes to tally Sara's register. I usually could expect to be at the store until midnight, and occasionally, one or two A.M., but it was nearing eleven and everything that needed to be done had been taken care of.

I placed the bundles inside a deposit bag, zipping it up and setting it on the counter as I prepared to go make a drop at the bank.

"Sara, if you're ready to go, I will walk you to your car."

Sara pulled the ponytail holder from her shoulder length strawberry blond hair; the bone straight mane fell to the collar of her Car Care uniform. "I'm ready," she said, pulling keys from the book bag she seemed to always carry. "I was even able to get some homework done during our down time."

"Yeah, I saw you drop that book under the counter whenever the door opened. What exactly are you studying?"

"Engine Fundamentals. Boring material, but it's part of the curriculum. I have to do it, though. I'll admit that I'm more into the hands-on stuff." Sara put her book bag on her shoulder.

"I've probably said this before, but you're the only girl I know in a mechanic program." Sara was average height for a young woman, but had a thin build. I couldn't visualize her underneath a car changing brake pads or dismantling a transmission.

"Yes, Scott, you say it all the time." She laughed at me as I held the entrance door open. "I couldn't believe how dead it was tonight."

I locked the door and said, "It has been fairly slow, but I'm not complaining because I need to go home and take care of some things," however unpleasant they were going to be.

"Yeah, and I have more studying to do. Two more semesters and I am done with this program."

Sara's classic midnight blue Cadillac Eldorado Coupe with a V8 engine that was rebuilt by her uncle sat near the front entrance of the Car Care building. Her tires touched the lines of a handicapped parking space. I waited for her to get in and start the car.

"Have a nice night, Scott," she waved. The car purred to life with a quiet hum as she talked to me with the door open.

"Thanks, you do the same and drive safe," I said as I closed her door.

Sara lived in Myers Park, on the South side of the city, an area that was recently on the news for having laws that prohibited ownership of homes by black people. The publicity made

Myers Park sound like a completely divided part of Charlotte. Supposedly, the laws dated post-slavery and were never revised to reflect current times. There were a couple residents on the news expressing their outrage that on the books, blatant discrimination still existed. One man dismissed the law and allegations of discrimination as past occurrences, and suggested people needed to stop playing the race card.

I waved at Sara as she exited the parking lot. I could hear "Just Fine," a new song by Mary J. Blige, from the Power 98 radio station blasting from her stereo system. I put the money pouch under my arm as I fished out my keys from my front pocket and pressed the keyless entry.

Because Germani didn't call back, I could imagine her sitting in the recliner of the living room waiting for me with her arms crossed and her foot tapping.

As I put the car in reverse and rolled backward, I felt the tire on the passenger side wobble. I placed the car back in park as I got out and went around to see what the problem was. After leaning down, I noticed that the front passenger side tire was so flat that the rim almost touched the ground.

"Ain't this a trip," I said to myself as I stood up and put my hand on top of the hood of the car. The light at the street was broken and the one further down didn't give off enough.

An indescribable twitch tugged at my spine as I could have sworn I heard footfalls nearby. My head jerked to the left of a vacant parking lot, vacant with the exception of a 1979 Chevy Caprice that had littered my company's property for the past three days. I kept telling myself to call the city and have it towed away, but as I've said before, distractions make you forgetful.

I glanced to the right where Farm Pond Lane sat amongst deserted cement, although I could hear traffic driving down Albemarle.

The tire needed to be changed. I went back to the driver's

side and popped the trunk then fished around in the unlit area for the dummy tire and jack. As I searched, I realized that there was no flashlight.

My emergency kit was in Germani's Cougar. I had given it to her for the trip to the annual women's retreat over the past summer. She'd driven to Atlanta with Taylor and Stephanie, her church friends. They didn't want to be confined to a bus for long hours.

The store had a storm lamp in the back office. I decided to go grab that and thought it might be wise to get a can of fix-a-flat while I was in there.

It didn't take long for me to change my tire. When I got back in the car, the cell phone I had left on my seat was flashing with missed calls. All of them were from Germani. I hoped she wasn't trying to start something else about the power bill before I got home. As I decided whether to call home, the phone rang again.

Germani spoke in rushed choppy words, and at once, our earlier argument was replaced by somebody else's problems.

CHAPTER TWENTY-NINE

GERMANI

Scott wasn't going to work my nerves.

That's all I was thinking as I pulled the take-out container from its bag and placed the contents on a thick Dixie paper plate.

I had dropped Elijah off at Momma's house before I went on a feed-my-soul mission. My emotions were all over the place after the argument with Scott. I was prepared for an ugly, heated conversation when my husband made it home, and if I felt like hollering my aggravation from the rooftop, I didn't want Elijah caught in the middle.

On the way back home, I stopped at Boardwalk Billy's. They had a hot wing special. Ten for five dollars. I thought about getting the ribs, but my appetite craved mozzarella sticks. Ribs just didn't go with fried cheese.

Once my plate was in hand, I angled a glass bottle of Sobe Tsunami between my thumb and forefinger, dangling my dinner on the way to the living room couch for an episode of *Grey's Anatomy*. Just like my momma to Howie Mandel in *Deal or No Deal*, I rearranged my schedule around Isaiah Washington in *Grey's Anatomy*. I admired his easy swagger as he gravi-

tated to emergency victims. The man was a complex cardio-
thoracic surgeon with an obvious dominant presence. Although always competent, his role choices had evolved since I
first saw him playing in the movie *Crooklyn* thirteen years ago.
Since they fired him, the show wasn't quite the same, but I
continued watching anyway and lived for the re-runs where I
would get to see Dr. Burke.

I took a swig of my peach mango beverage, savoring the *me*
time more than the drink itself. I placed the food on our end
table and curled my feet under my bottom as I cozied up in the
nook of the couch. I emptied my thoughts as I tried to focus
on my favorite show. My thoughts kept bouncing to the growing tension between Scott and myself, then I would focus
harder on television. By the end of the episode, I couldn't remember half of what the show was about.

The shrill sound of our house phone jolted me from my
self-conflicted mental zone. Cherish's phone number came
across the television screen caller ID.

"Hello." I tried not to smear buffalo wing sauce on the
phone console as I answered.

The hollowness of her voice almost made it inaudible.
"Germani, can I talk with you?"

I had called Cherish at least five or six times since the charity in hopes of building a friendship, but she never returned
my calls. I was glad that we were finally connecting.

"Sure," I said, pressing the phone against my ear with the
palm of my hand. Something seemed strange in Cherish's
voice.

"Why have you been calling me so much lately? I know you
don't like me," she whispered.

I straightened my back as a chill went down my spine. "Uh . . ."
I didn't know what else to say. Maybe I was pushing for a
friendship that wasn't meant to be.

"Germani, I know it shouldn't matter, but I was wondering
why all of a sudden you want to call me." She paused.

I explained, "When we were at the banquet you seemed to be going through some things and I felt bad for not being the type of person you felt you could confide in. Basically, you looked like you needed a friend and I haven't been good in that area. I used my feeling toward your husband against you and I was wrong for that. I wasn't trying to be nosy about your marriage. I truly was worried about you."

"Yeah, my marriage." Cherish paused again. I could hear her breathing. I thought she was on the verge of tears, yet her voice remained placid and detached.

"Are you okay?" I asked.

"I've been living all wrong, Germani. Damon's not the man I thought he was. Arrogantly selfish, that's my Damon." I could hear Cherish crunch on something. "The problem is . . . I was raised to please my man. That's how things were done in my home. My mom always told me that if I wanted to be happily married, then I had to make my husband's priorities my own. A wise woman lets her man do what he wants as long as he's taking care of home."

Cherish gulped. "My father always had other women and my mother always knew about them. She used to say that she had no reason to be jealous, because she was his wife, not his whore. A wife is priority, while a whore is temporary. I respected both my parents, but I wanted something different. I didn't want my husband to feel like he needed mistresses or like I needed to ignore what he might be doing when he wasn't with me. The chemistry I had with Damon was intoxicating. I knew that I would never feel that kind of electric intensity with another man. Completely uninhibited love."

I could hear that crunching again, like she was eating peanuts or hard candy. But with her words, I was beginning to understand Cherish in a different way. She wasn't that different than me, when I was experimenting with porn to please Scott and keep him interested in our marriage.

"I feel like I lost myself somewhere along the line," she continued. "Started doing things I didn't want to do. Believed that he could be my everything. Believed I could be his everything and all the people around us would be enhancements to our lives. Damon had me convinced that the more we pursued heightening the excitement in our lives, the happier we would be."

Cherish inhaled sharply before confessing, "I've been stealing drugs from his work supply, trying to numb myself for the past couple of years. Damon thought someone in his family was taking samples, but it was me. I feel terrible about it. I never meant for him to disown his mother and siblings, but I couldn't tell him what I was doing either. It all started when Damon and I became part of this swinger's club. We've been having sex with other partners and couples every weekend since before we got married. I mean . . . anything kinky and risqué, we've probably tried it."

I stopped her, because I didn't want to hear sordid details of their sex life.

"It's not necessary for you to share everything with me. I don't need to know details." To put it tactfully, I was saying TMI, Too Much Information.

"No, I have to get this off my mind. I've held it in for too long. Justified . . . too long. So, please, listen to what I'm saying. We were interacting with physicians of all kinds from cosmetic surgeons to orthodontists and family doctors. Damon met them through his job." I could hear a gulp like she was drinking. "We didn't take precautions, didn't think protection was necessary. The people we dealt with were highly respected, exceptionally intelligent, medical professionals for God's sake. How asinine." Cherish suddenly cackled.

I stayed quiet. The conversation had me off kilter.

"Somehow things went wrong. I love Damon and would do anything to please him, but he wasn't the type of man I could trust unconditionally. He was blinded by his ambition; began letting too many people into our swinger's circle. Damon refused to admit how out of control things were after I found out that I was AIDS infected. He refused to get tested himself and didn't want me to warn the people we were sleeping with. He wanted to act like things were normal."

My mouth dropped open and the phone slipped from my palm. I smeared red grease on the arm rest as I scrambled for the phone, which fell under the couch. I got on my knees to get it.

When I picked up the phone Cherish was still talking. "I can't go on with the guilt. I just can't."

Oh, Lord. I was stumped, baffled and seriously shocked. All I wanted was to enjoy my buffalo wings in peace. This confession took me into a whole other realm.

"Um . . . um . . . well," I couldn't think. This wasn't a conversation I felt prepared to handle. I silently prayed for God to help me to help her.

Before I could say anything, Cherish spat, "You're judging me, aren't you? That's why you're so quiet. Probably thinking how pathetic and despicable I am."

"That's not what's on my mind," I said truthfully as I tried to keep her calm.

"My, my, my, what a pretty little mess Cherish has gotten herself in," she said in a strange sing-song voice.

It felt like Cherish was edging off an emotional cliff, close to losing any rationale. I measured my options. My next words could make all the difference.

"No, Cherish, I think you're wounded. Life choices have severely wounded you. Often times, when I'm feeling like the world is weighing on my shoulders, I pray for guidance and I use my Bible for encouragement. I can't say that I do the right thing every time I go through some kind of suffering, but I know that prayer works and God listens. Look, let me get my Bible and I'll be right back."

I waited for her to say something, but besides light breathing, the line was silent.

I knew what person in the Bible I wanted Cherish to relate

to. Rahab stuck out to me. I searched my study Bible to make
sure I wasn't giving her the wrong interpretation of the Word.
In the Book of Joshua, in order to save her family, Rahab
helped Joshua and his men in their defeat of Jericho. My pastor taught us that Jesus was a descendant of Rahab, a former
prostitute who later married and became a virtuous woman. A
woman who used her body to please many men extended to
the greatest man in the Bible. She and Jesus shared the same
bloodline. I wanted Cherish to know whatever faults she had
now, any mistakes she previously cultivated didn't have to dic-
tate her future. Damon had Cherish's mind all twisted up.

I put markers in the books of Joshua and Matthew to confirm the lineage and then made my way back to the phone. She
was gone when I got there.

I quickly dialed her back with trembling fingers. I didn't
want her to think that she was alone or that I was condemning
her. If she called me with a conversation as personal as that
one, then she must have felt like I was her best option in her
time of need. I was more scared than I'd ever been in my life.
Petrified for Cherish. The voicemail clicked on. My nerves
were on edge. Instead of calling her again, I dialed Scott.

I said breathlessly, "I need you to meet me right now.
Right . . . now."

"What's wrong?"

My thoughts were moving too fast. "I can't talk, I need to
get over to Cherish's house. In fact, don't come home. Something is very, very wrong. Can you meet me over there?"

"Whoa. Tell me what's going on."

"I can't. We've got to get over there." My voice kept rising
as I jammed my feet into a pair of Sperry loafers and headed to
the door.

"I'm on the way." Scott's voice exemplified the worry I felt
as I headed to Cherish's home, unaware of what I was walking
into.

CHAPTER
THIRTY

SCOTT

Germani's Cougar was in the driveway when I made it to
Damon and Cherish's house on Pemswood. There were no
other cars parked outside, but that wasn't unusual. With the
rash of recent break-ins throughout the city, it was understandable that Damon and Cherish would have their vehicles
parked in their garage.

I stepped into the warm, dry night air and looked down the
quiet tree-lined street. Strolling up the walkway, I checked my
phone screen, hoping that Damon would get back to me. I had
left him a message after hanging up with Germani. I knew he
wouldn't be home, because Thursday nights he usually frequented the Gentleman's Lounge for an after hours nightcap.
When I spoke to him earlier, he told me that he had a busy
schedule and would be meeting up with a couple of new sales
reps at his favorite stripper's spot.

I walked up to the front door. I could see the shadow of a
light streaming through the stained glass window. The door-
bell chimed loudly inside the home.

Germani was nowhere in sight. I assumed she and Cherish

were having some woman talk. I even thought maybe my wife had over-reacted when she called me. Lately, she seemed easily riled and moody.

I waited several seconds for Cherish to answer, but nobody came to the door. I turned the knob, but the door was locked. I checked the time on my cell phone. After waiting three long minutes I dialed their house number. Germani should be expecting me.

"Where are they?" I murmured to myself as I stepped back and looked up to see if any other lights were on in the house.

Germani rounded the side of the house by the garage, squeezing between the garage door and the front end of her car. "Nobody's answering."

This was a declaration of what I already knew.

She made a circle with her finger. "I also checked all around the house and I don't see any movement. The back patio door was slightly open, but I was afraid to go in."

Still being a skeptic, I asked, "What made you think something was wrong enough for both of us to come over?"

"I don't know how else to describe my conversation with Cherish, but she told me a lot of personal information, and toward the end of our talk she sounded a little crazy." Germani whispered the word *crazy*. "Like she might be suicidal."

I frowned. "Cherish?" It just didn't sound believable. Damon's wife was a happy person. The kind of woman that kept a smile on her face; had a warm disposition. In fact, she was probably the most easy-going female I knew.

"Did you try calling Damon? Were you able to reach him?"

I shook my head. "I left him a message before I got here, but he hasn't called me back yet."

"Cherish isn't answering her phone either. You can't tell me that doesn't sound bizarre to you. "

"There have been plenty of times Damon hasn't answered my calls. We don't know what he could be doing. Sometimes people are too busy to get to their phones"

"Umph," Germani replied.

"What's that suppose to mean?"

"Look, we can't just be standing here . . . we need to do something quick." Germani flayed her arms in panic.

"Come on," I said as I took the trek around the house that I had seen Germani come from. I headed to the patio near a Koi pond with my wife on my heels. I stepped into the floor-to-ceiling glassed in sunroom and instantly felt chilled. The air had to be on full blast. "You know this is invasion of privacy, right?" I told Germani as we moved from the sunroom through their kitchen.

I turned on lights in each room I went through. If Damon was home, I hoped he had a sense of humor about the intrusion. He wasn't big on uninvited company.

Germani nodded as she linked her arm with mine in the darkened area. "It's the risk we have to take. Believe me, if you had heard her talking, you would understand why I'm here. Scott, I got a really bad feeling about all this."

She shuddered and I didn't know if it was from the cold or fear.

"Maybe they're sleeping," I said to Germani as I noticed a set of car keys on an accent table. "Anybody home?" I called out as we entered the lit hall entry.

"Cherish can't be sleep that quick. I just got off the phone with her less than an hour ago."

It was obvious that no one was in the downstairs area. I strained my eyes and could hear vague rhythmic thumping from above my head. The sound was so obscure that I had to strain to hear it; almost like music was playing, but I couldn't be positive.

"Do you hear that sound?" I asked Germani as she picked up the keys off the table.

She nodded her head with a deep scowl. "Uh-huh." Germani examined the set. "Aren't these Damon's?"

In the palm of her hand lay a wired ring with a miniature

VIP access card, his Lexus keyless entry button, a baby blue Charlotte Panther's emblem and eight keys.

"Yep." I was starting to feel that Cherish's panic had some merit. I turned on the hall light that led to the second floor and bounced up the stairs two steps at a time.

I went directly to Damon and Cherish's bedroom and what I saw made me stop dead in my tracks.

Both of them were in bed under a sheet covered in blood. Even from the dim light shining from the hallway I could see the circular smears across Damon's upper torso.

I don't know what made me think I could revive him. I guess natural response, instinct. Who knew, but I rushed over to his body and pressed my hand to the ooze of a gapping hole right below his sternum.

Germani let out a high-pitched scream as she remained in the doorway. She inhaled sharply and screamed again. Her entire body shook like she was convulsing.

With my hand pressed to Damon's chest, I searched the room for something I could use to stop the flow of blood.

When I was barely out of high school I wanted to be a paramedic. Thought that would be the coolest job without having to endure years of college courses with completion in eighteen months. I took CPR courses in the Adult Education program at the community college. When I discovered that I would be required to complete Advance Biology and Chemistry classes, I dropped the EMT program. Regardless, there were some things I still remembered.

It was too dark in the room for me to see clearly.

"Turn the light on," I told a hysterical Germani.

Her screams ceased. She slowly shook her head as though the rest of her body was paralyzed.

I reached up with my free hand to check for a pulse. I thought I felt a faint, slow vibration against my fingers, although his body was growing cold. Probably from the freezing central air.

I let out a small sigh of relief as I looked over at Germani again. "Call an ambulance. I think he's still alive," I requested, scared to move my hand from his wound.

She still wouldn't budge.

I hollered with pained frustration, "Dang it, Germani, snap out of it and help me. Get the telephone."

She jolted from her trance and began shifting her feet. "Okay . . . okay. Where's the phone?"

"Downstairs, I think." Damon didn't keep one in the room for his own personal reasons. He said the last place he wanted to be disturbed was when he was in bed.

Germani left the room and I could hear her running down the stairs.

I also heard a gurgled groan over the music playing from the other side of the bed.

"Cherish, everything's going to be okay. An ambulance will be here very soon," I said.

She mumbled something.

I leaned over Damon to listen.

I could only understand one word. "Bad."

I didn't know what else to say, so I simply replied, "Everything is going to be fine. Just hold on, everything is going to be fine."

Germani ran back into the room. "I called 911 dispatch. Help is on the way. They said an ambulance should be here in less than ten minutes."

"Good. Cherish was just talking. Can you see how bad her injuries are?"

Germani walked over to Cherish's side of the bed, then paused as I stared at the blood soaked sheet.

"I can't touch that sheet, Scott. I think we should wait for the paramedics."

"All I need you to do is see where her wounds are and how bad."

Germani frowned and shook her head again. "I'm not comfortable doing that. Cherish told me she has AIDS."

I snapped my head up and looked straight into Germani's eyes. "What?"

"AIDS. She said she has AIDS." Germani spoke slowly, accentuating each word.

I recoiled at the thought and almost removed my already red hand from the wound site, not knowing if he had the deadly virus as well.

"Did she say whether Damon had it too?"

"No. No, she didn't."

I tried to think of things I should do next and couldn't. I shifted the weight on my legs as I stayed bent down. My knee crackled. This was the worst night of my life.

I finally said, "Germani, go downstairs and wait for the paramedics to get here. The front door is still locked."

After she left the room for the second time, I checked Damon's pulse again. I didn't feel a vibration except from the slight trembling of my hand. I convinced myself that it didn't mean anything. I prayed that the paramedics would hurry up. I prayed harder than I had in my whole life that God would spare Damon and Cherish's lives.

CHAPTER
THIRTY-ONE
GERMANI

Damon Spears was pronounced dead at 12:14 A.M. after arrival at Carolinas Medical Center.

Scott seemed to become numb from the news.

The police hadn't allowed us to follow as gurneys were lifted into an ambulance and sped away from their house. We answered questions about what little we knew. I was hysterical. My words jumbled together like a wrinkled cassette in a tape player. Scott spoke for me, repeating things I had told him when we first arrived. He said I called Cherish crazy, but I couldn't remember what I told him. There had been blood . . . so much blood that I would be seeing red for the rest of my life.

It didn't help that the police thought that it was supposed to be the makings of a murder-suicide. They had suspicion that Cherish was the one who stabbed Damon. She didn't have any visible wounds and they bagged a wood carving knife under the bed. My sense of understanding was pillaged under layers of disbelief and guilt. I should have been able to talk her out of it.

Scott walked away from the attending physician, Dr. Ellison, and collapsed in a cushioned chair. A look of disbelief covered his face. I stood with the doctor as he explained the extent of Damon's injury.

His tricuspid valve was severely punctured. He bled out before the ambulance made it to the scene. There was no way they could have saved him.

Dr. Ellison looked as worn as I felt. His eyes had poofy bags under them as if he'd worked too many shifts without sleep.

"I believe Mrs. Spears is going to be okay. The medical team pumped out the contents of her stomach and they're working on stabilizing her vitals," he said. Dr. Ellison adjusted the face mask hanging from his neck. "I assure you that she is in the best care North Carolina has to offer. We don't know how long ago she ingested whatever she took. We still have to run labs to see what kind of drugs are in her system, so I can't honestly tell you how much damage was done."

I rubbed my forehead. My temples throbbed and exhaustion had me nearly dead on my feet. Things were going from bad to worse.

"I'm going to try and stick around for a while to see how she's doing. I'll be sitting right over there if anything changes." I pointed to the row of chairs by Scott. I had placed my purse in the seat next to him. The waiting room was full of people. Death, sickness and injury surrounded us.

After Dr. Ellison went back through the double doors, I sauntered over to Scott. His elbows rested on his knees, while stretched hands connected against the back of his bent head.

"You want some coffee?" I asked him.

He looked up and I felt like his gaze went straight through me. His expression was blank. I turned to see if maybe he was staring at something behind me, but besides a few people walking across the floor, I didn't see anything.

"Scott," I said with concern.

My husband blinked twice before his gaze met my eyes.

"Coffee?"

"No. I'm tired and ready to go home." He abruptly stood and stretched.

"They're still working on Cherish. I was planning to stay until I found out how she was doing."

Scott's face frowned up. "For what? She's a murderer. She killed my best friend. Why do we need to know how she's doing? If she's alive, she is already doing a whole lot better than Damon. We wouldn't even be in a hospital if it wasn't for Cherish being jacked up in the head."

He was snapping at me. I wasn't used to him snapping at me. I stepped back a few steps. It wasn't appropriate for us to have this discussion in the hospital waiting room, but I was the one that Cherish had confided in. I felt I had to rally in her defense.

"Do you have any idea what she was going through?"

"Whatever she was going through didn't justify her taking Damon's life."

"Damon wasn't blemish free. Cherish was tortured by her life with him. I couldn't believe some of the things she told me. They were going to sex parties and having orgies with doctors that Damon sold prescription samples to. And it gets worse. Even though she had AIDS, Damon didn't want her to tell anybody." I spoke quietly but there were still a few people nearby tuned in to our conversation. One woman who sat next to a pale sickly man in a wheelchair covered her little boy's ears. We walked over by a water cooler, out of earshot of the general public.

"He was putting all kinds of people at risk unnecessarily," I whispered.

Scott threw up his hand like he wasn't hearing me. "Nah, you don't know if that's true. That is just her version of what happened. Damon didn't have her doing nothing she didn't want to do. It wasn't like he was controlling her or something. They have been doing that swingers' thing for years."

"You knew?" I questioned Scott as my eyebrows raised. Truth

was a reflection of itself, and at that moment, I saw it as an ugly devouring beast. I saw my husband in much the same way. Mirror images. "Of course, you knew."

Scott ignored my statement. Automatically made me wonder what else he knew that I didn't. True enough, couples had secrets. Nobody told their partner everything, but it was the big secrets that could destroy a relationship, annihilate a marriage.

"Now you can stay if that would make you feel better, but I don't have a whole lot of sympathy for Cherish right now." There was acid in his voice. Scott began walking toward the glass doors with the exit sign.

I stood for a moment thinking, *What if I did stay, how would I get home?* My car was still parked in the driveway at Cherish's house. Right along with the purse I left in the front seat. In such a rush to get to the hospital, I didn't think I would need my car or my purse. They were blocked in by a fire truck, ambulance and two police cars when we left the scene. Even thinking 'scene' made me cringe. Death wasn't supposed to be so close. I could smell it lingering in my nose hairs.

I knew Scott had to be grieving. His best friend was gone . . . dead. The anger wasn't meant to be directed at me. I shouldn't take it personal.

As I watched his infuriated steps stomp from the building, I felt disjointed. Somehow, during tragedy, when Scott and I should have been closest, there seemed to be an evolving wedge. He was walking away and I was standing still. How much worse could things get between us?

CHAPTER THIRTY-TWO

SCOTT

If you don't respect where you came from, then you won't appreciate where you're going. Those were the words I would say to Damon when he complained about his momma, but he wasn't even remotely receptive. He resented being raised poor and was obsessed with having more than he was raised with. He constantly complained that his mother never stayed at one decent job. Her main income came from hustling. Ms. Ilene taught them to survive, but not to succeed. Ironically, he hated Ilene for being a hustler, yet he used those very skills she taught him to get paid as a sales rep. Wasn't much difference between a sales representative and a hustler. Both had to perfect the game of persuasion.

The brick ranch-style house in Hidden Valley was nondescript except for the row of cars parked down the street in front of it. The inside of the house was also full. There was a card game going on. Three men and Ms. Ilene were playing spades with money on the square glass table. A group stood around watching. Nay-Nay, Damon's older sister, was the one that led me through the maze of people. She looked almost exactly like Ms. Ilene, except she was about one hundred and fifty pounds bigger, with a raspy voice. Her eyes were half closed and she swayed when she walked. When we were kids, she used to follow me around, getting on my nerves. On that night, her gift for gab seemed to be locked away.

Ms. Ilene was addressing the other players of the game. A hill of dollars lay on the table.

"Ma, Scott came through and he wants to talk to you," Nay-Nay said before turning her attention to one of the card game on-lookers, holding a joint. She removed it from his hand and took a draw.

"Hamhock." Ms. Ilene looked up and smiled as she shuffled the deck of cards. "What a surprise. You came through to see me. Get comfortable and enjoy yourself. There's all kinds of liquor in the kitchen if you want a drink," she said to me.

I watched her flick cards around the table; one . . . two . . . three . . . back to herself and then around again.

Ms. Ilene trashtalked while she finished dealing out the deck. "Me and my partner ain't moving from this table. Y'all have sat down with the wrong ones. We about to send you home broke and disgusted. You might as well call yourself De La Hoya. In fact, if you want to just hand over the money and get up with your pride intact, I won't be mad at you."

I couldn't deliver the kind of news I had in that room full of strangers. I had hoped my solemn expression and unannounced visit would be warning that I had something bad to say, but she was too involved in her game and Nay-Nay was too high to care.

I walked over to her side of the table. "Ms. Ilene, can I talk with you alone for a moment? It's about Damon."

"Baby, I just sat down to play this game. Ain't no pausing in Spades. Speak your mind. I'm listening." Ms. Ilene had her set of cards fanned in front of her as she counted the three high clubs and two hearts. Her set was mostly black. I knew enough about the game to realize that she had a good hand.

"We got six. How many you bidding?" asked a chunky, dark-skinned man to her right.

Ms. Ilene looked at the man across from her. "Howel, I can pull six by myself. What you working with?"

I recognized Howel from the house I had dropped Ms. Ilene off at. He shook his head. "My hand is kinda ugly. I can pull out one for sure and maybe even two."

"Put us down for eight. Somebody about to bump heads," she said confidently.

I bent down close to her head. "This is important. I don't think you want to hear it like this."

Ace of diamond went on the center of the table, followed by a three of club and a five.

"Is he dead?" she asked bluntly.

It felt like the whole room shifted their eyes to me.

"Yes," I hissed through my teeth like I was in pain. And in a way, I was.

"Okay." She dropped a two of spades on top of the others and pulled the stack toward her. "Guess we got to plan a funeral."

I didn't expect the response I got from Ms. Ilene. I waited for it to sink in, but she kept playing the game like I hadn't said a thing. All I could figure was that she must be numb. Ms. Ilene wasn't the type to be cold over her children. Shoot, I was numb when I first heard. I had just talked to my best friend this morning. We laughed about our crazy schedules and how we didn't hang out like we used to before we got married. In less than twelve hours, he had been taken from this world. I couldn't figure it out. What could have happened at Cherish and Damon's house to make her snap so unexpectedly?

We left the hospital before we learned any more about Cherish and her condition. Germani was mad at me, but I didn't care. I dropped her off before I came to Ms. Ilene's place. She kept defending Cherish and talking about how depressed the girl had been lately. I was about ready to go off, so I felt it was in both of our best interests if I took her home. Damon was dead; my boy was gone. That knowledge diminished any level of good feelings I could have had about Cherish.

Ms. Ilene thumped out a cigarette from a Virginia Slim pack in her lap. "Nay-Nay, hand me your lighter."

Nay-Nay took one from her pocket and slid it across the table.

Ms. Ilene lit her cigarette. After taking a long draw, she blew cigarette smoke in the air from the side of her mouth and said, "I have a friend, Flossie, that works at Phillip Morris. They'll be closing down that plant over in Concord, and Flossie's thinking about moving to Richmond with them. She only has four years to retire. Might as well get her due. Anyway, Phillip Morris makes Virginia Slim. Flossie brought me a carton last Tuesday, I believe, and since they was free, I didn't turn it down, but I still prefer my Newport 100s."

"So, he's dead. You know he had no love for us," Nay-Nay said as she leaned one arm on the back of Howel's chair. I guess that part of the conversation was finally registering through her marijuana fog. "He didn't even act like we existed, why should we act he did?" Even with her eyes half closed, I could see the contempt in them.

She used to adore her big brother. When we were about eleven, Nay-Nay was five years old and the baby girl in the family. She had this pumpkin patch doll she took everywhere with her. She used to strap the stringy-haired doll to the pink bucket on the front of her bicycle and ride behind us. If she saw us leaving the house, she ran to get on her bike and follow us. Usually, Damon and I were going to the corner store to get candy and chips, or we would go to the elementary school up the street to play basketball. Without fail, Nay-Nay was on our trail. She was the only one. Ke-Ke and Mario had their own friends to play with and wasn't thinking about us. Brandon was still a baby, so he wasn't leaving the house anyway.

Damon used to turn her bike back toward the house and tell her to mind her business. She would turn the bike back around, then pedal up to us like we were in a clique. If Damon yelled at her, she'd run inside to tell Ms. Ilene, then we would get cursed out and were forced to baby-sit Nay-Nay. I'd bribe her to leave with a bag of red hot potato chips and some Boston Baked Beans. I knew that would get her to leave us alone the majority of times. Things sure had changed over the years.

Nay-Nay had passed the joint to a female with a bright orange waterfall-looking weave ponytail. The woman was light brown, but had blackheads all over her face. She stared at me with a buck toothed smile.

Nay-Nay was waiting for a response.

I kept a blank face, like I was playing poker. I didn't know none of them people staring at me and I wasn't going to put Damon's business out there.

When I didn't say anything, Nay-Nay lifted a beer bottle of Old English by its neck. She took a swig.

"Nay-Nay, come take over my hand." Ms. Ilene waved her daughter over to that side of the table.

Ms. Ilene took me to one of the rooms at the back of the house. It was packed with boxes, but I guess that was the only quiet place.

"What happened to my son?" Her attitude had softened.

"He was stabbed to death . . . murdered by his wife. I guess it was supposed to be a murder-suicide. At least, that's what the police think happened. Germani and I found their bodies. Cherish tried to kill herself with some pills."

Ms. Ilene puffed hard on that cigarette as she nodded her head. "I assume that we will be the ones to get his things together. Do you think he had an insurance policy to cover some of his expenses? I know I have a small one, about five thousand to help in the funeral costs, but we need to go through his things and see what all can be taken care of."

"You don't want to see the body and say goodbye?" That seemed like the first thing a mother would want to do.

"No. I want to remember him in the living. If you say he's dead, then I have no reason not to trust the truth of that and do what is necessary to provide a proper burial."

I sat against an old washer that was placed in the corner, and tried to absorb the reality of my friend's death.

Ms. Ilene took a long drag from her cigarette. Her hands slightly shook. "You know, Scott, I'm not sure how I'm supposed to feel about Damon being dead. When I lost Brandon I was devastated. He was my baby boy. My pride and joy. Damon had so much hatred in his heart for me, for his sisters and Devon, and for the hood. For everything he came from. I've been waiting for his heart to soften up, for him to make amends with his family, and now, that will never happen. And to think his last memory of us was that one of his family stole prescription drugs from him. I may not have always done right by my kids, but I didn't raise thieves. To know that he thought so little of us . . . I don't know how I'm supposed to feel."

Ms. Ilene was a strong woman, but I could hear the pain in her voice.

This was another reason for me to be pissed off at Cherish. While we were at Damon's house being questioned by the police, Germani told the officers that Cherish had been stealing samples from Damon's briefcase. She believed Cherish took some drugs before calling her.

"Cherish told my wife that she was the one stealing from Damon. She was supposedly doped up when she killed him. She's probably been doing it for years."

That cigarette halted two inches from Ms. Ilene's her mouth. Her face frowned up. "You mean to tell me that Damon's wife was the reason he kicked us to the curb?"

"Yes, ma'am."

She cursed under her breath. "I should have known. I should have known that, but I thought Damon was looking for an excuse not to be around. That his nose was too far up in the air. Kay-Kay didn't like that girl from the first time we met her. She was too quiet . . . devious. Soaking in everything we said and did, so she could use it to her benefit. And he thought we were the messed up ones. Ain't that nothing. You say she's in the hospital right now?" Ms. Ilene resumed her smoking as she looked at me. Her numbness changed to anger.

"Yes, ma'am."

"Okay." She paused. "Okay."

Her anger trumped mine.

She took one last puff before extinguishing the cigarette on the washing machine behind me. Ms. Ilene tossed the cigarette into a metal garbage can.

I didn't know what Ms. Ilene planned to do about Cherish, but I hoped I didn't become a part of another crime.

CHAPTER
THIRTY-THREE

GERMANI

I burned all of Scott's clothes that he wore that night. Set aflame everything down to his socks and Hanes briefs. After putting on a pair of industrial use rubber cleaning gloves, I took that heap he left on the bedroom floor, tossed it in a black garbage bag and dropped the bag on the barbecue grill in the back of the house, then lit a match.

It wasn't that I was an AIDS-phobic, but if something was hazardous and contagious, then I didn't want it openly displayed in my house, on my floor, near my bed. It was enough going on that I didn't need the added discomfort. The smell of his blood-soaked garments made me nauseous. It was so bad that I put rubbing alcohol on a makeup sponge and crammed it up my nasal passage, trying to get some relief.

Scott had long left to go talk with Damon's mother. He refused to take me back over to the house so I could get my car. I hadn't wanted to go back either, but I needed my vehicle and I wanted my purse. The entire trip home, he drove with his gaze set on the road and his eyebrows furrowed. Every word I spoke seemed to be rapidly dismissed with a *"Not now"* and tense silence. I might as well have been talking to myself. By the time we made it home, I was done saying anything to him. When he came out of the shower and changed clothes, he finally acknowledged my existence. Told me that he needed to inform Damon's family of what was going on. He didn't ask if I wanted to go, and from his foul mood, I didn't offer. What I did do was try to give him a hug, show him some love in the midst of his loss, but he said those words again, *Not now*. I was offended and felt abandoned. He brushed past me, knocking my shoulder with his. I could feel the grief and pain in his shove.

I gathered his soiled clothing and had a bonfire. Smoke circled the calm air as I sat in a lawn chair, watching the flames. The smell of melting plastic was repulsive, but it was a world better than the aroma of death.

The neighbor's dog two doors down, whimpered. I could hear him rattle against the small box cage like he wanted to be free. Ms. Maverick kept her German Shepherd, Warner, on a leash in that cage every night. I usually ignored the sounds, but a few other people had called the Home Owners Association on Ms. Maverick for not keeping Warner quiet.

Her son, Lucas, bought the dog as house protection, but she obvious didn't want a pet in her home. She was the epitome of old with a short silvery mane, frail limbs, wrinkled skin and a humped back. I had once heard them arguing outside about Lucas thinking she needed to go live in a nursing home where people could take care of her. Ms. Maverick told him that he just wanted to get rid of her and she wasn't going to no place that mistreated the elderly for profit. I rarely saw Ms. Maverick except when she answered the door for Meals on Wheels. Once in a while, Lucas would pass me while walking Warner as I strolled Elijah around the neighborhood. Didn't know much about him or Ms. Maverick. The houses in my neighborhood were close enough for me to learn vague information about my neighbors, but what do we really know about the people living next to us?

As black smoke took over the sky in my yard, I decided to contact Autumn. I needed to go get my car. Her house was twenty minutes away. I thought about calling Mekhi, but Momma lived too far away for me to wake him up and to come across town in the middle of the night. He would do it, but Scott would probably be back before Mekhi made it to my house and I was already antsy about my car still being at a crime scene.

Autumn sounded like she had been wide awake. Surprisingly, her voice was alert, "What's wrong?"

It was dang near three in the morning. Only people in crisis called their friends at that hour.

"Something bad has happened." I instantly felt déjà vu, by using Cherish's words when she had called me. "You will never believe my night. It is unbelievable. Do you remember Scott's friend that I'm always talking about?"

"Yeah, Damon. The friend you said Scott should hurry up and get rid of."

I winced. "Yeah, him."

Considering the circumstances, my previous comments about the man sounded kinda of disgraceful. Almost like I was heartless, which was the furthest thing from the truth. I didn't want Damon around, but I also hadn't wished ill upon him.

"Damon's dead. His wife is in the hospital. Autumn, they think she did it and Scott left to go tell Damon's mom."

"Back it up. Come again."

I knew it sounded bizarre, probably like some episode from *Snapped* on the Oxygen channel. People we knew weren't supposed to be involved in murders. That kind of stuff happened to other people.

The events of the night destroyed any peaceful thought I could have. I felt the hairs on my arms stand up like it was freezing outside, but the warm breeze, plus the heat from the barbecue grill touching my skin said different.

"Dead. Damon is dead." I paused, lifting my eyes to the sky.

"Supposedly, Cherish stabbed him to death. And that wasn't the worst of it. She called me earlier tonight. I knew something was wrong. I just didn't say the right thing . . . do the right thing. She hung up on me because she was trying to confide in me and I made her feel like I was judging her. And maybe I was. I hadn't exactly been treating her with kindness. Anyway, she told me that her and Damon were doing those swinger parties. You know what I'm talking about, right?"

"Yeah, orgies."

"Well, now she has AIDS. I think she took finding out pretty hard, but then Damon had her keeping it a secret, while they continued to have unprotected sex with other people. I think all that combined was more than she could handle."

Autumn replied, "I bet it was. It goes back to what I was telling you at the nail salon. If you keep sacrificing for the wrong people and wrong purpose, eventually, you will have nothing good left for yourself. It is awful that such a tragedy happened though. How did you get the news?"

"Scott and I were the ones that found them."

The fire had smoldered down to blackened ashes. Light ambers peeked from the bottom of the grill.

I stood up and took the lawn chair to the garage.

Autumn hummed into the phone, "Um . . . um . . . um, the devil is busy."

"Yes, he is. I can't even explain to you how messed up I am by all of this. But right now, I don't even want to talk about this anymore. I can't. I called you because I need to go get my car. It's still parked over in their driveway."

"Give me a few minutes to throw some clothes on and I will be right there."

"I'll be waiting."

I was so used to being the one to rescue Mekhi during his multiple dilemmas that I never imagined that I would be the one in crisis.

Fear was riding my back. Cherish had placed Damon on a

gold encrusted pedestal. Idolized him like he was God, but man could never replace Him. I feared for Cherish because the consequences of her choice were devastating whether she lived or died. If she lived she would have to face criminal charges and the guilt of knowing she killed her husband. And if she died, her soul may be damned. I only hoped God wouldn't punish her eternally when she was already living on earth in torment.

As I sat by the front door and waited for Autumn, an old song recorded by Fred Hammond came to mind. I sang part of the verse to "I Will Find A Way" to comfort myself and apologize to God for my own bad decisions.

"And though my life is broken I'll find a way to give you praise."

Thoughts of me and Scott, growing farther apart, scared me. I couldn't fault Cherish. I was out of order myself for some of the decisions I made to keep Scott happy. I had placed Scott above God and saw the result. I didn't know if I could handle a marriage with a man acting unsaved. Or his trying to get me to straddle the fence with him. Knowing that the company he kept was a reflection of him only made our relationship seem doomed. I couldn't sacrifice my sanity or soul the way Cherish had for Damon. The cost was too great.

CHAPTER THIRTY-FOUR

SCOTT

Exactly two weeks after Damon's funeral I watched porn at work.

I had been stretched so thin that I couldn't see straight. My nerves were shot from the stress of it all. Men weren't allowed to grieve. We were supposed to stand like solid rocks through any and all crises, but even mountains crumble when too much weight wears them down.

Cherish had fallen into a coma after Germani and I left the hospital that night. I think because Cherish lived, Ms. Ilene was on a war path. It started with the planning of a family gathering after the wake service. Ms. Ilene wanted it held at Damon's home—the same house he died in. She and my Uncle Gabe, her ex-boyfriend, got into a heated argument at the wake service. He told her she was trying to turn the family gathering into a spectator sport.

I was the one with Damon's house keys. Ms. Ilene knew I had the keys and although I refused to give them to her, the family gathering ended up being held at Damon's place to squash the drama. The very next day, Damon's family was trying to move some of his things out of the house he shared with

Cherish. Ms. Ilene said that she wanted items to honor his memory. For all I know, they could have grabbed some stuff during the family gathering. I suggested that they wait and get legal advice because Cherish had ownership of the home. Ms. Ilene had me call a lawyer to see what rights she had. I became her middle man when dealing with the legalities. I didn't want any part of it, but felt obligated.

On top of that, Germani had been constantly making little comments about the lifestyle of sinners and how she needed to get better in her Christian walk. Damon's death made mortality more real to her. She even kept a Bible on the nightstand and made reference to certain verses whenever we were in the bedroom together. She talked in general statements about people needing more intimacy with Christ and how they were missing an opportunity to get their lives in order; like I really wanted to hear that after I lost my best friend. And to make matters worse, we still weren't having sex. I wanted to feel her close to me. I needed some kind of physical connection with my wife. She was too busy standing by her asinine convictions.

It was easy to access porn sites from the back room at Car Care. As manager, I made up excuses to retreat to my office in the back room for an hour or two at a time. That first time was a Wednesday. I had Sara take over my register, because I wanted to go online and make price comparisons of some products for an upcoming sales promotion. After I got the information I needed, the temptation to peek at other things overwhelmed me. I convinced myself that I wasn't harming anything by getting a quick viewing. I stayed on for less than ten minutes. I felt guilty and knew it was wrong, but the temporary release became my 'high.' It wasn't enough to just watch porn at home after Germani went to sleep. My actions on my work computer became bolder as I increased my viewing time to twenty-minute increments a few times throughout the day. I realized I needed to be a little more careful.

It had been a slow night, so I sent Sara home two hours early. There was a new employee, Antonio, who replaced Torrance, scheduled to close with me. Antonio had worked a few years at an auto dealership as a technician before three of his fingers got mangled in a motorcycle accident. Left him with a pinkie and thumb on one hand. The auto dealership let him go because he could no longer do the job. He had been on my staff for about eight days, but had enough knowledge that I felt I could leave him unattended for a little while.

I made up a quick lie to have to go to the back once Sara walked out of the building. "Hey, Antonio, I need to call this manufacturer for some parts we have on back order. Think you can handle the front for a few minutes?"

"Sure thing," Antonio responded as he handed change back to a customer for their purchase.

I anxiously headed to the back room. I knew exactly which site I wanted to go to. After shutting the office door, I quickly clicked into the one that had longer free viewing time.

I felt something telling me to stop, but I didn't listen. Instead, I glanced up at the closed door as the video began playing on the screen. Told myself not to worry. I had everything under control. Before long, I was completely engrossed in my computer fantasy. Thoughts about my wife, about Damon's death and about anything that caused me stress, vanished.

I turned up the volume on my speakers slightly.

Got lost in the feeling.

Until . . .

"Scott, we have a problem," Antonio explained with a frown protruding from his brow as he stood right in front of the desk.

I nearly jumped out of my skin when I realized he was standing there.

I quickly clicked off the porn page, heart beating fast, thumped against my ribcage like an Amtrak train en route to Texas.

Maybe Antonio didn't hear the noises coming from my computer. I hoped he didn't. I could lose my job if he told headquarters that I was watching porn on the clock.

I tried to act oblivious to what I'd just been doing. "Wha . . . What's wrong?" I stuttered.

"Guy out here needs a diagnostic test and the code won't clear on our machine. I was wondering if you could reset it." Antonio was still frowning at me.

I bet he knew.

I glance at the cleared computer screen, pushed myself up from the desk and walked alongside him to go help out.

If he didn't mention seeing anything, I sure wasn't.

Fear had me in a vice grip. I needed to stop watching porn at work. I needed to stop right away.

CHAPTER THIRTY-FIVE

GERMANI

Two cops stood outside my door.

"Are you Germani Wilson?" the one in a short black winter jacket, asked from outside my screen door. He had a serious scowl. One of his hands was tucked in a coat pocket. Next to him, stood another cop with a gray overcoat. Short black guy with a bald fade. He was close to my height, maybe an inch taller.

"Yes, that's me. How may I help you?" I answered.

He pulled out a CMPD badge and flashed it quickly. "My name is Detective Hart and this is Detective Brooks. We're with the Charlotte-Mecklenburg investigation division. May I come in?"

I looked behind him at the police car sitting in my driveway. "What's this about?"

"I have a few questions regarding a homicide investigation that you and your husband were listed as witnesses to. We need to verify details from the incident." He saw me frown up as I held the screen door fastened. Him on one side of the glass with me on the other, hesitant to let him in.

I truly couldn't remember what I told them to fabricate a

story. Damon had been buried for three weeks. Cherish had awaken out of her coma only a couple days ago. I'm sure they'd spoken with her by now and wondered if Cherish had anything to do with them being at my house.

The wind whisked by, shifting the strands of his short ash blond hair. It was bone chilling cold out. Barely eight o'clock. I could feel the raw early morning chill touch my feet from beneath the metal screen.

"It will only be a minute, ma'am." I saw what I took to be a slight annoyance as Detective Hart put the badge back in his coat pocket.

I opened the door and escorted them to the living room. "My husband is upstairs. I hope you don't mind standing here for a moment while I go get him."

They nodded their heads.

I rushed up the few stairs and checked on Elijah who was playing in his room with an electric train set. I then went into our bedroom where Scott was still in bed. He hadn't gotten into bed until three this morning. I had felt the bed dip when he got in. Always knew when he was coming to bed after watching his porn. The computer got far more action from my husband than I did. Our intimacy had been reduced to pecks of kisses every now and then. The fire that used to burn between us was extinguished months ago.

I gently nudged him. Had to poke Scott three times before his eyes would open.

I put my face close to his. "There are two detectives downstairs that want to talk to us."

"Huh . . . for what?" he asked, slowly lifting his body to a sitting position.

"Something about the case with Cherish and Damon. I really don't know yet. I came to get you. They are downstairs waiting."

He slid out of bed, threw on a pair of jeans over his boxers and walked back down with me.

"Morning. How may we help you?" Scott asked as we met them in our living room.

I felt like we were being impolite. "Please have a seat," I said, pointing at both the couch and loveseat.

Scott was prone where the hall meets the living room, with arms folded.

"If you don't mind," said the short cop.

"No, not at all. I'm just curious about what would bring you out here on a Saturday morning." Scott came by the couch, but wouldn't sit down.

"We are here to discuss your statements made on October 11, 2007, regarding the subsequent death of Damon L. Spears," said Detective Hart.

Scott scratched his nose before folding his arms again. "Okay . . . and?"

Detective Hart pulled out a small yellow pad from an inner pocket. He leafed through scattered notes.

"From what it says here, when you got to the house on Pemswood Street, the front door was locked and you went through a patio door to gain access. Is that correct, Mr. Wilson?"

"Yes," Scott replied.

"It also says that you and Mr. Spears were best friends."

Scott nodded his head.

"Can you remember seeing anything unusual or out of place while you were there?"

"My best friend was laying in a puddle of his own blood next to the woman who murdered him. Everything about that night was unusual."

The detective ignored Scott's hostility. "What about you, Ms. Wilson? Did you see anything unusual besides the murder scene in itself, at any point after you entered the home?"

"I'm not sure what you mean, Detective Hart, but I hadn't been in their house enough to notice that something would be out of the ordinary," I cautiously explained with measured words, confused by the range of questioning.

"Do you know why Cherish Spears would have had reason to murder her husband?" Detective Brooks asked as the other detective jotted down more notes. His voice had bass, a tone I didn't expect from his size."

"No," Scott said quickly.

At the same time I said, "Yes."

I gave Scott a puzzled look. Didn't understand why he was acting defensive. He made it seem like we had something to hide.

"Ms. Wilson?" All eyes were on me.

"They were having problems," I stated. I didn't know what I should or shouldn't say. I was worried that they would think we had something to do with the crime.

Detective Hart asked, "What kind of problems?"

"You know . . . marital troubles. Same as anyone else, I suppose." I was starting to feel nervous, interrogated. I didn't mention the swingers parties. Thought it might place Cherish in prison for a longer period of time. Courts wouldn't have mercy on her due to her lifestyle.

"On the night in question you told the police that Mrs. Spears called you and you rushed over because you thought something might be wrong. That she was crazy."

Did I say that? I couldn't remember saying that. "I don't recall saying that about Cherish. Everything was crazy. The whole night was crazy."

"How about a Dell computer? Did either of you have access to the computer in the Spears' home? Or do you know of someone with access?"

"No and no," Scott responded.

I shook my head, biting the inside of my cheek.

Scott sat on the armrest next to me. "You already have your suspect. What's with all the questions?"

"There has been new evidence surrounding the case that we need to check into. Do the names Omar Jennings, Sophie

Duran, Jackson Parker or Martin Scalli mean anything to you."

Once again, Scott was abrupt in his answer. "No. Why? Are they suppose to be familiar to us?"

Scott should have recognized some of those names. We met Sophie and Omar at the stem-cell fundraiser.

Even if he didn't remember, I wasn't going to sit there and lie. "I know Dr. Jennings from a fundraiser we attended with Cherish and Damon. Dr. Jennings became my contact for hiring we do at the employment agency where I work. My knowledge of him is based purely on a professional level."

"And the others?"

"I also met Sophie Duran once at the same fundraiser, but I haven't had contact with her outside of the one introduction."

Scott stood back up. "Once again I ask, what's with all the questions?"

"For the last week or so, there has been a video circulating the Internet with the four people I named. It was a very explicit video of them in compromising positions. It was posted on I-Tube from the Spears' home computer on the same night that you found Mr. and Mrs. Spears. There were others in the video, but the four I mentioned are prominent figures in this community."

The story had been on the news. I remember watching the story on the news, but they didn't say names. That part was kept private.

"So, basically, you are here about an I-Tube video, not about Damon's death." Scott's eyebrows furrowed together.

"We're trying to find the link between the video and Mr. Spears' death."

Scott began walking toward the front door. "Well, I think we are done answering questions. You should really go talk to Cherish Spears about all that." He opened the door and stood there.

Detective Brooks and Detective Hart got up from the couch. Brooks pulled a card from his pants pocket. He handed it to me. "If you have any more information to help us with this case, it would be greatly appreciated.

After they left, I said to Scott as he walked upstairs, "Scott, you were rude to those detectives."

He walked into the bathroom. "I wasn't rude; I just didn't want them feeling overly welcome."

"What's going on, Scott? You know something you're not telling me?"

He pulled out his toothbrush and smeared toothpaste on the bristles.

"I know the police don't care about Damon or how he died. I don't need to entertain their questions. And they told on themselves when they mentioned those *prominent figures* of the community put on I-Tube. They're more concerned about some naked rich folks exposed on video rather than Damon getting stabbed in the chest. They wanted us to say Cherish posted the video or Damon did before she killed him, or better yet, they were looking for a confession from us. Ridiculous." Scott put the toothbrush in his mouth.

I rolled my neck. I felt a tension headache coming on. "Even if that is true, we looked suspicious by giving them conflicting answers about what we know. Me saying *yes* and you saying *no*. If I were those detectives, I would be thinking we were hiding something."

Scott looked at me from the corner of his eye while he brushed his teeth.

"What did you know about their swingers lifestyle? I'm sure Damon shared all the sordid details with you. Were you tempted to do the same thing?"

Scott spit into the sink and swished with a Dixie cup of water, before spitting again.

"Just because I respected Damon's right to choose how he

lived, doesn't mean I wanted to be like him. Now, if you will excuse me, I'm going to go get dressed for work."

The only thing playing in my mind were birds of a feather flock together.

I moved to the side and let him pass. He was hiding something; and as God as my witness, I was going to find out what.

CHAPTER THIRTY-SIX

SCOTT

I found Alex's number on a calendar attached to a refrigerator magnet at Beverly's house. As soon as I saw that number, there was no question that I needed to dial those digits. Beverly needed a break, so I offered to stay with Alexis while she went to IMAJ Salon. That singing bird, Fantasia, owned the place and paid for Beverly to pamper herself. Alexis' illness had her stressed out. Her hair was falling out in clumps. She had a bald spot at the top of her head that she was trying to hide, but the comb over wasn't working for her. She was looking like Donald Trump and it was disturbing me.

Germani acted like she didn't trust or believe in me anymore, but both Alexis and Beverly relied on me. Family was supposed to believe in each other. Family was supposed to have one another's backs through thick and thin. If Germani didn't appreciate me, I was glad somebody in my family did.

Alexis and Elijah were in the living room watching *Animal Planet*, while sharing a carton of Cold Stone Creamery's Founder's Favorite ice cream. We had stopped at the creamery's West Mallard Creek Church Road location an hour ago. I checked in on them before I tried to handle that other business. They sat together in an overstuffed recliner. Alexis held onto the red carton while Elijah used a plastic spoon to dig into it.

"You good?" I asked Alexis.

"Uh-huh." She was completely engrossed in the show she was watching.

"*Animal Detective*. They rescue tortured and abandoned animals in New York." She pointed to the television with her free hand. "Some guy was evicted from his apartment and left his guard dog chained to a fence in the courtyard. Look at him; he's starving. People are cruel."

She was looking and feeling better for now.

I needed to know where Alex's head was. Even though Beverly kept insisting that Alex refused to help Alexis and there was no convincing him, I had a hard time believing her. He did go through some tests and he had planned to come previously. He might have needed some male encouragement to actually do what he was supposed to do.

It took a minute for Alex to pick up the phone after I dialed his number, and when he did, it wasn't a kind greeting.

His first words were, "Beverly, I told you to stop calling my house so much. My wife is starting to get upset about this situation."

I had to check myself. My first instinct was to tell Alex a few things about dissing my sister like he did, but I decided against it.

"This isn't Bev. It's Scott." We hadn't spoken in eleven years; not since he skipped town on Beverly.

Still no warm greeting. "How did you get my number? Did Bev tell you to call me? Because if she did, I'm going to tell you the same thing I told her. I'm not risking my life and I don't have any money. Other than those two things, I'm willing to help anyway I can," Alex sputtered those words like I was calling to blackmail him.

"I'm calling for Alexis. You had planned to come to town and donate your bone marrow to help your daughter. Help me understand why you backed . . . decided not to show up. Alexis's condition is dire. She needed that transplant and you are the main one that can make the surgery happen."

"I don't mean to sound disrespectful toward Beverly, but I don't think Alexis is as bad off as Beverly makes it seem."

"You think Bev's lying about Alexis having sickle cell anemia? You both have the trait. There was no getting around Alexis contracting the disease. What are you talking about?"

"I know she has the disease, but I've been talking to some of my friends. I also have family members with sickle cell anemia and they've all been telling me that sickle cell anemia doesn't kill. Some of them get sick on occasion, but not to the point that they require constant hospital care or transplants. None of them believe Alexis is that bad off. And I'm inclined to agree with them."

"Do any of your friends or relatives have a medical degree?"

"Yeah, Garnett is a medical assistant. She has been working at a doctor's office for a couple years now."

All I heard was ignorance. "I'm not talking about medical assisting. I would bet money that none of the people talking to you have an advanced medical degree that they spent eight or more years to get."

"No, but they are living just fine with sickle cell anemia. Don't get me wrong, I want to be there for my daughter, but I can't let Bev over exaggerate to keep contact with me. I can tell she still has feelings for me."

"Alex, you give yourself way too much credit. Beverly isn't into you that hardcore. What she does feel is guilt about putting herself in a situation where she has to ask for your help and it's not looking too good for her to get Alexis well any other way. If you did some research, you would find out that sickle cell anemia doesn't respond the same in everybody. There are some people whose bodies can't handle the disease. Have you even talked to her doctor?"

"I don't need a diagnosis or prognosis from her doctor. For

all I know, Beverly could have that doctor telling me anything. He gets paid more money for each extra test he administers. As a matter of fact, you all should be careful what you believe."

"There has been more than one physician working on Alexis and they all say the same thing. She's in bad shape. Why don't you admit that you don't care what happens to your daughter. It's not like you have a close relationship with her. Call it like it is. You accidentally knocked up her mother and want both of them to stay out of your life."

Alex sputtered some more. "I've already explained to you the same thing I told Beverly. I don't have anything to give Alexis. If you insist on harassing me about her, then I will be forced to change my number and cut off all of you, including Alexis."

If that was the way he talked to Beverly, I didn't know how she put up with him. Alex was going to remain close-minded because he could. If I kept talking to him, I was about to get pissed off.

"I'm done with it. If you believe nothing is wrong with Alexis, then you have it twisted, but you better hope Alexis doesn't lose her life."

"Tell Beverly to stop calling me so much. Alexis can call, but Bev needs to stop."

We both hung up.

Talking to Alex was a waste of my time. Some men shouldn't be allowed to procreate. I was more of a father to Alexis than that imbecile would ever be. Yet, a sense of helplessness for my family fell over me and I couldn't shake it off.

CHAPTER THIRTY-SEVEN

GERMANI

I went to see Cherish after church, right after I left Momma's house. Mom had been upset because Mekhi got himself arrested again, and she asked me for help with bail money. Evidently, Mishelle's new man hit Camry and left marks. Mekhi confronted him about the bruises on Camry's legs and they got to fighting. The police were called and Mekhi was booked on another set of assault charges.

I explained to Momma that I didn't have access to any money on a Sunday. His bail would have to wait until the next business day.

I moved a blue curtain as I entered the hospital room.

They had Cherish's right wrist handcuffed to the bedrail.

It was the first time I'd visited her since it happened; had felt awkward at the thought of making casual conversation with a murderer. But I couldn't avoid the inevitable. She brought me into her drama and I had to deal with it.

I sat in the chair across from her bed. Her hazel eyes were sad, like she regretted the hospital staff had kept her alive. She looked as if she would try to kill herself again, given the chance.

"Surprised to see you here," Cherish said with a chalky voice.

I shrugged. I wasn't going to act like we were best buddies. "The police came to my house asking all kinds of questions about you." I pointed to the handcuffs dangling between her and the railing. "Um . . . you officially been arrested?"

"They came and read me my Miranda rights the day after I woke from the coma." Cherish picked up a foam cup and sipped from a straw.

"Have you seen a Detective Hart or Brooks? Those were the policemen at my house yesterday morning."

"They weren't the ones that arrested me, but I was questioned by Detective Hart on Friday."

"About the video posted on I-Tube?"

"Yeah, I-Tube. I also sent a list of the people we slept with in the Swingers Network. I planned on dying, but wanted the people involved with us to get tested. I wanted somebody to warn them. It was the coward's way out."

"The video sounds malicious, like you had an ax to grind."

"I did . . . with Sophie. She's a nasty, aging hag who filled Damon's head with ideas of grandeur. He ate her advice about getting to the top like lobster on a buffet table. He didn't become pompous until we met her." Cherish held on to her anger.

"She didn't make you kill Damon?"

"No . . . I take full responsibility for that. I lost my mind. I was coaxing him into giving up the lifestyle we'd been living. But then he called me stupid . . . said I needed to get with the program. I heard him degrading me and I snapped. I just snapped. Everything from then on happened so fast. I—" She stopped talking, covered her mouth and closed her eyes.

I felt her remorse. Decisions made in spontaneity.

I reached for Cherish's hand and did the one thing I thought I should have done when I was looking up Bible passages on the night she called me. I had tried to find the right words when the words were already inside me.

"Lord, I come to you on behalf of Cherish, seeking peace for a troubled soul. Through your grace and mercy, I know all things are possible."

I heard Cherish breathing heavy as she whispered, "Yes, Lord, yes."

"You guide us with a tender, but steady hand. You continue to love us in spite of ourselves and the things we do to bring you sorrow. When we are sad, you open your arms and hold us close to you. When no one else understands us, you do, because you knew us first and made us in your image. We delight in your creation. When no one forgives us for our transgressions, you say your grace is sufficient. When we fall prey to the wrong hands, you say come back home anyway. I ask that you show Cherish the mighty, omnipotent Father that I know you to be. Bless her, Lord, during a dark hour. She needs you now more than ever. Amen."

Cherish's eyes watered. "Thank you."

"We all do it at some point . . . allow our outer to influence our inner."

"Yeah, that sounds about right."

She smiled at me. I smiled back. It was the start of a new friendship.

"When are they transporting you?"

"In a few days, I believe. Paperwork needs to be done. My doctor has to verify that I'm well enough physically to be released from the hospital. I'll be in another county, because of the I-Tube publicity. I guess they're worried that good ole Sophie might put a hit out on me."

I felt extremely bad for Cherish. Her situation was all messed up. I had faith that God would intervene on her behalf.

"When your trial is scheduled, I will be there in support of you, and if you need a witness in your defense, I'm willing to testify too."

Cherish took another sip of water. "Javir or rather, Dr. Cavella, you remember him. He has gotten me a good lawyer. I'm hoping to plead out with a decent deal."

"Does he know about your condition?"

"Yes, he knows I have AIDS. He's not holding that against me. He's one of the good guys."

"Did Scott ever participate in the swinger's thing? Did he have any involvement in that lifestyle?" It was a question I desperately needed the answer to but didn't see an appropriate way to ask.

Cherish shook her head. "Never. You have a good husband. Don't put him in the same category as Damon."

I checked my watch. That was becoming a chronic habit. "Well, I'm going to head out of here. You have my address. Drop me a line when you find out your placement."

"Sure. And thanks again for praying with me."

"You never know. One day you may have to return the favor," I said fully believing in that possibility.

CHAPTER
THIRTY-EIGHT

SCOTT

The city put a restriction on all outside water use back in August due to the drought. It was November and we still weren't allowed to wash our cars or water our lawns until the restriction got lifted. Anybody caught with a hose in their hands would get between a $100 and $600 fine. They also encouraged residents to limit inside water consumption as well, but they couldn't enforce whether somebody left water running while they brushed their teeth or took too many showers. Considering the low levels of rainfall, the city was talking about imposing those restrictions with 493 penalties until next spring, or possibly longer, if it didn't rain more.

My grass was turning yellow and becoming crisp. It had grown only about an inch and a half since the last time I cut it. The ground was hard as the fertilized dirt dried too.

I had begun to cut the front yard, but ran over a rock or stick. I heard a noise against the blades before the lawnmower cut off on me. I went to the garage for my tool set, which I placed on the side of me as I loosened several screws and lay the green cover on the grass.

Germani came outside and watched me work on the lawnmower. "I should probably let you know that I went to visit Cherish today."

We had driven separate cars to church this morning. I thought it was because she didn't want to ride with me. Since Damon's death a month ago, any conversation we had was strained. It was strained to the point that we could go days without having a conversation.

After service, she handed me Elijah and told me she needed to go take care of something. That's all she said. I brought Elijah home with me. Didn't think nothing else about it. In fact, I assumed that she was going to see her mother, because Mekhi was arrested again.

I shrugged my shoulders when she mentioned seeing Cherish.

"I told her that I would be in court to support her at trial," Germani continued.

"You told her what?" I strained my ears because I couldn't have heard Germani right.

"I told Cherish that I would testify in her defense if she needed me to. I believe her motives were justified. I'm not saying the deed itself was right, but I could understand how it happened. She was going through pure hell because of Damon. You may not like what I'm saying due to your friendship with him. You were too close to see what he was doing to her."

I dropped the wrench on the ground that I was using to fix the lawnmower. I stayed bent over the rusting propeller. "I guess Cherish has no self-accountability. It doesn't matter that Damon's the one dead. You're gonna make Cherish into the victim." It sounded so stupid I almost laughed in Germani's face.

She crossed her arms as she once again tried to make an irrelevant point. "As I said, I don't justify the action, but I justify the person behind the action. She wanted to please her husband and he wasn't appreciative of her efforts. The more she gave, the more Damon took, until she didn't even have her dignity. He sure didn't have any respect for her. I think she felt trapped."

I placed the top back on the lawnmower. "Whatever. It's bad enough that you're on some sympathy kick for Cherish. But did you ever think she had the ability and choice to leave if she was that miserable? Her feet could have walked her out the door at any time. For all the bad you think about Damon, he wasn't the type to keep a woman tied to him if she didn't want to be there."

I used the wrench to tighten the bolts. "Germani, there's this thing called self-accountability. I don't know if you've ever heard of that, but it's when somebody is responsible for his or her own actions, be they good or bad. If they don't have remorse for wrong actions, then there is this judicial system that will force them to be accountable. While you are sitting on the defense side, I can guarantee I will be behind the prosecution, waiting for them to lock her tail behind bars for the rest of her natural life."

Germani huffed. "Scott, you're not even trying to understand where I'm coming from—"

I cut her off. "No, I'm not. I refuse to understand the insane point you are trying to make. You've been jumping down my throat over those videos I watch, but Cherish can plead crazy for killing a man and you are alright with that, quickly rallying to her defense." I could feel myself getting angry. I could feel my voice escalating.

She had another thought coming if she ever took on the notion that we would see eye to eye about Damon's murder. He might have made some bad decisions, like marrying that unstable girl, but he didn't deserve to die for them.

Germani stood there like she was thinking of something else to say and she couldn't.

I pumped the gas button on the lawnmower a couple of more times, then pulled the string, hoping I could finish cutting my grass.

"Before you come up with some other defense on behalf of Cherish, this conversation needs to end." My voice stayed stern.

Germani finally gave up trying to say whatever and she went back into the house.

I watched the front door close, thinking she had too many double standards going on and I'd had enough of all of them.

CHAPTER THIRTY-NINE

GERMANI

At four in the morning, I checked the clock on the night-stand. My husband still hadn't come home.

I held the yellow pages in my lap. *Hospitals-Hotels* was the heading in the corner of page 605. I anguished over whether I should start from the bottom of that page and work my way up, or at the top on down in search of Scott.

It was while I tortured myself over that decision that he walked into the room as if he had just gotten off work. Scott threw his keys on the nightstand and began to undress. His work shirt hit the floor followed by his pants. Not one word passed from his mouth to acknowledge that I was in the room. As he sat down on his side of the bed I could smell perfume and cigarettes.

Things had become intolerably tense since I told Scott that I would support Cherish at trial. He didn't take my decision well. I didn't want to budge on my principles and he wasn't trying to see things my way.

"Where have you been?" I asked with serious concern as I drummed my fingers against the phone book. He hadn't called to say he would be late or had made plans for after work. He had just left me in a worried daze, wondering if something tragic had happened to him.

Scott didn't respond as he got beneath our thermal blanket and tucked it under his arm at his waist.

I leaned over, pressing my body against the back of his frame. I asked again, "Where have you been?"

The stench of perfume and cigarettes lingered on his skin. I locked my mind from conjuring up assumptions and possibilities while I waited for an explanation from my husband.

When Scott ignored me yet again, the thought of who, where and when, seeped into my mind anyway. Scott and I both knew trust between us was virtually nonexistent. The strain from our differences tightened like piano wire.

"Leave me alone, Germani," he finally declared.

That comment made my head jerk.

"Leave you alone? You come home near dawn and I'm supposed to leave you alone?" I exclaimed incredulously.

Scott kept his back to me, but I heard the rigidness of his tone. "Yeah, that's exactly what you need to do. You need to leave me alone."

Oh, no he didn't.

I sank my teeth in my bottom lip to avoid speaking real nasty and out of turn. I rolled back to my side of the bed and sat straight up. He wasn't going to get the option he thought he had. Not coming into our home smelling like another woman.

The clock on my nightstand read 4:23 A.M. In roughly four more hours, I had a meeting scheduled with Liberty Mutual for a claims division they were opening in the area. With the loss of our biggest contract, Job Track needed all the business we could get. I needed to be sharp for my presentation, but that wasn't going to happen with me functioning on fumes from lack of sleep.

"Scott, you can't honestly think I'm leaving this alone," I said barely above a whisper. I really didn't want an argument.

He still wasn't talking, so I continued. "You need to tell me something, because you can't come in here whenever you feel like it. You're not single and if that's the direction you're gearing your life in, then I think I deserve the right to know that. As your *wife*, I believe you owe me that."

"A *wife* should trust her *husband*." Scott got out of bed, walked across the room and turned the light off as if that would end the conversation.

"If my husband has shown himself to have questionable ways, then I guess trust deserves to be an issue."

"Funny that my ways didn't become questionable until you changed the rule book of our marriage."

The insult came out before I could stop it. The start of an unnecessary tit-for-tat game. "No, Scott, you are shady. We are supposed to have a certain standard of morals and yes, you are correct. It's my job to put things in perspective if you don't know how to act right."

Tit.

"Germani, there you go sounding sanctimonious and ultra religious again. You might want to be careful, because I think those angel wings you're wearing have spikes in them."

Tat.

"Don't hate on me, because I'm trying to get it right and live according to God's design. We get only one chance before we die. I thought you would have learned that lately."

Tit.

"What I've learned is that you're so saved and filled with the Holy Ghost that I can't relate to you anymore."

Tat.

"What? So that gives you the right to stay out all night, doing God knows what with God knows who. At least one of us is acting saved."

"Urrgh!" Scott shook the bee as he flopped onto his back.

I brought up an observation. "You have a high sex drive and we haven't had sex in five months. Five long months."

Scott spat. "I'm so sick of this. Yes, I have a high sex drive and yes, I'd like my needs met. I don't care how saved I'm supposed to act. I will always be a man with manly needs. And you have made it crystal clear that you are not going to meet those needs, even as my wife. I'm telling you right now that I'm not going to stop being flawed and I'm not going to stop being a man. Germani, if you want to be mad at somebody, then be mad at yourself for making me get my needs met without you."

Too much had been said. I didn't get the explanation I sought, but Scott did answer my question.

Our partnership was nonexistent.

He wouldn't make me cry. I wouldn't give him the satisfaction. I got out of bed as hurt bled unwanted confirmation on the inside of me. I quietly left our room and went down the hall to Elijah's, where I crawled into the little toddler bed, curled around my son and rocked myself to sleep.

CHAPTER FORTY

SCOTT

Apprehension stopped me at the door of New Joy Christian Cathedral, where I was scheduled to meet Ahmad for a porn addict's recovery class.

Ahmad had stopped me before church service the Sunday following the big fallout between Germani and me. My wife wanted to believe I was cheating on her, so I let her assume exactly that. She and I were no longer on speaking terms. Our daily routine didn't even require us to have a conversation if we chose not to. My work schedule was attached to a planner board in the kitchen. I made sure to work most evening shifts at the store, giving my weekday hours up to my assistant manager, Craig. He was more than happy to have that time with his family.

I had spent the night Germani thought I was cheating on her at the Playa's Lounge. After more than a month of fighting the temptation to go back and see Pleasure, I stopped resisting. Initially, I had turned down the striptease from Pleasure when I was at the hotel with Damon before he died, out of respect for Germani and our marriage. But she wanted to believe I was messing around on her so badly that I stopped trying to convince her otherwise.

The unrest in my home stressed me out. I needed some relief. Seemed to need a lot more stress relief lately. Ahmad had told me that he saw me leaving the stripper's club on his drive home from a conference in Jacksonville, Florida. He also explained that he didn't know my home situation and he wasn't trying to get in my business, but he could sense I was troubled. I confessed my porn struggles with Ahmad. By the time we finished talking, he had convinced me to attend one Saturday afternoon meeting.

I stood outside New Joy for several minutes before I decided to leave. As I got to the sidewalk I saw Ahmad approaching.

"Good to see you, Scott. I was running a little late, but I'm glad you made it. The brother teaching the class is powerful. You're about to be blessed."

I wasn't convinced by his enthusiasm as we made it into the brick cathedral. Ahmad took me past doors with colored paper signs posted.

LIFE AFTER PRISON in purple . . . DRUG/ALCOHOL ANONYMOUS in blue . . . STRENGTH FROM DOMESTIC VIOLENCE in green . . . PORN ADDICT RECOVERY in yellow.

Ahmad pushed the door open and held it while a stream of men and two women filed into the room.

As everybody got settled in table topped desks arranged in a large circle, hand-outs were passed around by a man Ahmad identified as the session teacher. A tall, lanky, dark-skinned man in a green button-down shirt with black slacks, he looked to be around my age.

I read over the bold letters of the top page: XXXCHURCH.COM THE #1 PORN SITE.

The title alone threw me for a loop. I must admit that I didn't know what to think about the class Ahmad had me attending.

As the presenter noticed the myriad of facial expressions, he burst out laughing. "I love the looks I see on the new people's faces when I first give out these pages. Admit it, you think I'm crazy, don't you?" he walked over and asked a mocha-toned woman with a short afro, who appeared obviously mortified.

She nodded her head.

The presenter told her, "There is a method to my madness." He then addressed the entire room of attendees. "There are quite a few unfamiliar faces in the room. For those of you who are new to the class, I am Myles Corbin. Welcome to Porn Addicts Recovery. Please read over the second handout to make sure you are in the right location before we begin."

I browsed down the list of questions.

Do you use pornography to cope with life?

Do you get angry at anyone mentioning your porn use?

Has there been an increase in volume of porn use?

Do you have an inability to stop using porn, even if it results in a job or marriage loss?

"If you think you are in the wrong room, raise your hand," Myles requested.

No one raised their hands.

Myles further explained as he sat on the edge of a desk, "I am going to say right off the bat that I am an unconventional speaker. What I am not, is a pastor, Bible scholar, licensed therapist or any other label that someone wants to attach to me, as I've heard people ask what right I had to head a counseling class. But you don't need a degree to understand God's love and grace. A label won't determine whether I choose to honestly live by the Bible or not. The reason I bring all that up is because I've gotten used to judgment from whomever. I'm not going to lie to you and tell you I like it, but as a re . . . covered, re . . . newed porn addict, I understand how detrimental judgment from family, friends or the general public can be when you're fighting the weakness within. XXXChurch is a non-conventional Christian based anti-pornography website geared toward helping people with porn related struggles. The creators are on a worldwide mission and have innovative resources for dealing in everyday life."

I was feeling what Myles was saying. My expectations for the class had been limited by my experience with Germani. The fire and brimstone convictions . . . that approach had damaged our relationship.

Myles put his finger to his lips before using that same hand to point around the room. "Here, the focus is on fighting urges and building sexual integrity. The focus is on support in the midst. I'm going to let a few others in this room tell you the benefits of Porn Addict Recovery."

Ahmad spoke up first. "I had been watching porn since junior high. If you would have asked me three years ago if I had any major issues, I would have denied it. Porn wasn't interfering in my everyday life. I could take it or leave it. When my son, Quinn, became a teenager, I gave him access to my video collection. It was a right of passage from father to son, or so I thought, until I received a call from his guidance counselor to appear in the school office. Quinn had gotten caught masturbating in the boys' locker room after basketball practice."

The room was so quiet we could hear the buzz of the furnace. Myles went and sat in one of the empty desks of our circle.

I didn't realize that Quinn had a porn problem. During the conversation, when Ahmad invited me to the class, he had only admitted that he used to watch porn. He didn't mention his son.

Ahmad looked calm and collected, despite his confession about his son. "The principal wanted to suspend Quinn sixty days from school for criminal sexual misconduct. That would have put him behind the rest of the ninth graders. My wife and I stayed in that office for most of the afternoon hashing out other solutions with the principal and guidance counselor. Our parenting skills were placed under a microscope. We spent a great deal of that time defending our son and our morals. The conclusion was that Quinn could get the penalty reduced to two weeks' suspension if my wife and I got him in a rehabilitation program. Quinn's guidance counselor gave me a flyer for New Joy and that's how we ended up here."

A man three desks over asked, "If your son's the one with the problem, why are you here instead of him?"

Ahmad responded, "Because I'm part of the problem. I introduced him to something he wasn't equipped to handle. Quinn completed the required class and went back to school, but his attraction to porn continues to be a struggle. I stop in here every once in a while to keep myself in check on how I deal with him and to encourage anybody else going through."

I never realized that my love of porn could influence my own son in such a bad way. A whole new light was shed.

Someone else began to speak. A middle-aged man with sandy blond hair and a deep tan talked from his chair. "My wife left me because she could no longer compete with the fantasy I was caught up in. I don't blame her. It was a heavy burden to bear. I paid for her to have a tummy tuck, breasts enhancement and dermal abrasion so that she could look like the women in those porn videos, but in the end it wasn't enough. Her self-esteem was shot. We've been divorced for a year now and I miss her, but I respect her decision to move forward without me." He pulled out a tattered note card from his black leather billfold and held it in the air. "I keep this folded in my wallet. It's an inspirational quote from Todd Bolsinger, the author of a book entitled, *Showtime*. It states, '*If your mind is not filled with the Scriptures and your heart is not in the habit of obeying them, then to trust your gut and go with your own insight is to walk a crooked and perilous path.*' It reminds me of how destructive things get when I live in my own will and own desires. It reminds me to not rely on what feels good without questioning the cost."

As others told their stories I found myself comforted by

their flaws. And if I was made in God's image, then He was well aware of my flaws whether they were temporary or permanent. I realized that maybe I didn't have things as in control as I previously believed. Maybe my marriage didn't have to keep spiraling from our differences.

As I listened to triumphs and tragedies, I realized that the Porn Addict Recovery class was exactly were I needed to be.

CHAPTER
FORTY-ONE

GERMANI

"I am not going to let this be another bad day," I muttered to myself as I pushed open the front door. Things were out of control and there wasn't a thing I could do about it but go with the flow.

The day care charged me forty dollars for picking Elijah up half an hour late, even though I was never late getting him any other time. On top of that, Plas-tech decided to let a majority of our contract workers go by the end of the month after they merged with a Japanese company. Employees were already calling us worried about their next jobs. And worse yet, Scott was treating me like enemy number one. He walked around the house like he was living there alone; didn't want to discuss the murder. It was as if he was the only person going through changes after our discovery. Like he was the only one allowed to grieve.

I played with the light switch. I clicked it on and I clicked it off. I went to the kitchen. Clicked it on. Clicked it off. The time on the microwave was blank. I couldn't get over it.

I lay Elijah on the living room couch. He always fell asleep in the car on the way from the day care. Even with my plantain blinds open, I still could barely see. Darkness was fast approaching due to time being pushed back an hour by daylight saving time.

I picked up the house phone, and like an idiot, waited for a dial tone that wasn't coming. "Real bright, Germani," I said to myself as I placed the phone back on its base.

I pulled out my cell phone and called Scott at work.

Craig answered, "Car Care the automotive specialist for all your repair needs, this is Craig, how may I help you?"

"Hey, Craig, this is Germani. Is Scott busy?"

"Right now he is outside doing a battery check. Would you like for me to have him call you back?"

"No. I can hold," I said.

I sat in the dark waiting for eight minutes before he came to the phone.

"What's going on?" Scott asked in an agitated voice.

Instead of playing into his bad mood when I already had my own, I replied, "The power is off."

He apologized for forgetting the payment arrangement he made with the utility company, then he put me on three-way while he paid the bill. With it being after five in the evening, the electric company didn't know when a technician would be out to turn the power back on. I decided to leave the house and go see Kira.

Nu Taste Café had a calming, yet eclectic environment; the blend of Polynesian and Spanish cuisines that reflected cultures of both Kira and Jayat. They purchased the building three years ago. Brick red covered the walls, while tan wicker chairs lined the small tables. International jazz vibrated from the speakers. The contrasting smell of papaya soup along with saffron from paella lingered in the air as a waitress holding a plate went past me.

"Do you need some money?" Kira asked me as she sat across from me at a corner table.

I helped Elijah play a game on his Leafpad.

"No. Absolutely not." It was embarrassing that she would even feel the need to ask. Her finances were no different than mine. The money they made went back into sustaining Nu Taste.

"You know that pride is man's greatest downfall. Took down more than a few nations. If you need it, then you shouldn't be ashamed to ask. When we were teenagers we used to put our money together for those summer events at the Afro-American Cultural Center, Blumenthal Performing Arts and the Actor's Theatre. This would be no different."

"I'm a grown woman now. It's not your job to take care of me or make sure I have money for household bills. As much as I talk about Mekhi leeching off my momma, the last thing I would do is ask for that kind of help. Besides, it's not that we're broke. The money is in our checking account and Scott carries the debit card for the account. I should have requested my own card when I realized he wasn't using automatic pay for our bills. This wouldn't have happened if I were thinking. Duke Energy gives customers at least ten working days from the receipt of the notice to get the bill paid. Scott made a payment arrangement for three monthly installments. He paid the first amount, but ignored the second notice. It should have been taken care of."

"You two have had a lot happen in the past four weeks. Scott's mind was probably on the death of his best friend. If you didn't have that to deal with, I'm sure he would have remembered." Kira placed the salt and pepper shakers inside the menu rack.

"Don't get me wrong. I understand that Scott didn't purposely forget to pay the bill. I had forgotten about the bill myself with this whole murder-suicide uproar. But my point is that we would have never received a shut-off notice if he had continued to take care of business like he's supposed to.

"If it weren't for his obsession with porn, we wouldn't have a problem, because our bills would still be paid instead of him wasting *our* money—and I do mean ours, because that's my money in the bank too—on pay-per-view nude movies. Over four hundred dollars worth of porn, if I include the amount from the new bill. Who has that kind of money to waste on pay-per-view movies? We sure don't," I whispered, hoping that Elijah wasn't paying attention to our conversation.

"He used your bill money to pay for sex on television? You didn't tell me that was what happened." Kira sounded astonished.

"I know. We argued about the first shut-off notice on the night Cherish called me and . . ." I flayed my hand in the air. "Well, you know the rest."

"That's serious. I can see why you're so mad. Why would he even need to spend that kind of money on movies?"

"Exactly. That's my question too."

"Germani, he must need something extra in the relationship. Did you ever make it over to Kinky Ways? Maybe buy yourself a cute little French maid outfit."

"French maid outfit?" I scoffed. "I don't need to role play to please my husband. This is bigger than me dipping my body in hot chocolate, doing Chinese splits or spanking him with a leather paddle. Intimacy is a connection between two that goes beyond the physical. Scott should be able to touch my soul when we make love. You can't touch my soul with props."

"Germani, be reasonable, you're sounding like a prude. Why do you think men stray with mistresses and prostitutes?" Kira paused, but she didn't really want me to answer that. "Because their wives are afraid to explore sexual techniques that would keep the love fresh and interesting. I was listening to The Michael Baisden Show the other day and they were talking about this exact subject. Making love work. Several women called to say they are open to try new things. If they didn't keep their homes happy, then their husbands would find somebody who would. No matter how much you love God, you still have to keep Scott happy and interested."

He probably was already cheating on me, but I couldn't handle that subject with Kira on top of everything else. "Scott has a problem . . . a porn obsession. I've been doing research and there are a lot of women out there going through the same thing as me. Scott is going to have to get his sex movie obsession in check, or else."

"Or else what?"

"I haven't decided what the *or else* will mean, but if I have to dish out an ultimatum to get my point across, then I will."

"Okay. Hope that ultimatum thing works out for you." Kira gazed over at Elijah who had bread fries in one hand and his Leaf pad pen in the other. He was completely oblivious to our conversation. Her look made me feel like I was trying to break up a happy home, when my home was anything but.

"Did I tell you that there was a detective at our house asking questions about Cherish and Damon's activities? He wanted to know the extent of our involvement. Basically, what he asked was if we were into the same thing. Evidently, a video surfaced on I-Tube of some prominent figures in compromising positions. They linked the upload of the video to a computer at Cherish and Damon's address on the night of the murder, and since we were the ones who found them and were their friends, they thought we might have more information about the case than previously stated. You should have seen Scott cut me off before I could speak in our defense. He told the detective that we didn't need to disclose anything. Scott asked them to kindly leave our premises. Kira, it made us look guilty. I didn't have any involvement in their swingers' network, so why the hush?"

"Hmmm. What did Scott say?"

"He told me that Damon was his friend even in death, and the police just wanted information to further smear Damon's reputation and take the spotlight off the rich folks caught on video."

"He may have a point."

I looked at Kira like she fell off a dump truck. "I don't think so. Damon screwed his own reputation. He wasn't ashamed of his lifestyle. What are we hiding it for? Regardless of that, I feel more disconnected from Scott with each passing day. Like we're going through the motions of marriage to save face and—"

The ring tone "Lost Without You," by Robin Thicke began playing.

Scott was calling me. Maybe I should change that ring tone. Even with the croon of a falsetto, I felt more lost with him.

"Hey," I said, rubbing the line of the table with my finger after answering the phone.

"I got a call from the electric company. They won't be able to get somebody out there until the morning. They said the power should be back on first thing. I'm about to close shop and head home soon."

"I don't want to be in the dark. I'll spend the night at Kira's and come home in the morning before I have to be to work." I looked up at Kira for agreement.

She nodded.

"That's who we're with already." Even though it was almost nine at night and I could easily sleep in spite of the power being out, I didn't want to. I didn't want to act like I wasn't mad. I didn't want to undress Elijah or myself in the dark nor vacillate about the electricity not working. And I definitely didn't want to sleep next to Scott.

"Tell Kira I said hello," Scott said like we were okay, like our situation was all good.

"Scott said hello," I told her.

"Hey, Scott," Kira shouted into my phone.

"See you in the morning?" Scott asked me like I had a whole bunch of other options.

"Uh-huh."

What I was giving and what I was getting were far from equivalent. I couldn't keep up the charade.

CHAPTER
FORTY-TWO

SCOTT

I cruised down the almost vacant street of a normally well lit North Tryon in Uptown after work. Two patrol officers rode their bikes past me turning down East 5th, where a man vanished a week ago after leaving the Buckhead Saloon. His story received national attention on *Good Morning America* when his family sent out a plea for any information leading to his whereabouts. I would bet money that they don't find him, at least not alive. If a child goes missing, they may be taken by a disgruntled parent or the child might have run away from home. Worse possibility is they were snatched up by a child molester or some other kind of lunatic. When a grown man goes missing, it is almost always a case of foul play unless that person didn't want to be found. Considering the news hype that he telephoned several people on the night he was last seen, it was highly unlikely that he vanished intentionally.

I wondered how long it would take for the family's denial to fade and the full blown grief to emerge. How long would they keep his picture circulating before public interest faded too?

Damon got his ten minutes of spotlight in two days of news

broadcasts. Then it became sensationalized a week and a half later, after a few local doctors were seen streaming bare bottom through the web. Somebody leaked to the press that there was a connection to the murder-suicide in Highgrove. News was only glorified when it was bad.

I wasn't going home yet. I was a little irritated that my wife and son weren't there, although I didn't say anything about it to Germani. In the five years we'd been married, sleeping apart had never been an option.

Further down Tryon Street in the center of the Uptown condos named Ratcliffe, was a three-tier landscaped park with art pieces shaped like fish and a high tech water fountain. I proposed to Germani there in January, almost five years ago. We had come from an art exhibit in the Mint Museum and strolled along Tryon as I held her from behind to ward off the chilly winter evening. She had stopped at Dillworth Coffee on the corner of West Martin Luther King for a hot mocha latte, but they had closed an hour earlier.

She was ready to go find a Starbucks, but I convinced her to walk down Tryon to the Green. There was something special in the park that she hadn't seen before. I remember that she smiled and wrapped herself in my wool trench, my body heat merging with hers as we matched strides in our stroll.

She used to be so agreeable. She used to be easy to love.

After Aquavina, but before the Bank of America Stadium where the street changed from North to South, I parked my car and walked by the Ratcliffe underground parking deck toward international signs, stepping on riddles built into the ground, a hopscotch board several feet away. Right next to the water fountain was where I had gotten on my knee and requested that she spend the rest of her life with me. Her smile, with shivering lips, dropped as I pulled the ring out of my inside pocket. Throughout the evening, I had been checking on the ring, worried that it might somehow slip out without the box to protect it. But I left the box at my apartment so that she wouldn't feel the square bulge when we were close. She did ask me several times why I kept my coat on during the exhibit, but I would change the subject each time she mentioned it. She didn't linger on the subject.

Back when she was agreeable, before the times changed. Now everything was an issue with her.

My daddy once told me that the only thing consistent about a woman is her ability to be inconsistent. He gave me a speech after my sister, Sharon, slapped me for throwing away her raggedy Barbie dollhouse after she flushed my GI Joe. I slapped her back, figured she should be able to take a hit as well as she gave one. She went crying to Daddy, but I didn't expect nothing to happen since she started it.

Daddy came into the room and punched me right below the cheekbone. He made my jaw rattle. Then he took me to the back shed, where I thought he was going to beat me some more. Instead, he explained the rules of man versus woman.

Woman was the weaker vessel. He told me that it was biblical. Women did everything based on emotion. Women had a fantasy expectation of life, while men used logic to solve problems. He told me to never respond to a woman like a woman. The reason he hit me was so I would understand the difference between a woman's hand and a man's fist. Men were stronger physically and mentally, so we had to handle them with cotton mittens, address them like fragile jewels. Think when they don't. Walk away when they don't. If he ever heard about me hitting my sisters or another female, he would break both my legs and leave me with a permanent limp as a reminder of what he said.

Germani should have been my rock, but if what my father said was true, she was incapable of possessing the kind of strength I needed. The newlywed bliss was gone, and as much as I wanted to make things right, I knew I couldn't squeeze water from a dry towel.

I looked at the bronze and silver coins at the bottom of the fountain as I rose.

Headed back to my car, checking my watch.

It was 11:14 P.M. Torrance would be up. He hadn't picked up his last check today. It only had twelve hours, but I figured he still needed his money. I needed to apologize to him. In my stress, I came at him wrong and I was man enough to come correct.

Dillehay Court was one of the older subsidized housing complexes for low-income families. Due to a multi-million dollar urban revitalization Hope VI grant project, most of the properties were given a face lift by the Charlotte Housing Authority. The effort merged families in a residence with various income brackets; kept people without the means to afford the high priced condos like the Ratcliffe in a decent, safe standard of living.

Several complexes got new names to match their new look, but Dillehay remained the same with the exception of the creation of a new computer system in the youth center. It still looked like the projects, the ghetto, the hood.

I turned onto Pine Street and saw a group of kids, teenage boys, standing on the corner. Two of them leaned against a White Cutlass. The brake lights were on as one stood on the driver's side and the other on the passenger side. Bass bumped from a blue Deuce parked nearby; rims with spinners sparkling brighter that the night post on the corner.

I idled my car a couple of minutes, but the boys weren't moving. They acted like they had ownership of all of Pine Street. I pulled my 300 around the Cutlass. I didn't have gas to be wasting. The boy on the driver's side glanced up. It was Torrance with a hoodie on. I watched him from the rearview mirror as I parked on the curb directly in front of the other car. I knew what was up. He'd gone back to the streets, probably peddling crack instead of Jimmies.

I got out and we met in the street.

"Man, what you doing out here?" I asked as two of the boys watched from the blue Deuce.

"I'm doing me, what you doing here?" Torrance's chin was up. His body bucked up like he wanted to fight me. I had tested his manhood before; he wanted to reciprocate the deed.

I pulled the folded paper from my pocket and handed it to him. "I came to give you your check."

"Who dat?" one of his boys with a Phat Farm cap asked Torrance as he approached us. He had a baby face and looked like he should be in bed getting ready for school the next day.

Torrance didn't respond as he unfolded the paper. He laughed as he tapped the paper with his free hand. "Sixty-eight dollars?"

The joke must have passed me by.

"Man, you could have kept this. What I'm supposed to do with this chump change?" He showed baby face the check.

Two weeks ago, sixty-eight dollars would have paid his mother's rent or bought some groceries. Two weeks ago, he would have stretched that money to meet his needs. Two weeks ago, he was grateful for a check.

"Torrance, these streets can't do nothing for you . . . not long term," I told him, shedding a little wisdom.

"Pssh. You can only live one day at a time. I ain't worried about the future." Torrance blew my wisdom off, the vices of a fatherless young man talking.

"If you're not worried about the future, then what about your momma? Aren't you worried about her?"

Torrance's face frowned up. "Dawg, I know you ain't acting like you worried about my momma. You fired me, dawg. Then made sure the unemployment office denied me my benefits. Don't come over here talking about my momma like you care."

"I had nothing to do with your unemployment application getting denied. I tried to tell you before you left that you didn't have enough work hours to claim benefits. I was going to try to get you connected with one of the auto shops for a position—"

"Man, whatever. Go on with all that. I don't need nothing

you to got offer," Torrance balled up the check and threw it down. Stomped it with his tennis shoes. Watched the check become ripped and dirty. I stepped forward with no other intent but to get through to him.

He started walking toward the Deuce. "I don't need your advice or suggestions."

"Torrance." I had lost one friend and felt like I was losing a little brother too.

Baby face pulled a gun out; aimed it at my forehead.

I stared at him like he was stupid. "You gonna use it?" I challenged him. He had the wrong brotha if he was trying to scare me.

"Lemon, let's bounce. Those females on Leafcrest still waiting for us to come through," the other boy with Torrance said as they got into the car.

The little punk lowered his gun, laughing.

As I got into my ride, I thought about what I had to go home to. An empty, dark place. It felt like I was losing everything important.

Lord, what are you trying to tell me?

CHAPTER FORTY-THREE

GERMANI

I lay on a camper's twin air mattress, staring at the ceiling in Kira's living room, and for once, it wasn't Scott or his addiction to porn on my mind.

I was thinking about a man other than my husband. I was thinking about Tre. How there was no closure when he dissed me for Africa. Our relationship stopped abruptly, mostly on my part. I had given him an ultimatum after he went through airport security of the Charlotte Douglas Airport. *"Go into that ridiculous war zone to risk your life for nothing and I won't be here when you come back. If you're able to survive."*

He decided that my love wasn't as important as his destination. I stopped talking to him on that day his flight left. Refused to accept his calls, threw away letters without opening them. Did my best to block out my feelings for him. Nothing seemed to work until Scott took my pain away. I stuffed that need to speak to Tre, to hear from Tre, be close to Tre, in the corner of my heart.

It was the worst decision I'd ever made.

Kira and Autumn were my friends, Scott my spouse, but none of them could replace my bond with Tre.

I rolled over on my side and pulled my arm from beneath Elijah's head. An intense desire rushed over me like a tsunami hitting a small village. I suddenly felt like I was drowning. I couldn't breathe and I thought I was having a panic attack.

Slid on my shoes. Grabbed my purse. I tiptoed down to Kira's room at the far corner, knocking gently. I waited against the door frame. Looked down the hall, expecting my son to awaken. At home he slept like a rock, but we weren't at home.

When I didn't get a response, I cracked open the door and whispered Kira's name. My head lay against the opening, but I couldn't see inside.

She poked her head out, saw me in my coat, "Leaving?"

"I need to get some air," I told her, fanning myself. The house wasn't hot. Her thermostat stayed at seventy degrees, whether winter or summer. It was me. My inner temperature was rising, face flushed from scattered thoughts. "Elijah's still in the living room. He shouldn't wake up, but I need you to keep an eye on him until I get back."

"That's fine. Let me get you my keys." I waited outside her door with a lump the size of a grapefruit in my throat. I had never had a panic attack. Didn't know the feeling.

Kira saw the horrified look on my face as I wheezed like I had asthma. "You sure you okay?"

"I . . . just . . . need . . . air." It wasn't enough oxygen in her apartment to dislodge that grapefruit.

Kira fumbled with her keys, wrapped an index finger and thumb around one oval-shaped key. "Bottom lock, turn twice. Top lock. Pull the door toward you and turn the lock once."

I stared at her. They lived on the ninth floor of a secured building.

"Can never be too safe," Kira remarked.

I shrugged and left quickly. Thought about Damon and Cherish. Seemed to me more crimes occurred by loved ones than burglars on the prowl for free goods.

From the ninth floor on down, I tortured myself with decisions I had made six years ago after Tre got on that Boeing, until six hours earlier when I realized the power bill wasn't paid by Scott.

My life made less sense by the minute, with each labored breath. By the time I stepped outside, that grapefruit had dispersed into a thousand tears. Outside the Camden Grandview Apartments, I cried while the wind kissed my face. I put Kira's keys in my purse and pulled mine out. Needed some time to myself to think things through. Govern a worthwhile plateau. Level my life out. As soon as I got in my car, I knew where I was going. I had to go see him. I had to get some understanding of when my life stopped making sense.

From East Morehead to North McDowell to East Eleventh, stopping on North Davidson. Six years and he still lived at the same address in that small one bedroom studio above a vintage clothing store.

Tre opened the door in an Echo t-shirt with a pair of checkered green pajama pants on.

"Hey." It's been a long time coming.

"Germani, what are you doing here?" he searched the hallway like he was expecting somebody else.

I wiped at my puffy eyes. I knew I looked a mess. "I need to talk to you. I got some stuff on my mind I need to address. That I should have . . . me . . . we. I don't know," I sighed and closed my eyes as I felt tears soaking my ducts.

"I can't let you come in." Tre rubbed his face. His eyes focused above my head at the swaying trees on the ledge behind me.

"Did I catch you at a bad time?" I stepped back, feeling rejected again. "You know what, I shouldn't have come here. I'm sorry for bothering you. I wasn't thinking." I turned toward the stairwell. Just another bad decision. He couldn't give me closure, if I couldn't give it to myself.

I heard footfalls of bare soles against wood behind me as I rushed downstairs.

"Germani. Wait a minute. Don't leave like that."

I stopped with my leg landing on the third step from the bottom. Turning around, I said, "I was in the wrong for showing up unannounced. It didn't dawn on me that you might have company."

He had said at the store that he wasn't seeing anyone.

"There's nobody up there," he responded. Tre's shoulders were hunched like he was warming himself up. "I just don't think it's a good idea for us to be alone in my apartment."

"Oh." In the three years we were together, only once did we cross the lines of intimacy. If there was anybody that I could trust not to take advantage of me, it was Tre. Unless, that was flipped and he didn't trust me. "Listen, it's cold out here and I don't want to be responsible for you getting pneumonia. I'll go."

"Don't. We can go back up to my place and talk." He sounded reluctant.

"You sure?"

There was laughter and music coming from the club around the corner: the Wine-Up.

"Yeah. Something must be weighing heavy on you for you to show up at my door in the middle of the night." He began walking back up the stairs.

"Do you still go to the Wine-Up?" I asked as I followed him.

We used to go listen to poetry on Friday nights at our main hang-out spot. Sometimes he would do one of his poems. I'd watch him mesmerize the crowd with his prolific nuance, stringing words with unexpected meaning.

"Once in awhile. Not like I used to though. But when the mood strikes me, I go."

"I haven't been in years. Couldn't walk in there without thinking about you."

His head dropped briefly before he pushed his apartment door open.

I bit my bottom lip, regretting that I had said that.

"I was laid out, so I'm going to have to make the place presentable for you."

He moved his furniture. That was the first thing I noticed. His futon was gone and everything in the room was rearranged. The wicker rattan chair was facing a bookshelf instead of the television. The walls were covered with art work he collected from artist friends that used to be stacked in a corner.

"It looks different in here," I told Tre as he pushed in the let out mattress of his couch.

"I sublet the place out to a couple of college students while I was in Africa and came back to a few changes. My futon was missing a leg. They had a chunk of wood holding up the left side. Other than that, everything was kept in good condition. I used their deposit to buy a new sleeping area."

I scrolled through his collection of DVD movies, *Hero* with Jet Li. A Brazilian film called *City of God*. The made-for-television version of *Their Eyes Were Watching God*, starring Halle Berry.

No porn amongst his collection. Porn wasn't something that Tre ever entertained when we were together. Instead, he focused on thought-provoking movies. I appreciated that about him.

I noticed a movie I wasn't familiar with. I pulled out the cover with a boy below marching feet. The title read *Sometimes in April*.

"It's a good movie. Realistic depiction of death in Rwanda. Idris Alba played the heck out of his role." Tre came over and pointed to the case in my hand.

"I'll take your word for it," I said, pushing the movie back in place. It would seem like he had enough violence while over in Africa that his watching movies about the same thing seemed to be overkill.

I wanted to ask why he left me for war, but instead I asked, "What's it like? Darfur?"

264 *T.N. Williams*

"Chaotic. Hundreds of thousands dead. People trying to find refuge amongst the violence. They're scared. Uncertain of the future. What can you do when your country's killing you and the necessary help is just not there? People assume the United States isn't helping with relief efforts because there isn't any oil for us to claim as our own over in the region, but it's deeper than that. There is oil, but China's running that. In fact, China is to Darfur what America is to Iraq. The United States doesn't want to mess with China. They're just as much a super power as we are."

"I read in *Newsweek* that Darfur has become a repeat of the Rwandan genocide. Men, women and children being murdered in bunches like pig slaughters. It seems so senseless. When did life lose its value?" I sat down on his couch.

Tre plopped down on the opposite end. "When Cain killed Abel."

"It was senseless then and it's senseless now."

"It's about perspective. You have people with opposing views, so the militia eradicates the other. Ethnic cleansing."

I placed my arm on the curve of his couch. "I feared for you over there. I thought you weren't coming back. Did you fear for yourself? You were right there. Volunteered to be a moving target." I sounded harsh, blatantly bitter about a past I couldn't change.

Tre glanced at me and shook his head. "I didn't volunteer to be a moving target. I volunteered to help people the same shade as me get out of a distressed situation. We were housed in the neighboring city of Chad. The organization couldn't get in Darfur. Too dangerous. Germani, believe it or not, I wasn't on a suicide mission."

"My daddy died in a foreign land." Some hurts were impossible to let go.

"I know. And you were expecting the same thing to happen to me. I understand why you didn't want to wait for me."

He sounded way more forgiving than I was willing to be.

I closed my eyes as guilt tugged at my heart. I nervously ran my fingers across the back of the couch. "I think I made the wrong decision."

He sat across from me and stared for several minutes. His expression was blank. I couldn't read his thoughts. "Germani, what's going on between you and your husband?" he finally asked.

"It's not working. He's got problems. Big problems that are destroying any chance of us salvaging things."

"Everybody has problems. You have to work through them."

"I've been trying, but he's making it hard to do. He has this addiction. I don't know how to deal with his addiction."

Tre sat up with worry on his face. "Is he on drugs?"

"No. Thank God." I rubbed on my pants leg. "I don't know how much I'm supposed to say. You are my ex-lover."

He sat on the edge of the couch and looked me in my eyes. "Germani, you came to me. You obviously need to talk about it. You know that's something we used to be good at doing: communicating. I can't change your situation, but I can listen."

"Was I enough woman for you? Did you ever feel like I wasn't enough?"

That question jolted him. He frowned. "No, but this isn't about us or what we had or anything like that. You have a husband. Marriage isn't something to be taken lightly."

"Porn. He's addicted to porn." I didn't wait for Tre to respond. "You know what I learned? I discovered that if a man lusts with his mind, then he is an adulterer. That he has broken the covenant of marriage."

"Even a broken covenant can be repaired. Have you prayed about your situation?"

"Yes. I've prayed and prayed, then prayed some more. Futility. That's what it is. I think my efforts are in vain. I'm frustrated and tired. I didn't sign up for all this. You and I didn't have this kind of issue. I married Scott, but I wasn't prepared for this type of issue."

"Germani, you can't base the expectations from one relationship onto another." Tre stood up and walked to the kitchen area. "I'm not going to tell you to leave your husband, if that's what you're looking for."

"I knew you wouldn't," I sighed. "Tre, I just want to be happy again."

"Happiness is relative. That's an inner dilemma. You control that, I don't."

I heard what he was saying, but I needed him to understand my point, understand what I was going through.

"You're the only man I completely trust," I said with honesty. We could be transparent with each other. "I don't think I can trust Scott. You can't be happy without trust."

"*We may handle any how, if we only have a why.* Do you remember that quote?"

I had to smile. "Friedrich Nietzsche."

"Only you understand why you married him and only you can decide how to stay married."

"I disagree. My judgment was skewed. You were gone and Scott made it easier to move on."

"I don't think you married him just to have a warm body nearby or because you were mad at me. He had some qualities that drew you to him; that made it worth ending our relationship so you could be with him." He came over and handed me a cup of steaming raspberry zinger tea.

"Stop giving me Gandhi and give me Tre. The delicate approach is not your style. Tell me how you really feel."

He placed his cup of tea on the table and pushed the wicker chair so that it was facing me. "You made your bed, now you got to sleep in it."

His candor surprised me. "Well, I didn't mean be that harsh."

"Emotionalism will destroy you and everything around you. Your being obsessed about his addiction is just as bad as his having an addiction. You've got to stop trying to control the relationship, trying to fix it. Let God work it out."

"That's easier said than done."

"Only if you make it that way. You can't box people in and expect them to want to stay there. If you focus on your walk instead of his, then life won't be so difficult. God honors your relationship with Him. Your husband has to deal with his own struggles. Either you're going to be supportive or you're not. Just remember that whatever decision you make impacts more than just you." Tre paused as he took a sip of his drink. "Germani, you need to be talking to your husband, not me."

As much as I didn't like his response, I knew he was right.

CHAPTER FORTY-FOUR

SCOTT

I sat across the street from Germani's ex-boyfriend's place wondering how long she would be inside. I couldn't believe she was cheating on me after all her lectures about Christian values. It was all a bunch of garbage to make me feel guilty for her bad deeds.

She played me for a fool.

Instead of going home when I left Torrance with his crew, I decided to go clear the air with my wife. Just as I pulled up to Kira's apartment complex I saw Germani get in her car. I thought she saw me, but she drove right past. I turned around and followed her. Never could have guessed that she was going to see her ex.

I had watched the whole touching scene. Her going up his stairs, only to run down minutes later. Tre chasing after her. Their exchanging words. Him taking her back up.

I stayed in my car for fifty minuets, debating whether I would knock on his door and confront both of them or leave, go get my son from Kira and wait at home for an explanation. Give her time to figure out how to lie to me.

I wondered how long she had been seeing him on the low. Did it start before Damon died? Probably so. That explained her detachment from me, her constant complaining about my faults and the excuses not to make love. It all finally made sense.

After stewing for close to an hour, I got out of my car in a fighting mood.

I rushed up and banged on his door. If they were in bed together, I wanted to make sure they heard me.

When Tre opened the door, fully clothed seconds later, his appearance kept me from punching him in the face. He didn't look like a man interrupted in the middle of getting some. Instead, the brotha was welcoming, smiled at me and stepped aside.

Caught me off guard, but the night was full of surprises.

I stormed in and saw Germani curled up on his couch. She looked too comfortable.

"Well, don't you look cozy. Weren't expecting to see me tonight were you?" I asked Germani as the shock from seeing me settled on her face.

"Scott, I—" She quickly stood up stuttering.

"You what . . . you got a reason for being here? A really good one?" I stopped in front of Germani, wondering what kind of explanation she could give for being in her first love's house at one in the morning. I knew how she felt about him before we got together. If he hadn't left the country, she probably would have married Tre instead of me.

"Scott, we were just talking."

Tre responded, "There is nothing going on between your wife and me. She came to get advice about you, but I told her that she needed to talk with you about it."

I gritted my teeth before asking, "So, you were complaining about me to your ex?"

Germani looked over at Tre. "He's right. There is nothing

going on between us. Nothing like what you're thinking. Scott, you know how things have been between us. We don't talk anymore."

The whole scene was too strange for me to handle. I turned to my wife's ex. "Tre, no offense, but there really is no reason my wife should be at your place, regardless of what's going on with us." I then looked at Germani. "I don't want to have this conversation in front of your ex-boyfriend. If you have a problem with me, then we need to go somewhere and talk."

"Alright, let's go." She turned to Tre. "I'm sorry for bringing any confusion to your home."

He held up his hand like there was no need for her to apologize.

I walked back out the door just as quickly as I had come in.

Germani met me at my car. "Where do you want to go?"

"Anywhere but here."

"I'll follow you and let you decide the location." For the first time in months, she wasn't being combative.

"Alright." I got in my car and drove back down to the Green. I didn't say anything to her until we were back by the fountain.

"What are we doing here?" she asked as she stared at the waterfall.

I sat on a bench. She came over and sat next to me. Germani bit her bottom lip as she listened.

"Germani, I love you. When I asked you to marry me, it was a life long commitment. Lately, it has been sounding like you're looking for a reason to end our marriage, like you're digging for bad things to discredit me as your husband. Things that weren't a problem before are all of a sudden a major dilemma. I didn't get what was going on with you."

"I think I've made my stand pretty clear. I've compromised my values to please you and basically I have gotten tired of it. When I was sitting at that strip club, all I could think about was that environment didn't fit me. You seemed completely comfortable with those naked women surrounding you, and that just wasn't right to me. I felt like we weren't as connected as I originally thought. I felt like you saw women as purely sexual objects and the company you kept only reinforced my opinion."

I took a rock and threw it into the water. Her words made more sense after listening to Myles speak. I hadn't told her about the class I attended with Ahmad. I felt like she was going to judge me on that too. "You should know me better than that. I don't see women as sex objects. I mean, come on; I was raised in a house full of females. And you've seen how protective I am about my sisters and niece."

"Yes, but the people you associated with didn't have that same standard of living. Why would you hang with men that didn't respect women? That makes no sense to me. Plus, you seem to be obsessed with pornography. It all made me question your character. It's as if God was looking down on us shaking His head at our disobedience to His Word."

"Germani, you act like you don't have any struggles. Porn is a struggle for me and has been since way before we got together. Believe me, God knows my struggle. It doesn't mean that I see all women as sex objects. I would think that as my wife, you would be able to stand by my side during my struggle, even if you didn't agree with it."

"No. I can't stand by something I don't agree with. I can't justify what I know is wrong. I desire to get better with time, not deeper in denial. If something doesn't feel right, then that is the case for a reason. As your wife, if I see you are doing wrong, then it is my responsibility to mention it."

"I understand, but it's also both our responsibilities to know when something is not meant for us to control. I wanted Damon to live, but God took him anyway. I can stay mad at God or I can accept that my friend is gone. The same thing applies to you. This isn't supposed to be your battle; it's mine to deal with. You can either respect the place I'm in, or not."

Germani sighed. "I suppose."

Her words didn't sound all that confident about our marriage. "So what's it going to be? I'm willing to work harder on my struggle. Are you able to be supportive?"

She sat there, but didn't say anything. I took that to mean she couldn't be. I stood up and began walking out of the park. Guess it would end where it started. I couldn't force her to understand. She knew what she could and couldn't handle. I didn't want to leave without her, but . . .

"Scott, I love you." She stood up and walked toward me. "I love you enough to make this work. I will not sacrifice my beliefs to have you, but I can be supportive, because I believe God will deliver you from your addiction."

"That's all I ask." I wrapped my arms around her waist and gently kissed her lips.

Relishing in the commitment we had.

EPILOGUE

GERMANI

January 5, 2008

The New Year always brought a desire to change. Many made plans to eat right or workout more. Some became determined to get out of debt or give to charity. While others decided it's the perfect time to stop smoking or drinking. But all change ain't good change. I had read an article in a legal journal that said January was the highest divorce filing month. Supposedly, the holidays caused extra stress and magnified marital problems. Thus, throwing in the towel come January seemed like a logical solution for those in turmoil.

Scott and I had endured so much turmoil in the previous year that I didn't think we would make it as a couple. We'd both been stretched by our extended family obligations. Me trying to help Momma with Mekhi. Scott trying to help Beverly with Alexis.

Fortunately, we were able to put together some money and get the assault charges made by Mishelle's boyfriend, Cyrus, against Mekhi dropped. Child Protective Services were investigating Cyrus for the bruises on Camry. We were all still waiting for Alexis to get a bone marrow transplant, but her name had moved up to number seven on the waiting list. It wouldn't be much longer before she got the help she needed.

Damon's death took a toll on Scott. He had such a difficult time forgiving Cherish. He knows it's something he has to do for his own benefit. I don't even mention her to him anymore.

Cherish took a plea bargain of ten to fifteen years for second-degree murder right before Christmas. The publicity had already been brutal and she didn't want to go through a long trial under scrutiny. She gave her attorney permission to turn over Damon's belongings to his mother, and Cherish also planned to give Ms. Ilene part of the profit from the sale of the Ballantyne home.

For Scott and me, the New Year meant the renewal of our relationship. Biblically, the number eight signified a new beginning, the combination of resurrection and regeneration. We were determined to take the struggles of 2007 and strengthen our new beginning.

I glanced around the packed room at New Joy Christian Cathedral as my husband walked to the center of it.

"I want to tell my wife I'm sorry," Scott said in the room full of people.

Elijah sat next to me in a navy blue turtleneck sweater and dark jeans. His outfit matched his father's. When Scott told me that we would be going to his porn addiction recovery class, I thought it might have been inappropriate for Elijah. Scott insisted that we attend Family Support Day. He had told me about the class on Thanksgiving night. Scott had explained that he needed to sort out his thoughts before he came to me. I was ecstatic that he was doing something about his problem.

I listened to my husband apologize. I mouthed, "It's okay."

Scott saw my lips moving and smiled affectionately. "No. I'm sorry. For all the times I made you hurt. For all the words I said in anger. For rejecting your input and denying your beliefs when you saw me getting out of control. I heard you even when it looked like I wasn't listening. I loved you even when I didn't show it. If God had not given you to me, I don't think I could have become the man of integrity I was meant to be."

"Oh, gosh." I could feel tears slide down my face at his admission.

His eyes stayed locked with mine. "With every struggle there is the opportunity for growth. When you're not willing to acknowledge a problem, or in my case, an obsession, you're not willing to grow. I didn't realize how hard I was making my marriage. I didn't realize how I was compromising my walk with God. Thank you, Germani, for staying by my side. I know it wasn't easy. Baby, I get it."

I nodded. Things definitely hadn't been easy. Through it all, I had to reach my own level of understanding. I tried to force Scott to serve God my way. I didn't get that his struggle started in adolescence. That it wasn't something he knew how to just quit. I had to learn to respect the place he was in.

Whatever battles we faced in the future, were battles we would face together.

Readers Group Guide Questions

1. Germani said early in the story that she agreed to watch porn because she thought it was part of submission. Do you think her intentions were honorable?
2. Both Scott and Germani spent a lot of time dealing with problems of their extended family. Did that prevent them from focusing on their own issues?
3. Scott maintained friendships primarily with men who had derogatory views of women. How does that play into his own actions? Did those relationships hinder Scott's Christian walk?
4. Scott's sister, Beverly, tried desperately to convince Alex to donate bone marrow to their daughter, Alexis. What would you have done in her situation?
5. Mekhi wanted to stay with Mishelle despite their abusive history together? Does the Bible have an answer to abusive relationships?
6. Germani was shocked and hurt that Scott didn't want to give up porn. Should she have been surprised? Should she have responded differently?
7. Today's culture glorifies eroticism and sexual independence. Is the culture a hindrance to Christianity? Why or why not?
8. Germani called Scott unsaved because of his refusal to give up watching porn. She judged him by his addiction. Was she justified? Is one sin worse than another?
9. Germani and Scott sought advice about their sex life from friends, including Tre, Germani's ex. Are there some personal issues that friends shouldn't talk about? Does it depend on the type of friend?
10. How does the story affect your perception of married Christians with similar problems?

BIOGRAPHY

T.N. Williams is the author of the debut novel *Something On The Inside*, which made Black Expressions and Black Christian News bestsellers lists. She has received several awards for recognition and collaborated poetic work in the published collection entitled *Traces of the Infinite*. T.N. Williams graduated from Grand Valley State University with a Bachelor degree in Sociology. She currently resides outside of Charlotte, NC with her husband and three children.

Urban Christian His Glory Book Club!

Established January 2007, **UC His Glory Book Club** is another way by which to introduce to the literary world, Urban Book's much-anticipated new imprint, Urban Christian and its authors. We are an online book club supporting Urban Christian authors by purchasing, reading and providing written reviews of the authors' books that are read. *UC His Glory* welcomes both men and women of the literary world who have a passion for reading Christian based fiction.

UC His Glory is the brainchild of Joylynn Jossel, Author and Executive Editor of Urban Christian and Kendra Norman-Bellamy, Author and Copy Editor for Urban Christian. The book club will provide support, positive feedback, encouragement and a forum whereby members can openly discuss and review the literary works of Urban Christian authors. In the future, we anticipate broadening our spectrum of services to include: online author chats, author spotlights, interviews with your favorite Urban Christian author(s), special online groups for *UC Book Club* members, ability to post reviews on the website and amazon.com, membership ID cards, *UC His Glory* Yahoo Group and much more.

Even though there will be no membership fees attached to becoming a member of *UC His Glory Book Club*, we do expect our members to be active, committed and to follow the guidelines of the Book Club.

UC His Glory members pledge to:
- Follow the guidelines of *UC His Glory Book Club*.
- Provide input, opinions, and reviews that build up, rather than tear down.
- Commit to purchasing, reading and discussing featured book(s) of the month.

- Agree not to miss more than three consecutive online monthly meetings.
- Respect the Christian beliefs of *UC His Glory Book Club*.
- Believe that Jesus is the Christ, Son of the Living God

We look forward to the online fellowship.

Many Blessings to You!

Shelia E Lipsey
President
UC His Glory Book Club

**Visit the official Urban Christian Book Club website at *www.uchisglorybookclub.net*